RAYFORD'S GARDEN

RITA HAAG

Wood Lane Books

To Charlie
For Believing

Contents

I

A Bear And A Jackrabbit

Georgia Hill Country
Spring 1864

There is a thing in the air I can't put my finger on. It appears to be resting on Pa, but he ain't one to trouble others so I been looking for the cause of it. I felt it strong after breakfast, but couldn't see naught that was different. My brothers, Hugh and Mule, had gone up to the field and Granpappy headed to the outhouse. Uncle Rayford sat big and still at the table, staring out the window like always while Ma worked around him carrying plates and cups to the dry sink and throwing mean looks at me. She ain't the forgiving kind and that is a shame for both of us, especially on mornings like this when before I was even settled in my chair she asked did I know why her hairbrush has a peculiar smell to it.

I reckon I need to explain there are three ways to get into trouble around here. One is lying, of which I only take it up when there ain't no other way to get around it, like with that hairbrush. I had an idea how it came to smelling peculiar, but if I was wrong it would be like lying, so I just put a confused look on my face.

Then there is stealing, of which there ain't nothing around here worth stealing, so there is no temptation to do such a thing. I didn't steal the hairbrush, I just borrowed it to clear the brown lumps out of Beauregard's tail seeing as how I have in mind to make a scarecrow. Mule tail would be just the thing for hair but I didn't want my scarecrow's head full of turds.

The third way is to do something of which there is no harm in it to begin with, or there is even an idea it could come to some good, but it still gets you on Ma's bad side of which that is generally where I land seeing as how I ain't been able to find any other side.

It ended up I told Ma I was making a scarecrow to keep the critters away from the garden so there'd be more food for her to cook—that part I came up with on the spot—and I needed some hair for the head.

I looked to Pa, who is generally one for seeing my side of things, but this time it didn't work. "Is that why Beauregard ain't got nary a hair left on his tail?" he asked. I didn't have time to come up with anything more before Ma got in it again.

"YOU BEEN USING MY GOOD HAIRBRUSH ON THAT MULE'S TAIL???"

Hugh and Mule busted out laughing and before long Rayford got caught up in it, snorting and carrying on and Pa had to hustle him outside for a bit lest he break something. Ma took me out back and used the hairbrush on me, and not on my head, neither. I still had to clean the hairbrush and time I got back to the kitchen Rayford was ready to head out, so I didn't get breakfast this morning.

Rayford is Pa's twin, but he can't go nowhere by himself without he'd get lost. He can't talk and he ain't right in the head, so we have to keep an eye on him, but there ain't a body in all of Georgia what can whittle likenesses better than Rayford. Ma don't care a lick about that. All she thinks about is chores and hounding me til I'm miserable, of which she is good at.

I've about given up on running away with Rayford—he ain't much for walking on his bad foot—but it crossed my mind this morning. Pa's too, I reckon, seeing as how he pulled a promise from me before he headed up to the field.

"Looks like it's dry enough to plow," he said when I followed him out to the porch. "You keep an eye on Rayford, and help your ma. No running away, neither."

I put my hands behind my back, crossed my fingers, and said "Yes, sir," but it backfired. Pa looked at me squinty-eyed like as if to see was I thinking what he thought I was thinking, of which I reckon I was. "But Ma'll run me ragged," I whined, pulling a pitiful face.

"I'll be riding into town in a day or two. You stay out of trouble and help your ma, and I might see my way clear to pick up some lemon drops and horehound–"

"And peppermint sticks for Rayford?"

Pa's eyebrows came together in a look of worry and he stared off into the day like he could see something bad awaiting. It set me wondering again, but before I got to asking on it, he laid a hand on my shoulder. "Puts me at ease to see you watch after him." He headed off to the barn and time he got to the road, his walk took on a liveliness again, so I let it go and went back to the kitchen.

I wiped Rayford's face clean, grabbed his quilt off the parlor chair, and led him outside. On nice days we set him up in his garden. It's fenced all around and if he had a hankering he could climb between the rails, but he does his coming and going through a six-foot gate Pa set up on the north end. When we got to it Rayford let go my hand, the way he does every morning, and pulled the gate open and pushed it up against the fence, grinning so as you'd near most think he'd got hold of a spoon and a crock of huckleberry jam. That gate squeals like a piglet yanked from its mama's teat, so we suspicion it's the sound Rayford likes, seeing as how he don't appear to hear nothing that ain't loud. Then he grabbed it and I got in the garden with him and he pulled it closed and I latched it. Pa hid the hasp in such a way that Rayford can't see it, so he can't let himself out. Leastways he ain't done so yet.

I walked him to his twig rocker, laid his quilt over it and set his bucket of wood on the left side. Pa built a stand for holding a pitcher of water and such, and that sets on his right. Once Rayford settles into his chair he leans over and picks through the chunks of wood. He works pine and basswood mostly, being as that is what Pa and I gather. I spotted the half-finished wagon and handed that to him, but he looked at it and set it on the stand like he had in mind to whittle a new thing today.

I grabbed a hoe and dug in the garden for worms coming

alive in the warmth. Mule gives me a sweet for every five I dig, but he's some particular and says the skinny ones don't count. When I found five fat ones, I tossed them in the worm bucket, covered it good and set it in the shade. Time I got back to Rayford, he'd found a piece of wood to his liking. He pulled his knife out of its raggedy leather pouch and set to whittling.

All that digging had got me heated up some so I flopped down by the hackberry tree that shades the clearing on the east edge of the garden. I had in mind to make a hitch for the wagon Rayford was making so I pulled out a piece of twine and set to working on it. But after a minute or so, I stuffed that in my pocket, sat back and rested my head against the trunk. I no sooner closed my eyes than Ma hollered for me, like as if she heard my eyelids shut. I sidled around east of the tree and when she hollered again, I dove to the ground, rolled under the fence rail, and crawled for the woods, of which it ain't easy with a dadblamed dress on. Ma won't let me wear britches no more. She aims to get me growed up quick, but that ain't like to happen.

"Tatum Louise Wiley! Don't you go sneaking off." A blue jay shrieked and soared overhead to a hiding place in the pines and I wished for wings like that. "Come get this basket and fetch some sassafras root afore dinner," Ma yelled. There was nothing for it but to make the best of it, as Pa would say.

"Can I take Rayford?" I hollered back. The sassafras patch edges the woods across from the field Pa was plowing, so Rayford could watch him while I dug the root.

"You get on over here and leave Rayford be." I ran up to her lickety split and took the basket, like my sister, Melanie, would've done if she still lived here. Sometimes Ma is kindlier if I move fast.

"Please can he come?" She winced and closed her eyes, of which that likely meant one of her headaches was coming on. "I'll hurry him," I promised.

"Oh, just get then. But mind you be back quick or I'll take it out of your hide."

She rubbed her forehead and went back inside, hunched and slow-moving. She says she is a woman gone old before her time and it is because of me. I reckon I am a child bound to be old before my time and that is because of her, but leastways I know better than to say such a thing so as she can hear me.

I climbed into the garden through the fence rails, ran over to Rayford, and held out my hand. He'd switched to whittling on the wagon, eyes hard on it. I put my hand under his nose and he looked up and grunted, like as if to say he'd be ready in a minute. He took a few more cuts, then blew off the shavings and brushed his fingers along the outside of the box. He set it on the stand, then picked it up and held it in my face. "That's real nice, Rayford, but we got to get some sassafras root. C'mon." He set the wagon down and closed his jackknife, careful, like as if it might explode if he made a move sudden.

That's why Ma don't like me to take him when she is set on having a thing done in a hurry.

Rayford tucked the knife in the leather pouch and pressed it in the palm of his right hand, closing his fingers around it. I grabbed his wrist, walked him to the gate, and let him push it open. I looked over toward the porch and waved to Granpappy so he'd know it was me taking him out. Ma says that squealing gate is like to make her crazy, but Pa won't grease it. He says if Rayford ever takes a notion to leave, we'll hear the gate and catch him.

Granpappy watched us come up from the garden. When we passed the house he leaned forward in the willow rocker and looked at us peculiar like his hip was paining him.

"You feel alright this morning?" I asked. "You got a sorry look on your face."

"That's a thinking look! Seeing you two coming up the path puts me in mind of a bear and a jackrabbit," he said, and he rocked back and grinned. "You heading up to the field?"

"Ma wants me to gather sassafras." I held up the willow basket.

"You best get a move on, then." He pushed himself up from the rocker. "I reckon that oak rocker ain't like to make itself, neither."

He's got himself a bad hip so he don't get around good no more, but he keeps busy making chairs from oak splits or willow branches. He headed across the road to the barn, and me and Rayford took the path on the south edge of the woods that lies between the house and the field. We'd gone about twenty feet when Rayford stopped and pointed and I saw there on the slope a trillium just opened. Rayford got down on all fours and looked at it close up, then grunted at me, so I squatted next to him.

"You hear what Granpappy said? Reckon you're the bear and I'm the jackrabbit, seeing as how I'm fast and you're big. He's funny, ain't he?" Rayford sniffed the flower and touched a petal. "Maybe you should take it to Ma after what you done to the bed this morning." Rayford looked at me and back at the flower, to keep in mind the shape of it I reckon. Even if he did understand, there ain't no way he'd take a flower to Ma. He stood and I took his wrist again and we moved on. He lumbers side to side when he walks, and he's big and round. Tall, too, like Pa, but Pa's built more like a string bean. I reckon Rayford does look some like a bear.

Time we got to the field, Pa had already made two rounds and the damp cool earth of the turned furrows steamed in the warm air. When Pa passed he waved and Rayford waved back. I set him on a stump at the edge of the woods, took the hand shovel out of the basket and got to work. The sun felt good. A light breeze rustled the new spring leaves like bits of shiny paper and carried smells of broke-up earth, sassafras, and dogwood, all so true and fresh. Hugh and Mule cleared brush at the other end of the field and didn't pay us no mind, but the next time Pa passed he stopped Beauregard. He came over, squatted next to Rayford and touched his arm, then pointed to a mature sassafras in full bloom, covered with greeny-yellow flowers spreading their spicy smell everywhere. Rayford got up and took to sticking his nose into the blossoms like a big old bee moving from one cluster of flowers to another.

"Ma let you bring him?" Pa asked

"I promised I'd hurry."

"Hard promise to keep with Rayford."

"But he ain't been out much with all the rain of late. Did you see the wagon he's making? He just finished the box. I was about to tie a hitch when Ma called me."

"You try to get him to use that new knife pouch Granpappy cobbled?"

"He won't have naught to do with it." I could see a half inch of tattered leather fringe sticking out from Rayford's fist. He ain't one for new things or doing a thing different. He likes things the same of which I reckon that is why he takes his knife everywhere. At night he sets it on the wooden stand between his bed and Granpappy's, moving it this way and that til he gets it laid out to his liking. Excepting for when he's sleeping or eating or working in his garden that knife is in his hand. I suspicion he's afeared somebody will take it, but we wouldn't never do that to him. Well, Mule might. He's got a mean streak. But if he did Pa would lay into him, of which that only happened once that I recollect, when he and Hugh tied up the cats. Pa said Hugh should've known better because he was older—nearly sixteen then—but he would've got into it just to see how it worked. Hugh's one for spending time in Granpappy's workshop making contraptions, but he generally keeps to himself and he ain't mean, so we knew the idea came from Mule.

Pa and Granpappy were in the field when it happened. If it was up to Ma, Hugh and Mule would've been there, too, but Pa says they need time to be boys so he always gives them an hour to do as they please after dinner. That day I came on Mule filling a saucer with milk, calling "kitty, kitty," so I knew they were up to something. While Cleopatra and some of her tamer half-growed kittens lapped milk, Hugh and Mule made a big old poke from one of Ma's sheets, of which she was not real happy when she found it out. Then they grabbed all the cats, threw them in the poke and tied it up. "That's mean," I said. Hugh looked at me like as if I could have been right, but he didn't want to think on it, whereas Mule heaved a clod of dirt my way and told me to skedaddle.

I ran to the house to tell Ma, but she had gone to lie down, so I let her be. But when Hugh and Mule weren't looking, I ran behind the barn, peeked around the corner, and saw Mule clambering up a hickory tree. He shinnied out on the end of a limb, and Hugh handed him the poke, bouncing and wailing like a banshee. Mule hung it on a nearby branch, then jumped down. They took hold of the branch, pulled it low and let go, and that poke flew up and as it came down, it bobbed off, went flying, and hit the ground hard. With all them cats howling and snarling and fighting in it, it looked like a big old haint come alive and rolling on the ground. I ran to the field and told Pa and he came tearing back like as if the house was afire. Hugh and Mule were still carrying on, laughing and jabbing the poke with a stick. Pa hollered at them to stay put, and he came up and collared them and marched them back of the house and I ran right behind them. I would have given supper to watch, but when we were near most to the woodshed Pa turned around and told me to set them cats free. I would've leastways enjoyed listening to all that whupping, but the cats were so snarly I couldn't hear nothing else.

A few minutes later Hugh and Mule came out from behind the woodshed sniffling and walking peculiar. They headed straight on up to the field and Pa said if they so much as looked at me funny for telling on them, they'd get it again twice as bad. I hung right close the rest of the day, and I reckon my tongue even came out a time or two, but they didn't lay a hand on me. Pa must have whaled on them good.

That was a little more than a year ago, about the time Mule turned thirteen and took to calling me a girl and a baby even though I was eleven years old and already a good runner. Me and Pa like to sprint from the house to the barn or the field of which it is good practice for races after prayer meeting. Ma don't want me to run with the boys, but Pa says I'm too fast for the girls and I won't get no faster if I ain't got no one good to run against. But Mule still wouldn't hunt squirrels and rabbits nor throw stones with me no more. Now I go with Rayford. He takes some caring for seeing as he won't wear a straw hat. You got to watch that the sun don't burn his head. And he runs after critters and such, but he whittles things for me, whatever I ask.

"Sun feels good this morning," Pa said.

"I like how it sets the fog to rising when you plow. What you reckon Rayford thinks about that?" I asked.

"I surely don't know," Pa said, shaking his head. "What do you think?"

"I suspicion he thinks it's smoke, and the ground is hot, like wood on fire, and he wonders if it burns your feet." Pa looked over at Rayford. He twirled a leaf between his fingers, watching it turn like as if he was thinking on it.

"Hard to know what's going on in that head. Well, I got to get back to work and Ma is likely waiting for them roots." He stood and ruffled my hair, then he took a long drink from the jug he'd set in the shade. He pulled a handful of grass and grabbed a bucket of water for Beauregard, then went back to the field. I dug another root to top off the basket and took Rayford's wrist, but he wouldn't budge. When I pulled he let loose like a screech owl and Pa turned to us. "I can handle him," I hollered. I broke off a branch of sassafras flowers and shook it in Rayford's face. Pa tapped his head, as if to say that was a right smart idea, and he headed back to work. "You come along, and I'll give this to you," I said, waving the branch. Rayford followed me like a big old puppy.

We came back by the north path and when we got near the creek I caught a whiff of a heavy smell I thought might be spicebush. I set Rayford down on the bank and gave him the sassafras branch and told him to stay. I aimed to see if the spicebush was ripe and surprise Ma with it. I spotted some about twenty feet away and hadn't no more than pushed a willow branch aside to get at it when I heard a rustling sound. I looked back at Rayford and saw he had his eye on a squirrel digging in a pile of leaves over on Driscoll's side of the creek. I hollered at him to stay put, tore off a handful of twigs and tossed them in the basket. When I looked back he was on all fours pushing himself up. "YOU STAY, RAYFORD," I hollered again. He stood and I dropped my basket on the bank and ran for him. Just as I was about to grab him, his foot caught in a patch of vines and he tripped and tumbled and ended up flat on the creek bottom, one whole side of him covered with mud.

"Rayford! I told you to set still, dadblame it! Every durn time we head out I end up in trouble, and here we are again." I could see the look on Ma's face when he came in dirty, especially since he messed his sheets during the night and they had to be washed, not just hung to dry. Leastways I had filled that basket so before Ma got riled, I'd remind her how she likes to sit on the porch of an afternoon with a cup of sassafras tea and a spicebush twig for stirring.

"Rayford, come out of there," I called, but he flopped in the mud like a big old sputtering trout. There wasn't nothing for it but to go after him, so I hiked down the bank. He ain't one to have dirt all over him, but he wouldn't lay still long enough to let the mud settle so I could scoop clear water and rinse him off. Time I got him on top of the bank, there was near as much mud on me as on him. I went back for the basket and as we made for home, I thought as how I'd best take him back along the path that goes behind his garden instead of heading straight to the house, so we could clean up at the well before anyone saw us. That squealy gate was a problem. Then it came to me to wait for Ma to ring the dinner bell to call Pa and my brothers in from the field. You can't see Rayford's gate from there, and if I opened it while the bell was sounding, she wouldn't likely hear it neither. I'd quick pull up water from the well and clean off the worst of that dirt so leastways we'd look a little better. When we went in, I'd hand Ma the basket and tell her I'd wash our clothes, of which she'd make me do it anyway, but it'd come to a better end if I said it without her hollering it to me, and she'd be so happy with that sassafras and spicebush, she wouldn't hardly pay us no mind at all.

It was a good plan until Rayford spotted something in the woods and started off after it. Generally he ain't ornery, but when he sets his mind to something, he gets stubborn. I held tight, but he took to thrashing around, so I had to set the basket down and grab both wrists and sing loud about the chickens who outsmarted the fox. After a few seconds Rayford turned from the woods and moved his head side to side and jabbered along. Pa wouldn't let me take him nowheres at all, excepting that Rayford is partial to my singing, of which that is one way

I keep him in line. Pa says he's right proud of how I handle Rayford even though I'm not much taller than a wagon wheel.

After I sang it once through, Rayford forgot about whatever it was he had in mind to chase and I pulled him along and told him I was going to wash all that mud off. I made the motions with my hands so he'd get the gist of what I was saying, then he got to walking by himself. We got close to where the creek path meets the one that heads over behind his garden by the outhouse when it came to me I'd left the basket back where Rayford got feisty. I nearly called it quits and gave in to all that trouble. By the time I dragged him back to get the basket, dinner would be on the table and Ma and Pa would be out looking for us, and I wouldn't have a chance to clean us off. Then my luck went good again seeing as how I recollected I still had some twine on me. I generally try to keep a piece in my pocket. If there ain't nothing else to hold Rayford's attention, you can knot it and he will try to get them knots out. I tied it up good and handed it to him.

"Rayford, you set on this stump and see to this twine. I'll be back right quick."

He turned it over in his hands and I took off. It wasn't no more than a quarter mile, and I was near most back with the basket when I heard Ma howling. I hightailed it as fast as I could, leaping over roots and rocks on the path and ducking under low branches. I passed the stump where Rayford had been sitting and saw the twine straightened out with nary a knot in it. When I came through the clearing behind the house, Ma came out from nowhere and grabbed my arm and twirled me around, the basket went flying, and I saw Pa whip a sheet off the clothesline and bolt through Rayford's gate. Just before Ma pulled me into the woodshed, I caught a glimpse of Rayford tearing around his garden buck naked.

"You best get explaining, girl," Ma yelled, all red-faced, eyes squeezed tight.

"I found the sassafras like you--"

"Rayford's clothes is covered in mud. Ain't no sassafras growing by the creek."

"First I got the sassafras, then we went to the cr--"

"Ain't a thing in that basket," Ma said, pointing to it tipped on its side near the woods, while she held me tight with the other hand. "It's bad enough you brung him back all muddy, but taking the clothes off him . . . landsakes, it's the work of the devil that brings a young girl to such as that."

"But Ma, I didn't--" and by that time I was bent over a stack of wood, gritting my teeth and listening to the hickory switch whistle through the air before it landed. Ma was so riled, she didn't even stop to pull my dress up. She must've thought of that herself, because she generally only gives me a half dozen swats but she kept at it until she didn't have a breath left. Time she set the switch down and told me to get the wash pot boiling seeing as how I had a mess of muddy clothes to clean up, she was wheezing hard. She leaned against the woodpile to catch her breath and called to Pa with shaky words, "Will, bring them clothes of Rayford's over." She turned to me. "Don't you go light on the lye soap, neither."

My hands had got some scratched and I could near most feel how they'd burn after the lye got to them. I put together another plan for running away, of which those plans never come to naught seeing as how I ain't about to leave Rayford, but my brain don't always think on that. It goes right to a picture of me heading down the road with a poke full of food and a smile on my face, and Ma crying because she made me leave. Then Ma cuffed me and the picture in my brain disappeared. I looked over and saw the coals still glowing from when she had washed Rayford's bedding so leastways all I had to do was stir them up and put more wood on.

Pa hollered over to me then. "Tatum, you best throw Rayford's shirt and britches over the fence rail and let the mud dry, then shake the worst of it out." He tossed Rayford's clothes in a pile outside the garden. "It'll make a bigger mess to wash them now. Looks like you need to do the same with your clothes. Just wash his underclothes now."

Ma had headed back toward the house but when she heard that she turned. She'd been so riled over Rayford, I reckon she didn't even notice the front of my dress. She started in about how it wasn't enough she had to take care of him, she also had a lazy, shiftless, trouble-making daughter on her hands. I let her go on some, but when she took a breath I hollered for Pa. He had Rayford wrapped up in the sheet and they were heading into the house, and he stopped and turned. "Pa! Tell Ma how I had that whole basket of sassafras when Rayford and me talked to you in the field."

And he no more than said, "Well, Mae," when Ma lit into him for taking my side all the time and she grabbed my ear and pulled me back over to the basket lying on the ground. "Tatum Louise Wiley, do you see a lick of sassafras in there?" I felt along the bottom until I found a small piece of root that had got caught in the reeds. "Well, I reckon I can make me a nice drop of tea out of that," she said in a sing song voice and she tossed it in the woods and Pa shook his head.

"This sheet'll have to be washed again," he said, like he didn't have no will to fight with Ma, so I'd best do as I was told. "I'll bring it out after I get Rayford dressed." Seemed like Ma stood a little taller then. She turned and went in the house, and I headed to the wood pile. I fetched kindling, stirred up the coals, and got the fire going again. A few minutes later Ma came out and threw the sheet on the ground next to me. "I want this one clean as the other," she said, pointing to the sheet still hanging on the line. She wiped her hands on her apron like as if to say she was through with that mess, and stomped back to the house.

I picked up the sheet and Granpappy hobbled past with a bucket. "What'd you get into this time?" he asked in a quiet voice. He flicked some wood chips off his shirt, and took his pipe out of his mouth. He generally keeps it in while he's talking and takes it out when he's listening, of which it don't make sense, but that's the way he does it. I tried to talk with a stick in my mouth but either it falls out or I can't make out a word I say.

I told him about Rayford falling in the mud and the rest of it and how if a body was to look, they'd likely find clumps of sassafras root and spicebush twigs all over the ground from home to halfway back to the creek. He looked over toward the house and tapped his pipe on the back of his hand. "You think I'll be as ornery as Ma when I grow up?" I asked.

He put his pipe in his mouth and squinted like as if he was thinking on it. "Well, I suspicion you take after the Wileys. Your Ma's a Stirling and they're a feisty bunch. I knew some Stirlings what came down from the mountains to work the gold mines at

Dahlonega in the thirties when I cobbled boots over there. The men were tall and red-headed and the women were short and red-headed, and every dadblamed one of them was feisty. They were hard workers, I'll give 'em that."

"I know Ma works hard, but Pa does, too, and he don't let it turn him sour. Pa gets atop it but Ma lets it drag on her like she's hauling a mule sled through a plowed field. And she's so mean to Rayford, I can't see as how she and Pa ever got hitched."

"I reckon he was drawn to that spunk. Kind of evened things out. Your Pa has always been easy-going. And I recollect she was some softer starting out. You know they were living the other side of Harpersville with her kin then. If she'd known she'd be taking on Granny and Rayford and me one day, might be she would have turned your pa down. It's been a hardship, and the Stirlings never were a forgiving bunch. Your Ma is strung a might tight. I reckon that's what brings on them pains in her head. Well, I got to fetch water and get some oak splits soaking afore dinner."

I took the sheet to the battling bench and beat on where it had got muddy. I got to thinking as how it might be Ma's hardness that laid heavy on Pa of late, but another part of me piped up she's been ornery for years. Then I smelled lard frying and recollected that Ma had picked some poke sallet earlier and about then my stomach rumbled and I stopped to take a good whiff, when Ma hollered.

"Tatum! Ain't you got that sheet soaking, yet?" Her head stuck out the back door so I quick gathered up the sheet and took it to the wash pot. Then she stepped out and looked over on the fence rail. "You ain't got Rayford's clothes laid out either.

You best get to it, seeing as how we ain't waiting dinner. If that poke sallet is gone time you get in, I reckon you ain't like to get none."

2

Ma Will Work Me To Death

Ma put a fire under the wash pot first thing this morning and told Pa it looked like a good drying day of which that meant she was in a cleaning mood, so I hightailed it to the barn. I holed up in a corner behind a pile of hay, of which I wouldn't have done excepting I had a plan. That hay itched the inside of my head like as if it had crawled up my nose. Pa says if a sneeze is coming you better let it go or your eyeballs will pop right out, but I reckon he's putting on about that. I didn't want him to know I was there, leastways not until after he got Beauregard hitched up. Whilst he went in and told Ma he was set to head out to Harpersville for supplies and seed and to get corn ground, I aimed to jump on the back of the wagon and hide amongst the feed sacks, and in a few hours I'd be picking out sweets over to the general store.

I ain't never in a cleaning mood, but most especially not on days Pa is heading to town.

Melanie is more one for such as that. When she lived here, if Ma was in a cleaning mood, Melanie was in a cleaning mood. If Ma was in a quilting mood, Melanie was in a quilting mood. She did everything Ma did without no fussing. She can sit at mending all day long, and put her hands in the hottest water and knit as good as Granny, and her biscuits are always tender.

I reckon I ain't got sitting-still blood, I got fast-moving blood. I like to run races with Pa and chase the squirrels around the tree for him when he's hunting, and it don't turn my stomach to pull the skin off them while Pa holds their legs. I like the way you yank at it, and it pulls clean off the meat, like as if that was the way it was meant to happen. Melanie didn't want to see none of that, and wouldn't never pull feathers off chickens nor help gut a deer nor butcher a hog nor cut up a possum for cooking. If ever you were to ask her, she would scrunch up her nose and turn her head. "I don't want to see none of that til it's a hunk of meat ready to coat with flour or corn meal or toss in a stew," she'd say.

It ain't that I like killing critters, but I ain't never been one for house chores. Pa says I got me a knack for hoeing, but truth to tell, it's just that I'd rather work with him than Ma. If he said we were heading out to the woods to chop down a tree and haul wood all day, even if he tried to set me against it by saying it would be hard work and we'd get tired and thirsty, I'd still hop right on the wagon just to be by him. That's why I aimed to go to town. Well, truth to tell, I like sweets, too.

Trouble is, Pa wouldn't never get there the way he was going at it. He treats that dadblamed mule like Missy's Ma treats her little brother, Hereford, when he gets ornery at prayer meeting and takes off and runs hither and yon and the whole time he's hollering and putting on. If it was my ma, she would've had me hanging by my ear, but Missy's ma sets to chasing Hereford all over whilst the preacher eyeballs her with the wrath of God. Finally she grabs hold of his shirt and picks him up and says, "Now, Hereford, you set right still and don't you be bothering all these nice folks what's trying to hear the good Lord's word." Missy says her ma can't bear to take a switch to a child seeing as how loving is a better way. Pa is like that, too, of which I am grateful, or I don't reckon I'd have any hide left at all.

But Beauregard is just a stubborn old mule, so I don't know why Pa puts up with him. I couldn't see from behind the hay, but I heard Beauregard heeing and hawing and prancing, and Pa pleading "C'mon, Beauregard" as if that mule would listen to polite talking. "We got a long trip," he said. I couldn't barely keep my sneeze in, but it was a might harder to hold my tongue. Every time the harness shook I wanted to yell out and set Pa straight. Sometimes he can be downright exasperating. Then Pa rose his voice and said "Hold still, now," and I couldn't help myself.

"Give him a good kick or you'll be here forever," I called out.

"Reckon that kind of treatment'd work on you?" he said. Truth to tell, Pa wouldn't hurt a fly. "What're you hiding here for, Tatum? Don't suppose you were planning to hop on the wagon afore I left."

"ACHOO!"

"Bless you."

"Pa, why can't I come with you? Ma will work me to death, and I ain't been to town for months."

When Melanie was still here, Pa took me to town a lot and whilst he was at the mill getting corn ground, I ran to the general store and gave his list to Mr. Wright. He filled it and I looked at the bright jars of red and black licorice whips and smooth peppermint sticks and honey-colored horehounds and puckery yellow lemon drops. My mouth filled up with spit just looking at them. When he had the rest of the order together, Mr. Wright came over and ripped off a sheet of brown paper and spread it out on the counter and he'd look over the counter at me.

"Hey there, Tatum. How is your Ma feeling these days?"

I had to be polite and tell him she was fine, even if she wasn't, of which she never was, but Pa heard me tell the truth once and said that people asked just to be kindly and I didn't have to go on—just be polite and say everyone was fine. Then Mr. Wright would ask about Rayford and I'd say how he was still partial to peppermint. I always hoped he'd say, "Then I best throw in an extra peppermint stick for him," but he went on to asking after Melanie and Hugh and Mule. It near most drove me crazy to talk kindly til he got around to asking did I care to pick out any sweets seeing as how Pa had a half pound written on the list. Then he'd take his time and if someone else came in and Pa hadn't come back from the mill yet, he'd say, "Excuse me, Tatum, Mrs. Beasely looks as if she's ready to be waited on," of which I already knew seeing as how her wheezing gets real loud when she wants attention.

When Mr. Wright finished with her, he'd come back and he'd say, "How's your granpappy's hip?" like as if he saved that just to tease me more, and I'd tell him how Granpappy still had the limp, but he didn't complain. I sure wanted to tell him how Ma complained about her head pains all the time and I helped her a lot with the work so he'd feel obliged to throw in an extra licorice whip or two seeing as how I was such a good child. But if Pa walked in in the middle of such as that, he'd likely tell Mr. Wright we didn't need no sweets this time. After more talking about the weather or some such, Mr. Wright finally picked out what I wanted and wrapped it up, but he held on to it til he saw Pa coming up the steps. Then he handed it over the counter and told me I was lucky to have such a Pa.

But since Melanie left, I hardly ever get to town, and it didn't look like I'd be heading out today, neither.

"Town's no place for a child these days, what with talk of war stirring up regular folks until they get to acting crazy," Pa said.

"Stupid war. It's ruining everything." I stood up and brushed straw off my dress, but I stayed put.

"Can't argue with you there." Beauregard brayed again and tossed his head and lifted his hoof and near most stomped Pa's foot, but Pa just patted his neck and finally got the harness straps together under his belly. Pa is the most patient man in the world. 'Course he gets a heap of practice with Ma.

"But Ma put the wash pot to boiling and I reckon she has in mind to take the beds apart and undo the rope and boil it and empty the mattress ticks and wash 'em and lay out the straw to air in the sun and do all the quilts. I can't bear to think of a whole day listening to nothing but water boiling and Ma complaining how her head hurts and her back is paining her and then she'll have to rest a spell, and it'll be me hanging the quilts and retying the rope on the beds and stuffing all the straw back in and you know how it always makes me sneeze."

Pa was quiet. It came to me he was probably fixing to say something to make me feel better. He rubbed Beauregard behind the ears, and I waited for them kindly words like how Ma shouldn't be so hard on me.

"Ma said you were chasing chickens again this morning," he said, still petting Beauregard. Sometimes Pa surprises me.

"I wasn't chasing chickens." He turned his head and lifted an eyebrow. "I wasn't. Not *lots* of chickens, just *one*, and it was that feisty russet that pecks on all the others. She's just the meanest old hen, she puts me in mind of--" I near most said Ma, but I caught myself, "--of one of them witches in them stories Granny used to tell." Granny never told a story the same, but every one had a witch in it and they were always mean to children and whupped them, or ate them, or scared them, or made them work real hard and wear rags and she never gave them anything to eat. Truth to tell, Ma lets me eat and Ma wouldn't make us wear rags, but if I ain't out hoeing cotton or hiding somewheres, she ain't happy until I am miserable doing chores. And it don't do no good to stick to them and get them done so I can have some time to myself, no sir, she just gives me more. I already done enough to last me til I die, of which it ain't like to be long the way Ma has been working me.

"Why d'you let her yell at you, Pa? She hollers at you near as much as she hollers at me, and you don't say a word. Are you afeared of her?" He took off his hat and brushed his hair back. I wish I had hair like Pa, a good dark brown with a turn to it here and there. Melanie and Mule got hair like that. Hugh's got some red, from Ma's side of the family, but most of it came out on me. Pa put his hat on again. "You're bigger than she is, Pa. She won't take the switch to you if you talk back."

"That ain't respectful," he said and before I could defend myself, there came a wild whooping sound the likes of which near most curdled my blood.

"There you are!" Ma roared into the barn like a runaway fire, eyes blazing, tongue whipping around like the devil had got hold of it and I ducked back into the pile of hay. "Tatum Louise Wiley, I surely hope you ain't got it in your head that you are going to town!"

"Now take it easy, Mae--" Pa said, but he don't never stand a chance, no sir, not against that wild woman.

"Well, I surely would like to take it easy," Ma hollered back, and I knew we were both in for a good talking to. "As it is I get up when the rooster crows and by dinner time, my back is paining me so I can't barely walk no more and the day ain't but half through. There's work everywhere I look and this young woman—no sir, William Wylie, don't you go calling her a child— she's a young woman and best take on her share lessen you and the boys aim to help with the cooking and the garden and the wash and everything else that has got to be done round here." I know better than to try to talk sense to her when she is riled, but it sounded like Pa needed help. "Rayford plants the garden," I called out, but I stayed hidden.

"And when I need sweet taters or greens I go out and get em," she yelled back. Then she laid into Pa again, so I figured I'd best get whilst I had the chance, seeing as how her last words would be a mess of chores for me. "Rayford takes all day to do what a regular man does afore breakfast," Ma said like as if we ain't heard this same speech every week since I was born. "For every bit of work he does, he makes four times that. You treat him like a baby and you treat that girl like a child." I pushed through the pile of hay along the edge of the barn and crawled for the door. "You're working me to death, Will, and there ain't no need of it. I took care of your ma til she died and it looks like I'll be nursing your pa til he's in his grave, too. We got two full-growed boys who do half a day's work then go off fishing and hunting and come home empty-handed. You're too easy on em, Will. You're too easy on em, and it's me that's paying the price."

Poor Pa. Just once I'd like to hear him say he never should've got hitched to that cantankerous old pea hen. I had my eye on the door, but my dadblamed escape was taking forever. I peeked out from behind the hay. Ma was bent toward Pa, red-faced, still hollering, one hand on her hip and the other pointing to where I was standing when she came in, of which that was a good sign if she thought I was still way back there. Then Pa patted Beauregard, his mouth open like he was waiting for Ma to hush so he could say his piece. I felt sorry for him. If I was Pa and not just a child, I would've hollered right back at her.

Then Ma took a breath and Pa put his arm around her, like as if she had just brought him a sweet potato pie. They were facing the back of the barn, so I kept crawling until I got to within twenty feet of the door, and as I stood, I heard Pa say: "I suspicion the Lord had in mind for there to be more to this world than working from the time we are old enough to walk til He lays us back down. Children grow up too fast as it is." I should've thanked him, but there was a voice in my head telling me to keep my mouth shut. I reckon it was the devil come by to tempt me to his evil ways, and it was working. I was near most to the door when Ma set to hollering again and I scooted behind the wagon. I couldn't see her face, but I had in mind what it looked like, all hard and squeezed tight with her lips ramming together like two fighting worms.

"You hear me now, William Wylie, if Hugh put as much time and calculating into working as he does into pounding nails into boards, we could double our stand of corn and cotton, and Mule ain't far behind. If Hugh has such a good mind, I don't see why you let him waste it on pulling jokes and building worthless contraptions that never amount to nothing. Will, they are *men*—not children. When you were as old as them you were out working from dawn til dusk and caring for Rayford besides. And you'd best take a good look at your daughter. She's a young woman, whether you treat her like one or not."

"Mae, she's only twelve."

It was quiet for so long I finally peeked out. Pa's hand worked Ma's neck like as if to calm her down, then Ma's shoulders rose and she pulled away from Pa. I stood and hightailed it for the door, but my foot kicked something and it screeched and I tripped over it and as I hit the ground, I heard her holler, "Tatum!"

"Dadblame it, Cleopatra! You could've made a noise. Five more steps and I'd have been out the door." I stood and brushed hay off my clothes. Ma looked at me with a face like sour milk and stomped past me and out the door. I turned to Pa and gave him a friendly smile. "That was a close one," I said, quiet so Ma wouldn't hear, but he didn't look none too happy with me, neither. He folded his arms and stared at the ground. Then he looked over to the house, and I knew there wasn't going to be no sneaking on the wagon.

"Go help your ma," he said.

I thought on all the things I could say as to how she is the meanest, most orneriest, most cantankerous old biddy that ever lived in the whole wide world, but seeing as how he tried to tell Ma that I am still just a child, it came to me that I was obliged to do as he said. And I didn't suspicion this was a good time to bring up those lemon drops and horehound candies neither.

3

Aint He A Wonder?

I hauled a bucket of ashes to the barrel in the woodshed, dumped them, and stood back while the soot rose like smoke. Ma had told me to clean the hearth and build a new fire so it would burn down in time to make a pan of cornbread for dinner. The woodshed ain't no more than an open lean-to at the back of the house so after I pulled a few logs from the pile set against the east wall, I peeked over to Rayford's garden. He eyed something on his water stand, so I ran over for a quick look. As I climbed through the fence rails, I told Ma in my head how it wouldn't take more than a minute or two.

He had pushed his drinking bucket to the back of the stand and set up a line of whittled critters that put me in mind of pictures I'd seen of a circus parade. He had a mule, a chicken, a hound dog, a pole cat, two squirrels—one big and one little—a rabbit, and two racoons, of which one had a fish in his mouth.

Rayford whittled that one last year when the water was high and we went to the creek to watch Mule fish. Near dark a racoon came out of Driscoll's woods about fifteen yards away, scurried back and forth on the bank, then dashed in the water and grabbed a fish. I reckon it would've stayed and ate it, but Rayford got to caterwauling and scared it back into the woods. When Pa took him out to his garden the next morning, Rayford found a piece of wood to his liking and by the end of the week he had whittled that raccoon with a fish in its mouth.

Rayford can't think the way other folks can, but he has his own way of looking at things, like how he is partial to critters, and it don't matter if they are tame or wild. One morning last week I was toting empty buckets from the house to the well in his garden, and there he was, kneeling hunched up on the ground with his hands cupped together. I crept closer til I could make out he had a baby thrasher, feathered, but still young. It must have flown from a nest in the thicket beyond his garden. He held it for the longest time, then tilted his right hand, and the bitty thing hopped and huddled in just his left hand. He petted the tiny feathers and those big fingers of his turned soft as wisps of cotton. I waved and he looked at me, so I tiptoed over. He held his hand out and I saw how the little bird rested easy like as if it knew it was safe. He held it for two, maybe three minutes, then he stood and set it on a fence post at the edge of the garden and went back to his chair. He sat and watched that bird, and that bird sat and watched Rayford. As hard as they were eyeballing each other, it was like they were talking back and forth without words. About the time I reckoned the poor little bird's wing had broke, it flew up into the hackberry tree. Rayford's eyes followed it, then he went back to his whittling.

Generally he ends up with a critter, but he can make a likeness of anything he has a mind to. He picks up a piece of wood and takes his knife to it, and in a day or two it's a hen, or a flower, or even folks. You should see the one he whittled of Preacher Abernathy, of which Ma took it and set it on her dresser. With that scowl carved on him and his mouth open, you near most expected him to set to preaching, even if he was just made of wood. Then there was the one he whittled of our neighbor, Mr. Foster, with long straight hair so real looking, you knew right away who it was. And you wouldn't think as how a body could whittle nice, or happy, or such as that, but Rayford has the knack of it. Like on the carving of my sister, Melanie. She is pretty, but she is also good-hearted and when you look at that likeness, you can see it. I reckon it's how he whittled her eyes, big, and with a crinkle or two in the corners. Some of his carvings we give away but I kept the one of Melanie. She got hitched to Joram Foster and lives with his family over past McCreedy's Hill and down the road south three miles. His ma, Miss Clara Foster, ain't been well, so even though Joram lit out and joined the Confederate Army last fall, Melanie stayed on to help take care of her. Ma says she'd best be helping here, but if I was Melanie I wouldn't want to come home, neither. Miss Clara ain't a lick like Ma, so I reckon she and Melanie have a fine time.

Ma don't care none for Rayford's whittling. Once he was carving on a thing that wasn't a critter nor a flower nor a person. When he finished I saw it was the leg bone of a chicken, as natural looking as if he'd just ate the meat off and set it on his plate. "Can I have this?" I asked. He ain't partial to anything he whittles. It's the whittling he likes, but I never take one of his carvings unless I ask him. Pa says it's respectful and Rayford deserves respect like regular folks. I even try to give him extra seeing as how Ma is short on respecting him.

Like with that chicken leg. That day I ran to the yard where Ma was sweeping the hard dirt bare with Granny's old corn shuck broom. "Hey, Ma, look what I found." She stopped the broom, looked at the carving, made a sour face, and went back to her sweeping. "Ma, look!" I said again.

"If you ain't got nothing better to do than bother me with old chicken bones, you best take this broom."

I had got her! I jumped around a time or two, laughing, and held it up again. "See? It's just a piece of wood. Rayford whittled a real-looking chicken leg of it. Ain't he a wonder?" I waved it in her face, and she swung at it and knocked it to the ground. Then she turned her head away like as if that bone had a stink and went back to her sweeping. As I picked up the carving and brushed it off I heard the chink of a mallet on a nail, so I crossed the road to the barn. One side is for storing hay and sheltering Beauregard and Belle, but I headed to the side Granpappy turned into a workshop where he and Pa and Hugh tinker and such. He was at his cobbler's bench working on a new pair of boots for Mule. I flopped on the ground and he looked up, then went back to his work. He had two short nails in his mouth and pounded them into the heel, then he set his mallet down and reached behind on the bench for his pipe and put it in his mouth.

"What you got there?" he asked and I showed him. "Chicken leg? Is that for good luck?"

"It ain't real. It's wood. Rayford carved it. See?" He took it and eyed it.

"Hmmm," he said. "Don't see as it's good for much, but it surely is a fine likeness." He handed it back to me. "I saw you through the door. Is that what your ma was riled about?" I nodded. "You oughtn't to bother her with such as that."

"Well, if she'd just once allow as to how he is the best whittler ever, I reckon she'd go easier on him. And she wouldn't get so riled when he wets the bed."

"Ain't no use fighting it. She ain't like to tolerate him til plants grow root-end up. You best let it be." Of a sudden, the way Ma is mean to Rayford got to paining me like as if I had just found it out. I don't know as I ever felt so sad. I hid my face in my hands, and Granpappy let out a deep breath. "Come," he said. I wiped my eyes and went to him and he put his arm around my shoulders. "Ain't no use carrying on about your ma that way. She don't bother Rayford none. He's my own born son but since you took to him, I don't give nary a thought to worrying on him no more. Couldn't nobody love him more nor better than you."

"But what's the good of it, when it hurts so."

"Tatum, the heaviest load a body can carry is the weight of a tender heart." He brushed his hand over my hair, again and again, and I felt the truth of those words come out in tears on my face. After a bit, he took out his pipe and pulled a hanky out of his britches pocket and handed it to me, then put his pipe back in his mouth. "It's clean," he said, and he winked, and I laughed and wiped my face with it. I hugged him and he grabbed me round the waist. "Now, you go get me that piece of leather so

I can make a set of laces. Rayford ain't the only hand at making things round here."

I recollect that time a lot when I get sad. Granpappy's kindly like Pa and like to take my side, lessen I done something really mean of which I ain't one for meanness. I reckon Ma is waiting on him to die but I hope he waits til I'm grown and gone off on my own, of which that will never happen because I ain't like to leave Pa. I ain't like to grow up neither seeing as how Ma will just make me work more. It's a sorry thing to think on.

I felt a nudge and took the cup of water Rayford poured for me, but with my mind on that leg bone it jumped right to recollecting how Ma won't even let him give her water. It is another thing about Rayford that he likes to give people things. There is a stand setting by his twig chair that Pa first built for his whittling knife and bucket of wood and the things he carves. Then Pa taught him how to bring up water from the well and he set a small bucket and a ladle on the stand for Rayford to dip his own water when he gets thirsty. When Pa came to talk to him, he'd take a drink himself, and before long, when Rayford saw Pa coming, he'd dip a ladle of water for him. Now everyone who comes into his garden gets water, excepting Ma.

"Rayford, can I keep this coon with the fish in its mouth? It is such a good likeness." When we tell how he done a good job it always puts a smile on his face. Next time Mule goes on about how stupid Rayford is, I aim to tell him about how there can be knowing without words. There's times even words can't tell how you feel, like when you're so sad all you can do is cry, or when you're so happy, the laughing spills right out of you.

When we get too many carvings we take them to prayer

meetings at Colter's on days there's a picnic after. We go outside and Pa is like to hold Rayford's hand so he don't go running off after the Colters' chickens or cats. Pa sits him on a stump and folks bring a bench over and Rayford takes out his carvings and sets them up on the bench like he did on his water stand today. The children gather round and the smallest one walking comes up first, and it is likely to be a Cobb seeing as how they have a large relation. If I was to set it up, I'd let the oldest one who wanted a carving come first, seeing as how the little ones likely don't care what they get.

A few years back Rayford carved a mess of wish bones and we brought them to give away. Driscoll's boy, Silas, who is the same age as Hugh, took one, and no one thought nothing of it, but there was some whispering. Then every boy took one and Leroy Cobb got back in line and turned in his hound dog for one, too. Next week at prayer meeting, Mr. Cobb told Pa he best not bring no more wishbones, seeing as how Leroy nearly took out little Annabelle's eye with it. I was standing with Pa and he gave Mr. Cobb a funny look. "Them boys turned all them wishbones into sling shots," he said, and Pa looked straight at Hugh. Hugh made a face like he didn't have nothing to do with it, but then his shoulders came up a bit and his head sunk down, like a turtle trying to pull back in its shell.

Ma hollered then and I quick ran back to build up the fire. She says I'm lazy but that ain't the truth of it. I told her how I get to thinking on one thing or another and forget what I was working at. She don't see it that way. I've heard them ladies at prayer meeting talk on how the first-born girl is special. That's Melanie. She can darn stockings and is a good hand at mending and knitting and crochet, and I ain't much for none of that. I suspicion Ma wishes it was me that was off and married and that I'd take Rayford with me. To me she is looking at it all wrong. Near most every girl or woman for miles around can do fancy work, but it's only us who have a body in their family that can carve a chicken leg bone so good you have to look twice to see it ain't real.

4

Why Is There A War?

Pa went to town again today. When he told Ma at breakfast, she laid into him something awful. Seems to me if you want someone to stay, you'd best not holler at them all the time, but I don't reckon Ma wants to hear such as that from me. I ain't never surprised that Pa leaves, I am only surprised that he comes back.

She kept at me all day and I never even got one chore done before I heard, "Tatum, come sweep the yard," or some such. Mid-day she got wound up when I didn't get the peas shucked fast enough and came after me with the battling board. We ran around the yard and when we got near the barn, she threw it at me, and I leapt aside, and Granpappy hollered, "Mae!" She stopped dead in her tracks and burst into tears. Granpappy hobbled up to her and took his pipe out of his mouth to talk, of which I ain't never seen him do before. He pointed it at the front porch. "You git up there and set. You know you ain't to get yourself all het up like that." He stood right there and so did Ma. "Git!" he said, louder, and he motioned to the porch with his head. Ma took one step, then another and her shoulders shook. The way she dragged her feet it looked like it took all her strength just to move them. "I mean it," Granpappy said. "You'll land up sick again. I'll have Tatum bring you your piecework if you want or you can just set."

He didn't take his eyes off her til she was at the steps. "Tatum, you go find some mullein and dig up the root and fix your ma some tea. You know mullein? That tall spiky-top plant with the wooly leaves?" I nodded. "You look over where the road curves and follow it on up the hill. Should find some thereabouts."

I like chores that get me away from the house and moving some, so I headed right over and got the hand shovel from the shed in Rayford's garden. I would've taken him with me, but he was bent over the melon patch looking for bugs and worms. He won't kill the bugs with his hands. I suspicion he don't like the way it feels. Hugh made him a contraption that looks like a cup with a bottom made out of a piece of tin with a whole mess of tiny holes punched in it and an inside piece of rounded wood near as big as the cup. Pa showed Rayford how to put the bugs in there and press the inside piece against them so they'd come out the bottom and go back into the ground and make things grow. Them holes get plugged up quick and nothing never gets through but Pa said that ain't the idea. "It helps if Rayford gets the bugs off, but if he just throws em back on the ground, it don't do a lick of good." So me and Pa and Granpappy open it up every day and scrape out all the squashed bugs. Now that is a thing Melanie wouldn't never do but I don't hear Ma boasting on me over it.

I went out to where the road curves and found the mullein right away, but I took my time walking along the road like as if I didn't have a care in the world. About the time I reckoned Granpappy would look for me, I dug up a couple of plants, and took them back to the well to rinse the dirt off. Rayford came over with his toy spinning top and pulled on my arm like he wanted me to play. "Rayford, I got to fix tea for Ma, then I'll come back." He grinned, but he didn't move, so I reckoned that many words were too hard to figure.

Cleopatra came over then with two kittens and rubbed up against his leg. He petted her, then tried to grab a kitten and they ran, and Cleopatra took off, too. He went after them, and they'd leap away, then stop and sniff at a plant or eat a piece of grass. Rayford would just about catch them, then they'd leap and run a little further. If Granpappy was up on the porch sleeping in the chair and Ma was resting, I would've caught one of them kittens so Rayford could pet it, or we could've made pictures in the dirt or played with his top. Rayford's garden is near most my favorite place to be. It's always what comes to mind when we sing them hymns with words like peaceful and calm and such as that.

Ma don't set store by them hymns. She's partial to meetings where the preacher talks a might on the devil and his evil doings, and where he gets himself wrought up some. Preacher Abernathy, who comes up every once in awhile, is her most favorite. He gets to carrying on, hollering and such, until his face turns red, then you know it's coming. He stops and lets us stew whilst he takes out his hanky and blows into it so as you'd think a sorry old goose took over the pulpit. When he gets his breathing back regular, he picks up where he left off and his preaching gets louder and louder. Then he stops again, only this time he stretches his neck up, somewhat like a tom turkey, and makes himself tall and his cheeks puff out and he hangs on to the pulpit and leans over, and if you are close you'd best watch out for flying spit, and everyone hushes. When it's so quiet you can hear Loretta Beasely's wheezing, he hollers that if we aim to see the inside of heaven we must be fearful of the devil and shout, GET THEE BEHIND ME!

I don't hold much with that idea. If the devil is up to no good, I reckon he'd best be right there in front of me so I can keep my eye on him.

Truth to tell, them prayer meetings ain't near as entertaining since the dadblamed Yankees took to heading our way. All folks ever want to talk about is war and Yankees, and it don't make no sense whatsoever. Even Pa and Granpappy get in it. One night this week they were sitting on the porch watching the sunset and Granpappy said, "I ain't got no use for war, and you best not get no foolish ideas in your head. My hip is getting worse--"and then I came out to hear better and they quit talking. I suspicion that's where Granpappy hurt his hip, in a war. When I ask Pa about it, he says ask Granpappy. When I ask Granpappy he says he don't like to talk on it none.

Pa says war's a terrible thing, but Hugh and Mule can't wait to go and get their licks in. "If I was Pa, I'd be at the war right now," Hugh told Mule when they were climbing up to the loft last night. I told him you have to be seventeen to join up with the Confederate Army, but he said he has a mind to lie about his age like some of his friends who've lit out and joined up already. "And if you tell Pa, you'll be wishing *you'd* run away and joined up," he said. I stuck my tongue out, but he didn't see it, so it didn't make me feel better. Can't say as I'd miss him. He generally don't pay me no mind, just goes about his business, sawing and nailing on some contraption or other.

I asked Pa why is there a war and he said there's two reasons, mainly. One is state's rights and the other is darkies. I don't know no darkies, but once when we were in Harpersville I saw one driving a wagon and another one hauling feedsacks by the mill. Pa says there's lots of them farther south in Georgia and in other states. I asked Pa what did the darkies do, and he said they're owned by other folks and work for them. "Like how Ma owns me and I work for her?" I asked, but Pa shook his head and said some of them are treated like animals or worse. "Well that surely does sound like me," I told Pa, but he didn't pay no mind to that, he just went on talking. He don't think it's right for one body to own another, but he said he don't see as how it's right for the northern states to tell the south how to run their business, neither.

Most of the traveling preachers don't hold with the idea of owning folks, but some, like Preacher Abernathy, say, "Why, the very Bible itself tells us that slavery is part of the natural order of things." The preachers tell us to pray and put it in the Lord's hands, but I reckon that ain't working seeing as how it's come down to where war is near most the only thing folks ever talk about, excepting at our place. Ma says mealtimes ought to be quiet unless we are talking to the Lord. "Maybe the Lord don't want to be bothered none when He's eating, neither," I said once, but Pa coughed and told Ma she looked right pretty in that dress. Ma pulled a face. "This is the same dress I've been wearing nigh onto six years, so I don't see what makes it so pretty today." She near most hollered them words like as if he was all the way out in the barn instead of across the table. He told her that it was her that made it pretty, and the end of it was that I didn't get a whupping.

Last week at prayer meeting I asked Missy Tarkan—of which I was sorry I did seeing as how the only reason she's my friend is there ain't no other girls my age—I asked her what did she know about darkies. "They're made by the devil," she said to me in that prissy voice of hers that she puts on like as if she knows everything in the world. "And they grow like cotton or tobacco on them big plantations." She set her face just so and poked her chin out at me.

I reckon she's got it in her head that's how you act when you're smart, but truth to tell, it just made me want to bust her a good one. Missy has told me lots of things that ain't true, so I didn't know whether to believe her or not, and then, like as if she knew what I was thinking, she asked me, "Why do you reckon their skin is so black?" Before I could think on it, she set her face an inch from mine and hollered, "From the dirt!" I got spit all over me and near most went deaf, and I reckon I would've whaled on her, but what she said set me to thinking. I have had a go in with the devil a time or two myself and he always comes out ahead, so if he made them darkies, I set my mind to it that I didn't want nothing to do with them. When we got home, I asked Pa about the darkies that grew in the ground. He said he could see how Missy might think that, but, truth to tell, it was the Lord that made them, and likely they were like us, only with darker skin, but it was a thing folks couldn't agree on. "I generally go with the idea that a man is good until he shows me otherwise." Pa is one for saying such as that.

Ma tells me it ain't polite to listen to the grownups at prayer meetings, but Missy's ma, Anna Tarkan, she talks real loud about the war, and unless you clop your hands over your ears and scream, there ain't no way not to hear about it. Last prayer meeting she said, "Them bluecoats weren't so bad when they were playing games over at Fort Pulaski, but they're in Georgia now, up near Dalton. Our boys can't hold em." It came to me she might be inclined to tell stories like Missy. Pa ain't said nothing about it so I ain't worried. Besides which, I got my hands full steering clear of Ma.

I don't know a lot about the world, but I don't see as how there could be a finer place than Rayford's garden. Well, I like our whole farm. We got a big south-facing house. When we moved here, Granpappy and Granny and Rayford lived in a one-room cabin that ran east to west up against the woods. Granpappy traded some land to Mr. Driscoll, our neighbor on the north side of the creek, for help building on to the old cabin. They took off the south wall and put in a kitchen and parlor to the east, three bedrooms to the west, and a loft down the middle under the rafters. Ma and Pa got the north bedroom. Granpappy and Granny and Rayford got the middle bedroom seeing as how it was the biggest, howsomever when Granny got real bad, they set her up in the kitchen. I recollect sitting on her bed with the fire going hotter than hell, but I stayed because she could tell a good story. Her spinning wheel was in the kitchen, too, but after she passed on, they moved it to the loft, where the boys sleep. Ma still uses it some, but Granny was a better hand at it.

I reckon that big house was Ma's idea seeing as how she had worked for some rich people when she was my age, taking care of their children. She still talks on that some, and about the house and all the rooms they had and how she always wanted a big house some day.

Me and Melanie had the other bedroom with our window on the south wall, of which it meant we were first to see morning light. Our beds are beneath the window and our dress hooks are pegged into the wall acrost. Pa nailed a shelf above them where I put my favorite carvings of Rayford's, like the one of Melanie, and the coon with the fish in its mouth, and Bee Boy, our hound dog that died when I was eight.

From the porch you can see the barn and corral across the road. Rayford's garden sets off to the east, and if you look past it, you can see where the road curves and heads on up to McCreedy's Hill. The cotton and corn field is on a hill the other side of the woods to the west and there's the woods back of the house with two paths that lead to the creek. If we didn't have to put up with Ma I reckon we'd have the best place in the whole world, but Pa says since I'm only twelve and ain't been farther than Harpersville, I might change my mind someday.

I shook the water off the mullein root, went to the kitchen and made the tea. When I took it out to Ma I asked did she want anything else. She shook her head. I headed back to Rayford's garden and heard a door slam. I suspicioned she'd gone in to lay down.

When Pa came home, he looked in on her and told me to put supper on. She didn't even come out to eat.

5

I'll Be Counting On You

I reckon this morning Pa finally had his fill of Ma, seeing as how he sent her off to Fosters to visit Melanie. He said she needed a day away, of which that is fine with me. I need a day away from her, too. But after she left, he didn't head up to the field, like I reckoned he would. Instead he poured a cup of coffee and went out on the porch and sat and rocked. I put it up to how Ma has been lately.

She had set out chores, but I had most of the day to get them done so I wasn't in no hurry. As soon as she cleared the curve of the road, I got the wagon Rayford carved for me, of which it's near most as big as Pa's shoes. It has a tongue for hitching and Hugh attached the wheels so they'd turn. I tied a cornshuck doll in the wagon and aimed to hitch two hens to it, so they could take the doll for a ride. Ma don't like me messing with the chickens. She says it's the devil that puts such ideas in my head, but Pa says it's good to think and come up with ideas, as long as you don't hurt nobody. After Ma yells at me, Pa is likely to come up and say, "You know why your Ma got riled about that don't you?" Then I nod and he says: "Well, you got to respect her, so don't do that no more. But I am glad to see you are using your brains." Truth to tell, I ain't got no trouble coming up with ideas, but making them work is a might harder.

I tied two lengths of twine to the wagon tongue and headed over to where a half dozen chickens were pecking for worms and grubs between Rayford's garden and the road. I walked around real slow and picked up a handful of dirt and tossed it so they'd think I was throwing out corn or such as that. I kept circling them like as if I was thinking on what a nice looking bunch of hens they were and as soon as I got close, I snatched one. I had in mind to hold her good until I got both legs tied, but as soon as I pulled the rope tight on one leg off she went, leaping and squawking and flapping like the wind had picked her up and tossed her in the air, and that wagon looked like it was hanging on for dear life. You wouldn't think a hen could move that fast with a piece of wood tied on her leg, but I reckon she had in mind that wagon was after her. I couldn't get nowheres near her for five minutes or so, then she tired some and I dove at her and grabbed the wagon. She flapped hard enough she nearly lifted me off the ground. I pulled her closer with the wagon, but every time I touched her leg to untie the twine, she set to squawking and flapping all over again. I was nearly deaf when a hand came down and sliced the twine with a knife and the hen flew off. I ain't never seen a hen go that far without touching down.

"You keep bothering the chickens, we won't never see another egg."

"Thanks, Pa. I tried to get the twine off her but she wouldn't hold still." I stood and brushed the dirt off my knees, and showed him the wagon. "Rayford sure whittles a good wagon, don't he?" I said to Pa with a big smile on my face. He nodded, but I could see he was thinking on something else. I looked over at Rayford. He was sitting in his twig chair with his mouth open and a piece of wood in one hand and his knife in the other, like he couldn't believe what he saw neither. I tried to think of something more to say about Rayford, or the wagon, or anything, but all I could think about was that this was going to be the first whupping I ever got from Pa.

"I didn't mean no harm, Pa." He didn't answer, he just looked around the farm like he hadn't never seen it before. He stood there so long, I got to worrying. "Pa!" I said, pushing his arm.

He pulled in a deep breath through his nose, and blew it out, then he shook his head and looked at me. "You should've had some schooling. You got a good thinking brain. I reckon if it had more book learning to think on, you wouldn't be tying chickens to wagons."

"But you taught us to read and cipher. And you bought us all them books on history and geography and such."

"Wasn't enough for you. You took to book learning right from the start. I didn't mind so much that the others didn't go to school. Melanie was always one for working with your Ma. Hugh has a good brain, too, but he don't need to learn from books. And once Mule sets his mind for or against something there's no changing it. That's how he got his nickname you know."

"Well, he sure don't seem like a Harley."

"No, he don't. But he works like a Mule, too, when he has to, and it's a thing he can do right by. He'll get through life just fine. I reckon they got what they need to get by, but you should have had more learning. With Rayford and Granny and Granpappy to care for and the farm to run, and you children, I just couldn't see my way clear to get you to school and back each day. I reckon I should've tried harder."

"Ma wouldn't have let me go anyway."

"Well, your Ma's family didn't set store by book learning. Never saw the need of it up in the mountains." He stooped over and picked up a rock and looked towards the woods. I reckon he had his eyes on a tree seeing as how he threw it hard and when it hit he nodded his head, like as if he'd done what he had in mind to do. Then he made a weird face. "Let's take a walk down by the creek." He took off towards the woods, and I followed him.

"Can we go to our tree?" I asked it in a soft voice like as if to let him know I was still sorry about chasing the chickens, but truth to tell, I wasn't.

He didn't answer but we were headed that way. We've been going to the stand of hickories to pick nuts for as long as I can recollect, and one tree has come to be our favorite. It has two good sitting branches low to the ground, and when we have us time to spare or we need a rest from Ma we go sit in that tree. Ain't nobody knows about it but us, of which that is how it came to be my favorite place. Rayford's garden is my other favorite place excepting that it is right under Ma's nose. I'd like for Rayford to come with us and sit in the hickory, too, but he ain't much for climbing and he'd likely fall off. But Pa and me, we have us a time. He gets up in the tree, leans back against the trunk, pulls out his mouth organ, puts one leg up on the branch and taps his foot to keep time. He plays tunes Cransus Rhodes teaches him at picnics after prayer meetings. I make up songs telling about bears dancing in the moonlight and frogs with hiccups and such as that. Ma don't look kindly on music, lessen it's prayer-meeting hymns, seeing as how she suspicions the devil might have a hand in it, but I don't reckon the devil has doings with Pa. There ain't a lick of evil in him.

"Pa, ain't we going to our tree?" I asked as we passed the path that led to it.

"Not today." He took a few more steps and asked, "Don't you reckon you're getting too old to chase chickens?"

"Just getting fast enough to catch em," I said, thinking that was a right smart thing to say. I reckoned it would bring out a smile from Pa, but he kept his eyes on the ground as we walked.

"Well, that may be, but one of these days you'll wake up and see you grew into a young woman."

"Can't see as how growing up is worth nothing. Leastways for girls. Hugh and Mule said I can't join the Confederate Army, nohow."

"Don't reckon you'd want to."

"Well, I don't want to grow up none, neither," I said. "I'll just run away."

"Can't run away from growing up."

"What about Rayford? He ain't never growed up." Pa kicked a clod of clay that burst into little pieces and scattered along the path. I didn't know was he riled over what I said or just thinking on it, but I reckoned I'd best apologize. "Sorry, Pa," I said.

"No. No cause to be sorry. Truth to tell I wanted to talk to you some about Rayford. I reckon it's high time we learn him to plow with Beauregard so as he can help plant the fields."

"Rayford!? Pa, are you funning me?"

He shook his head. "One of these days he might get a hankering to hire out somewheres."

"Pa! Rayford can't do that. He'd get lost if he wasn't with us. You recollect that time someone left his gate open and he got out and we couldn't find him. He near most died. And he couldn't handle Beauregard no more than he could handle a bolt of lightning from the sky."

"What if your ma wanted Rayford to leave?" My stomach knotted up and I got a picture in my head of how Ma jumped up from the table and near most pushed him off his chair when he spilled the cream at breakfast this morning. "She's the one who fixes his food and takes care of his clothes. He wets his bed leastways two or three times a week, and then it's Ma that's got to wash out the quilts and bedding and hang em all to dry."

"But I help. Oh Pa, don't make Rayford go. I'll help with everything. You know I will."

"What I know is you wake up every morning bound for mischief. That's all right for a child what don't know no better, but you're as tall as Mule but for an inch or so. Won't be long til you're growed up." When Pa said that I got to thinking maybe I could get to the war and get my licks in, too, and I got all tangled up with a picture in my head of carrying a gun and shooting at them Yankees. I could just see them hightailing it all the way back north where they came from and swearing they'd never come back, and then I heard Pa say, "...and that's what it takes to handle Rayford."

"Rayford wouldn't hurt nobody." Excepting Ma, I near most said.

"But when he's scared or gets his dander up, he can be a handful." Pa put his hand on my head and rubbed my hair. "You better watch out or you'll have a nest of thrashers hatching young ones in that red mess." We had come to the end of the path and up to the creek that separates our land from the Driscoll's. Pa sat on the high end of a log that had fallen part way into the water and I sat next to him.

"I ever tell you about the time we were in Harpersville, me and Granpappy and Rayford. We set Rayford to whittling outside Wright's store. His pa ran it back then. Town folk knew Rayford and either let him be or were kindly, but one of Cobb's relation came from over North Carolina way, a boy not much older than me and Rayford were then. He tried to talk to Rayford. Figured Rayford was being uppity and gave him a push, leastways that's how he told it. Lancey Cobb it was, if I recollect."

He got a look in his eyes like Rayford when he's getting shaved and don't see nothing but what is going on in his head. Then Pa patted the tree limb, like he came to, and went on.

"This Lancey fellow must've been hankering for a fight because Rayford just sat there and Lancey hauled off and punched him in the jaw. By then old man Wright came out and set Lancey straight. He felt a might sheepish, they said, and he had in mind to apologize. He went back to Rayford, but Rayford didn't understand and put up his hands and took to screeching so loud I heard him over at the mill. When I ran up and saw Rayford

with blood on his mouth and his hands up like he was protecting himself, I went for Lancey like a wild man. Took old man
Wright and Delmar Cobb and Granpappy, all three of them, to
pull me off him. I was the one felt sheepish when I heard it all.
Rayford has always been so good-hearted. Had your Ma doing
for him and was so kindly to her first off. Then the work got
to be too much, and your Ma got the headaches and her back
took to paining. Granny couldn't do for herself and Granpappy's
hip got bad, and for awhile Rayford's bed needed changing near
most every night. Wasn't long til your Ma hardened to him—it
wasn't just him, a' course. It was all the work. Seems all my life I
been torn, and now...well...it ain't changed."

He put his hand in his pocket and pulled out a piece of paper,
tattered and wrinkled like it had been opened and folded a
hundred times. He stared at it, then looked to the creek. "I been
meaning to talk to you about the war," he said and he picked up
a hunk of clay and threw it in the water. When it hit it made
rings and we watched them head out and grow bigger and break
along the edges of the creek. It was a pretty sight, but I got a bad
feeling the way Pa was talking. Then he handed me the piece of
paper and I read:

> *All able-bodied men between the ages of 20 and 50*
> *are earnestly called upon to join the Southern Army.*
> *Rally to the call of the countrymen in the field. One*
> *united effort, and those Northern Hirelings will soon*
> *be driven from our sunny south.*

I felt his hand on my shoulder and then he said, "Signs like
this have been posted all over Harpersville. The Confederate
Army put out a call for men up to thirty-five back a year or

more, and I was past the age then by a year, but now...I got to go, Tatum. I don't want to, but I can't see my way clear to putting it off no more. Leaving you and Rayford and everyone...it'll be the hardest thing I ever done in my life, but I got my duty. You need to take care of Rayford for me whilst I'm gone. Ain't many got the patience to handle the likes of him. Surely not Ma nor Hugh nor Mule. And Granpappy's getting on in years."

It took a minute to sink in, like my ears didn't want to hear the words, but they kept at me like gnats til I couldn't ignore them no more and I went crazy inside. I screamed and ran and hollered and pounded Pa and threw myself into the water and held my face under as long as I could. Well, it seemed like all that happened but I never moved. Then it felt like a boulder fell on my chest and I suffocated, and my life ended and left me, and I was nothing. My pa. My pa...gone. It hurt to even think about it. Then I felt his arm around me and his warmth and strength and goodness forced the life back into me and made tears fall, painful as blood.

"I'll be back soon's I can," he said, and he drew his arm tighter around my shoulders. "But I'll be counting on you to take care of Rayford. Granpappy will help, but you know he has got trouble with that hip. And I suspicion your Ma'll be a might ornery for a while."

"She's always ornery," I said, wiping my cheeks.

"You know, your ma used to sing just like you do now. That was afore we moved back here. Some folks can start each day new and let go of what's done. Others hold on to it, even if it's a thing they don't want. I don't reckon they do it a' purpose, it's just the way they're made. Granpappy calls it sticky skin. Whatever comes along latches on, and afore long, they get lost inside all that and you can't see the good in there no more. It don't help none to hold it against them. I reckon you're like me. You make the best of things. That's why I need your help, Tatum."

I wouldn't have been against that, but I didn't know how I'd get along without Pa. When he left for a day to get supplies, time dragged, and I never had a lick of peace. "She'll work me to death, Pa. I'll never have a dadblamed minute to myself."

"I'll talk to her afore I leave. This is gone be hard on her."

"It'll be worse for me." He took his arm away and folded the paper and put it back in his pocket. He picked a thick piece of bark off the log and turned it over in his hand like it was something special.

"But it's different for you. Your time with us is just a short part of your life. You'll meet a fella and be off on your own some day."

"No! I ain't never getting hitched."

"What I'm trying to say is you got a whole life ahead of you, but lessen we find gold in the fields, this old farm and a heap of chores is all Ma'll get for the rest of her life."

"Pa, I'll never leave you, honest. I hate fellas, and I don't even want to grow up." He threw the piece of bark off into the woods and it fell with a thud into a pile of leaves.

"Not much of a world to grow up in right now, but it'll be better. Tatum, look at me."

Never before in my life did I not want to look at my pa, but I reckoned I'd bust out crying, so I kept my head down. He put his hand under my chin and pulled it up til I looked him square in the eye. "Tatum, there's something special waiting for you. I promise, surely as I'm sitting here. And I don't never want you to forget it. "

"Don't go, Pa. We need you here." I grabbed him and hung on tight and he put his arms around me.

"I know you can't understand all of this, but I can't hold my head up in town no more." I heard in his voice that he'd made up his mind and there wouldn't be no changing it. I sniffed back my tears and took a deep breath.

"Reckon you ain't told Ma yet."

"No. And if you tell her, I'll be obliged to give you such a whupping you won't sit for a week. When I go to town to-morrow, I'll bring back extra supplies to help you get by. I'll take Hugh and Mule with me--"

"And me, too, Pa, oh please. If you leave, I won't never get to town and I'll be stuck here with Ma every day. If Hugh and Mule can go, why can't I?"

"I can't take you, Tatum. I said what I have to say and that is what has got to be and there ain't nothing for it. I'll see what Mr. Wright has in the line of books and I'll tell Ma you need some time to read and play with Rayford. I'll bring another bag of sweets--"

"Peppermints and licorice and horehound and lemon drops?"

"Long as you promise to help your Ma."

"I will Pa, but why can't I go, just this time. If Hugh and Mule get to--"

"Hugh and Mule have to see everything that's got to be done--"

"But not Mule. Why does Mule get to go, too?"

"What if Ma needs supplies and Hugh is ailing?"

"What if they're both ailing? Then I could go."

"Tatum, you ain't going to town today and if you don't stop pestering me, I ain't gone bring no books nor sweets back. Mule has got to know what to do if...well, if there's a time Hugh can't get there. Now hush. I aim to join up tomorrow and get my orders. I reckon I'll be heading out by the end of the week."

The end of the week. Of all the bad things that could happen, Pa had told me the worst. I reckon I love my ma seeing as how she is my ma, and leastways I don't hate her as much as I hate the devil and I don't want nothing bad to happen to her, but I love my Pa more than everything else in the world, excepting maybe Rayford, of which I love him the same. I reckon if Pa leaves, the sun don't need to bother coming up no more. This whole world can just shrivel up like an old plum and then some big old giant like we read about in that book of fairy tales Melanie gave me, he can come and toss it away in the river. It wouldn't matter none to me. And I was thinking along those lines when Pa took my hand.

"I worry about Rayford. You got to take care of him. Can you do this? For me?"

I barely had the strength to nod.

"Now you keep quiet. I'll have to put my mind to finding a way to tell your ma so it ain't so hard on her. That way it'll be easier for you, hear?"

"Yes, sir. When you aim to be back?" I couldn't get my words to come out louder than a whisper.

"Hard to say. We just got to turn them Yankees around and get em heading back north again, like the poster says. Reckon I'll only be away a few weeks. A month or two at most."

"No, Pa, please don't go. Please." He took my hand and patted it.

"I got an idea. Every night afore you go to bed, look up in the sky at the stars. There'll be a message from me waiting for you."

"But, Pa--"

"Hush. You got a good imagination. Now you got reason to use it. And when I send my message up there, I'll look for one from you."

"We could write letters."

"We can do that, too. But this way we can get the message right away."

"It won't work--"

"Hush!" Then Pa let go of my hand and put his arm around me again and looked at me. "What am I thinking?" I could see in his eyes how much he loved me, but I couldn't say it. I couldn't keep the tears in no more either. "See?" Pa looked so happy over his idea, I didn't say no more against it, but I can't see how it'll do any good to look at stars. The plain fact of the matter is that when we really need Pa, he won't be nowheres near.

"I've got a hankering for some homemade biscuits," he said, and he stood. I reckon he expected I'd get up, too, but I didn't feel like moving. "Think you could muster up a batch?" He pulled out his hanky and wiped my eyes and kissed my forehead.

"Not as good as Ma or Melanie."

"Just takes practice," he said. "You know, when I get back, we'll go to the circus. We'll see clowns and elephants doing tricks and big growly tigers in cages. How would you like that?" I nodded and he went on about how the baby elephants hold their mama's tails with their trunks and how Rayford carved a whole circus full of critters when they saw some circus posters at Wright's store years back and how Rayford's carvings were near most better than what was on them posters.

"What if the war comes here?" I asked.

"Ain't no need to worry about that." He grabbed my hand and pulled me up and started walking back along the path toward home. "That's why there's a big push for more men right now. We'll stop them Yankees, and I'll be back afore you know it."

I ain't saying Pa lied, but what he said about being back before I know it ain't the truth. I will know every minute that he is gone.

6

All I Did Was Listen

I knew something was up when the smell of rhubarb cobbler woke me before first light. I dressed quick and went out to the kitchen and there was Melanie, home from Fosters and sitting at one end of the table. She never looked up, just kept staring at the table like as if it would take off and head out the door if she didn't keep her eye on it. Pa had Rayford up and ready to shave, and then the rooster crowed, like he was the one that woke up late. It was most peculiar.

"Morning, Tatum," Pa said.

"Morning, Pa." Hugh and Mule leaned against the wall, and Ma worked some biscuit dough over and over like she plumb forgot what to do next. There was a powerful feeling in that room and I reckon my brain could've figured it out, but the rest of me didn't want nothing to do with it. I just headed to the outhouse singing like as if I was trying to calm Rayford, but when I pushed the front door open and saw a big old pile of darkness on the porch, I let out a yelp and hopped back inside. Pa came up and I grabbed him. "There's a bear sleeping out there." Pa pushed the door open and looked.

"Ain't no bear, Tatum. That there is a blanket."

Pa ain't one to tell stories, so I peeked out and gave that pile a good looking at. It was the brown blanket that's always on the parlor chair, but now it had got itself rolled up and set in a heap. Melanie came over and put her arm around my shoulder. "Ma put a change of clothes and some corn pone and ham and such in that blanket," like as if that would explain everything, and I reckon it would have, but I still didn't see fit to think on it. "Oh," I said, and I stood there in the parlor while Melanie and Pa went back to the kitchen, and I took to singing again, softly to myself, and went back out the door and gave the blanket a kick to be sure. Then I saw Pa's musket leaning up against the porch and the truth of it grabbed me like a haint and whispered in my ear: "This is the day Pa leaves to join the Confederate Army."

I took off running to the top of McCreedy's Hill but the awful feeling was still there. I ran back and made it to the curve, then tripped on a stone and hit the ground hard. I laid there with a picture in my head of Pa heading out on Beauregard, and I didn't see no reason to ever move again. But the ground was cool and hard, so I got up and, not twenty feet ahead of me in a little pile of leaves at the edge of the woods I saw an egg. It was my job to fetch them, so I did, and the rest just happened, and even though I was the cause of it, it wasn't none of it my fault. I didn't look for trouble, the whole thing came right to me. All I did was listen, and you can't hardly stop a body from listening.

I gathered an apron full of eggs and even though the last one I found was closer to the front door, I went around to the back so I wouldn't have to look at Pa's musket and the parlor blanket all heaped up and waiting. I went in and put the eggs in the basket on the sideboard and went back out to the chicken coop to check under the hens that were setting. I reckon even they knew something wasn't right seeing as how they were downright ornery about me reaching under them and I got pecked something fierce. Or maybe it was that the sun was just peeking up over McCreedy's Hill and they weren't ready to move yet, but they were a feisty bunch. When I came around the back of the house, I bumped up against the woodpile, and heard a sound that brought to mind one of Beauregard's hee haws, and then up out of nowheres came the idea. Now as I have had time to think on it, I reckon what made the noise was one log brushing against another and I suspicion it was the devil that put the idea in my head, but it got there all the same.

By that time Hugh and Mule were moving, Ma had got the biscuits to baking on the hearth, Pa was shaving the last of Rayford's whiskers, and I heard Melanie waking Granpappy. No one paid me no mind, so I headed out to the garden and dug up some carrots that were still mighty young, of which I had to dig a mess of them just to get a handful. I rubbed them on the ground to get the dirt off, then snuck around back of the house, along the west end, and over to the barn. Beauregard was outside in the corral and looked over as I opened the gate and pushed it back against the fence. I held a carrot to his nose and he snatched it out of my hand and chomped it up good, his big old yellow teeth working it like as if it was a great big sweet. A mule surely does enjoy carrots. Then I stepped back and when he opened his mouth to bray, I held up another carrot and he forgot his complaining and chomped again.

I didn't want to head down the path in front of the house where everyone could see us, so I got Beauregard to follow me into the woods. I had in mind to get him out on McCreedy's Road and give his hinder a good kick, so as he'd take off and we wouldn't find him for weeks. Then Pa wouldn't have to go to no war, leastways not today, and time we found Beauregard, the war'd be over and Pa'd be grateful he didn't waste time trying to get out there and join it.

With no path worn down it was rough going through the woods and Beauregard ate those carrots a might faster than I had reckoned. Before long they were gone, but he didn't believe it and took to snuffling me all over. I couldn't do much but keep ahead of him, and leastways he followed, but then I got turned around and lost track of where I was. I stopped to get my wits about me and next thing I knew there was a tugging on my dress, I heard a rip, felt a sting on my behind, and whirled around to see a hunk of homespun hanging out of that old mule's mouth. Just as I reached back and felt a big hole that went right down to my hinder, he tossed his head and brayed and came after me. I took off hollering to high heaven.

Seconds later I heard Pa call my name. I ran to the sound of his voice and hightailed it through the last of the brush, coming out not three feet from where I went in, with Beauregard right behind me. I ran to Pa, but he dodged me and grabbed Beauregard around the neck. Beauregard kicked out his hind legs and threw his head around to nip at Pa, then took off. Pa hung on, swung a foot up and booted Beauregard a good one in the jaw. Beauregard stopped dead like as if he couldn't believe Pa would do such a thing, and Pa went flying. As he hit the ground, Beauregard took off for the road. By then Hugh and Mule had come out and Pa scrambled to his feet and yelled, "Head him back to the corral," and they all got in the chase. A little voice told me I'd best get in there and help and as I turned down the road after them, out of the corner of my eye I saw Ma's hand fly to her mouth and Melanie squeaked, "My word, Baby, your behind is a showing its face!" She came running. "Don't move," she yelled. She got back of me and grabbed my shoulders. "AAAGH! Are them teeth marks on your backside?" She turned me and pushed me along. "I'll cover you and we'll get back to the house."

I reckon Beauregard ain't never run so fast, and Pa and Hugh and Mule chased him and hollered and in the midst of all the commotion, I saw as how not only was Beauregard still here, but I had a mess of mending to do, and if Ma took the switch to my backside she'd be whaling on bare skin that was already stinging from where Beauregard's teeth nipped it. And after all that Pa was going to leave anyway, of which that meant he wouldn't be around to say, "Now take it easy, Mae." Pa whooped and I looked back to see him chase Beauregard in the corral and Mule push the gate closed. About then Beauregard gave one more good kick, and when his hooves crashed against the gate, it swung out and knocked Mule flat. He ain't like to forget that neither, nor who was the cause of it.

"I swear I didn't mean no harm. I just didn't want Pa to leave and join no dadblamed Confederate Army." I didn't know as it would help, but leastways it was the truth, and I hoped it would bring some pity from Melanie. She was quiet for what seemed like a long time, and I didn't know as she was working up to yell at me, or thinking on what a poor, sad child I was, and then I felt her hands on my shoulders from behind.

"Baby, I know you are the youngest, but it's time you took to thinking on what you're doing. Pa don't want to leave. It's honor and pride that's taking him and we don't want him to spend his whole time worrying on us. When Joram told me he was heading out, I had in mind to tie him in bed so he couldn't leave, but I had to be brave and let him go. Just like we got to be brave for Pa and not make trouble for him on the very day he is leaving."

I'd been looking over to the barn where Mule had pushed himself up on all fours, then tipped over. He looked dazed some and Pa bent and took his arm. He helped him up and hung on to him til he could walk on his own, but he was still weaving and Pa had to steady him a time or two.

Melanie let out a long sigh and started in again. "All that commotion and Pa didn't have in mind to take Beauregard anyway. Silas and Jeremy Driscoll are coming for him. Now you best get your other dress on, and learn to carry on like a young woman instead of a child that ain't got no brains." Pa and Mule were at the steps by then, so Melanie pulled the front of my dress around to cover my behind and stuffed it in my hands and headed back to the house.

My face burned and I would've taken off and never quit running, but when it came to me that my plan was a waste from the start, and only made everything worse, I couldn't move. Then I got a picture in my head of Ma taking the cane to me. I reckoned a face full of tears would've done me some good, but the shock must've stopped them. I stood there a minute or two til it came to me I'd best get in there and take my licks so I could be with Pa some before he left. I feared Ma was waiting in the parlor to whup me in front of everybody so I went around back and this time I steered clear of that wood pile so as not to get no more dadblamed ideas. When I got to my room and took off my ripped dress, I felt my back side. Little welts had popped up and burned like I'd backed into a boiling washpot. Ma called to get into the kitchen so I quick pulled on my other dress, and hightailed it in there.

Ma had set out Granny's vase with flowers and laid out a spread like breakfast and dinner both with enough eats to feed us and the Fosters, too—ham, biscuits, new peas, fried sallet greens, and that sweet-smelling rhubarb cobbler with fresh cream to go atop it. Rayford dug in, but everyone else sat as stiff and still as if they had frozen in their chairs. I took my place and when I sat it was like landing on a hot iron, but I gritted my teeth. Pa bowed his head and tapped Rayford's hand so he'd set his fork down, then Pa took his hand on one side and Ma's on the other, and she took Mule's hand and so on, all around the table. Then Pa said grace.

"Lord, I reckon there ain't no man what wants to go to war, but I been praying on it, and I reckon it's Your will that I go." Pa took a deep breath then like he was thinking and I snuck a peek at Hugh and he was sneaking a peek at Mule and I know they were thinking they were two that couldn't get to the war fast enough and would've given their eyeteeth to be heading out with him, then Pa cleared his throat. Pa ain't one for a long grace, he generally just gets it over with, but this morning he put me in mind of a preacher. "Look after my family, Lord, and keep em safe. And…and watch over me and give me strength to fight them Yankees…and bring me home soon. We thank You for all this good food, amen."

We kept holding hands. Even Rayford. We sat like that for three, four minutes, then Pa set Rayford's hand on the table and kissed Ma's hand and held it to his cheek. We all let go of hands, then Pa picked up his fork and said, "Mae, you set a fine table," and Ma busted out crying.

That food didn't look so good of a sudden. Ma hushed her carrying on and Granpappy cleared his throat. Then Pa picked up his fork and said we best all eat and keep up our strength. I don't recollect a quieter meal. Once Hugh said, "Don't worry none. Me and Mule will get the corn and cotton in." That would've been the last thing on his mind most days, but seeing as how he would be the man of the family, I reckon he wanted to ease Pa's mind. Hugh is handy, probably better with a hammer and nails than Pa, but it'd be easier to get milk out of a well than to turn him into a farmer. His heart ain't in it. But I reckon Pa was glad to hear that leastways he was willing to try.

"I can't do the work no more, but I can tell how to get it done," Granpappy said. Then it was quiet again but for the sound of forks and knives hitting plates, until Pa stood.

"Boys, there's things we need to tend to. Let's go." He put his hand on Ma's shoulder while Hugh and Mule got up, then they all headed out. I had in mind to follow them, but I reckoned that was where Pa would say goodbye, not in front of everyone. I suspicion they went out to the field and Pa talked on farming some, and I reckon Hugh nodded and Mule cried. Hugh wouldn't, but

Mule might. I've seen tears on his face before, like the time Pa was chopping down a tree at the edge of the woods near the woodshed. He didn't know it was rotten, and it split and came crashing down. One of the branches knocked him over, scraping his arm enough to get the blood running good. When he fell he threw it up over his head, likely to protect it, but the blood from his arm ran over his face. It looked worse than it was, and got Mule riled so that he ran up to the house hollering that Pa was a goner. Time we got to Pa, the tears were streaming down Mule's face and he cried out, "Oh, Pa, Oh, Pa," until Ma yelled at him to hush up. I reckon as mean as Mule can get, there's still likely some good in him.

By the time Pa came back from the barn, Rayford and me had picked a bucket of peas and he had settled in his chair to whittle. I brought the peas out to Jenny's Stump to shuck so Ma wouldn't make me go set up the washtub or some such so as I couldn't see all that was happening. Jenny's Stump is on a little rise between the house and Rayford's garden and when you sit there, you can see near most the whole farm. When Granny reckoned she had to keep an eye on things, that's where she sat. Granpappy took to calling it Jenny's Stump, seeing as how that was Granny's name. It's low to the ground so it's good for sitting work done out of a bucket, but those peas could've turned to maggots and I wouldn't have noticed. I kept my eyes on Pa. He walked straight from the barn to Rayford's garden, opened the gate and went over to him. He looked around back to the barn, to the house, out to the road, then he squatted and pulled out one of Rayford's carvings. "You near most got this kitty finished. You do a fine job of whittling, Rayford. Ain't none better. You make me a whole bucketful of critters while I'm gone." I reckoned Rayford'd have a big old grin on his face, because he wouldn't understand, but he just sat in his chair looking at the ground.

Pa knelt and put his arms around Rayford and tears rolled down my cheeks. It put me in mind of when Lucretia Morgan lost her baby last spring. She didn't leave her house for weeks, but when she finally came to prayer meeting I would've known something awful had happened even if Melanie hadn't told me. She walked around like a haint, like as if someone had pulled out her insides and threw them away. Melanie said losing a baby is the worst thing in the world seeing as how it's part of you. Being twins, I reckon Rayford and Pa were near most as much a part of each other as folks can be. Pa stood and turned and hurried to the fence, then stopped. It was open enough for him to get through, but he pushed it all the way open, then walked around it and pushed it closed slow, like Rayford does. I reckon he wanted to get the sound of that squealing clear in his head so he wouldn't forget it. Or maybe he made the sound for Rayford.

Pa went up on the porch and leaned against the house a few feet behind Granpappy. Granpappy kept rocking. I couldn't hear, but I don't reckon much was said. Most of the time their lips weren't moving. Then Pa went over and put his hand on Granpappy's shoulder, and Granpappy stopped rocking.

A few minutes later Pa went down the steps and looked around again, then came back to Jenny's Stump and plopped on the ground beside me. "Sorry I let Beauregard out," I said. "I didn't mean no harm. I just thought as how if he wasn't here, you wouldn't have to join no dadblamed Confederate Army."

"No harm done. You'll need him here and the Driscolls can

spare a wagon." It seemed my whole head filled with tears, but I took deep breaths to keep them in. "You understand why I got to go?" I shrugged. "There's times you got to do a thing you don't want to do. But it's the right thing and you do it so at the end of the day you can sleep in peace. It ain't always easy. I reckon that's why I been trying to protect you from it. But there's a good feeling that comes of doing what's right, and maybe I kept that from you, too. Whilst I'm gone, I hope you come to see what I mean. There's two things I want you to know. The first is that when you do what's right, even if it's hard, good comes of it. The second is that no matter what happens, even after I come back and years go by and I pass on to the hereafter, my love will still be with you." He squeezed my hand and stood. "I reckon it will be a fine day today. Air is dryer than what it's been."

I jumped up and grabbed him and he put his arms around me. If I live to be a hundred, I'll still recollect that hug. Then he kissed the top of my head, and said, "You keep growing like this, I reckon time I get back you'll be kissing the top of *my* head." I got that picture in my mind and laughed and before the tears got back in it, Pa said, "Let's see how fast them long legs of yours is. First one to the oak at the curve," and he took off running and I chased after him and we laughed and carried on and I forgot all about him leaving. We ran full speed and I nearly caught him. As soon as we got to the tree, he hollered, "To Rayford's gate," and he took off again. I couldn't quite catch him, but when we got back, we leaned against the gate to catch our breath and Pa said, "I reckon you'll beat me in a race, too, time I get back. Now I got to say good-bye to Melanie and your Ma. You got to be happy for Rayford, you hear?" He had such a big grin on his face, I couldn't help but smile. I kept it on my face til he turned, but as I watched him walk away I recollected the Driscoll's were coming and there wasn't no way to stop them. All I could do was wait for the sound of the wagon wheels creaking down the road.

I went back to Jenny's Stump, picked up a handful of peas, and time stopped. Not a bird chirped, not a chicken squawked, not a squirrel chattered. I know that likely ain't the way it was, but all I recollect is how my ears were straining for the sound I wanted most not to hear, the only sound that mattered.

Then I heard the faint squeak of wheels turning on an axle, growing louder and louder. I looked over and saw Melanie sitting on the porch steps and Granpappy still in the rocker. Pa hadn't come out so I reckoned he and Ma were sitting at the table. I went round back into the kitchen, but they weren't there. Their bedroom door was closed, but I didn't hear no talking nor moving. I reckon they were sitting on the bed together, Pa with his arm around Ma telling her like what he told me, Ma dead still like a stone. I stood at the table, the wagon sounds ringing in my ear like as if they were inside my head and a few minutes later the door opened and out Pa came, Ma behind him white as a sheet. He took Ma's hand, they went outside and I followed them. Melanie got up from the steps, and Granpappy pushed himself out of the rocking chair and hobbled over to Pa and hugged him and snorted. I ain't never seen such a thing before. Then Pa grabbed the rolled-up blanket and his musket, kissed Ma on the cheek, gave Melanie and me another hug and told us to wait there. He gave Ma one more hug and a kiss on the lips, then he went down the steps. Hugh and Mule came over from the barn, walking slow, like they didn't know what they were doing. Pa met them in the yard and shook their hands. He hugged Hugh, then Mule, and went to the wagon.

We weren't a bit neighborly. None of us even waved. Pa tipped his hat to Silas and Jeremy Driscoll, but he didn't say a word, neither, of which that ain't like my pa. He threw his blanket on the wagon, then his musket, and he hopped on the back.

They took off and I kept my eyes on him, in his straw hat and onion-dyed homespun shirt, sitting on the back of the wagon, getting smaller and smaller until he rounded the curve at the bottom of McCreedy's Hill and was gone.

7

❧

Nothing Ain't Been Right Since He Left

Pa had best get home soon. It's been a week now, and we are doing poorly. Granpappy gets Rayford up in the morning and shaves him. After breakfast he takes him out to his garden, but Rayford just sits in his chair. He don't pet Cleopatra when she jumps up on his lap. He don't move at all. "Stupid Rayford," I yelled at him. "You gotta get in the garden and pull them weeds and keep them bugs off." I grabbed his arm, but when I let go it fell to his side like a dead limb hanging on a tree.

Last night Ma said he was lazy and she wouldn't give him no supper. I had to sneak biscuits and bean soup to him after Granpappy put him to bed. Everyone is either too ornery, like Mule and Ma, or too quiet, like Granpappy and Hugh and Rayford, and it's all Pa's fault. Last night after I snuck the food to

Rayford I went out and looked up at the stars and put a message in them for him: "I hate you and I hate everybody!"

I was still riled this morning, but I saw as how I don't hate Rayford none. He don't know no better. I can't hate Granpappy neither. He lost his balance going down the porch steps three days ago and fell on the hip that bothers him some. He don't complain, but he takes his steps careful and makes a face if his foot lands wrong.

But I surely do hate Mule. Ma tells him to milk Belle and he walks away and she don't take the switch to him, but she gets her dander up. Granpappy tells her to let the boy be seeing as how he's missing his Pa and he'll come round, so Ma makes me take the bucket and milk Belle, and still do all my other chores. I'd like to walk away, too, but I reckon Ma wouldn't never feed Rayford again. I ain't about to let nothing happen to him, like I promised Pa.

I've been waking up when the birds set to singing at first light. I take my quilt out and wrap it around me and sit in Rayford's chair, pretending that any minute Pa'll come out the door and head to the cotton field. The last thing I think of at night is that Pa's gone, and it's the first thing that comes to mind when I wake up. I don't care none about the Confederate Army, and I don't see why they need my pa out there. If they are looking for tough, mean, ornery fellows like Mule, they best send Pa back, seeing as how he ain't like to be a real good soldier. He ain't never been mean in his life. He can't even kill a deer without he gets all worked up over it like it was a pet dog. When he brings a deer down, I go right to thinking on roast meat and venison stew and how we can get the hide tanned for new shoes, but Pa bows his head and tells the deer he is grateful to feed his family. First time he did that I thought he went simple-minded.

"Pa, that ain't like to do a lick of good," I said. "That deer can't hear you nohow."

"But the Lord hears and if he knows we are grateful, he'll keep sending deer our way." I asked Pa if the Lord hears everything. "I reckon he hears everything He needs to."

"You figure He listens to Ebediah Johnson at prayer meeting? When he starts in singing I got to put my hands on my ears. I reckon the Lord is up there with His ears clopped shut, too."

I don't see why He can't make a miracle and take away Ebediah's voice, leastways in church, and whilst He is at it, he could bring my Pa home. Nothing ain't been right since he left, and the worst of it is a feeling I ain't never had before. At first I put it up to all that hate I got riled up for Pa, but now I see it is something different. I reckon it is somewheres in my stomach. What it comes down to is I just can't sit in Rayford's garden every morning hating Pa. It ain't come to no good yet and I can't see as how it ever will.

I think on how I promised I'd take care of Rayford and help Ma and not pull pranks and all such as that, but there is a pot inside me set to boil. I got a notion it's the devil that has built a fire under it, and this morning I couldn't sit a minute longer. I got up and took a step, then another, and another. I didn't put no thought to it, I just let my feet go and they headed to the barn. I found a rope and before I knew it, I was twisting and turning and tying until I had a respectable noose. It brought to mind a story Mule told about a boy not older than him, who'd run away, and was out on his own and hungry. He stole a chicken from some Hallowells on up north a ways and they caught him and strung him up by his neck in a hickory tree until he died and when his Ma and Pa found out, they wailed and mourned and carried on and wished they would've treated him better.

That's when the idea came to me.

8

I Put In A Word Or Two Of My Own

Pa sent us a letter from near Resaca, northeast of here. He told us about birds he's seen, and the pretty hills along the way, and the folks that feed them, like as if he is on an adventure. Near the end of the letter he said it might take longer than he thought to get the best of the Yankees, but he reckoned he'd be home before cotton-picking. That ain't til September so he'd best be back before that.

He asked was I taking care of Rayford and I recollected as how in my head I was taking good care of him, but betwixt the scheming and the steering clear of Ma, it came to that I ain't done right by it, and I thought as how I will get to it real soon and do better.

I reckon I must've read that letter near most ten times at

dinner. Ma would eat some and say, "Read it again." It got so I didn't even have to look at the words, I just looked right at Ma and said them. She asked me to write a mess of words back to him and I near most said, "Now ain't you happy Pa taught me to read and write," but I reckon she already knew that's what was in my head and if I said it she might take it as cause to whup me, but if I just thought it, she couldn't do naught about it.

"You write how as we miss him, and we are thinking about him."

I wrote the words on a sheet of stationery Melanie gave us, but it didn't look right to see that great big piece of paper and just them few words. "We got to write more, Ma. These words are too puny and it don't look good. Say some more."

I reckon that's the first time I ever told Ma to do ary a thing. She looked down at her hands, then cleared her throat. "I miss you something awful, Will. It's so lonely and there's so much work to be done. And I'm sorry for ever being hard on you." She stopped and I waited. "You got all that?" she asked. I nodded and showed it to her, then I read it back.

"Ain't much more than there was afore. We still got a page that's near most empty." It didn't seem right to me to send that letter off to Pa half empty.

"Well, I can't say no more--" She stopped and left the table, but I heard the tears in her voice. I'd like to sit down and cry, too, but I don't see as how that will do Pa no good, but when he gets letters, it might make him happy and maybe he'll tell the Confederate Army his family can't bear it that he's gone and he needs to get home. I reckon by now they see as how he ain't no kind of soldier and they are just keeping him to be polite. I asked Hugh and Mule if they had ary a thing to say to Pa and they said, tell him "Hey".

"You can't just say, 'Hey', in a letter. Don't you have nothing else to say to your own pa?" They looked at each other and shook their heads and left.

"I'll tell you a thing to put in there," Granpappy called from the parlor. "You tell him to be careful, and don't do nothing brave and get home soon." I wrote that, too, but I still had part of the page left, so I set to writing a few words of my own and then a thought came to me: Ma can't read. And the next thought was that Hugh and Mule don't care for it none. And Granpappy can't read but a few words. I recollected the day Pa tried to teach Granpappy to sign his name, but his old hands shook so, it put me in mind of a stick chasing a squirmy little bug all over the paper. It came to me I could write whatever I set my mind to without no one knowing what it was! Likely it was the devil who put those thoughts in my head. Once he sees you are weak, I suspicion he don't let go real easy.

But I wasn't of a mind to think no more on that seeing as how when I have the paper and pencil in my hand, Ma lets me keep on writing, of which that's better than hiding because excepting for my tree, Ma knows where to look and then I am back doing chores again.

"What're you telling Pa now?" she asked and I read how the sun's been out most every day and we did the wash and Rayford brought in some beans and such as that. And Ma said, "That surely is a heap of writing on them pages for just them things," and I told her as how I was writing it with lots of words so he could see it in his head like as if he was here. Then she let me write some more. Well, what I told her wasn't the truth of it entire, but it was somewhat what I had wrote, excepting I put in a word or two of my own so Pa'll know what my life is like with him off at the war. Of a sudden that pencil took off like as if there was a devil inside of it and it wrote how I get up every morning and fetch the eggs, get the water, milk Belle, and such as that with the cooking, scrubbing, and all the chores.

Today I took out a new piece of paper and wrote on how Rayford missed him something awful at first but since he got back to his whittling and his garden he was better. At first I felt some bad about all that extra writing I done on that other letter, but it went away, so I wrote how I been gathering all the ashes and cleaning the fireplace and how yesterday we set up the new ash hopper Hugh built, and how we dripped ashes in it all day to make lye. Then I wrote as how I tended the fire and stirred the tallow and put the lye in and minded it until it thickened to soap, of which it was near most the truth, seeing as how I did part of all of those things. When Hugh or Mule or the Fosters go to town, they take the letters. I reckon when Pa reads them, he'll want to get home to thank me for all I been doing to help out.

There was one thing that happened of which I didn't tell Pa. This morning when Granpappy took Rayford out after he shaved him, his gate didn't make a sound. Granpappy asked if I greased it, and I told him no. He didn't say nothing more, but I reckon he was not too happy about it. I went out and pushed the gate open and sure enough, the squealing is gone. Rayford won't like pushing the gate open near as much seeing as how it don't make that noise no more. I reckon it was Ma that done it, seeing as how she says the squealing makes her head hurt. Maybe she will be some kindlier now seeing as how she got her way about it.

9

Help!

Summer 1864

I finally got a chance to work on the idea I got the day I
played with the rope and made it into a noose. It didn't turn out
the way I pictured it, but leastways I'm still alive. After dinner
one day last week, Hugh and Mule begged for the time Pa used
to let them be after dinner and Ma put her hand to her head and
hollered they should get out and leave her alone. Two minutes
later they weren't nowheres in sight and Granpappy was asleep
in the porch rocker so there wasn't nobody to see me head over
to the barn. There was an old door that's been setting against the
back wall of Granpappy's workshop for years. I pulled it back of
the barn and hid it in the tall grass.

A few days later no one had said nary a word on it, so I got
up early one morning and dragged it to the woods west of the

house. Then I tried to drag it closer to the hickory tree, but it was heavy and clumsy and didn't slide easy through the brush. I studied it, then tied a rope around the girth of it near the top and attached both ends of another rope at the middle of the front and back so I could pull it somewhat like dragging a sled only it was just the back end that slid along the ground. That helped some. When I got tired, I covered it up with leaves and brush. It was slow going, but whenever I could sneak away from Ma I'd drag it farther. Yesterday morning I made it to the hickory tree. I climbed on one of the low branches to rest and got to thinking that if it all worked out, the next day that door would be up in the tree, and I'd be sitting on it with Pa's letters, and a little tin with sweets and leftover biscuits and whatever else I wanted to bring. It was a good idea all around and the devil didn't have no part of it neither. Leastways I didn't think he did.

This morning I got up early and milked Belle and got the eggs and made biscuits. They were burnt around the edges, but I sopped them good with bacon grease, so no one would notice. The smell woke Ma and when she came in the kitchen, I asked how did her head feel and she said it was real good. I said maybe I'd best find some Pink Lady Slipper, in case the pains came back, and she put her hand on my shoulder, of which it has been a long time since she's done such as that, and said that would be right kindly of me.

"It might take time to find. Seems sparse this year, but I'll keep looking til I find some." It made me feel growed up to say such as that, even though it was all just talk to give me time to get that door up the tree and sit there and enjoy myself some.

When Ma let me go, I tore down the path and ducked in

the woods and headed to the hickory. I was so excited, I forgot to bring the rope with the slip knot that was still hidden in the barn. I looked to see was there a way I could get by without it. I been up that tree nigh onto a hundred times before but I couldn't climb and hang on to the door, both, so I ran back and when I came to our yard I saw Ma had set up outside to patch some britches.

"I forgot the basket," I said, and went in the house through the back door and got it off the sideboard. I ran out the front door and across the road to the barn, found the noose, coiled it up, and hid it in the basket. Then I went over to Granpappy to see how his chair was coming, so Ma would think that's why I went to the barn.

"Can't work fast as I used to," he said, and before he got all caught up in telling me how he used to put a chair together in a week of evenings at Dahlonega, I told him I was off to get Pink Lady Slipper for Ma.

"You best get, then," he said, like I knew he would.

"Granpappy sure is coming along on that chair," I called out as I ran past Ma. She gave me a look like she suspicioned I was up to something, but she let me be. I hightailed it back to the tree and took out the rope. It was a might long, but I didn't have a knife so I tied one end to the other rope already on the door, pulled the slip knot over my head, and settled it at my middle. With my hands free I crawled up on the first limb, stood against the trunk, got a handhold on a higher limb, and crawled up on that one. The rope got tight but it wasn't nothing I couldn't stand for a few minutes, and the good feeling I got from thinking about having my own place made it so I barely gave it a thought. I climbed higher and higher and the door kept coming behind me. When it got caught in the branches, I planted my feet hard and twisted the rope and pulled til the door slid by them. It worked so slick I got to thinking the Lord Himself must've decided to help me out, since I wasn't in cahoots with the devil this time. When I got the door ten or fifteen feet off the ground, I rested and looked out into the woods. Birds flitted all around me and three squirrels chased each other around the trunk of a nearby tree then ran off. I reckon it was the happiest I'd been since Pa left.

After I got my wind back, I looked above me to where I was aiming to set the door on two limbs across from each other so there wouldn't be no way for it to fall off. I climbed up onto the branches, got a good foothold, and pulled the door the rest of the way hand over hand. That was the hardest part, seeing as how that rope was a might scratchy and it hurt, but I got the door up and settled and had it near most flat on the branches, excepting that my foot was in the way. I took a small step backwards and heard a creak, but my toes were still right under the door where I wanted to set it down. I stepped back no more than an inch, and of a sudden there was a loud crack, and down I went, leaves and branches clawing and poking at me like as if that old tree was riled at me for trespassing. Well, truth to tell, I didn't think none of that at the time, I just grabbed every which way but there wasn't nothing to hold onto, then I jerked to a stop five feet from the ground, scratched from one end to the other and near most cut in half by that rope around my middle. Leastways I wasn't dead, howsomever, my middle hurt so much, I near most wished I was. I tried to work the knot but my weight kept it tight. It came to me that if ever a thing was the devil's work, this was it, and here he had stumped me good making me think the Lord was helping me out.

I reckon that old devil had himself a good laugh seeing as how I was smack dab betwixt the two branches Pa and I had always sat on and no amount of kicking and squirming and thrashing was getting me closer to either one. Then I got to thinking what would happen if that door wasn't stuck up tight in that tree. I got real still and asked the Lord please not to let those branches that the door was setting on break, and if they broke, not to let the door come loose, and if the door came loose, not to let it fall on me, and if it fell on me, not to let it kill me, and if it killed me, to make sure there was somebody to take care of Rayford. I was near most prayed out when I got the picture in my head of what would happen if Mule found me and I called on the Lord all over again. I said if He could just make Granpappy's hip better for today and whisper in his ear about where I am, I would be kindly to Missy and do what Ma says without complaining ever again, and I knew it wasn't right for me be asking no favors, but if He'd get Granpappy or even Hugh to find me, that'd be best. And if that wasn't like to happen, he could send Ma, and if there wasn't no other way, he could send Mule, but please not Mule if He could get to one of the others.

"Help!" I yelled. "I'm strung up in a tree." I listened, but all I heard was critters, no voices, and my stomach took to paining me something awful. I reckon the Lord could've helped but maybe he saw how that predicament could be a lesson for me. I hollered as loud as I could without moving so I wouldn't make the door come down. "Hey, there! It's me, Tatum. I'm stuck. Help!"

The rope got tighter and tighter and I didn't see as how I could stand it much longer without I'd end up in two pieces. It wasn't long before all that hollering turned to plain old crying and then I reckon the Lord took pity on me. I heard tromping through the woods and hollered, "HELP!" and a minute later I was looking eye to eye with Melanie.

"Tatum Louise Wylie, you are a sight. You are cut up from one end to the other." She looked up at the tree. "Ain't that the door to the old outhouse?"

"I'm gone die, Melanie, if I don't get this rope off me right quick. You got a knife?"

"No. I didn't plan on cutting you down out of a tree. Can't you get that rope untied?"

"It's too tight."

"Here, I'll grab your feet and pull em down so's I can--"

"Aaagh. Don't pull. It's making the rope tighter."

"Well, land sakes, I got to do something. Here," she said, grabbing my ankles. "I'll set your feet on my shoulder and you try to stand and maybe that'll loosen the rope so as you can get your hand in it and work it some." I told her to be careful in case the door came down on both of us. She cranked her head around and looked up again. "That door ain't going nowheres," she said, of which it got me thinking about that saying in the Bible: "Pride goeth before a fall," but I couldn't help being proud. Leastways part of my plan worked out.

"Just get around and loosen that rope," Melanie said, but my fingers wouldn't barely work, it hurt so much, and despite I was proud of the door staying up there, I cried the whole time and I swear it hurt worse once I got the rope loose.

"You got it?" Melanie asked. She hung on to my ankles so I wouldn't fall, but when I pulled the rope over my head, I lost my balance and went down, and Melanie hung on tight and came down with me. I smashed my face on the ground, but leastways I was out of the tree. And I had that dadblamed rope off.

"You all right, Baby?" What didn't pain me from falling through the branches pained me from hitting the ground. It felt like my front and back had been crushed together in the middle, and when I looked under my clothes, there was blood where my skin had rubbed raw from the rope and it all got to smarting twice as much when I saw how it looked. "Poor Baby. I reckon Ma's got some pine tar salve or such to put on it."

"NO! You can't tell Ma about the tree--"

"Well, I reckon I got to tell her something." She scowled. "You're scratched and bloody and you can't barely walk right."

"This is the tree Pa and me always come to. Don't nobody else know about it. Please don't tell." She made a face, then gave me a look like an angel and put her arm around me. Melanie never stays riled for long.

"You miss Pa, don't you?" She said it so sweet, it brung tears to my eyes. "I know Ma is hard, and I reckon you ain't never seen her no other way. When I was your age, she didn't have headaches and them pains in her back, so I reckon I look at her different. I feel sorry for her. She ain't well, and I reckon she takes it out on you some. It ain't that she don't love you. She's just too wore out to care for a child. Of which that is why you got to grow up some. She's like a wild stallion that finally got broke. She don't have that kick to her no more. And Pa's leaving just broke her more."

"It broke me some, too."

"No baby, you ain't the breaking kind. You're the bending kind. As soon as the weight is gone, you pop right back up."

"But Ma is like to work me to death."

"Now Tatum Louise Wiley, you know that ain't the truth. You just ain't accustomed to doing as you're told seeing as how Pa always went easy on you. I suspicion you done more work pulling that door from the barn and getting it up in the tree than you done all last week. If you'd do a little extry for Ma, I reckon she'd simmer down quick." I gave some thought to all that, but I reckon the real truth is that Melanie always finds the good in people, like Pa, and she just ain't like to see how Ma works me. I wished she still lived with us.

"I'm glad it was you found me. Why aren't you at Fosters?"

"I came for a morning visit and when Ma said you'd been gone awhile I reckoned I'd best look for you. I was afeared you tried to run away again." She brushed leaves out of my hair and off my back. "Let's get on home and get something on those cuts. I reckon you'll be hurting worse tomorrow."

"I promise I'll never do nothing mean again. And I been helping Ma real good." I picked up the empty basket, wishing I'd found the Lady Slipper before I headed up into the tree. The handle was smooth-wrapped in flat strips of willow, but it still burned on my palm and fingers where the rope had rubbed the skin raw.

"Now I ain't riled over what you done, but you can just save all that there nice talking, if you think I am going to tell Ma a lie. I'm not the lying kind. I reckon when she sees you, she'll take pity. I don't aim to make more trouble, but if she asks outright, I got to tell her the truth."

"Wait. If I leastways had some Lady Slipper that might do me some good, and I think I see some." I turned into the woods.

"Baby, there ain't like to be none here." I took off into the woods, then let out a cry and laid on the ground.

"Baby? Baby, what are you up to?" she said. I kept quiet. A minute later I heard her step through the brush. When she found me she asked, " What's got into you?"

I opened one eye and looked around like I just woke up. "Well. Ain't this a wonder," I said. "Here I am just lying on the ground. Did I faint? Or did I trip over some roots whilst I was looking for that Lady Slipper? Well it surely is a good thing you found me, seeing as how I am scraped and cut up from one end to the other," I said getting up and brushing myself off. "And durned if it ain't the truth."

10

It Starts With The Water

It is a peculiar thing that the more you set your mind against something bad, the more it is like to happen. It is all because of the letter we just got from Pa, but it started with his last letter of which that one came about two weeks ago. When Mr. Foster brought it, I hollered to everyone like always and they came and sat around the table, Mr. Foster, too, but not Rayford seeing as how he don't understand letters. It makes me proud that I am the one to do the reading. I reckon Pa is the head of us all, then Granpappy—I reckon he was the head of us until he got so old—then Ma, then Hugh, then Mule, and when it comes to the chickens and Belle, I'm the head of them, of which they are not much to be the head of, and Rayford don't count. But when I read Pa's letters, I reckon I'm the head of everybody seeing as how I am the onliest one that can read them right.

Generally Pa starts off telling how he's glad to hear from us and how I am a fine hand at writing. Then he tells where he is, and in that letter he was traveling on the wagon road south of Resaca, of which that means they are getting closer. All he wrote about guns and battles was that he was fighting under General Joseph E. Johnston, of which he called him a good man. It didn't matter none to me, but Hugh and Mule were a might disappointed. After I read the letter, Mule told me to write Pa and tell him to put in some parts about the fighting, of which I did. But seeing as how I am the one doing the writing, I also asked Pa what does he think of how hard I've been working.

When Mr. Foster rode in today with another letter, I had in mind this was the one where he'd tell about that. I couldn't wait for everyone to hear what he said, so as soon as they all gathered round, I took to reading with my eyes running across the words like they were leading to a great big old sack stuffed with peppermints and horehound and licorice whips.

"Hugh and Mule had best be keeping up with the hoeing in the cotton, and it's near time to breed Belle again," I read, and my heart banged along lickety split while my eyes raced from line to line. "I'm sorry to hear that Granpappy's hip is getting worse," Pa wrote, and I kept on and when I got to the bottom of the page, I quick turned it over and the next words out of my mouth were, "...so I reckon it's time Tatum learned to shave Rayford." I came to a dead stop. My mouth hung open, and whilst everyone else had time to think on that idea, my brain darted around like a scared jackrabbit trapped in my head and slamming into thoughts like how shaving is men's work, and how I got me enough chores already, and what if I hurt Rayford. If I could've grabbed those awful words I'd just read out of the air, I would've opened my mouth wide, took every one back in even if they were covered with Ma's spring tonic and rolled in dirt, and I would've chewed them up good, and swallowed them down. I should've said I read them wrong, but that is one thought that didn't go through my brain at the time.

When I got my sense back I read the rest of the letter, and there wasn't nothing about no one else doing no extra chores to help me out, no sir. Pa went on about the war and how there's a lot more sitting and waiting than fighting, and once the fighting starts, there ain't no glory in it, truth to tell, and Hugh and Mule should be glad they ain't got to be out there seeing as how the food ain't so good and there ain't no beds to sleep in and lots of times there ain't even a place to shave and wash up. Then Hugh and Mule got to talking about the war and how they ought to be out there, and how they'd show them Yankee bums. They went on like as if their ears had been stopped up and they hadn't heard a word Pa wrote, so I told them that seeing as how Granpappy's hip was ailing, they best stay right here and shave Rayford for him.

"That ain't what Pa wrote," Hugh said, and out the door they went.

The next morning when I came back from the outhouse Granpappy collared me. "You get in here and watch this shaving." I said I didn't particular want to watch besides which Ma would take one look at me sitting, and I'd be out washing clothes or sweeping the yard or some such. He told me to get in the kitchen or he'd tan my hide. I don't reckon he could catch me, but Granpappy is a lot like Pa in that when he talks, you listen if you know what's good for you.

"First you heat the water," he said as I followed him to the kitchen. "You set down, I'll show you how."

"I *know* how to heat water." I reckon there was a touch of sass in them words, but I felt worse off than a calf roped and bound. Then Granpappy got real still and it came to me as how you can holler a thing without raising your voice.

"But what you got to larn is how to shave him," he said, without so much as turning his head, "and it *starts* with the water."

"Yes, sir," I said. I looked at Rayford sitting on the stool, and I recollected how I promised Pa I'd take care of him. I reckoned it had to do with passing time in his garden, and playing with him and keeping him out of trouble and it didn't made a lick of sense for me to learn shaving when Hugh and Mule were already doing it every morning. I told Granpappy as much and he turned to me. His eyes were squeezed near most shut and his mouth was set tight, and even though he didn't hardly move, it felt like he'd whaled on me with a fence post. I reckon I'm lucky I'm still alive. I sat, mad as a wet hen, but I had in mind to get up earlier the next day and be far from the house before he even opened his eyes.

"Like I was saying, first you get the water het up, of which I already done that. Then you pour some in the cup with the soap and you steer it up to make a lather." His hand was so shaky he spilled half the water when he poured it. Then he took the brush and instead of a nice stirring, like Ma does when she beats the eggs, he banged that brush against the sides and the porcelain handle hit the cup with such a racket I thought it would break. "Now you get some of the lather on the brush and smear hit on his face. He's got whiskers about two fingers under his eyes, over to the side of his face and down on his neck. You come closer so you larn this." He pointed to the floor beside him and his hand shook so, I got the picture in my head of him picking up that straight edge—of which they always kept it sharp—and I didn't want to watch no more.

He got Rayford all lathered up so he looked like an old man with a great white beard, and it was near most funny, excepting I was afeared for him. Granpappy picked up the straight edge and I held my breath. Rayford never moved. He just sat there like he did all those other mornings—thousands of them I reckon. It came to me that Granpappy had shaved Rayford ever since Pa left and never hurt him, but when he put that straight edge to Rayford's face, my hands flew up over my eyes and I gritted my teeth and waited for the screaming to commence.

"You can't see what I'm doing with your eyes closed, you ninny."

I peeked through my fingers and saw that a swath of lather had been scraped from Rayford's face near the ear and there wasn't a speck of blood nowheres.

"You move his head round like this," he said. "Then you push the skin to make it tight, and take the straight edge and turn it like this and run it right along his face. Ain't nothing to it. He sets good, long as he has his knife." Rayford's hand rested on his right leg and he rubbed his thumb back and forth along the smooth ivory of the handle. "Puts him at ease, so he sets still. I reckon if you took all morning he'd get ornery, so you make sure you stick to it and get it done quick."

It soothed me some to see Rayford work that knife handle. I took a breath, sat back, and saw that when Granpappy got close to Rayford's face, the shaking slowed and his hand steadied some. Soon as he pulled away, his hand shook again so you'd think it was a miracle he didn't draw a lick of blood. I watched Granpappy's face and saw how he worked hard to steady that blade.

"Betwixt the shaking and my hip, I can't do this no more."

"But Hugh and Mule already shave their own faces every morning. They should do it. I am just a child!" I said.

"If your Pa was still here, I reckon that'd be fine and dandy, but we all got to make do. High time you grew up. Rayford's partial to you. He ain't like to set still for the boys and he sure as hell won't let your ma near him. Now I don't want to hear no more of that there baby talk. This was your pa's idea and when he gets back, I reckon you want him to see as how you done like he said." He finished the job and cleaned off Rayford's face with a cloth. "You get him settled in the parlor and come back."

I set Rayford up with a circus book, seeing as how he likes to look at all them animals, and when I came back to the kitchen, he pointed to Rayford's shaving chair. "Sit here," he said.

A voice came up inside me and hollered, "Run for your life," and another voice said, "Now Tatum, this is your own granpappy and there ain't naught he'd do to hurt you." And the plain truth of the matter was he had taken aholt of my arm real tight, so I couldn't go nowheres anyways. "Now I got an idee. You set still and watch." He picked up the mug and dipped the brush in it and whisked it along my arm. "You get the lather on, then you tilt the blade like this," he said, "and you scrape that lather off." He dragged the straight edge down my arm, and it cut the hairs off clean and didn't pull, nor sting, nor nothing and there wasn't nary a drop of blood left behind. "Here." He handed me the mug and brush. "You try it on your other arm."

I got the lather on, scraped the straight edge and, truth to tell, I liked the way it swiped everything off clean. I thought how as with a week or two of practice, I could learn to shave Rayford. And maybe by then Pa would be home, and I wouldn't have to do it anyhow. Or maybe by then I'd want to show Pa and make him proud, and that got me fired up to run to our hickory tree and write to Pa how good I'd done, then Granpappy said, "You try it on me now," and my stomach rolled.

"On you? But I ain't--" He pulled me out of the chair and fell back in it, and looking straight on him, I saw the pain in his eyes.

"Can't hardly even stand today. Lather me up." I stood there for a minute, wondering how I'd got myself in such a mess. "Now!"

I picked up the mug and the brush and covered his face with lather like I'd seen him do to Rayford. Then I grabbed the straight edge and I reckon I shook near as much as he did. I held my breath, took my first swipe, and he jerked and the blood came running. I took off for the back door and would've run til sundown, but he lunged and caught my arm. Sometimes he's a might quicker than he looks. "Get back here," he said and before I could get a word of blubbering out he told me to hush. "You hit a scab I got from when I fell agin the door. I could've drawed blood there with my fingernail. Now finish the job." I wished I was anywhere but there, even stuck at the wash pot on a hot day. "You got to do this."

The blood dripped making pinky stripes in the lather, and I

told him how it got me riled to see it. "It don't hurt a lick. Just steer clear of that spot and do the rest." I moved slow as molasses and he wasn't none too tolerable about it, neither.

"Time you get to the other side, the first whiskers is gone be growed back," he said.

"I don't want to cut you."

"You hold the blade right, like I showed you, it won't cut me."

Time I took the last scrape it felt like I'd just done a day's work. If I thought I could've got away with it, I would've gone to bed.

"Now you see how it works," he said and he took the looking glass and turned to the light and rubbed the side of his face I didn't cut. "You done a fine job." A feeling came over me, of which I reckon it was pride, and right then I thought how as growing up might have a good part or two. Granpappy put the looking glass down and pushed himself up. When he got all his weight on his feet, he let out a little cry.

"You shave Rayford tomorrow," he groaned, and though I heard the hurting in his voice and watched him limp to the sideboard and lean against it, all I could think about was blood.

"Tomorrow! I ain't ready. You got to let me try it on you again."

"Tatum, the morning is gone come, and it's coming soon, when I can't so much as get outen my bed. Your Ma is a might short of patience when it comes to Rayford, and the truth is, your brothers are like to run off and join the dadblamed Confederate Army first chance they get, no matter what we say. It's you what will be shaving Rayford from here on out, and that's that and there ain't no more to say about it, *AMEN!*"

He Was Always There Between Us

I didn't sleep so good last night, and when I did my head was filled with nightmares of Rayford in his shaving chair with a cut-up face and blood everywhere, and Pa sitting at the table crying. When Granpappy pounded on my door this morning, I let out a yelp and near most fell out of bed.

"Tatum! Time to get up. Rayford's in his chair for his shaving. Hear me?"

"Yes, sir." I reckon I would've been sleepy then but the fear had me wide awake. I pulled on my dress, ran to the outhouse and came back in and there was Rayford, sitting in his chair, rubbing on his knife, staring off into space. "He likes things the same," a voice inside my head whispered. "And you ain't the one been shaving him." I needed Granpappy one more time. I looked in the parlor and on the porch, then I peeked in his bedroom. His back was away from me, and I thought as how I should let him sleep, but I was too riled.

"Granpappy. Can't we just let his whiskers grow?"

He rolled over just enough so he could look at me. "We talked about this already. His beard would always be full of food, and while it's growing, he fights it and tugs at it and near most gets his face to bleeding. I ain't got the strength to argue."

"Please come and watch so I don't hurt him." He rolled back over, and let out a deep sigh.

"It was all I could do to get him up and dressed. Bring me a chamber pot and get to it and no more whining."

I went out to the woodshed to get the chamber pot we keep for if somebody gets sick. Ma don't like them in the house and won't let us use one lessen we're sick, so when Granpappy asked for it, I knew he was paining bad.

"Chamber pot's here on the floor," I said when I brought it. He was nigh onto forty years old when Pa and Rayford were born and Pa was near most forty now. That made Granpappy a mighty old man. "Sorry for pestering you," I said, but he didn't answer.

I put more wood on the fire and swung the kettle over it. Whilst the water heated I set out the shaving mug and sharpened the straight edge on the strap like I'd seen Pa and Granpappy do, and I told Rayford how I'd be shaving him today. I picked up the brush and tried to put a brave look on my face for Rayford's sake, but it didn't matter none. His eyes were open, but he was somewhere else inside his head, his thumb polishing the knife handle. When the water warmed I mixed the soap in for lather and picked up the brush but before I got to his face, Ma walked in. I didn't turn and she didn't say nothing. I had an idea of the look on her face and instead of putting the lather on Rayford, I kept mixing the soap and water, mixing, mixing until the lather came close to spilling over the top of the shaving mug.

I don't know as I had in mind to keep mixing that lather until she left, but I didn't want to do no shaving whilst she was right there, and about that time my stomach took to churning. I heard the chair scrape against the floor as she pulled it away from the table. I reckoned she sat and it came to me I was knocking that porcelain handle against the edge of the shaving mug as hard as Granpappy so I told my hand to stop. I near most had to tell myself to breathe, too. I turned around then. There she sat, still as could be. Scairt me half to death.

"Your pa tried to learn Rayford to shave," she said, the words so soft I turned to her again. Sure enough, it was my ma. I couldn't recollect the last time I heard her talk like that.

"Pa took over shaving Rayford right away when we moved in here, and after we'd been back a couple months, he said, 'Seeing as how Rayford is so good with a whittling knife, I reckon shaving'll come natural to him.' It was just after Mule was born. Pa'd get out the straight edge and touch the blade and make a face so Rayford would get the idea it was sharp like his whittling knife and he had to be careful. He'd lather up Rayford's face, and talk about his critters or working in the garden or some such. Then he'd pick up the straight edge and pull it acrost Rayford's cheek, slow, not like when he shaved him regular. Two, three weeks he done it like that, then one day he put the straight edge in Rayford's hand and held his own around it. Pa wanted to know if Rayford'd let his hand be guided, seeing as how he can get stubborn. Every day for a month or so, Pa shaved him that way, with his hand around Rayford's. I told him Rayford wouldn't never learn, and he was a fool to waste his time, but your Pa has got more patience than a dead man."

I couldn't scarce believe it was my ma telling this story. She had a look on her face that put me in mind of Mrs. Driscoll when she's hauling her grand-baby around and everybody wants to hold it and she don't give no one else a chance, like it's her own borned baby. And then I recollected how Pa said that Ma was different when they first got hitched and it came to me as how he might've been right. It was the dadblamedest thing. Seeing her like that calmed me down and I wasn't near as rattled as when she first came in.

"He's been looking out for Rayford all his life. I heard tell Rayford didn't walk til he was nigh onto three years old. Even then he couldn't hardly stand up. But your pa'd take his hand and off they'd go."

The water had cooled some and I thought as how if I didn't get started I'd have to heat it again. I got a picture in my head of Rayford as a baby again, and a tiny Pa grabbing his hand and the two of them toddling all over. Ma got up and made a cup of grain coffee, then sat again.

"I was telling about shaving. One morning Will, I mean your pa, reckoned it was time to let Rayford try it alone, so he put the straight edge in Rayford's hand. Rayford shook his head, so Will put his hand around Rayford's like he'd been doing. After a few strokes, he let go and put one hand on Rayford's shoulder and the other on his elbow to guide him. He kept talking in near most a whisper, but of a sudden, Rayford swung his arm and the straight edge came at Will's face. He put his hand out to stop it and caught the blade. It cut him deep. Blood poured out and Rayford took off running."

I heard the smallest sound as Ma took a sip of coffee and set the mug down, and I saw that Rayford had stopped rubbing his knife. He had a look like he was listening, like as if he knew what Ma was talking about.

"Will never got riled. He took a towel, wrapped it round his hand and pulled it tight and took off after Rayford. Rayford likely was aiming for the creek, but he didn't get on the path. He ran through the woods, howling like a wild critter and the branches and bramble bushes scraped him all the way. He won't never grow up. I tried to be better to him for your Pa's sake, but he was always there between us. Always keeping Will from me."

She stood and went out the back door. When she had to move here and Pa had to do for Rayford, I reckon she felt as trapped as I did when Pa wrote I should shave him. And least-ways I love Rayford. I threw out the cold lather and heated the water again. I thought on all those times I wished we didn't have a Ma around. I reckon she feels the same way about Rayford. I noticed he'd took to rubbing his knife again. Poor Ma. She has her headaches and backaches and Pa is gone and Rayford is here and he won't never change.

I put the towel around Rayford's neck, smeared the lather over his whiskers, and scraped the straight edge along his face. I saw as how I'd get the hang of it. He sat so still and I wished he could tell me what was in his head. Regular folks put each new thing they come acrost with everything else and that's how they learn about the world. But I spect Rayford sees just one thing at a time and puts it back inside and keeps it like it is. It don't get tangled with all kind of other things. Like how he carved that raccoon, the fish in its mouth curved, like it was whipping its fins to get away. I suspicion Rayford still saw it behind his eyes the next morning like a picture painted in his head, and I reckon ary a time he had a mind to, he could whittle another raccoon that looked as real as the first one. It surely is a talent, seeing as how Granpappy has whittled all his life and you don't know he's finished with a piece until he says so, and you don't know what it is until he tells you.

It'll Be Over In A Few Hours

Pains hit my innards mid-day, not like a bellyache of which a good retching would have cleared it, but like a fire had got to blazing in there. The pains got worse and worse, but I kept on. Before supper Ma sent me to the garden for carrots and greens, and time I got back I had to hang on to the table it pained me so. Ma stood over the sideboard scraping a potato and when I told her my innards were on fire, she scraped faster. "You ain't getting out of no work. Now you get out and milk Belle afore--"

Of a sudden she stopped and looked straight ahead at the row of candles hanging by their wicks on a wall peg. She stood that way so long I near most expected her to talk to them. When she finally turned to me she had a peculiar look on her face, somewhat kindly around the eyes, but scairt-looking around the mouth. Then she asked was I bleeding.

"Bleeding?" I got a scairt feeling myself.

"You look see."

I went to my bedroom and pulled up my dress. Nothing but faint red streaks around my middle from the rope burns. I went back to the kitchen. "There ain't no blood, but I swear a haint jumped inside me with a hot knife and set to slicing away." She stopped scrubbing again and turned to me.

"You go set, then. There's stockings in the mending pile to keep your mind off the pain. I'll milk Belle." I suspicioned Ma had gone simple-minded, then she looked at me with a kindly smile. "It'll be over in a few hours."

That's when it came to me I was dying.

I reckoned it was because I got strung up in that tree, and now Pa wouldn't be able to tell me how proud he was of me getting that outhouse door up to where we had a place special to go to. I wished I could see him before I passed on, but I figured unless he came back from the Confederate Army before nightfall it wasn't like to happen. I took out the basket with the stockings, and Granny's darning needle, and a ball of yarn and sat in the chair by the hearth, the one Rayford usually sits in. I stared at that needle and yarn and tried to recollect what to do with them, but the pain brought tears to my eyes. It hurt so, I laid on the floor in front of the hearth. I took to asking the Lord to see his way clear to put me in heaven, but then I thought about Rayford and had in mind to do some studying on it first.

I didn't want him to be alone. I thought on how Pa would go to heaven seeing as how he is such a good man, and with all that

Bible-reading, Ma would likely get there, too. Besides which I can't see as the devil would let her into hell no how. From what I hear he's in the custom of doing things his own way, so I don't reckon he has in mind to go up against the likes of Ma. She'd put an end to his pranks right quick. I'd lay odds she'd turn the whole place upside down and have the devil himself studying at the Bible.

But I was worried about where Rayford would end up seeing as how he ain't one for praying. At prayer meetings he sits and plays or whittles or such as that, whatsoever we can find to keep him quiet. Maybe whittling preachers counts for something, but if you got to pray and believe the Lord is your salvation so as to get to heaven, I reckon Rayford ain't going to make it, and I don't want him to be without nobody wherever he goes.

I suspicion the devil has two spots already staked out for Hugh and Mule so if Rayford is headed to hell, they could keep him company, excepting they ain't never been no comfort to him. 'Course Rayford ain't got no evil in him so I don't reckon the Lord has in mind for him to burn in the eternal fires of hell, of which Ma says that means forever. It came to me there might be a place special for folks like Rayford that ain't heaven but ain't hell neither, like as if Ma set me up a dose of her spring tonic and Pa brung me home horehound candy from the general store. One tastes like a polecat smells and the other is so good my mouth is coming up with spit just thinking on it. But most times I don't get neither. Maybe there's a place like that when you die. If there is, I reckoned that's where Rayford was going. I surely wished I could ask Pa.

There was a break in the pain about then so I got up and sat in the parlor chair and dug out the darning gourd and pulled a stocking over it. Time I got the needle ready and took a couple of stitches, my insides heated up again. As I set the whole mess down, Granpappy came in with a peculiar look on his face and it came to me that he was feeling a might better today.

"Either my eyes is failed or your Ma is out there milking Belle." He went to the window and looked out. "It shore is a wonder."

"She is being kindly. My innards is paining me." The pain bent me over, and near most brought tears to my eyes. "I laid down before, but it don't help. I reckon I'll be passed on by nightfall."

He cupped his ear. "Passed on?"

I took a deep breath and nodded. "I'm dying," I was so close to tears from the pain and the sadness of passing, I couldn't barely get the words out.

He quick turned his head away and took his pipe out of his mouth and tapped it. It appeared his shoulders shook a bit. From holding back tears, I reckon. He cleared his throat and turned back to me.

"You do look a might peak-ed," he said.

"Ma told me to mend these stockings. I been trying but I can't hardly think on nothing but the burning. You reckon Rayford is going to heaven?"

"Is he passing, too?" He turned away again. Poor Granpappy, he couldn't even look me in the eye. I reckon I should have given him words of comfort, but I had my mind on Rayford.

"No. But I promised Pa I'd take care of him, so I want to know should I ask the Lord to put me in heaven or hell. Lessen there's a middling place for the likes of Rayford seeing as how he ain't the praying kind, but he ain't evil neither."

"I suspicion the Lord will take him in. He might could use a good whittler up there." I saw how Granpappy was likely right, and it made me feel some better. "You hang on," he said. "I reckon once the Lord has him, Rayford'll be fine, but while he's on this earth, he needs you. Your Ma talk to you some about this dying business?'

"No. She came in once and asked if I been to the outhouse. I told her I been, and she asked if my drawers had blood on them yet. I told her I ain't got no blood nowheres besides which it was making me plumb scairt, such talk about blood in particular to a body what is dying. I reckon she just wanted to see what a dying person looks like. Or maybe she was looking to see how my mending is coming."

"Hmm. Has Melanie talked to you about...about woman things?"

"Some on crochet and knitting, but not on darning." Melanie is a good one for all them sitting chores and a good one for teaching seeing as how she has more patience than Ma.

"Next time you see her, you ask her about woman things...troubles and such."

"Next time I see her, I reckon I'll be already passed on."

"Well. You work on that mending and keep breathing. We need you around here." He put his hand on my shoulder and left.

It was the worst predicament ever. Here I had learned to shave Rayford and I wasn't going to be around to do it no more. Granpappy's talk on Melanie put me in mind of asking her to come back and help with him after I pass, but I didn't see as how

I'd get to Foster's. I asked Ma last week could I go visit her and she said Melanie could just as well come here and lend a hand seeing as how we got ourselves so much work. Then an idea came to me. Might've been the devil who put it there. Seems like he's the one gives me most of my ideas, but I didn't see as there was no other way but to try it.

I just had to drink all the water I could hold and live through the night.

13

I Wish Everybody'd Just
Let Me Be

I woke up an hour or so before daybreak and had to use the outhouse quick, like I suspicioned I would. I lit a pine knot off the fire and took it with me to light the way to Foster's. When I used the outhouse, I saw the blood. It came right out my bottom. I tiptoed back in the house and took an old stocking and wadded it up to stop the blood and asked the Lord to give me strength to make it to the Fosters. I headed out along the road but it was slow-going seeing as how I had to keep pushing that stocking back in place. Leastways the pains were nearly gone. I didn't know did that mean I was near the end. I hoped I had a little more time.

When I got to Foster's Whiskers ran out to meet me, jumping

and barking. I reckoned he'd wake everybody, but he's such a barky old dog, nobody pays him no mind no more. He sniffed me and we walked to the house, then he went off to the barn and I went to Melanie's window. I called her, but before she woke up, dried leaves crackled behind me, and I jumped and turned, and there was Mr. Foster pointing a gun at me.

"Tatum?"

"It's me. I got to talk to Melanie."

"Couldn't it have waited leastways til the sun came up."

"No, sir. It can't wait. I'm dying and I need to talk to Melanie afore I pass," I said.

"Dying?" He came up closer and looked at me squinty-eyed. "You look all right to me."

"No sir, I ain't. Truth to tell, the life is passing right out me. I don't know as I got much longer, so I got to talk to Melanie."

"Well, I reckon seeing as how you're near most dead, I best let you in. Come along. But you got to be more careful. I like to've killed you myself. Middle of the night ain't no time to be sneaking around. Yankees been through Harpersville and they're swarming over there like bees. Ain't come round here, far as I know, but I don't like to see you out roaming."

"Well, I'm right sorry, but this is a dadblamed predicament and I need Melanie to make me a promise." We went in the house and I had to push Melanie near most ten times before she opened her eyes.

"Baby?"

"I ain't got much time, so I'll get right to it…I'm dying." She sat up, and grabbed my hand.

"What're you talking about?"

"I got blood in my knickers and it just keeps coming. I reckon I ain't got but half of it left and afore I die, I need you to promise you'll take care of Rayford."

"Your insides hurt?"

"Plumb awful yesterday. Couldn't barely walk. They ain't so bad this morning, but I'm still bleeding like a butchered hog."

"You tell Ma about this?"

"I did and she set me in the parlor mending stockings."

"Mending stockings?"

"She milked Belle. I reckon seeing as how I am nearly passed on, she is being kindly."

"Poor Baby. Come sit." She patted the bed.

"I'm like to get blood on it."

"Well, here then." She went to a drawer and took out a rag. I pulled the stocking out of my knickers, and she gave me the rag and helped me get it settled. "Ain't that better?"

"No. It feels like I got a rag stuck in my knickers."

"You'll get used to it. Now, sit." I sat next to her on the bed and she put her arm around me and squeezed my shoulders. "You ain't passing on. You're just becoming a woman."

"A woman? I am becoming DEAD!"

"No, that blood means you got your monthlies and your body is growing up and now you are a woman."

"How can I be a woman if all my blood runs out and I am dead."

"No. It's just a little. You got a whole lot more inside."

"Well, if it keeps running out, I ain't like to have a whole lot more inside. Fact is, there ain't gone be none inside."

"No. It don't all run out. It just comes out for a few days

each month, then it stops. And it's blood you don't need. It means now you can have babies."

"Babies!" I near most fell over dead right then just to hear such an awful thing. "Well I better not get me one. It's all I can to do take care of Rayford. I can't take care of no baby, too."

"It don't happen til after you get hitched."

"Hitched? Well, I ain't getting hitched, so I reckon I ain't getting no babies. How come you ain't got no babies yet? You're hitched."

"I will. It just ain't happened yet."

"Are you funning me?"

"No. Miss Clara done told me."

"Well, how does the baby get in there? I surely hope it ain't like Missy said. She told me this most awful story. She says that a feller puts...he puts one of his parts into a girl and then a baby gets in her. I told her she is a blabby-mouthed liar."

"She ain't. That's the gist of it."

"Well I ain't never getting hitched, and I most surely ain't about to let no feller come nowheres near me with ideas such as that."

"I reckon that's a good idea for now," she said, rubbing my back.

"Forever!"

"Whatsoever you say. I don't reckon Ma knows you left."

"No. I was afeared she wouldn't let me come. She asked me was I bleeding but at first I thought she meant from where the rope was tied around my middle."

"No, she meant out your bottom."

"Well, why didn't she tell me about I was becoming a woman!"

"Ma ain't one for such talk. About babies and all. I reckon she will be happy you came here and now you know about babies and such. Letting you sit and mend was her way of taking it easy on you seeing as how you were ailing."

"Well, if she was trying to take it easy on me, she shouldn't have come in with all that talk about blood. I swear she was getting ready to lay me out."

"Baby, that ain't true. You just ask her for rags for your monthlies and tuck them in your knickers like I showed you. They'll soak up the blood and then you rinse them good and wash them with the other clothes."

"And if all of that there blood runs right out me, you don't reckon I'm gone die?"

"No. I told you, it ain't dying blood. It's monthly blood that you don't even need."

"Then why have I got it in the first place?"

"Tatum Louise Wylie, you can be most exasperating. I already done told you everything I know. If you don't have the blood then you can't have no babies. That's just the way it is." She took a loud breath and pulled away.

"If I can't have no babies lessen I get hitched, why is the dadblamed blood coming now?"

"It's just part of being a woman! Now hush and forget about it."

"Well, it ain't enough that Ma is telling me I got to grow up, and Granpappy is making me shave Rayford, now you tell me the stupid blood that's coming out means I am a woman and I ain't ready to be a woman yet. I wish everybody'd just let me be."

I set to crying so fast, it even surprised me.

"Poor Baby." She put her arm around me again, and I let the tears come. "I reckon it seems like you got the whole world on your shoulders. Here. You come sleep with me til the sun comes up, then we'll get us some breakfast and I'll ask can I take Major Tom and the wagon and get you back. Maybe I can stay the morning and help with some of the chores. We don't want Ma and Granpappy to wake up and find you gone and worry to death."

At daybreak Melanie got another rag and went to the outhouse with me and showed me how to fold it and tuck it so it'd be more like to stay in place. We went back in and had us a fine breakfast of flapjacks that Melanie made, then Miss Clara told Mr. Foster to pack up a ham from their smoke house and some cornmeal they'd just got ground.

After he left, she said, "Come here, Tatum," and I went by her bed and she gave me a big old hug and she said, "It's right nice that you become a young woman and I hope some day you find a nice feller and have lots a babies."

"Well," I said, but before I could tell her I didn't like fellows and I didn't want no babies, Melanie kicked me. I reckon Miss Clara didn't mean no harm by them words. She is too kindly, even though she is not very strong and flat on her back in bed. "Thank you for them nice words," I said and Melanie gave me a big smile. "I hope you are feeling better soon."

As we headed out to the wagon I got to thinking that maybe if my Ma didn't have such a hard life, she'd be more like Miss Clara. Course Miss Clara had a real hard life, what with her always ailing, and she still was good to other folks. I reckon there's some women that can have children and whole families and still be happy and some that can't, but seeing as how I don't know which one I am, I won't take no chances and have no babies. I just hope Melanie is right about you got to be hitched first and one don't come by surprise. Maybe if a baby comes and you don't want it, you can send it back some place, or give it to someone. If one comes by surprise, I reckon I'll send it to Melanie.

I4

This Is My Home

I got a peculiar feeling when I woke up this morning. I laid there thinking on it, listening. I heard Granpappy in the room next to mine, snoring regular, but it still seemed too quiet. I put it up to not hearing the wind. When I heard Ma stirring the fire on the hearth, I got up and as I dressed, she yelled up to the loft, "It's morning, boys. We got chores afore breakfast." I searched the yard for eggs and found five. As I walked into the kitchen, Ma came behind me with cream she brought up from the root cellar. She set the cream on the sideboard, then picked up the broom and hit the floor boards of the loft. "Boys! Get a move on." There still wasn't a sound.

"Maybe they got up early and Hugh is out in the barn and Mule is off to the creek fishing," I said.

Ma didn't move for a minute, then she set the broom against the wall and ran her hand over her hair. "Run out to the barn.

Tell Hugh we got corn and cotton to hoe and he can't be messing with his contraptions today." I stood there a second, wondering should I say what I was thinking. Ma rubbed her back low and scowled at me. "Git!" she hollered and I ran out the door.

There wasn't nobody in the barn. I came back and told Ma. She set up the butter churn next to the table, and poured in the cream as Granpappy came into the room. Ma eased herself into the chair and grunted, then turned to him.

"You know where them boys is at?"

He shook his head. "Did you check the field?" he asked me. "I told them yesterday we had a hard day of work ahead."

Ma slammed the top on the butter churn and gave me a look like as if this was all my doing. "You run up to the field and see are they there," she said. I ran off again knowing I wouldn't find them and I'd best enjoy every minute of peace. I headed along the path, noticing how the drops of dew glistened in the brush at the edge of the woods. A mourning dove cooed and I recollected Pa imitating them, his bottom lip and chin rolling forward following the sound. Up ahead a squirrel rustled leaves but when I got closer, I saw it was a towhee and it flew away, streaking reddish through the sky. Birds sang and called to each other while a woodpecker hammered away in the woods behind the barn working for his breakfast. Halfway to the field I turned toward the sun, closed my eyes, held my arms out, and let it warm me. It was a thing Pa and me did on nice cool mornings like this, and I hoped that somewhere at the war he was facing the sun spread out like a scarecrow, too.

I rounded the curve at the top of the hill and looked that field up and down. It was mostly cotton with a few acres of corn. Well, there was a mess of weeds, too, truth to tell. I pictured myself as tall as a giant and swinging a big overgrown hoe, weeds flying in every direction. With Hugh and Mule around, and me tending to Rayford, I only hoed when I wanted to be with Pa, but he learned me how to do it right, how to swing the hoe and use the whole of my body to bring the weeds out easier. Watching him move along a row put me in mind of a bird floating through the sky looking for gusts of wind to ride on. I thought of Ma rubbing her lower back, Granpappy hobbling out to the barn, and Hugh and Mule heading up to the ladder and whispering long into last night. I thought of running away, but in my head, when I got to the road, I met Pa and I ran to him and he opened his arms and hugged me. We didn't say a word. We were too happy to see each other. Then I pictured us walking up the path together to the field and him putting his arm on my shoulder. "I'm proud of the way you kept those weeds down," he'd say, and thinking about that, I got tears in my eyes. "We'll get two, three more bales of cotton thanks to you and it looks like we'll have enough corn to last through the winter for Belle and Beaure--"

Beauregard! The picture in my head flew out and I saw myself walking through the barn earlier and looking out into the corral. Belle had been drinking at the trough, but I hadn't seen Beauregard anywhere. I reckon my brain was so hard on Hugh and Mule, I didn't think on it at the time. I turned and ran for home and up the porch steps, through the parlor and into the kitchen. "Beauregard is gone!" I hollered, and Ma rammed the dasher into the churn so hard it like to've split apart.

I waited for Ma to commence yelling and truth to tell, she looked so pitiful, I was more sorry for her than scared. She opened her mouth like as if she was set to lay into me. Of a sudden she pulled the dasher up and eased it back into the churn, staring at it, holding her breath. Hugh turned eighteen last week and Ma told him not to get no ideas about joining up with the Confederate Army, especially with Pa gone and us needing him here. Granpappy came in the back door with Rayford and Ma took a deep breath, like as if she recollected she had to keep breathing.

"You tell Will them boys of his ran off." Her eyes went back to the dasher but she didn't move. "He's too easy on em. You tell him this is what it come to."

Granpappy looked at her peculiar, then took Rayford to his chair and set him down in it, and nodded at me to get shaving him. He hobbled over to Ma and put his hand on her shoulder.

"Mae." He talked just above a whisper. "Mae, Will is at the war. I reckon that's where Hugh and Mule is now, too." Ma let go of the dasher and slumped against the chair back. Granpappy pulled the churn over to another chair and set to work. I took the heated water from the hearth and gave Ma a quick look. A tear rolled down her cheek.

Ma sat for ten minutes or so. Then she got up, cooked a breakfast of fried eggs and cornmeal mush, set it on the table, made some mullein tea and went to her bedroom. Granpappy ate and headed out to the barn to work, but there was no pounding nor ary other noise so I suspicion he sat out there chewing on the stem of his pipe. I would have thought I'd be plumb tickled to be rid of Hugh and Mule, but instead of being happy my mind went to thoughts on how we'd ever get the cotton picked and seeded and the corn in and shucked, and how would we get it ground for meal without Beauregard. Mule wouldn't be hunting anymore and Hugh wouldn't be there to chop wood to cook what food we had.

Whilst Rayford ate, he'd stop and stare at Hugh's chair or Mule's chair and point. I told him they'd gone off to the war and he looked at me, like as if he was trying to figure what those words meant. Then he'd put his spoon in his bowl and eat a bite and look at their chairs again. A few weeks after Pa left, we put his chair out in the barn so Rayford wouldn't see it empty and think on him. I reckoned we'd have to move two more chairs out.

Ma didn't come out for dinner. Afterwards I settled Rayford in his garden and he took his knife out of its leather sack and picked up a carving. "What're you making?" I asked. He looked at me and I pointed to his carving. He smiled. Maybe he can't hear at all, but he knows what we mean by pointing. When I think and talk to myself in my head, I use words and I got to wondering how you think if you don't have words. If you don't know what the word "happy" means, you can't say in your head, "I'm happy." I reckon Rayford has a feeling like this thing, or this day, or this food is the way it should be, or it isn't the way it should be. He wouldn't know why. He couldn't ask questions. Maybe when he was being shaved, or when he was eating, or whittling, or working in his garden, things were the way they were supposed to be. But he knew something wasn't right because Hugh and Mule weren't in their chairs. Maybe when Pa left, it felt to him like it wasn't right, but after he was gone for so long, it got to feeling like Pa being gone was the way it should be. I'll never feel that way seeing as I got a regular brain and words that tell me no matter how many days he's been at the war, I know it ain't right. Some days I don't know if having a brain is good or not.

"Do you miss Pa?" I asked him. I wondered what happened in his head when I said "Pa," and then I heard the thud of hooves coming down the road, lickety split, and around the corner came Major Tom, Melanie astride him, not even sidesaddle, both her ankles showing. She jumped down, tied the reins to one of the fenceposts around Rayford's garden and ran to the house, skirt flying, never even looking to see was I there.

"Melanie," I called over and she stopped and turned to me.

"Oh, Baby!" she wailed and rushed over through the gate and I wondered what awful news she had brung. I stood and she grabbed me and my heart pounded. I held my breath while she stood back from me.

"Pa Foster told me Hugh and Mule headed out! Oh, Baby! What will you do?"

"Land sakes, you had me shaking. I thought you brung more bad news. How'd you find out so soon?"

"Everybody knows. Pa Foster set out to get news of the war today and ran into a feller whose arm was all wrapped up and he said he was wounded in fighting along the Etowah River, and probably wouldn't have made it at all but two boys on a mule gave him food. He recollected their names were Hugh and Mule."

"Melanie!" Ma called from the porch.

"Ma!" Melanie cried. She ran to the porch and grabbed Ma in a hug. Rayford looked to the house and I wanted to stay with him, but I had a feeling I should get up there and listen to what they were saying. As I headed to the porch, Granpappy came out of the barn. I hadn't given much thought to how he had been so hobbled, but it came to me that ever since I been shaving Rayford, seems like he is better. 'Course, even when Pa was here, he'd have spells where he wouldn't get out of bed. I had a quick thought about asking him to shave Rayford again, but it came to me to let it go. And leastways when I was shaving Rayford, Ma let me be.

"Glad you came, Melanie," Ma said, and they held each other. "You best move back here now. With them boys gone, we need you home."

Melanie looked over and motioned to Granpappy. "C'mon, Granpappy. Baby! You, too. We need to talk on this. Let's go in."

In the kitchen Melanie told us to sit, and it felt like as if we'd been waiting for somebody to come and tell us what to do. She pulled out Hugh's chair and sat, and looked at each of us, then she asked Ma, "Did you suspicion them boys were heading out?"

Ma shook her head and I saw the anger rise in her eyes. "I told Hugh that turning eighteen didn't mean he could go traipsing off to no war. Reckon he thought he knew better."

"I swear, when it comes to war, men don't have a brain in their head. Sorry, Granpappy, but Pa Foster told me how it is in town when our boys head out. It's like it's a circus they're going to, hollering and cheering."

"Reckon I'm of the same mind," Granpappy said. "You tell a feller to go out and hunt a man like they would a deer, they'd think you'd gone crazy. Call it war and get them fifes to blowing and them drums to thumping, and they can't wait to get in line. Reckon I'm just too old, and I've seen too much."

Melanie looked riled, of which there ain't been many times I'd seen that on her. "The worst of it is, it ain't like to do no good no more," she said. "Pa Foster says the Yankees are hellbound for Atlanta and are pushing our boys back steady. Hugh and Mule should've stayed home where they'd have done some good. We best pray for them, and in the meantime, we'll have to make do." She stopped and appeared to be thinking. She shifted some in her seat, kneaded her left hand and started in again. "Many's the time I wished we were closer to town, but now I'm glad we're so far out. Pa Foster says we likely don't have to worry none about Yankees. Trouble is, he's got to drive all the way out to Hay's Mill now to get corn ground. Yankees find out where the mills are and steal the grain then bust em up or burn em down." She clasped her hands and stared at them, like she wanted them to be still now, then looked at Ma. "You say as how I'd best come home, but I ain't one for no wood chopping nor field work. I ain't afeared to do my share, but them things don't come easy to me. Besides which, Foster's is my home now. I'm hitched to Joram and that's where I belong."

Ma jerked like she'd been slapped, and I wanted to look at her face, but it didn't seem right.

"I'm sorry. Those are hard words to hear. I'd be in both places if I could, but I can't and Fosters is my proper home. That don't mean I don't care about none of you." Melanie grabbed Ma's hand across the table. "Me and Fosters been talking. You best come live with us." She looked at each of us, to see how we were taking it, I reckon. I got a picture in my head of us being there with all that good food, and Melanie there to talk to and kindly Miss Clara and them nice painted-up walls in their house, and all the pretty things them daughters of hers were always bringing. But since I wasn't the head of nobody there, I knew my place was to keep quiet, and for once, I did.

"That's kindly of you," Granpappy said. "But long's I can get around, I aim to stay. This is my home. My hip is some better lately." His hip ain't better. It was pride talking, not sense, of which I was some surprised after what he said on the war. He looked down at the table. "And truth to tell, I don't know how Rayford would do. He don't know no other home."

"Foster's garden is fenced. We can set him up just like here," Melanie said.

"It don't feel right. Maybe I'll see things different tomorrow. Reckon I need to think on it some, but it just don't feel right. Mae, how do you see it?"

Ma looked surprised, and I reckon I did, too. It ain't no secret that Granpappy don't see eye to eye with her. It made me recollect how Pa told me I had to respect her. I suspicion I could learn some from Granpappy on that. Ma looked around the room, and her eyes settled on Pa's going-to-meeting hat hanging on a peg next to the door that went into the parlor. "When your pa comes down that road, I aim to be here to meet him."

"But, Ma. You got to eat." Melanie argued. "I know the boys ain't workers like Pa, but leastways they helped some and Mule was a good hand at fishing and hunting."

"I can hunt," I said. "Pa was set to learn me to shoot. I watched him. I reckon I can shoot a gun as well as I can chase squirrels for him. And there's coon down by the creek, and quail, and turkey, and rabbits."

"Well, Baby, that all takes time. And a gun. You got to have feed for Belle, and I reckon she needs to be bred and their ain't a bull left around here nowheres, and just to care for her and the chickens you need some grain and feed and such." She turned to Ma again and gripped her hands. "Ma, you got to listen to sense."

"Pa could come home tomorrow. If Fosters would spare some meat for us once in awhile, I reckon we can make do til he and the boys get back."

Melanie opened her mouth, but nothing came out. She shook her head. "If you ain't here when he gets home, Pa will come to Fosters'," she said to Ma, then she turned to Granpappy. "Pa Foster and Miss Clara are partial to Rayford. We'll take good care of him."

"When I'm laid up in bed, I reckon you can drag me wherever you need to. But long's I can get around, I ain't going nowhere else. Your Ma's right. I aim to be here to see my son come down that road, and my grandsons, too. It ain't just Rayford that takes comfort in things being the same. I ain't of a mind to leave my home neither. Them Yankees ain't pushing me off my land." Melanie clucked her tongue and gave him an exasperated look. He gave her a look back. "We need to, we can hire one of them young Driscoll boys."

"But they ain't like to work for nothing. What've you got to trade?" Melanie asked.

"They got a passel of sons. I reckon they'd be happy to trade work for more land. I still own all that to the west of their place up to Brace Mountain."

"But they got three or four that's still too young to help much and need to be fed themselves. I reckon you mean Hiram and Lee, but I don't know as Mrs. Driscoll would let them go. You and Ma got to think on how it will be if this war goes on much longer. Supplies are running low and Pa Foster says even rich folks are going without. You'll need a new milk cow if'n you can't breed Belle and there ain't none around, nor hogs for raising come spring."

"The Lord will take care of us," Ma said. She closed her eyes and I thought she was praying, but when she made a face I knew it was a headache coming on.

15

Happy Birthday, Baby

Last night I got in my head the idea for how it would be when I woke up this morning. First I'd look over to Melanie's dress hook where I'd lay eyes on the yellow ribbon with lacy edges that Pa sent, of which it would be near most glowing in the morning light. Then I'd recollect that the letter with just my name on it was under my pillow, so I'd shut my eyes again and pretend he'd come in to wake me. He'd stand by my bed and he'd say, "Tatum," and I'd pretend I didn't hear him, so he'd say it again, louder, "Tatum." And I'd wake up to see him bent over me, a smile on his face, his hair damp, one hand on the wall, and the other behind his back. "What're you hiding?" I'd ask and he'd make me guess and I never would guess a yellow ribbon with lacy edges, so finally he'd show me. And he'd make everyone be nice to me the day long and before dinner, Granpappy would ask him if he gave me my birthday bumps yet, of which it was a thing they did in Granny's family. And Pa would haul me upside down and bump my head on the floor once for each year.

Howsomever, that ain't the way it happened at all. I got in bed facing the dress pegs, but during the night I must've turned over. Before I opened my eyes I heard the rooster crow of which that made me think I'd best get up and get the eggs before Granpappy set Rayford up in his chair for shaving. With my next breath I smelled strong pee and that made me think how Rayford wet again and Ma would be ornery over it and I'd have a mess of washing to do. I got up sleepy-eyed and took my dress off the hook, and that's when I noticed the ribbon and recollected it was the sixteenth of July and I was born thirteen years ago on this day. And Pa had been gone nearly three months, and Hugh and Mule nearly two weeks.

I took the ribbon and rubbed my fingers over its smooth shininess, then sat on my bed and took out Pa's letter and read all those nice words on how he was thinking of me and leaving messages in the stars. He wrote he was proud of me and my fast running and my taking care of Rayford and that he'd be home as soon as he could. I got a whiff of pee again, put the letter under my pillow, and the ribbon back on the hook. Last year Pa said I'd likely be too big to turn upside down and bump this year, anyway.

I reckon Ma forgot what day it was. After morning chores and breakfast, she took a hoe and went up to the field. Ma ain't one for field work but she gave Rayford a fierce look when Granpappy brought him out this morning. Even with her back and her head paining her, I suspicioned she might head up to the field instead of washing Rayford's bedding. Granpappy was out in the barn cobbling a new pair of shoes for me seeing as my feet have been growing some. With everyone gone and not paying me no special mind on my birthday, I decided to have a time of it by myself. After I got Rayford settled in his garden and gathered his peed-up bedding, I washed my hair so as it would look nice with Pa's ribbon in it. It came to me to take a handful of dried leaves we gathered for tea—beebalm and chamomile and mint and such—and brew them to rinse my hair with so it would be nice smelling. Then I took out my brush and worked my hair until I pulled near most half of it out, but leastways I made my head a respectable place.

I recollected Pa saying it put him in mind of a bird's nest and whenever I caught myself in a looking glass, I saw the truth of it. There's some that have hair that hangs, like it don't have naught but hanging to do, but my hair ain't like that. One day when I was studying on it, it came to me that all them ideas in my head must be the cause of it. They come right out through the top and make my hair go every which way and it gets cantankerous and stubborn, making a mess of tangles. Whenever Ma threatens to take the shears to it, I recollect the day I went to town with Pa and we made a stop at Alameda and Brigham Charles's place over in Pine Ridge so Pa could look at their sheep.

They were dying, one or two every week. Mr. Charles had been raised on a sheep farm in England, but he'd never seen the likes of it before. He tried everything he knew, but they kept dying. Pa said it was likely caused by something they were eating on pasture, but I suspicioned they were dying of pure shame. Old Brigham must've been a might riled when he sheared them seeing as how he took every inch of wool off them and they looked like the sorriest bunch of naked critters I ever saw. I ain't never likely to be pretty, like Melanie, seeing as how I am too big-boned, and too red-haired, and I ain't much for acting ladylike, but I reckon I ain't about to go around looking like no sorry sheared-up critter neither.

I pulled my hair together and tied it up in the yellow ribbon. In Ma's looking glass I looked better than regular, but it was a waste with Pa gone. Thirteen sounded older than I was ready for anyways. Twelve is a no-count word, but thirteen has a growed up sound like there's more chores that go with it. I reckoned I'd best let it be and keep on like as if I was still twelve.

I went to the drawer in the sideboard where we keep Pa's letters and took out the one that came a few days ago and read it again. When Mr. Foster brought it he told how we should be on the lookout for Pa and Hugh and Mule seeing as how they were likely passing through due west. But I reckon Hugh and Mule wouldn't stop even if they were. And maybe Pa would be afeared that if he stopped Ma wouldn't let him leave again.

He wrote that he got in with a group of boys from Tennessee and the onliest thing they could talk about was food. When I read that, I got a picture in my head of Pa laughing. When Pa takes me to Harpersville, we have us a high old time. Folks like to talk to Pa. We walk down the street in front of the general store and they yell, "Hey, there Mr. Will Wylie. How y'all doin'?" and, "Hey, Will, how's your pa? He still nursin' that hip?" and all kind of talk such as that. I asked him why folks are so kindly to him and he told me that's the way the world is. "Folks like to be kindly to other folks. It makes 'em feel good," he said, but I reckon most of that is Pa's doing. I've seen it at prayer meeting, how he sets folks at ease. Even quiet folks get to jawing and telling jokes round him. I don't reckon he's doing a lick of good in the Confederate Army seeing as how he is so kindly.

Next he wrote about when he found a nest of robins a while back. He said the mother bird brung worms and them little beaks opened wider than her head, and she'd drop a worm in and a second later that beak snapped open again and he wondered how she kept track of who she fed. "Maybe it's like hogs," he wrote. "The pushy ones get the most." He still didn't tell about the fighting, but he wrote on how he's been learning new tunes to play on his harmonica and how he'll play a whole mess of them for me when he gets back. He will be so surprised at what I got set up for us in our hickory tree. I wrote back that I'm near as good as Granpappy at shaving Rayford. I didn't say naught about how Hugh and Mule lit out and joined the Confederate Army seeing as how Ma said she'd give me a whupping if I did. I told her he could look for them at the war if he knew they were there, too, but she didn't want him to worry none about them nor about us as he has enough worrying. I don't know how long I sat holding that letter, but when I heard a noise on the porch, I like to have jumped out of my skin. Here Ma was back from the field and I hadn't even got the fire going under the wash pot. I quick put the letter back and headed out the back door when I heard a voice call, "Anybody here?"

Melanie! I ran back to the parlor and there she was, all done up in her good dress and running to me and hugging me and of a sudden, it was a good day again.

"Happy Birthday, Baby. Why look at you," she said. "You're getting so growed up, and you got a yellow ribbon in your hair.

You ain't looked this pretty since my weddin'. And what is that smell? Puts me in mind of something," she said and I told her how I rinsed my hair with tea water. "Well," she said, "I might just try that myself one of these days. That is a good idea. I ain't forgot what today is so I got two things for you—one to eat and one what ain't to eat."

"Peach cobbler!" I hollered out seeing as how that's my favorite.

"Why you ain't a lick of fun, guessing right off like that." But I suspicion she knew that's what I'd guess. "You wait right here."

She went out and brung the cobbler in from the porch and the minute I smelled them peaches and cinnamon, it came to me as how it was near most the dadblamed best day of my whole life excepting I wished Pa was here. Then it would've been the best. And I would've liked for Hugh and Mule to be home, too, so as we could all be together for Pa to see, howsomever on my account it didn't matter none that they had gone, excepting that I had to do more chores. Melanie must've read my mind. She put the cobbler on the table and pulled out a chair. I sat across from her. She looked up at the loft then turned back to me.

"Where's Ma?"

"She went up to the field. Rayford wet everything last night and Ma said she'd rather hoe than clean up after him."

"Well, I'll go tell her I came and brought a rabbit for dinner. And I got something else for you that ain't to eat."

"Is it on the porch?" She shook her head.

"No, it's hid real good, and you got to find it. But you have to wait til after dinner."

With an extra body at the table, it felt like we were more of a family again. Rayford got excited and ate too fast and choked on a spoonful of sweet potatoes. When Melanie brought over the peach cobbler, Rayford reached out his spoon to dig in but Granpappy grabbed his hand and pushed it back by his plate. It is the custom to give the birthday person the first bite, but I told Melanie to give some to Rayford so he'd calm down and Granpappy said how that was kindly of me.

Melanie gave me the next piece and as she handed it over she said to eat it slow seeing as how she had dropped a piece of peach pit in the cobbler and couldn't find it, of which that wasn't like her, but I didn't give it no more thought except I bit into it easy. She served Ma and Granpappy and herself and we all got quiet enjoying that nice sweetness. I had the piece near most eaten when I bit down on something hard, but it surely wasn't a pit.

"Careful," Melanie warned. When I took it out, I saw it was a red stone. "That there is your birthstone. It's a ruby. One of Pa Foster's relatives from up in North Carolina found it and gave it to me on my wedding day. Ma Foster told me it was a birthstone for July and I been saving it for your thirteenth birthday. It's an English custom to hide something special in a cake, but I reckoned it would work with cobbler, too. Do you like it?"

Now a red stone is pretty, but it ain't worth a lick to my way of thinking. Ma had her eye hard on it, so I reckoned I'd tell her later she could keep it for me. It looked like a thing growed up ladies are partial to, of which it put me to thinking how thirteen was looking worse all the time. But I turned that ruby every which way like I thought it was beautiful, put a thankful smile on my face, and asked as polite as I could if the stone is what she hid so good that I had to find. "No, that's for later," she said and a real smile came on my face all on its own.

"Now, I don't know as I told you all," Melanie started in, "but when Miss Clara's daughters come for visits, they bring us books and I been reading to her." Melanie's eyes lit up and I thought how even though it was just our house and Pa was gone and Hugh and Mule weren't there to help with chores, there was such a happiness that came from her being there. If I ever grow up, of which I still ain't ready, I hope I am as kindly as she is.

"The book I'm reading now is called Jane Eyre. It's about a girl that worked for a man cleaning his house and such and fell in love with him. But she didn't know there was a woman in the attic that was touched in the head who was his wife. I'm at the part where she is leaving, seeing as how she can't bear to be with the man she loves as he is already hitched." And before I could ask why they kept that woman up in the attic and why couldn't they let her have a garden, like we did with Rayford, Ma got after Melanie.

"That don't sound like a Christian man, leaving his poor wife in the attic and taking up with a young gal," Ma said.

"But it ain't like that," Melanie said. "They are all so kindly to each other and it is so sad, we just cried after the last part, like as if Miss Jane was right there telling us the whole story."

"If that reading makes Miss Clara happy and takes her mind off her ailing, I reckon it's a good thing to do," I said. It came to me I should read to Granpappy to make him feel better, but not that Jane story about love and such as that. I'm partial to stories about witches and haints and goblins and such, even if they do scare me.

"It's like being somebody else for awhile and feeling all new things. Truth to tell, I can't wait til reading time," Melanie said.

Ma wouldn't let go of that sour look, but Melanie kept her smile, and set to talking about what kind of food and other things them friends of Miss Clara's brung, like real coffee and wheat flour, and spices we hadn't been able to get since the war started. And when we were done eating Melanie said it was time to look for that hidden thing. "I near most gave it to you last Christmas, but I reckoned it was a good present for a girl turning thirteen, who is become a young woman." She winked at me of which I knew why she did it and it made me recollect that stocking I put in my knickers. I hoped that present wasn't a mess of rags.

"You young 'uns go on. It's time for my nap," Granpappy said. He walked around the table, stiff from his sore hip but he kept a smile on his face and ruffled my hair like Pa would've done. "Reckon I'll have to do some fancy work on them shoes I'm making for you, Tatum, seeing as how hit's your birthday." He put his hand on my shoulder and kissed me on the cheek. "You set Rayford up in the garden for me, and later you tell me about this present."

"We'll take him out," Melanie said. She asked Ma to come along, but she wanted to lie down. Melanie scraped the plates while I cleaned up Rayford, then we headed out and went at it like a couple of chirping birds.

"I know Granpappy's hip has been acting up, but Ma walked stiff-backed, too." Melanie took hold of Rayford's hand while we walked to his garden, and I got a good feeling to see it.

"She still gets them pains. I reckon we'll have to get lots of mullein dried and set by for winter. Ma says it helps some. You best let Rayford pull that gate open." Melanie stepped back and Rayford pulled it open all the way, went in, then pulled it shut again and headed to his chair.

"No more talk on Ma. You got a present to find. You start in looking and I'll holler out 'hot', when you're getting close and 'cold' when you are heading the wrong way."

"Me and Missy play that game after prayer meeting sometimes, only she don't always say the hot and cold right. Then when I find it and tell her she was cheating she says she forgot, and I know it ain't so."

"Well, I ain't Missy and I ain't about to say it wrong. Now get looking."

I headed for the root cellar and she said, 'hot,' so I went on, then she hollered 'cold!'

"But I ain't even by the root cellar yet."

"It ain't there."

"But you said hot!"

"'Cuz you were going the right way but now you ain't. You best come back a few steps and go a different way." So I did and she kept up with the hot and the cold until I got to the outhouse and she took to yelling 'Hot! Hot! I can near most smell the scorching.'

"I can smell it too, but it ain't scorching. You hid me a present by the outhouse?"

"You weren't about to look there lessen I helped and I didn't want you off sneaking around and finding it when I wasn't there. I aim to see your face when you get it. Now keep looking. You ain't found it yet."

"Is it inside?"

"Well, you just move a little and see do I say hot or cold."

I opened the door and she hollered 'cold' of which I was glad to hear, seeing as how I didn't want no birthday present that had been setting in the outhouse. I went north a few steps and she hollered, 'Hot! Real hot!' I looked around in the brush and there was a little package all wrapped up in tan paper with a piece of twine tied around it and made into a bow on top. It was the size of a book, but it didn't have the feel of one. "I can't figure what it is."

"Open it and see."

I ripped the string off and tore at the paper, but Melanie said to take it off careful, so I could use it again. The paper was wrapped round and round and I took it apart until I got to the present of which it was a red tin box, not quite a foot long. "Is it to put things in?" I asked. It came to me that it would make a good hiding box to keep food in at my tree.

Melanie shrugged her shoulders, like as if she didn't know. I pulled the top off and there was a folded-up white lace hanky. I was thinking on how it was not a good sign to get another growed up present, but when I took it out, what I saw near most took my breath away.

"Paints?!"

"And brushes, too," Melanie said.

"Are they real?"

Melanie nodded.

"I never thought I could get such a thing as these." Then I thought how as Rayford would surely take to a thing such as painting. "Can Rayford paint, too?"

"It's your present. You can do whatsoever you want with it."

"It'll be like how you get to do the reading to Miss Clara. That's what these paints'll be like to me. I'll paint pictures of our house and yard and the barn and Belle, and the place down by the creek with a log in the water." Then I had a bad thought. "You think Ma will let me paint? She's like to call it foolishness."

"I got an idea on that. We'll go up to the field and hoe, and come back and put Rayford's bedding on. Then we'll make tea for Ma and call her in and tell her what all we done. Then I'll tell her about the paints."

I would've liked to get started right in with the painting, but Melanie was right. We took Rayford with us up to the cornfield and set to hoeing where Ma left off. Melanie talked about books and how Jeanie brung perfume from France for her and all kind of things such as that, and I was talking about what I could do with them paints and I didn't even care that the sun was hot and the sweat was dripping off us.

When we came back Granpappy was sitting in the shade on the porch and asked what thing it was that Melanie had hid for me. I whispered about the paints and how we'd been hoeing and working so as to soften Ma so she'd let me use them.

"Paints, you say. To make pictures?" I nodded. "Sounds like a thing I'd like to see," he said, and of a sudden a strong feeling of love came over me and I gave him a hug. He ain't like to call them paints foolishness and I suspicion he'll help us get Ma to look kindly on them. I still wish Pa was here, but leastways I still got the best granpappy in the whole world.

Melanie took Rayford back to his garden and picked some flowers and talked to him and watched him with his whittling.

When she came back we made biscuits and put together a stew of leftover rabbit and sweet potatoes and peas and set the table all up and put flowers in Granny's vase and stuck it in the middle. Rayford's sheets were dry by then so we put them back on his bed. When it was time for supper, Melanie got Ma up. When she came into the kitchen, and saw how we had the table done up with flowers and a hot stew and fresh-made biscuits, her eyes lit up some. We ate and talked and just as we finished eating, Melanie said, "Baby, why'nt you go get that present I brung and show Ma." Whilst I was gone I heard Melanie saying as how I was getting so growed up and I knew she was getting to where she'd ask Ma to let me have some time. I set them paints on the table, opened up the tin box, pulled out the hanky, and when I saw those shiny pots of color again, I held my breath and looked at Ma.

"Can't eat em, nor wear em," Ma said. "What're they good for?"

"For having fun, Ma. For making something pretty. C'mon, Ma," Melanie pleaded. "I know everything ain't perfect, and there are troubles. But it don't mean we give up on being happy. We have to try harder is all. We have to make fun."

She sounded just like Pa.

16

A Little Tin Of Paints

I reckon Ma has a touch of mule blood in her. It's near most like we got our own war going on right here, only I ain't got no say in it but to let her win, seeing as how she is the ma, and I am just a sorry child who got a little tin of paints for her birthday that Ma hid somewheres. If I ever get hitched, of which I ain't, and if I ever have me a mess of children, of which I ain't, I will be kindly to them, and if they get paints I will let them paint pictures on things that are old and sorry looking and need some sprucing up, and I will not get all riled over it.

When I got up this morning, I just looked at them paints a little. It surely is a wonder how you can get a little brush full of paint and make the color come off onto something else and it looks right pretty. My hands were just itching to get at them, but when Melanie left last night she told me to work hard all day today and not ask Ma on them til after supper when she had a chance to rest. That's what I aimed to do and I was just thinking on it when Ma came in and said not to get no ideas about frittering the day away.

"You get them eggs yet?" she asked.

"I'm getting," I said, sweet as could be and I headed out. Some days she is more kindly than regular but I could see this wasn't like to be one of those days. I gathered what eggs I could find and brung them in and set them on the plate on the sideboard, and milked Belle, and got Rayford up and shaved, and I did it all lickety split, no daydreaming nor naught as that. When we sat down for breakfast I asked in a most polite and kindly way if there might could be some time after supper when I could paint with Rayford. Granpappy shot Ma a look then, like he had in mind to say, "I reckon this poor little child who's been working so hard and doing chores and taking care of Rayford so good and shaving him and what all, I reckon she should get to play with them paints."

But Ma wasn't looking at Granpappy. "I don't know why Melanie ever gave you such a thing--" and she set to with one of her complainings. I would have put my hands up to my ears, but I had sense enough to know that wouldn't have done me no good, so I tried to shut them on the inside. It near most worked seeing as how she kept on a spell whilst I was thinking about me and Rayford painting in his garden and how we'd have lemonade like what Miss Clara done made for us once when we visited of a Sunday on the way home from prayer meeting. Then Granpappy snorted and gave her a fierce look, and banged his fist on the table.

"Why even a dadblamed mule gets a few hours rest ever day,"

he said. Ma slammed her fork down and it hit the side of her plate and that jumped up like a critter and tipped over and even though there wasn't no more food on it, it was a sight. There was a voice inside of me saying "Tatum, you best keep a straight face," but a giggle came up out of my throat like a cough and made me spew milk like the springs on the side of McCreedy's Hill and Ma pushed back her chair and stomped out. I tried to say I was sorry, but them giggles were too powerful and it was all I could do to catch my breath. I took to laughing so hard I like to have fell off my chair. I looked over and Granpappy was laughing, too, then Rayford got into it and all the while a little voice kept saying "You'd best hide those paints afore your Ma does." I reckon it was the devil come back to get me to do pranks again, but I thought as how that was a good idea, whether it came from the devil or not. I was thinking on it when Granpappy took out his hanky and wiped his eyes and blew his nose.

"You best go talk to your Ma. She can't help herself. It comes from too much hard work and not enough good times and the sorry thing is there ain't never been nothing for it. Seems like she'd figger out she's doing to you what's been done to her, but I reckon she just can't see it. Don't help none that your Pa ain't here and your brothers run off neither. She's a might scairt for us and for them, too, and you put all that together, it's a wonder she ain't gone plumb crazy."

"I didn't mean no harm. I tried to hold it in, but it was a might peculiar the way that fork jumped on top of that plate." I barely got it said before I started in again and me and Granpappy laughed til the tears rolled down our cheeks. It surely felt good to laugh like that again, like how you feel when you just done a heap of hard work and the sweat is running down your face and arms and back and it's time to stop and sit in the shade and have a cold drink of water and rest. Then Granpappy said sometimes we do things we don't want to do now so that things are better later, and this was such a time and he'd take Rayford out to his garden and I'd best run and find Ma and tell her I was sorry. I said I'd just scrape off the dishes, then I would. He said that laughing seemed to help his hip somewhat and he aimed to walk up to the field after he got Rayford settled and it came to me if that laughing helped him feel better, I was glad we done it, even if it got Ma riled.

As soon as Granpappy and Rayford left the kitchen, I took them paints off the sideboard and hid them outside in the brush acrost from the wood pile. Then I cleaned up all them dishes from breakfast and headed out. I found Ma on a stump in front of the root cellar taking skins off onions.

"You gone dye some more of that yarn up in the loft?" I asked. She nodded. "You want I should help you?" She shook her head. "Ma, I'm sorry about that carrying on. I reckon I just needed to laugh and when that fork hit the plate, it all came out."

"You make up some corn bread," she said. She didn't say naught about me sassing, so I got to thinking everything was all right and I might get some time to work with them paints yet.

After we ate dinner I cleared off the table and went in to the parlor. Everybody was sitting: Rayford whittling, Granpappy carving out a design for a chair back, Ma stitching away at a shirt she had in mind to send to Pa. "Can I take Rayford in and try out them paints?" I asked.

"You got everything cleaned up?" I nodded. "You get the table cleared off for breakfast after you mess with them paints," she said, and I took that as a yes.

I went out to where I hid them paints and brung them in. I put Rayford in his chair and I opened all them paint jars and he picked one up and sniffed it. I reckon he was thinking that was peculiar-looking food and where was the spoon for eating, so I told him they were for playing, not eating. "I'll show you," I said. I took out the paper that Melanie had wrapped the paints in and tore it in half. Rayford's eyes were on my hands and the brush and I kept at it until I reckoned he had got the gist of it. Then I took one of the brushes and stirred it around in the pot of yellow paint until the bristles were covered in a bright, shiny, yellow and I gave it to him. "Take it Rayford. It's paint. You put it on there," I said, pointing to the paper I had set in front of him.

He stared at the brush, then twisted the handle and touched the paint part and rubbed it twixt his fingers, then he smelled it and got yellow on his nose. I wiped it off. "You watch me," I said and I dipped the brush in the brown paint.

"See Rayford," I said. I pushed the paper closer to him so he could see the squirrel I'd painted. Well, it was meant to be a squirrel. The tail was nice and fluffy seeing as how that part was easy to do with the brush. The rest of it could've been a cat. I reckon I got a good likeness of the ears, but it wasn't easy to make that little squirrel body, and the feet were plumb awful, like four little splayed out forks setting neath the belly, which didn't look naught like a belly neither. It was too big for the rest of the body. "It's a squirrel," I said, but I don't think he figured it out.

I looked around for something else to paint and saw Granny's vase on the shelf above the sideboard. I took it down and set it on the table and painted a likeness of it, light green with purple and yellow flowers, then Rayford got the idea. He dabbed his brush on the paper a few times, then he went for the purple. I grabbed his hand and showed him how to clean the brush in the jar that had a smell of turpentine, then wipe it on a rag, like it said on the paper that came with them paints. He started in with the purple and made another flower, of which it smeared at first, but then he made tiny strokes of color. He went for the green, but I caught him and pushed the paintbrush into the turpentine and wiped it on the rag. He painted stems and leaves, and went for the purple again and I went for his hand, but he stopped, pushed my hand away, and rinsed the brush himself. Then he made another flower and another until his paper was near most covered. It was a wonder.

"Rayford, that is so pretty. I surely wish I could paint like that," I said. A minute later, in came Granpappy, holding his corncob pipe. He stood watching a few minutes, then sat.

"That boy has him a talent, all right," he said. "Your Pa was a good hand at likenesses, too. Just never had the time to dawdle with em." I suspicioned Ma would come in any minute. If I heard such as that about what a good picture someone made, I'd have come and looked, even if I didn't much like the one who made it. Pa calls that being curious, when you want to know about something, of which Ma is not, lessen she gets curious if you are doing your work or not, and to my mind, that is a plain waste of curious.

"What're you making?" Granpappy asked and it came to me that I wasn't even painting any more, I was watching Rayford. I showed him the squirrel.

"Well. That's nice," he said.

"It's a squirrel."

"Hmmm," he said and I looked over at Rayford and he was making a mess, brushing blue into white and mixing them all up. I grabbed for his hand and said, "No!" then Granpappy pushed my arm.

"Let him be. He's got a feel for it." After a few minutes, you could see a blue jay. It wasn't like pictures in books, but you could tell it was a bird and he had different shades of blue. "I reckon he had in mind to mix those paints a' purpose," Granpappy said, and both of us sat and watched him until it was time for bed.

Then tonight, after I done all the chores, and we ate supper and I cleaned up the kitchen, I set out the paints, brought in more paper Fosters had given us, and we started in again. My head was near most spinning with all the thoughts in it, like how lucky we were that Ma let us paint again, and how fast we were using them paints up, and it was good that Rayford was going at it slow. Then it came to me that I wasn't as much painting as I was watching Rayford to see how he done it, like I had my own teacher. I took to painting like he was, not pressing hard with the brush, but just touching it to the paper, and then we heard a bellaring sound. Belle ain't one for bellaring regular, and Granpappy called in from the parlor and asked me to take a look. I went out and didn't see her but she bellared again and I followed the sound. I found her behind the barn caught up in an old piece of fence post that had a wire on it. I reckon she got curious and stuck her head down by it and somehow it got caught on her rope with the bell on it. I tried to pull the rope out, but she was a might ornery and I had to be careful seeing as how every time I'd get near she'd throw her head and near most knock me down.

I came back and told Granpappy and he said to get the broom and use the handle to knock the rope out of there. Well I tried one way, then another, but I just couldn't get her loose of that post and then I thought as how maybe the pitchfork would work better, so I got that. I had to be careful not to poke her with it, but them pointy ends made it easier to get in there. I snagged the wire and pulled it away and Belle got free. By then she was all cantankerous and I don't reckon she did it a' purpose, but she came at me. I stepped backwards, stumbled, and near most fell, and then I was thankful I had that pitchfork and not some worthless broom handle, seeing as how I gave her a poke and she bellared again and jumped back. I was scairt she'd take off, but she shook her head like she couldn't believe I'd dared to stick her—like I had hurt her feelings—then she got over it, took a few steps, and went back to eating grass.

I rolled the wire tight around the post and laid it next to the barn, then took the pitchfork back by the woodshed and went right to the kitchen. I reckon my mouth hung open and my brain quit working for a minute. When a thought came to me, it was that a miracle would happen and Pa would walk through the door so he could say, "Now, Mae, just take it easy. He didn't mean nobody no harm." And Ma'd get that look on her face and she'd set to hollering but leastways I wasn't the onliest one she'd be hollering at. But Pa wasn't there and me and Rayford had to face her alone.

It was the sideboard. Whilst I was out getting Belle loose of that wire, Rayford had painted flowers on the top of it. I wanted to think on how pretty they were, but I couldn't, seeing as how it felt like there was someone right by my side poking me again and again, and whispering, "Ma's gone get him." I reckon it was the devil. It don't seem right that if there's as many folks in the world as Pa says there is, I'm the one the devil always comes to bother. But I reckon it was him, seeing as how that poking feeling got bigger and bigger until I couldn't hardly make myself think on how nice them flowers were, only how much trouble they would bring. I let out a little holler and told Rayford to stop, and then I heard Granpappy say, "No, you set and rest, Mae, I'll go have a look see." I didn't know should I oil a rag and wipe them flowers off, or would that paint smear, so as maybe I'd best leave the sideboard alone seeing as how flowers are better than smears.

Granpappy hobbled in and took a pretend puff on his pipe. I couldn't rightly tell what he was thinking. He turned around and hobbled out and there was part of me that said, "Now your Ma will be happy we got Rayford, seeing as how that is the prettiest sideboard I ever seen," and another part of me said, "Tatum Wylie, you best hightail it for Tennessee."

I heard Granpappy shuffle over to the rocker and sit in it. It creaked, then it was quiet, and I reckoned Granpappy was chewing away on his pipe and thinking. Then the creaks came regular, so as I knew he was rocking, and a minute later I heard, "Well, you are one lucky woman, Mae." I got the picture in my head as how Ma might be setting down her mending and looking at Granpappy like either he was touched in the head to say such as that or he was looking for a fight. "You got something now that lots a gals'd give their eyeteeth for," he said. It was quiet again except for the steady squeak of the rocker on the floor.

I suspicioned Ma was thinking as how she didn't have nothing that anyone'd give their eyeteeth for, excepting a sorry family without no Pa and too much work. Another minute passed and he said, "You got flowers on your sideboard that spruces hit up some," he said. "Makes hit look right cheerful."

Then there was stomping and screaming, and Rayford backed into the wall and covered his ears. I went to him and Ma grabbed the paints and took the brushes and headed out the back door. I ran after her and she turned and hollered "You stay right there," and I yelled after her that them paints was from England and was sent here special for Melanie to give to me, but I don't reckon she heard none of that, seeing as how I ain't seen them paints since. I looked everywhere, but she found a good hiding place. I aim to keep on looking but unless she tells me where they are, I don't reckon Rayford and me will be doing no painting for awhile. That's all right for now, seeing as how I ain't sitting no more than I have to. The only good that came of it was that she broke the cane. I ain't a bit surprised neither seeing as how she hit harder than she ever done before, but I never cried once. Ma was crying enough for both of us.

17

It's Like The Whole World Is Ailing

Granpappy ain't been out of his bed for two days now, excepting to use the chamber pot. Whilst we washed clothes today, Ma grumbled on it, so I said I'd take care of it. I reckon them words caught her by surprise. She took supper to Granpappy without a bad word, so some good came of it.

Of late it is like we are walking a long, flat road and there ain't no hills and there ain't no valleys and there ain't no pretty little streams to sit by, of which talking to Pa is like that. There ain't no more good things. And Melanie can't come round much with Miss Clara ailing so. To my mind, it's like the whole world is ailing. Even Rayford ain't been whittling regular. Maybe he's sad seeing as how Ma done took them paints we were having fun with. When I am in his garden, I talk to him regular and I pretend Pa is working in the cotton, Ma is rolling out biscuits, Granpappy is building a chair, Hugh is in the barn hammering away, and Mule is fishing.

But then it's time to help Ma with the cotton and I can't pretend no more. Cotton is a mess of work. All summer long you hoe the dadblamed weeds, of which they come back anyways, then you got to harvest, of which it means you got to pull off the bolls and they prick your fingers. Now we are cleaning it to get the seeds out, of which Pa'd make it fun and he'd tell me about he heard there was a circus coming through Georgia or how someday he aims to take us to Savannah. Or he'd tell about that dog that he had when he was a boy that could jump high as his head. Ma don't say nary a word, and I try to keep thinking on things that are interesting but without no one talking to me, it's the work that I am thinking of. Then I recollect how I ain't tried to run away in a spell and maybe it's high time I set out again and my head fills with ideas and I reckon I will just get on the railroad and get to a place where there is a ship and I will get to England and buy ten whole boxes of paints and Rayford and I can paint all we want, seeing as how there won't be no Ma to hide them and when they are all gone, we will just get us more. And I will bring Rayford and Pa. And if Ma promises not to complain nor tell me what to do, she could come, too, seeing as how Pa wouldn't want to come without her anyways, and then a cotton boll pricks my finger and I am right back on this here farm.

18

I Had Got As Tall As Ma

Last night the fiercest storm set in right over our place the whole night, crashing and banging and lighting up the sky steady. A thunderbolt hit close, and Rayford cried out. When Pa says there ain't no need to be afeared of storms, I feel better, but I suspicion it ain't his words that comfort me, but Pa himself. The thunder kept up, bang, bang, bang, so loud I feared the next one might knock me right out my bed. Rayford kept hollering but I reckoned Granpappy would take care of him, so I climbed down under my blanket and I swear, the lightning came right through it. With the next crack, the house shook and I recollected the story Missy told me about the little girl whose ma and pa got struck down by a lightning bolt that set their house a fire, and the girl's name was Tatum.

When the sun is out and it is daytime and it ain't storming, I know it's a story she made up in her head. But last night I thought as how every word must be true and I reckoned if the house caught fire, I'd best be ready. I pulled on my dress, and as I closed the last button, there was a crack that sounded like ten of the one before it, like all the thunder in the world gathered in our sky and hit at once. My stomach rolled and I had to swallow fast to keep from retching. Rayford screeched through it all and I wondered if Granpappy had gone out to the porch to watch like he sometimes does. If I was scairt even after all the good things Pa told me about thunder and lightning, then Rayford, who can't understand such as that, must be near most dead with fright. I lit a lantern and went to Rayford. He was hunched up in the corner and wailing like a wild critter that was getting ate up. His bedding was everywhere, and he'd been so scairt he'd messed himself. And there was poor old Granpappy, sleeping right through it.

I talked to Rayford but I reckon he didn't know it was me seeing as how I patted him and he jumped and near most knocked me over. Then the thunder hit and he started in again and I don't recollect it being so, but now as I think on it, I must have forgot all about being scairt because I set to singing. Rayford cried so loud, I near most had to scream the words. I thought as how Granpappy would sit straight up in bed any minute and tell me to hush, but he didn't move. I suspicioned he took himself a good dose of the medicine Doc Waitly give him for his pains. I recollected how when him and Pa talk about it, Pa says, "Now you take some of that there treatment Doc Waitly brung over," and Granpappy says, "I ain't gone take a lick of it, seeing as how hit makes me so groggy I can't even stand up. I ain't gone spend the rest of my days in bed." The pain must've got so bad he finally took it and now there wouldn't be no waking him. If I'd have known where he kept it, I would've given Rayford a dose and took one myself.

The storm kept up fierce, rain hitting hard against the roof and windows, but the loud cracks died down. I sang and patted Rayford and he was near most settled when lightning hit close again and Rayford let out a howl. I rubbed his arm and sang louder, and about then Ma came storming in, her voice high and screechy and the words pouring out her mouth so fast I couldn't make hide nor hair of what she said. Then she yelled "Shut him up, shut him up, I can't listen to that eejit no more," of which it only made Rayford set to again with a steady wail. I told Ma to hush so I could quiet him and she laid into me like that whole storm and all that lightning was my doing and it was me who set Rayford to yelling and waking her. I reckon the devil hasn't seen fit to let go of me, seeing as how I grabbed her arms and shook her. "Get out! You're just making him more scairt.," I hollered.

"You watch your mouth, Tatum Louise Wylie," she yelled back. She tried to get loose of my hands and her elbows jerked every which way but I hung on tight, and it came to me I was staring straight into her eyes. Somehow I had got as tall as Ma without even knowing I done it, and I could tell by the way I had a hold on her that I was stronger, too. "Ma! He was near most quiet. I ain't sassing, I'm just saying that if you want him to keep quiet, you best keep your own voice down," I screamed in her face.

She shuddered and quit fighting me. I loosened my grip on her arms, and she pulled away. "I can't take this stink no more," she sobbed, "I just can't take it." She bolted out of the room and a minute later a door slammed shut.

Rayford had crawled under a blanket, but leastways he was quiet. Then I recollected the chamber pot and lowered the lantern to the floor. It was on its side and one of Rayford's sheets had fallen on the floor beside it and was soaking up all the spilled pee.

I felt for a dry spot at the foot of the bed and sat for a minute, taking pity on myself and waiting for the tears to come, but the stink was too bad to sit for long. There was nothing for it but to go out and get the wash pot going. I'd have to keep a fire burning all day to dry everything, and it tired me to think on it. Leastways the thunder and lightning had finally passed on so they weren't over our house no more.

I shook Granpappy and he finally opened his eyes. "I need your help," I said. He mumbled something and turned away. "Rayford wet bad. He needs cleaning."

"You do it," he said.

"But he's got to be cleaned all over."

"Tatum," he whispered, turning toward me and grabbing my arm. "I can't get out of bed now. You clean him up."

"But--" He let go of my arm, and when he took a breath he shuddered. "No, I can't, I can't," I begged. "You have to help. Please."

He just shook his head and rolled over facing the wall.

I didn't see how I could do it all: start a fire under the wash pot, get Rayford out of them clothes, clean up the room, wash him off. It all swirled through my head like wind-whipped dust. I sang about a horse that was stolen and got back home again seeing as how he was so faithful, part of me wishing I could run away, and part of me thinking on where to begin. Rayford still whined, soft, like a mewing kitten, but he wasn't thrashing around. I decided to clean him up first. Seeing as how the storm had quieted by then, it was likely being in messed clothes that still made him uneasy. It would've taken too long to heat water to fill the wooden tub we use for baths, so I went to the kitchen, filled the cooking kettle with water, and set it over the fire to heat. Time I got Rayford in the kitchen and took off his britches and shirts and drawers, the water was warm enough, so I poured it into a bucket, refilled the kettle and went to washing him off. I didn't look more than I had to. Truth to tell, he wasn't made much different than the bull Fosters had before they gave it to the Confederate Army. Time I got the top part of him cleaned up, the water needed to be tossed and the kettle was hot again. I refilled the bucket with warm water, and poured more into the kettle to heat.

I closed my eyes when I did his man parts, of which that was where the worst of the mess was, then tossed the water, and filled it again from the cooking kettle. I was wiping off his legs—and was near most finished—when there came a shriek. I jumped and Rayford turned quick and crashed into me and I lost my balance and stumbled against the bucket, splashing water across the floor. Rayford set to screeching and as I put my arm out to comfort him, Ma grabbed it and swung me against the wall. Rayford went to the corner next to the sideboard and pounded on the wall and screamed and Ma came at me again, swatting at my head like I wasn't no more than a pesky fly. I screamed at her to stop, and Rayford turned and pushed Ma hard. She fell against the table and landed on the floor. Of a sudden it was quiet. Rayford looked at her peculiar, like he couldn't figure why she was down there. He lumbered off into the parlor, and I grabbed his clean clothes and glanced at Ma long enough to be certain she was breathing. I dressed Rayford and as I sat him back in his chair, I heard Ma wailing, soft at first, but then louder, a sorry, lonesome sound more like a coyote howling than a body crying. She sounded so poorly that even after what she did to me, I felt bad for her.

19

I Felt The Darkness Like A Cold Hand

I took out one of the good chunks of white pine we save for Rayford for times like this of which I hope there ain't no more of them. "I'm getting a might low on dogs," I said, handing the wood to him. I barked, like our old hound dog, Bee Boy, would have, and Rayford smiled. Then he put the pine to his nose and sniffed. I recollected his knife was still on the stand by his bed. When I went into their bedroom I saw that Granpappy's coverlet had fallen off. I pulled it up over him, took Rayford's knife, and left.

I sat with Rayford til he took the first cut with the knife, then I went out and washed his sheets and blanket, and wrung them out, and washed his peed-up clothes, too. As the water boiled away I refilled the pot and in between I looked in on Rayford and put a stew of ham and carrots and leeks and potatoes on for dinner. It looked like it had set in for an all-day rain, so I strung ropes across the parlor and kitchen to hang the wash. I brung in two loads of wood to get through the day, then dropped into the chair next to Rayford and looked at his face. I had forgot to shave him, but I was plumb wore out, not just from all I done, but from fighting with Ma. It takes a lot out of a body to be fighting and disagreeing all the time.

After ten minutes or so, it came to me I should go to Ma and say I was sorry and ask if she was all right, but I was afeared she'd lay into me again. I reckoned if I made breakfast and she smelled it, she'd come in of her own will. I hadn't even gathered eggs, but I knew with the storm, the chickens'd all be in the coop and leastways I wouldn't have to hunt for them. I swung the soup pot out from the hearth and built up the fire, then went out and found six eggs and fried them with potatoes and onions. I brought Rayford in, too, and he dug in like he hadn't eaten for days. He would've finished the whole pan if I'd let him, but I saved some for Ma, in case she got up. Of a sudden I recollected Granpappy hadn't eaten neither, and something came over me and I hugged Rayford. He stopped whittling for a minute, and looked at me, somewhat. He don't ever hug back, but I think he has a feeling about it. Leastways he don't fight it, generally. But the way he looked at me, I suspicioned he knew more why I hugged him than I did.

I looked in on Granpappy. It still smelled powerful strong like pee in there. Rainy days make it worse. I don't reckon I could've slept in that room.

"Granpappy, you want something to eat?" With only a small

window, it's always dreary in there on a grey day, but of a sudden, I felt the darkness like a cold hand. I shook him. He was still. I put my hand by his nose, but there was nary a breath. I touched his face, and a recollection came to me of the day he and Pa loaded up six chairs to take to the hotel in town. Granpappy had the knack of water-bending the wood to make nice rounded backs, and he got himself a name on it. I've never seen him look so proud as he did that day when all them chairs were up on the wagon, each one as good and perfect as the next. I kept that picture in my head and went back in and sat by Rayford.

He chipped away at the chunk of wood, working slow like always. After three, four minutes he closed his eyes and sat, then opened his eyes and turned the wood and rubbed his fingers over it. Then he started whittling again. He didn't look at me. It was near most like he got caught in the wood once he took to working on it. I wished I had something I could get inside of, so I didn't have to think on nothing else.

I went to the kitchen and put the rest of the fried eggs and potatoes on a plate and took it to Ma's room. "You want something to eat?" I asked. She didn't answer, so I set it on the stool next to her bed. "I'll leave it here for when you get hungry." Her back was to me, but I suspicioned she was awake. "Ma?" I was afeared she'd get up and swat at me, but I had to tell her. "Something's wrong with Granpappy."

"And there's a war on, and my Will is gone, my boys run off, and I can't help none of it."

In my head I said the words, "Granpappy's passed on," but I didn't know if that was the truth, and I didn't want it to be my words that made it so. I like when he talks to me and tells me about growing up and about hunting and fishing and how he helped his pa clear the land where we plant the corn and cotton. My favorite story is the one he tells about how Pa took off with Rayford and they couldn't find them, and when he's of a story-telling mind, I ask him to tell that one. I know it myself, but he tells it good, about how he and Granny looked all morning:

"...down to the creek and in the woods back of the barn and up to McCreedy's Hill and all through the house. We looked in all the places where they might've hid, and they wasn't no-wheres. We only had the two young uns and Granny fretted something awful, said she couldn't stand to live no more if they had drownded and I said there warn't no way they could of drownded seeing as how the creek was low, but it looked like it was coming to that.

"We started out for the woods behind the barn when we heared a wagon coming. We run out and it was Lem Foster and setting on the wagon was your pa and Rayford. 'They come for a visit,' he yelled out. I hightailed it out there all set to lay into your pa, and Lem—he was such a kindly man—he come over and put his hand on my shoulder and whispered, 'Now you take it easy on em. Your young Will was proud as a rooster about how he come over and brung Rayford. My Annie put out some sweet corn-bread and they set and talked a spell and we was plumb tickled over it. Annie asked if you knew they'd come and your Will said, 'Aw, it's all right. We just set out for a bit.' Then Annie said, 'Don't you reckon they're a might worried about you and Rayford?' and Will says, 'I reckon they know Rayford's with me, so they won't worry none.' He asked how was the corn coming, just like a little old man, and me and Annie, we like to split, hear that young feller talk crops that way. I said I'd bring them on home, and Will said, 'Ain't no need to trouble yourself none, seeing as how we done walked here. We can walk back.'

"Then Lem said, 'That's quite a boy you got there,' and I warn't quite so het up no more, and by then your Granny had just about smothered them boys to death with loving. I reckon if Lem hadn't of talked me outen the whupping, your Granny would of put a stop to it. 'Course we had a talk with Will. He always told us after that afore he set out. For the most part anyways."

And Granpappy tells me how he met Granny and what a pretty gal she was and how he had to fight off this one and that one to get her hand. I reckon he is funning about some of them stories, especially the ones where he was fighting off two at a time, both big as bears.

I made a batch of Johnnycake to go with the soup, seeing as how there wasn't nothing else I could do with the rain still coming down, and I had to keep a fire going anyways to get Rayford's blankets dry. The fire got too hot and I burned the Johnnycake, but leastways that got Ma up and moving.

"What'd you burn? How you gone take care of your own family some day," Ma asked.

"You best look in on Granpappy," I said. She gave me a look like I was simple-minded, but she headed off to his room. Time passed. I put more wood on the fires and turned the bedding so the heat could get to the other side. I took the beginnings of a honeysuckle basket in to work on while I sat by Rayford. I looked for things to think on and my mind settled on them paints. Ma took the paint jars, but not the covers. If they were outside somewheres, the rain was likely washing all that paint away. Rayford had fallen asleep. The only sounds were the crackling in the fireplace and the dripping rain. A few minutes later the floorboards squeaked and Ma stood in the door way to the parlor.

"Why'nt you tell me?" Her hair wasn't combed and little tufts stuck out all over her head.. Her face was grey and veins showed through her skin. She looked peculiar with her tiny hands and feet, her little nose and mouth, and those big eyes. It was like seeing her for the first time in a long time. She's changed a might since Pa left. I changed too. It ain't just that I can stand eye to eye with her, my whole body is bigger than hers. Even though I am still just a child.

"I didn't know certain," I said. She looked fierce at first, then softened some, so I asked, "Can Pa come home now?"

"How we gone get word to him?" she snapped. "Time he gets a letter, Granpappy'll be in the ground."

She stood there a bit, then went to the kitchen. I heard a chair scrape and knew she'd sat at the table. I didn't know did she want me to come in or not. I wove a row on the basket, then went to the kitchen. I looked for something to say, and all I could think was to ask about the breakfast I'd set by her bed.

"Did you eat, Ma?" She stared at the table. I didn't think she heard me, then of a sudden she jerked her head toward the back door. Then she grinned, like as if someone had walked in, and her eyes lit up. I would've thought she was funning excepting that ain't her way. She smoothed her hair, like she was gussying up for someone, and my stomach rolled.

"Ma!" I shouted and slapped the table. She startled and looked at me regular. "What're we gone do?" She looked around like she didn't know how she got to the kitchen, then back at me, her eyes lost. "Ma, Granpappy has passed on. What're we gone do?" She opened her mouth and looked toward his room, then covered her face with her hands. "I don't know . . ."

"I reckon I best go to Fosters."

She looked at me and nodded. "Mr. Foster will know what to do."

I put on my coat and pulled the oilskin tablecloth over my head to keep dry and set out. The rain had died down to a mist, but the ruts had puddled over and it was hard to walk. I thought on how it was as wet and dreary inside me as out, but if I was to find the good of it, like Pa would want me to, I reckon it would be that Granpappy's hip ain't paining him no more.

20

It Made Me Wish I Was A Baby Again

At the bottom of McCreedy's Hill I turned up the road to Foster's and Whiskers came running to meet me like always, barking and jumping every which way. I petted him and he licked my hands and face and whined like he was trying to tell me he'd missed me. That sad feeling faded some with old Whiskers hopping round like a big furry black and white frog, but I thought as how it wasn't right that there could be such happiness with Granpappy passed away. I hushed Whiskers, but he ran the rest of the way with me, yipping and carrying on. He puts me in mind of one of them toys Missy's brother Hereford brings to prayer meeting. You wind it up and it goes and goes then it runs down and you wind it up and it starts all over again.

Excepting that Whiskers don't never wind down. Time we got up to the house, Melanie was on the porch wiping her hands on her apron.

"Hey there, Baby." She brushed her hair back dotting it with specks of whitish yellow from the corn meal on her hands. Seeing her brought it all back to me how I put my hand to Granpappy's nose and how his face felt and of a sudden, the tears burst out.

Melanie ran down the steps and put her arms around me and patted my back and asked me what was wrong, and I carried on so I could scarce catch my breath. It wasn't just Granpappy, it was everything: Pa gone, Hugh and Mule run off, Ma acting peculiar, and Rayford afeared of the storm. It was like as if a big sack of meal fell on my head and near most knocked me down. Melanie is so kindly, she never yelled at me like Ma would've, she just let me get all that crying out. She pulled me over to the porch out from under the rain and she just held me. "It's Granpappy," I whispered when I could get the words out.

"It's okay, Baby. It'll be okay. Let's go sit."

She pulled the porch rockers close together and even though I'd been to Foster's so many times before, it came to me that those bent wood backs were Granpappy's doing.

"Now what about Granpappy? He took bad sick?"

I couldn't tell her. I couldn't say the words.

"You want me to send Pa Foster for Doc Waitly?"

I shook my head and then her eyes got big. Her lips twitched and she took a deep breath and tears ran down her cheek. But it is like Melanie to cry quiet, and not bother anyone with it. "I'm sorry, Baby. I'm so sorry." She reached over and held my hand.

After a few minutes she stood, pulled me up, put her arm around my waist and we walked in the house.

Inside it was warm and the smell of food set my stomach to growling. I eyed them real walls they had done up in a soft green that I always wished we had in our house. A dish of custard steamed on the sideboard and some kind of meat roasted on the hearth. My sadness for Granpappy got all mixed in with wishing we could live with the Fosters and Melanie, and thinking how there would be folks to help with Rayford and to talk to and different things to eat and maybe Ma's headaches and back pains would get better and she wouldn't miss Pa so much. Then we were in the parlor and there was Miss Clara, wrapped up in a blanket and sitting on a chair with a mess of fancywork in her hands.

"Why, Tatum. I didn't know we had a visitor."

"It's Granpappy," Melanie said. "He passed on early this morning." And then Miss Clara gave me a look like I ain't never seen on Ma, like she knew what I felt inside, and her eyes were full of love. And even though she was just sitting there, all spindly and sickly, she opened her arms.

"Come here, child," she said. "Come, Melanie," and we went to her, one at each knee, and she put her arms over us, like as if she could protect us from all them awful, sad feelings. "I am so sorry," she said, like it was her fault and she was bound to do what she could to make us better. "Poor girls," she said and such as that until I near most forgot what I was feeling sorry for and just thought how nice it was to have someone hugging me and holding me and letting me get all them tears out. When I got dried up, it came to me as how I might could have felt peculiar coming in and wetting all over her blanket with my tears, but she wasn't like that a lick. "Maybe now your Ma will see clear to move in with us. There's lots of families doing that now, for protection and to help each other." She let us be for a few minutes, just rubbing our backs and humming, like as if we were babies. It made me wish I was a baby again, without a care or worry or even knowing what was happening around me.

"Melanie, you pack up your things, then fetch Mr. Foster and set us up an early dinner and we'll talk about what all has to be done." She went off, and Miss Clara kept rubbing my back, making me more and more sorry for Granpappy gone, and Rayford without a pa or a brother, and most of all for me. It was a comfort to be crying, and the tears ran steady like they didn't have the heart to stop.

By the time Melanie came back, I'd dried up some, but I couldn't barely breathe. She gave me a rag to blow my nose into and it cleared my head some, leastways enough to smell meat and onions, and my stomach took to growling, of which it made me red-faced, but I didn't know how to stop it. Melanie helped Miss Clara to her chair and I followed her to the kitchen and a minute later Mr. Foster came in. It didn't seem right to sit down to roast squirrel and a heap of turnips and onions and potatoes fried in bacon fat when Granpappy had passed and Ma and Rayford were alone, but once my mouth tasted such as that, truth to tell, I enjoyed it. And I reckon it helped that I had already got so many tears out. Miss Clara talked on all kind of things like how the weather has been harsh and how Jeanette's boys were growing and such as that without a word on Granpappy, of which I know she did it to be kindly. Then Miss Clara told Melanie to bring the custard she'd made that morning, and she brought over the dish from the sideboard. When she broke into it with her spoon, a sweet, warm smell burst into the room. She dished some out for all of us and I picked up my spoon and put some in my mouth and even though I'd started to think on Granpappy again, it tasted good. I pretended it was the food that went with a burying. But I wished Rayford and Ma were there, too, so time Mr. Foster left to hitch up the buggy, I was ready to go.

"Melanie, get your things together, then pack some corn meal and molasses, and some of that there lard, and get them a ham. And put the rest of that custard in a crock for your supper."

"I can help," I offered.

"I'd like it if you sat with me awhile," Miss Clara said and she reached over and grabbed my hand and squeezed it. "I'd like to know how everyone has been at your place. I don't mean no disrespect to your granpappy, but I reckon he is in heaven and won't mind a lick if we just visit. How is Rayford? I surely would like to come and see what that man has been carving lately. He has a gift, that's for certain. And what about them paints Melanie gave you? I could send more paper along. Got me a cousin up in Massachusetts, you know. Her ma, Auntie Ruth, and my ma was together for a summer once when they was just girls, and they came to be good friends. Then, when I was seven years old, Auntie Ruth invited Ma and me up to visit, seeing as how I was the youngest and still at home. And my cousin Sadie Ruth and me, we came to be good friends, too. She sent me them paints and books and paper. Got em all the way from England. When this war is over, I got a big order to send to her."

I reckon she saw how I needed them kindly words and how

I couldn't say much back without I'd start in crying again so she done all the talking. I didn't want to tell her what Ma did to them paints, and it was near most like she knew that, too. She made me feel like I was an important person and not just some sassy child who was always trying to get out of work. I reckon if she was my ma, I'd do whatever she said and not try to get out of work ever. Even the sad part of me felt better, like the sadness was as good a part as the happiness, and it wasn't naught to be ashamed of. The onliest thing that made me feel bad was that I kept wishing she was my ma. She knows all kind of things, some-what like Pa, but different. She talked on visiting up north and all them nice fancy buildings, and them pretty dresses women wear and how they got stores with every kind of toy and pretty in them. Then Melanie came in and said Mr. Foster was near most ready.

"Take some of that writing paper that Miss Sadie Ruth Calloway sent, and maybe you can get Rayford to paint some-thing for me. Something with bright colors, all cheerful." And I thought how if Melanie told Ma what Miss Clara said, maybe she'd go find them paints. "Now, Melanie, if you would be so kind as to help me up, I reckon you can set me back in my chair by the fire."

I saw how Melanie helped her up by her arm, so I took the other one and she wasn't heavy, but I knew she wasn't strong neither, so it seemed like we were near most carrying her in to the parlor. She sat down a might hard on the chair, of which I felt bad for it, seeing as how I reckon I let her go too soon, but she just thanked us. Then we pulled a blanket around her shoulders, so thin and bent over, and she hugged us like as if we were her favorite daughters. "You tell your ma you're all welcome here, anytime," she said. "It would be an honor to have you with us til your Pa comes home, and Melanie would be tickled to see you every day. If I weren't stuck in this tired old body, I'd send Melanie home for good, but I can't do without her. I hope you and your Ma see fit to let her stay here." I choked back tears and Melanie took my hand and I blubbered how much I appreciated that good meal and her kindness, and then we walked out to the yard.

Mr. Foster helped me up on the buckboard wagon, then Melanie, then he climbed up and settled and clucked his tongue and Major Tom took off. Being outside got my brain going and I set to thinking on how Major Tom was born the same year as Hugh, but he surely was a good gentle horse. I even rode him a time or two after Melanie got hitched and I visited her regular before all this war got started. Joram near most took him, but he reckoned the Confederate Army would think he was too old, of which I am glad. Horses are smarter than mules. I wished we had us a horse instead of Beauregard, of which we don't even have him no more. Then I thought on how the Fosters are the richest folks I know seeing as how they have a horse and a big house. Melanie told me that if you are truly rich you have a plantation to live on, but for these parts, Fosters is rich.

Melanie took my hand and we rode quiet for a ways, then Mr. Foster looked over at me. "I've been studying on how to do right by your granpappy," he said. "We'd best lay him in the ground now and have a proper burying ceremony when the war's over. Or leastways when the Yankees move on. They're in camps all over up by the Etowah River and east of here down to Marietta.

It ain't smart to go stirring up trouble by asking folks to come to a burying. I hear tell the Yankees won't let no one travel without a pass, and that all takes time. I hope that sets with your ma. I just don't see no other way without getting us all killed." We rode on in quiet again, looking out into Fosters' fields as we passed and into the woods when we got up to McCreedy's Hill. I'm generally one for talking, but I reckon the sadness soaked up all the words.

When we came down the road to our place, I got to thinking how different it was from the Foster's. There wasn't no Whiskers running out and Ma didn't come out on the porch with an apron on and corn meal on her hands, and seeing as how it was rainy, there wasn't even no Rayford in his garden. It looks lonesome when he ain't there. Mr. Foster tied the horse reins to the fence rail, handed the crock of custard to Melanie, grabbed the sack of provisions she'd packed, and came in after us. The house was quiet but for the sound of the fire crackling in the kitchen hearth. When we walked through the parlor Rayford looked up and smiled. Mr. Foster set the sack inside the door and went over and looked at the dog he was carving for me. Ma came in and took one look at Melanie and burst into tears. She couldn't even say "Hey" to Mr. Foster. Melanie steered her into the kitchen.

"You want to see Granpappy?" I whispered to Mr. Foster. He nodded and we went on in. When we got by the bed, he put his hand on my shoulder, and that bit of kindness nearly set the tears to running again. We looked at Granpappy a few minutes, then Mr. Foster put his hand on Granpappy's, like as if to say good-bye, then he backed away.

"He needs to be laid out, soon." He turned his hat in his hand three, four times, like he should've done something right there. Ma was still crying, so we went back to the parlor, and Mr. Foster squatted by Rayford. Rayford sat still, holding his knife on one leg and resting the partly-whittled dog on the other. He still don't look Mr. Foster in the eye, but leastways he don't turn away. Mr. Foster went through the carvings in his bucket and talked on them, telling him how nice they were. He was partial to one of the flowers, a trillium, and went on about it, and Rayford took a quick look at it, then at Mr. Foster.

"He means for you to take it," I said.

"Can I take this to Miss Clara?" he asked. Rayford grinned and looked down at his lap. Then Mr. Foster said he'd best get start digging the grave.

"I can help," I said.

He looked like as if he was studying on it.

"I think you best stay with your Ma and Melanie."

He headed out, and I went to the kitchen. Melanie had pulled a chair up close and was rubbing Ma's back like Miss Clara done to us. I recollected the bag Mr. Foster had brought. I got it and dumped the corn meal into a barrel and set the crock of molasses on the sideboard. Ma never looked up. I took the ham out to the smokehouse, laid it on top of what we had and poured on the last of the salt and packed it like I'd seen Pa do with the venison. On my way to the house I looked across the road to where Mr. Foster was digging back of the barn next to where Granny was buried. It wasn't far from the tree where Mule hooked up all the cats. My mind had been so busy thinking on other things, I hadn't given him and Hugh a thought, and of a sudden I missed them. I went back to the parlor and sat a bit, then went out to the kitchen. Ma looked up and I said Mr. Foster was out digging the grave. Melanie told her what Mr. Foster said about waiting for a proper burying. Ma nodded.

"I made mountain tea, so we got something to offer him when he comes in," Melanie said. I had a notion to take a chair by Ma and sit, but I got the feeling she just wanted to be by Melanie, so I went out to talk to Mr. Foster

He had a place maybe six foot by three foot dug out to about a foot deep. He put me in mind of Pa, long and lanky. He worked steady and didn't notice me til I'd been there three or four minutes. And when he looked up I said, "I got a thing I want to ask you."

He leaned on the shovel and wiped the sweat off his forehead of which it didn't do no good with the rain coming down to wet it again. "Ask away,"

"You reckon Granpappy will be sad if no one comes to the burying?"

"Times are different," he said. "Driscolls are close. They might come by. I aim to stop and talk to them when I leave, but even if I could get around and tell folks, they wouldn't be of a mind to travel."

"I recollect when Granny was alive, and we first moved here, we had visitors regular. I ain't gave it much thought, but folks don't visit so much any more. Even afore the war came."

Mr. Foster looked to be studying on it, and once or twice he opened his mouth like as if he had a thing to say, but it never came to nothing.

"You reckon it's because of Ma?"

"When folks is ailing, like your Ma, with headaches and such as that, other folks tend to stay away. They don't want to be a bother." He grabbed the shovel and went back to digging.

I suspicioned it *was* Ma that kept folks away, but I don't know as it was because they didn't want to be a bother. Even at prayer meeting, Ma kept to herself. She'd make up a plate of food and go off and sit alone. The kindlier women, like Mrs. Holter and Mrs. Morris always sat by her and talked some, but it was never Ma that struck up the first word.

I went in to sit with Rayford. I watched the fire and thought on how Granpappy didn't always say much, but he kept Ma from being too hard on me, and he talked on Pa and Hugh and Mule, like as if to help us recollect how they were. After awhile I pulled my chair close to Rayford and whispered so Ma and Melanie wouldn't hear, "Do you know that Granpappy has passed on?" He showed me his dog, still not much more than a rounded block of wood with four legs and an egg shape where the head would be. He probably thought Granpappy would walk in any minute. Of a sudden, we three seemed so alone. I had to get Ma to move to Fosters.

21

I'm Just a Child

A few minutes later I heard steps on the porch. Mr. Foster came through, nodded and went on to the kitchen, and I followed him. "I got the grave half dug. I'll come tomorrow and finish it. We'll aim to carry him out and do the burying then. With Yankees overrunning the countryside, I don't reckon there'll be much visiting. Maybe Mrs. Driscoll can come and set with you tonight."

Ma shook her head. "Ain't no need, with Melanie here."

"You want I should carry him out of that room? I don't reckon it's good for him to be in there with Rayford tonight."

"We ain't got a place that Rayford won't see him."

"Well, I don't mean no disrespect, but I reckon the woodshed will do."

Ma rubbed above her right ear and got a pained look on her face. She closed her eyes and nodded. "I'll set up a place and we'll take him out. I reckon it's best with Rayford not knowing what this is all about. It's what your granpappy'd likely want."

I went out to help and found two long boards in the barn. We set up a table using Hugh and Mule's chairs on one end and stacked wood on the other. I took Rayford out to his garden, so he wouldn't see Mr. Foster move Granpappy out there. I wondered what he'd think that night when it was me that would put him to bed instead of Granpappy. After I got him settled, I went back in just as Melanie offered Mr. Foster a cup of tea.

"Thank you, but with Miss Clara alone, I'd just as soon get on home. There is one thing, though. Miz Wiley, I need to show you something out by the wagon." She gave him a peculiar look, then followed him. They weren't gone but a minute or two when Ma stomped back in and went to her bedroom without a word. Mr. Foster came behind her with a disgusted look of his own and a shotgun in his hand.

"I reckon I upset your Ma some, but there ain't nothing for it. You girls best come with me. I ain't leaving til someone around here knows certain how to shoot this here shotgun. I don't reckon there'll be need of it, but you ought to know how to use it and not need it than the other way round. The Yankees are spread out along the railroad all over northeast Georgia. Ain't likely you'll ever see one, being so far from the line, but if you do, you best be ready."

"I don't know as I could shoot a person," I said.

"Might come down to where it's you or him. Then what?" Mr. Foster asked.

"I'm scairt," I said, and Melanie took my hand.

"Me too," she said. "But I'd be more scairt if a Yankee came up to me and I didn't know how to use that gun. Come on, Baby." she said, and she pulled me out the door over to the wagon where Mr. Foster had laid out a little sack of black powder and the ramrod.

"I was hoping your Ma would be the one to learn. I know this don't set right with you, but I can't leave til you promise that if ary a Yankee sets foot in this yard, you'll pick up this here gun and aim it at him til he gets it in his head you ain't one to be messing with. And if he don't, then you best know how to pull the trigger." He looked at me. "I reckon the worry of it will cause you more harm than ary a Yankee, but you got to learn. Then it'd be best if you go out in the woods and practice a bit. Daytime, that is. Stay close at night and bar the doors. If ever the time comes that one of them tries to get in the house, you pick up this rifle. If he don't take to running, you shoot."

Mr. Foster showed us how to pour in the powder, pack it down with the ramrod, and set the cap. Then he handed Melanie the gun and she aimed at a knot in a tree east of the barn. When she pulled the trigger, the gun bucked like there was a mule inside it and the shot didn't get nowheres near the tree. "Puts me in mind of Beauregard," she said, rubbing her shoulder. "You try it, Baby."

She was talking all growed up, but when she held out the gun to me, she was shaking, and I shoved it back at her. It was bad enough I had to learn to shave Rayford, but now they wanted me to learn to shoot a gun so as to kill folks? What would they ask me to do next? When I had in mind the gun was to shoot our dinner and Pa wanted to teach me, it looked like a good thing. I even recollected how I had the picture in my head of shooting at Yankees and them running back north, but of a sudden it was a different picture that came to me of a Yankee that looked like my pa and it scairt me good. It didn't seem right seeing as how I am just a child that shouldn't have to know nothing about such things. "You got to do it," Melanie said. "Inside, you can be as scairt as you want, but outside, you got to get ornery. You learn how to use this here gun. Rayford can't, and Ma won't. I know Pa would want to spare you such as this, but the plain truth of it is he ain't here. Are you listening to me?"

"I am listening but I don't like what I am hearing. I am just barely thirteen–"

"And you're bigger than Ma and near as tall as me already."

"Well, I can't help that, none. Outside I reckon I'm bigger but inside I'm just a child."

"Tatum," Mr. Foster said, "you take that gun. If them Yankees come round here and see Rayford, they ain't like to stop and learn if he's slow, they'll take aim and shoot. This ain't just to protect you. You need to learn for Rayford's sake, too." When I got the picture in my head of a Yankee pointing a gun at Rayford, he didn't look like Pa no more, he looked like the devil. I picked up the sack of powder and shook in a bit of it and stopped it in with the ramrod a time or two, like Mr. Foster showed us. "That's the way Tatum, you got the idea of loading it. Now shoot it. Pretend that tree is a Yankee that's heading over to Rayford's garden and poor Rayford is sitting there just whittling. You got that thought in your head? Now what are you gone do? He's getting closer. He's near to the gate and he's looking over at Rayford and he's drawing up his own gun–"

And I didn't hear no more of what he said. I set the cap

and pulled the gun up like I saw Mr. Foster do, all squinty-eyed, and I looked at that there tree and near most saw eyes and an evil face upon it. I pulled the trigger and heard the shot hit the tree just as the gun kicked into my armpit, but I was ready. It knocked me back a bit but it wasn't near as bad as when Melanie done it. Smoke drifted out the end of the gun and I reckoned that Yankee was dead.

I looked over at Mr. Foster. He stared at the tree. "Lordy! You got a good aim on you. You be careful so's you don't shoot nobody you know." I wouldn't have figured it, but having that gun in my hand and knowing what it could do made me not scairt so much, and not sad so much neither. It was the most peculiar feeling, like I had growed up a bit on the inside right then and I didn't even think about it. Leastways I reckoned I made it to where I felt like I was thirteen. And I had in mind to holler, "You best not come round here you dirty, filthy Yankees seeing as how Tatum Louise Wiley is ready for you." Finally there was a thing about growing up that made sense. I reckon Mr. Foster wouldn't have gave me that gun and told me to shoot if I was just a twelve-year-old child.

"You set that gun up by the door inside the kitchen and keep it packed with powder. Some Yankee comes along, he might not be willing to stand there peaceable whilst you fill it. It best be ready for him when he comes."

"Yes sir, Mr. Foster. I ain't so scairt no more. I reckon it's the Yankees that best be scairt now."

"I reckon so," Mr. Foster said. "Your Pa'll be right proud of you. I suspicion it don't seem fair that all this is falling on you, but there ain't nothing for it. Truth to tell, I didn't think your

Ma would take to shooting a gun, but I pushed it so as to get her thinking on moving in with us. She didn't want to hear none of that talk, neither. Melanie, you best try to talk sense into her." He looked over at the house and made a face that gave me to think he didn't have much hope of getting Ma to move. "I'll be back tomorrow." He waved his hat and went over and untied Major Tom and turned the wagon around and left.

At supper I split the rest of the custard into two crocks. Ma ate it without saying a word and it made me sorry I didn't give it all to Rayford. He poked at it a time or two, then leaned over and sniffed it, stuck his fingers in it, then licked them. Generally Ma would go on about that, but she wasn't paying him no attention. Then he picked up his spoon and dug in. I watched Rayford enjoy that custard. It is a thing about him that he always eats, excepting when he's afeared of something. After he ate he looked up at Melanie, then at Ma and me, like he was studying on something. I reckon he had that feeling things weren't right, seeing as how Melanie was here and Granpappy wasn't.

After dinner, Melanie and Ma laid Granpappy out. I set Rayford up in the parlor, gathered his blanket and sheets and made up the bed, then fluffed up Granpappy's mattress and laid all the bedding back on it, so it looked nice. An hour later I took Rayford in to get him ready for the night. He went straight to Granpappy's bed and sniffed at the pillow and the blanket and quilts.

"Granpappy's in heaven," I said. Rayford looked at me like he was trying to understand. Granpappy's pipe was on the stand at the head of the bed, and Rayford picked it up and sniffed it. I put my hand on his shoulder and told him Granpappy's hip didn't hurt no more and he was happy. Rayford put his leather pouch with the knife in it on the stand, and positioned it like he always does, but he kept the pipe in his hand. Then he set it down next to the knife, moving it this way and that til he got it set to his liking. Then he got in bed. I sat on Granpappy's bed and blew out the candle and sang til I heard snoring. It was a lonely sound.

The kitchen was dark. I expected Ma to be sitting up, even if Granpappy was in the woodshed, seeing how it is respectful to sit the night through when folks has passed on. My candle was near most burned down so I lit another off it and went out to look at Granpappy. The pennies on his closed eyelids glinted in the candlelight. Of a sudden I thought of Pa. He's like to hurt twice as much when he learns he couldn't be here to say goodbye to Granpappy.

"Ain't Ma going to sit up?" I asked Melanie. She had brought out a chair from the kitchen and wrapped up in a light blanket. She took her time answering.

"Her head pains her."

I heard the tears in Melanie's voice and put my hand on her shoulder. It felt peculiar. I reckon it was the first time I ever reached out to comfort her. Generally it's the other way around. "I'll bring a chair out and sit with you."

I went back in, pulled the light blanket off my bed, got another kitchen chair and went out. We were quiet for awhile, then I told Melanie how the first thing I thought of was how proud he looked the day he and Pa took that load of round-backed chairs to the hotel. Then we got to recollecting funny things he said, and the toys he made for us when we were younger. Soon it was quiet and I heard Melanie breathing regular. She was in the corner and had rested her head on one of the woodpiles. It was a moonless night, the sky clear and thick with stars and I stepped out and looked up at them. I wondered were they the same ones Pa saw, or were they different where he was. I sent him a message in the stars that Granpappy had passed on. Then I recollected I never told Melanie to ask Ma where she put them paints. Forget a thing like that, I surely hope I ain't already getting like Ma.

22

His Spirit Is Gone

"You two been out here all night?" I heard. I opened my eyes and saw a log, then recollected I had leaned against the woodpile and fallen asleep like Melanie.

"I wanted to do right by Granpappy," I said. It seemed peculiar that he hadn't moved a lick. Melanie opened her eyes.

"You still got pains this morning?" I asked Ma.

"My back is real bad." She looked at Granpappy like it was his fault. "Day is on us. We best get moving." She headed back inside, bent over and slow-walking.

"Ma," I said. She stopped, and rubbed her back. "You reckon it'd be best to move on over to Fosters?"

"I can't think on that, now," she said and went in. I felt a chill and nearly threw my blanket on Granpappy. It was hard to keep in mind he didn't have feelings no more.

I got ready for the day then went to get Rayford, but he was still sleeping. He generally wakes early and waits for Granpappy to get him, but I reckon he had missed out on sleep during that thunderstorm and was making up for it. I shook him and he opened his eyes. He sat and struggled some with his bedding, so I got him untangled. He went for his knife first thing, then he noticed Granpappy's empty bed and pointed.

"He's passed on, Rayford. His spirit is gone." He looked at the pipe on the night stand. "Can you feel it?" I asked him. He moved to Granpappy's bed and I sat beside him and took his hand. It's big and soft, not hard and knuckle-y, like Pa's. He pulled his hand away and picked up Granpappy's pillow and sniffed it, like as if he could figure out something.

Mid-morning I heard a wagon instead of just a horse and I figured Mr. Foster had got hold of a coffin, but when we went out, we saw Miss Clara sitting in the wagon held up by blankets and such. He helped her down easy and Melanie got on her other side and they brung her to the kitchen.

"Nice of you to come, Miss Clara," Ma said and that put me at ease. It was the first thing she'd said since she'd come out to get us and I was afeared she might not be kindly toward Miss Clara. Especially seeing as how she holds it against her that Melanie ain't home with us.

I looked out on Rayford. He was standing in his garden by the fence watching Mr. Foster dig. He likely thought he was working on a garden back there.

Melanie poured tea for us and Miss Clara talked some on what they'd heard about the war, and how there were Yankees taking over houses up north of us and heading toward Atlanta and it wasn't safe to be out. "Will is coming back soon. I feel it,"

Ma said. She barely looked up, just stared at her tea cup. About then Mr. Foster came and asked for a cloth or sheet to wrap Granpappy in, so I got one off his bed.

"You want to bring Rayford in while I take him out to the barn?" he asked.

When I went out to get Rayford, I grabbed his bucket of carvings, too, so he could show Miss Clara. I set him up in the parlor next to her and set his bucket down. It was like he knew what he was supposed to do. As he pulled them out and set them on the table, she carried on like as if they were pieces of gold instead of pieces of wood. He ain't never been shy around her, like as if she's one of our family. He looks at her and makes sounds and she answers him back like as if she knows just what he's saying. Rayford had set up two kittens, one laying on its back and the other sitting with its paw up, like as if they were playing. Miss Clara picked them up and looked at them close. When it was time to put all the carvings back in the basket, Rayford pushed the kittens acrost the table to her.

Later we set up a chair for Miss Clara by the grave site and helped her outside and wrapped her up good seeing as how she gets cold easy, even though it had got warm by then. We left Rayford in the house whittling. I didn't know if that was the right thing to do by Granpappy but Rayford had got to working on something and didn't pay us no mind as we left.

We gathered round and Mr. Foster preached a few words on what a good man Granpappy was, hard-working and honest. "I reckon the Lord needed a good chair-maker and took him," he said.

It was shorter than most preachings but I reckon that'd be all right with Granpappy. He'd likely say the Lord had better things to do then fuss over an old man what's just coming home, and they both wanted to get it over with. After the burying, Miss Clara grimaced as we helped her up. It took some doing to get her on the wagon, but once she was up there, Mr. Foster had his mind set to go. "Well, I'll be back in a day or two to get Me--" he started, but Miss Clara laid her hand on his. Then he tipped his hat and she waved and he turned the buckboard around and left.

Late afternoon when my chores were finished, we got out Rayford's animals to play. It wasn't near as much fun as I thought it would be. I don't know if that's because Granpappy died or because Pa is gone, or just because I am getting older, of which I hope that ain't the truth.

23

I Went Out With A Good Feeling

Melanie stayed the night and after a breakfast of eggs and ham from the Fosters, I settled Rayford in his garden. Then Melanie brought out molasses and spices to make gingerbread. I still felt sad on account of Granpappy, but it helped some knowing he wasn't no longer in pain. With Melanie home to visit he would want us to be happy and I thought Ma would get in it too, seeing as how there'd be a mess of talking and laughing with Melanie home, but Ma said she had to gather plants for tea, of which that is a thing that could've waited. But it was a bright, sunny day, so I put it up to her wanting to be outside.

Truth to tell, I was happy Ma left. Melanie told me about the new book she was reading to Miss Clara about a girl they called Little Nell whose granpappy was a kindly man but gambled away all their money, and she talked on dresses from France that they saw in a catalog, and Driscoll's horse that up and disappeared, and how Doc Waitly's son built a whisky still and talk was the Yankees found it, drank the whisky, then busted it up. The only time one of us wasn't talking was to take a breath, and it came to me as how with folks like Melanie, talking about regular things is near as much fun as going to town.

After we baked the gingerbread, we went on visiting. Time Melanie stoked the fire again to make supper, it came to me I had forgot about Rayford. I went out with a good feeling, thinking on all what Melanie and me had talked about and was near most to the gate before it came to me that it was wide open and Rayford's chair was empty.

24

What'll We Do?

I closed my eyes and saw Rayford beaten and hog-tied and thrown on a wagon heading north with a pack of evil Yankees. Pa came down the road, looking over at the empty twig chair in the garden, asking, "Where is Rayford?" and I ran to him crying, "He's gone, Pa. Stole by Yankees." Pa's knees buckled, and I tried to hold him up, but he was too heavy and we fell to the ground--

"We'll find him," Melanie said, coming up beside me. "He can't be far."

We searched the yard, the barn, the woodshed, the outhouse, even the chicken coop. I didn't see as how he could have got in the house without we'd have known about it, but we looked anyways: in the parlor, under his bed, and through the sheets and coverlets piled on top of it. As we walked back in the kitchen, Ma came in holding her apron.

"Rayford got away!" I said.

She shook her apron over the dry sink, spreading out a pile of leaves she'd picked to dry for tea.

"We got to find him."

"There's work to do," she said, her head down.

"We'll look, Ma. C'mon, Baby," Melanie said. She took my arm and pulled me out the door. My feet flopped after her, like there weren't no bones in them at all, but truth to tell, my mouth still worked right good.

"Ma is the most hateful, orneriest woman ever. She is even more hateful than some of them evil old hags in fairy tales."

"Which way you think he would've gone?" Melanie asked, like as if she wasn't paying my words no mind at all. When it came to me I might of forgot to latch the gate, the idea pained me so, it near most took my breath away.

"Baby! Are you listening? You think he would've run down by the creek?" Melanie shook my arm and I got the picture in my head of Ma messing with them leaves.

"Ma should help," I said.

"Listen!" She turned to me, grabbed my shoulders and looked me square in the eye. "Ma wouldn't be no help. If she found him, he'd likely run from her. Now, which way you reckon he went?" I pulled loose and looked around. He never went anywhere without one of us. The latch opened easy, but it was on the outside of the fence, where he can't see it. He only knows to push or pull on it and if the gate won't open, he lets it be. Might be one of them Yankees snuck around and opened the gate and dragged him out. And it was my fault for not keeping an eye on him.

"I reckon he'd take the path from the garden to the woods

and the creek. But he might have headed out to McCreedy's Road, too."

"You know the woods better," Melanie said. "When you get to the creek, come back. I'll walk along McCreedy's Road for a quarter mile or so. He's likely setting somewheres, sleeping."

"Melanie, what if someone came along and took him away. What if he's hurt--"

"We ain't got time for such talk. We got to find him afore dark. Now get!"

She headed out to the road and I took the path to the creek. It started out wide, then narrowed with overgrowed brush. With the rough ground it was hard to spot footprints. The rustle of leaves pulled me into the woods time and again, but it was only squirrels. When I got to the creek I walked it west, then east aways, still calling his name, but there wasn't no answer, just the cry of birds. I turned toward home and when I heard Melanie holler for me, I ran back.

"I seen tracks, Baby. Tracks with a foot dragging, like Rayford does when he gets tired. They went off the road and I lost 'em. We'll look together." I took off, but Melanie grabbed my arm. "We should tell Ma. I don't want her to worry. And, Baby...you best let me do the talking."

Ma was still at the dry sink, scrubbing carrots, now, like everything was fine and she was set to cook us a nice supper. Melanie said to her in a kindly voice, "I seen Rayford's tracks out by the road near McCreedy's Hill. We're heading out to look for him."

"No," she said, without turning. "Ain't safe out there no more."

"Ma, we got to find him. He'll be scairt," Melanie said.

"You look in the morning. Mr. Foster said stay close at night."

"It's not night, yet," Melanie said.

"And we'll be together," I said.

"Don't you sass," she said, and the way them words came out of her mouth put me in mind of a hissing snake.

"Ma, she's just worried about Rayford," Melanie said.

"You set and eat."

"But, Ma--" I said, and she came at me with her arm up like she was going to swat me.

"Hush! I won't hear no more about it."

Melanie glared at me and whispered, "We'll look later," and pointed to my chair. I could hardly make myself sit, but I reckoned she had a plan.

The night passed quiet. Melanie hemmed some quilt pieces and Ma patched one of her dresses. I pulled out my honeysuckle basket, but I couldn't keep my mind on it. Ma put out the candles early and we went to bed, Melanie coming in to sleep with me, like before she married Joram.

"What'll we do?" I whispered.

"Keep quiet til Ma's asleep," she said. I got in bed but I squirmed like a worm pulled out of the ground and the longer I laid there, the more awake I got. Pa figured it wrong. He should've made Ma promise to take care of Rayford, seeing as how I would've done it anyways, but the only way Ma would've done it was because he asked her to. I must've laid there thinking for an hour or two, then Melanie rolled over and touched my shoulder.

"The moon is out and there ain't no clouds. We won't need no extry light. You go and wait by the outhouse. I'll make sure your leaving don't wake Ma, then I'll come out."

I threw a shawl over my shoulders and put on the new shoes Granpappy'd made for me. Every time I put them on I thought about him, and all he did for us. If he was still here and Pa hadn't gone, Rayford would likely be in his bed right now.

The moon shone like a big old lantern, and I could see Belle sleeping by the water trough. I stood by the outhouse to wait. A few minutes later Melanie still hadn't come out, then light flickered in the kitchen window. Ma must've woke up when she heard me leave. I snuck up to the house and squatted under the window and heard them talking. Melanie was saying she'd just come back from the outhouse, so Ma must've said she heard the door. I ain't never heard Melanie tell a lie before. I reckon it says how much she loves Rayford, too, to say such as that. Ma talked some on how she missed Melanie and wished she lived here again. Once she got Melanie's ear, it was likely she'd go on, and Melanie wouldn't be able to get away. I didn't see as there was naught I could do but set to looking for Rayford myself.

I pulled my shawl tighter around my shoulders and headed to McCreedy's Hill. It was hard to make out footprints on the ground, but there were times I thought I saw the mark of a foot dragging. I peered into the woods along both sides of the road as I made my way up the hill. When I got to the top, where Ma couldn't hear me, I called Rayford's name. It was near most quiet but for the sound of a light wind rustling oak leaves and the call of a whippoorwill. I listened for night critters and tried not to think on bears, but there they were: bear thoughts. It don't seem right that it's my brain, but there's times I got no say in what ideas it works at. Pa says when you see bears they are afeared of you so they head on their own way, and that's what I wanted my brain to think on, but no, it had got stuck on a story Hugh told me about a pack of bears that came upon two little girls and growled something fierce and attacked them and tore away at their skin and ate them alive. I got to thinking on them poor little girls, and my stomach took to rolling. Leastways I wasn't little. I was near as tall as Pa. I thought as how when I called Rayford I should make my voice sound like a growed up man and not a girl, but then maybe he wouldn't know it was me. I asked the Lord to keep them bears away, but every time I said bears in my head, the picture of them poor girls came to mind again, so I wasn't no better off.

The woods were thick all around, so if Rayford went in he wouldn't go far, but he could've gone in anywheres. Every so often an owl called and when I heard him say, "whooo, whooo," I wished I could have told him "Rayford, Rayford." I heard a skittering behind me and jumped and yelped and turned. When I didn't see nothing, I reckoned it could be only one thing. Haints! Pa says there ain't no such thing as haints and when he is standing next to me in the daytime, I believe him, but it's a might different thing when I'm by myself at night. Then my brain got riled and brought up pictures of evil witches that are hungry for tender little girls, and it got to where I couldn't hardly breathe, like as if I just ran two miles. I found a broken off branch and held it up where haints and ghosts and such could see it, so they'd know I'd put up a fight if they tried to get me.

I thought on how if I didn't find Rayford by morning, I'd ask Mr. Foster to bring his wagon and we'd drive along ringing the dinner bell. Rayford'd know that sound and he'd come to it. I no more got to feeling good about that idea when I heard something peculiar. It came from over the hill, but it sounded like it came from the north, not Foster's way, and a minute later I made out it was voices. *Men's* voices. I stepped back into the woods and kept quiet, excepting my heart got to beating loud as thunder. I reckoned there weren't no southern men left between the ages of fifteen and fifty all the way from our house to Harpersville. Then I recollected what Mr. Foster told us about them Yankees and how to aim that gun at them, and it wasn't no comfort knowing it was back in the kitchen, propped up by the door.

My teeth got to chattering so hard I had to put my hand in my mouth to keep them from knocking together. It came to me that with all that talk about Yankees, I didn't never hear a thing about what they looked like excepting they had blue coats. It wouldn't have surprised me none to hear they were ten feet tall, like in that Jack and the Beanstalk story. I wished Pa would've said more about them in his letters, so I'd know what I was up against. Of a sudden it seemed like there were two of me and we argued back and forth should we stay put or hightail it for home. I recollected how fast I ran when Pa and I raced, but if giant men came after me with long legs, maybe I wouldn't make it. And what if they had horses! I listened again, and didn't hear nary a whinny, but they were getting close real fast and the part of me that was for staying put won, seeing as how I was afeared they'd hear my feet hitting the ground if I took off, so I crouched down in the brush and listened.

I made out three voices, certain. One stuttered, somewhat like Arlo, Missy's next older brother. One was deep and sounded older. There was another voice, or maybe two more. Every time the one that stuttered opened his mouth, the others told him to hush.

The voices got louder and I pushed back into the woods so no one could see me. A branch snapped and I let out a little whoop. It was the smallest sound, hardly more than a peep, but I reckon I wasn't more than twenty yards below them on our side of the hill, maybe five feet into the woods. When I swallowed, I swear my spit passed my heart at the back of my throat. I peeked through the trees and in the moonlight at the top of the hill I saw the outline of two men, and whilst they stood there looking around, a third man come up beside them.

"Nothing!" one of them hollered into the night and I jerked and fell on my side on the ground, of which it sounded loud as a clap of thunder to my ears and it was all I could do to keep from retching. "Swear to God I heard something," he said. I inched forward, just enough so I could make him out standing there with his hands on his hips and shaking his head like he was a might disgusted.

"There ain't a house in sight," a different voice said. "That's the last time I listen to you. Come all this way for nothing."

"You s-s-s-s-said you heard it, t-t-t-t-to, H-H-H-Henry."

"Thought I did. Probably a wild animal. I bet there's cougars and bears in these woods."

"But this road must go somewhere," the first voice said. "Let's head down it aways."

"I told you this is an old road and a waste of time. We've been walking for two hours. We don't get back soon, we won't get any sleep."

"C'mon, let's go back. Stupid to do this at night anyway."

"B-b-b-but s-s-s-tuff we g-g-g-get in the d-d-d-daytime we g-g-g-got to sh-sh-sh-share."

"Shut your trap! Takes half as long to get twice as much, so even if we share, we still come out even, and we get our sleep in the bargain."

"Bunch a quitters."

"Go ahead, you and Stutter Boy go on by yourself."

"Aw forget it. Let's go back."

They kept at each other as their voices faded. I waited until I reckoned my shoulder might come right off, then I pushed myself up and tried to stand, but I was so weak—part from fear and part from being all crouched together—that I had to stay on all fours until my legs quit wiggling. I crawled to the edge of the woods and looked out. An owl hooted steady and another answered. I stood and tippy-toed to the top of the hill. Every time I set my foot down, I listened to make sure them voices didn't come back. When I got far enough to see down the other side I stayed close to the edge of the woods so if they looked back, they wouldn't see an outline of me like I had seen of them. Leastways there was no Rayford with them. Unless they already took him away.

About then, something big-sounding thrashed around in the woods on the south side of the road, and my heart set to banging. There wasn't no time for the two parts of me to think on it, seeing as how the one that was for going took off for home. I must've been tearing down that hill leastways as fast as Beauregard the day I let him loose. Of a sudden my foot hit something, I went flying and hit the ground hard enough to knock the wind out of me. I laid there for a minute, working to get my breath and when it finally came, I felt pains where the road had scraped my knees and hands and chin. I pulled myself up on all fours and recollected the noise. I turned slow, afeared I'd see the outline of something evil. There wasn't nary a thing behind me but the moon. I stayed on the ground til my breath came slower. I rubbed my chin and moved my shoulders, and then I saw a break in the woods on the south side of the road about twenty feet away.

I had lost my big branch when I heard the voices and skittered into the woods, but I looked around and found another one, and held it up as I limped to the break. I stepped in a few feet and there was Rayford, lying on the ground. I whispered his name and pushed him and he got to caterwauling without opening his eyes. I was still jumpy so it took a minute or two to recollect that singing would calm him, and let him know it was me. I kept my voice soft at first but Rayford couldn't hear me over his howling, and I had to sing louder and louder. Even though I'd seen those men head out of sight, I pictured them turning and running back and grabbing us, but I had to shut Rayford up, so I kept at it, singing about the horse that came home, of which that's likely Rayford's favorite. He finally opened his eyes and moaned like he was glad to see me. I took his hand to pull him up, and it was sticky.

"What'd you get into?" I touched his face. It was sticky, too. I sniffed. Peppermint? I put my finger to my tongue, to be sure. Mint grows all over, but not peppermint. And mint ain't sticky, nor sweet. It was downright peculiar.

I helped him up and we headed back along the edge of the

woods. I had to pull him until we came to the bend and he saw the house in the moonlight. He walked steady, then, but set to jabbering and moaning and I feared Ma would hear him. It was like heading straight for a bee's nest, but there was nothing for it. Then Melanie came around the back of the house and ran up to us shushing all the way.

"I can't keep him quiet."

"Get in the house and get in bed quick. If Ma wakes up, I'll say I heard a noise and found him out here–she'd be more like to believe it of me. Where'd you find him?"

"Up McCreedy's Hill. Saw three Yankee soldiers too." In the soft light, I saw Melanie's eyes grow big.

"Coming this way?"

"They came up the hill from the other side and when they got to the top and saw nothing but the dark road and the woods, they went back. I reckon that curve in the road is what saved us. My heart was hammering so it like to have banged right out of me. When I thought they were gone I went to the top of the hill and looked down and saw them walking on toward Harpersville. Then I heard another noise and near most wet my drawers." I told her how I ran and fell and saw the break in the woods and found Rayford. "There is one thing peculiar. Smell his hand." I put it up to her nose.

"Oh, Baby," she whispered, putting her arm around my shoulders.

"What?"

"I suspicion...I suspicion Ma let him out."

I couldn't believe she'd say such a thing. Even Ma ain't that hateful, I thought and I shook my head.

"You recollect how she greased that gate?"

I let out a squeak and my hand went to my mouth. "You think that's why she done it? But he wouldn't go with her." I didn't want to believe Ma would be so cruel.

"He would if she held out a peppermint stick for him. Now, Baby, we have to make like he got back on his own…then maybe she won't take the trouble to try and lead him out again. You get in the house and I'll get him to bed."

I ran to the house, but then an idea came to me, and I turned back to her. "If I tell Ma about the Yankees, she might be willing to go to Fosters."

"I don't know. Ma has taken on a stubbornness I don't recollect. The worst of it is, she'll know you were out looking for him and he didn't come back alone. Could be next time she'll just lead him farther away. We best stick to our plan. In the morning I'll say a noise woke me and I came out and found him." She put her hand on my shoulder and sighed. "Truth to tell, I reckon it ain't the Yankees you got to worry on, but Ma. Is that blood on your chin?"

"Likely so," I said, touching a sore spot. "I tripped on the road."

"We best say you tripped on the way to the outhouse."

"But, what if them Yankees come back?"

"It ain't like to happen."

"But they already came once."

"And now they think there ain't nothing back here. I didn't want to tell you this on account of it might scare you worse to think on it than not, but I reckon it'll put your mind at ease. Pa Foster has been brushing away his tracks and scattering rocks at the crossroads where McCreedy's meets the Harpersville Road, so it looks like an old road that ain't used no more. He said it'd fool Yankees and Rebels alike, and we best hope our own kin ain't fooled out of coming home. Now get in the house quick."

I ran in, wishing I could change everything, or that there was something good somewheres so I could think on it and say, "Well, leastways we got that." Before I got in bed I took a last look outside at the stars. I pretended to fly up and see had Pa left a message for me. Seemed like there was one thanking me for finding Rayford. Then there was another one telling me it was time to grow up.

I can't say as I'm ready, but if Ma is set on getting rid of Rayford, it looks like there ain't nothing for it. Leastways I'll give it some thought.

25

I'll Get The Gun

It's the middle of August. We ain't heard from Pa for weeks, but Mr. Foster said there's been steady fighting east of here and the Yankees are set on taking Atlanta. I reckon Pa has finally got busy with the fighting and ain't had time to write.

The heat is fierce this afternoon so we are sitting on the porch stringing up shucky beans to dry for winter eating. We brought Rayford's twig chair over and he's whittling on a doll of which I suspicion it will be Mr. Foster seeing as how he sat with Rayford some when he brought Melanie two days ago. Jeanette and her boys got a pass to visit with the Fosters a spell, so Melanie is like to stay here another three or four days. With the heat, we just ain't none of us felt like working hard today. Ma had me bring up fresh water from the well and mix in vinegar and molasses, for keeping us cool while we work, of which that made it near most like a party. Excepting that all of our menfolk but Rayford are gone. Mr. Foster said the Confederate Army is more retreating than fighting, and he don't see as how the war will last much longer. I told him I couldn't wait to see Pa come down that road. "And Hugh and Mule, too," I said, and truth to tell, I meant it. But Mr. Foster said we best keep an eye on who it is if a body comes down that road seeing as how there's Yankees and rebel deserters and such, thieving and looking for food, and even though we are way back on this old road, we best be wary.

That's the thought my brain had settled on when we heard wheels creaking down McCreedy's Hill. I knew Mr. Foster wouldn't be back for Melanie for at least a day or two, so my brain brought up a picture of a wagon full of Yankee soldiers. I reckon Melanie got the same idea seeing as how we both jumped up and she hollered, "I'll get the gun," and Ma's head jerked. "Get inside," I yelled. "Yankees!" She looked out at the road then, and I reckon she heard them wheels too. She jumped up and her lap full of beans fell to the porch. Melanie came out and pulled the gun up to her shoulder, shaking and crying, and then the wagon turned the corner and I saw who it was. "No!" I hollered, but it was too late. The gun went off before she could brace herself and it knocked her back against the house. Ma screamed and Rayford put his hands over his head and set to wailing and took off and ran smack into the door. Major Tom reared and the wagon jerked and Mr. Foster pulled the reins tight and hollered, "Whoa!"

Melanie dropped the gun and shrieked, "Pa Foster! You all right?"

He cooed to Major Tom, got off the wagon slow, and looked at Melanie. "A howdy would've been better," he said. I didn't know was he funning or not. Major Tom still tossed his head and skittered. Mr. Foster patted his neck and talked to him soft for a minute and when that poor old horse had settled, Mr. Foster walked him over to Rayford's garden and tied the reins to the fence rails. "Puts my mind at ease to see you ain't afeared of that gun, but you got to look first to see who you're shooting at. You best work on your aim, some, too. That shot didn't come within twenty feet of me. Them Yankees ain't like to stand still til you hit 'em."

"But I reckon I would've scairt em," Melanie said as he came over.

"Yes, Ma'am, that you would've," he said, nodding. "You surely scairt me." He wiped the sweat from his forehead, then broke into a grin, and by that time I had got Rayford turned around so he could see it was Mr. Foster and not no storm. Then something came over me and I got to laughing, of which I reckon it was relief that it wasn't no Yankees. I surely didn't mean no harm, but Melanie glared at me and got all red-faced. She is such a good person, it don't seem right to make her feel bad, so I made myself think on what would've happened if it had been Yankees. At first it made me feel scairt again, but then I got the picture in my head of how the shot nearly hit the barn and how Melanie got thrown back against the house. If it had been Yankees, I reckon they would've fell on the ground and busted out laughing, too.

"Did Miss Clara take bad sick again?" Melanie asked, all serious like as if leastways there was one person around here who still had a lick of sense.

"No. Ryker got shot north of Atlanta, and Jeanette is bound

to go home to him." Melanie grabbed the porch railing to steady herself. "No need for alarm. It ain't bad, but he needs nursing. I told her he could come stay with us, too, but she says there's doctors tending wounded up in Rome, so they can get him there, need be."

"Where'd the shot get him?" Melanie asked.

"In the shoulder. The left. It's tore up some, what we hear, but the doc who worked on him said he won't lose his arm. And Miss Clara said to bring your Ma and Rayford and Tatum. She said that's an order."

"Tell Miss Clara we're much obliged," Ma said. She still looked white and shaky, but she sat and picked up the beans like as if it wasn't a thing worth talking on. "We'll be fine here."

Mr. Foster looked at the ground, then at the house. "Well, I know it ain't easy to leave your home." Howsomever, I don't suspicion that's what he was thinking.

"Ma, it don't make sense to take a chance when you could be safe with us," Melanie said.

"I have faith the Lord will watch over us and bring Will home. I ain't leaving."

Mr. Foster had a look on his face like he had failed.

"You best keep this loaded and handy," Melanie said, handing the gun to me. "I'll get my satchel." When she passed me she put her hand on my arm and whispered, "You be careful."

"Oh, I near most forgot," Mr. Foster said. "You got word from Hugh." He went to the wagon and I sat Rayford back down on the porch and got him to whittling again. Mr. Foster came back and handed Ma a sack. "Plums. Our tree's got more than we can use." He gave me the letter as Melanie came out. "It's from Hugh," I said, waving it. I pulled it apart and read:

"Dearest Ma and Tatum,"

They put us to hauling cloth and lumber from the Roswell Mill til the Yankees took it back in early July. Now they got us pulling supply wagons all over, steady. First off I wished Mule would've stayed home, but I got used to him being here and we look out for each other. War and fighting ain't near as much fun as we thought. I reckon he'd ruther go fishing and every morning when I wake up and look around me, I wish I was back there working in the barn. There's too many folks and too much noise. I reckon them folks that live in Atlanta and such are accustomed to commotion everyday, but it is too much for me. We are doing the best we can, so we can get home when it's over.

We were sorry to hear about Granpappy. We been looking for Pa. We talked to some men from the 63d Georgia, but they got scattered at Kennesaw Mountain and ain't seen half their regiment. We hope you are keeping well, and we aim to be home soon. Our friend, Jake, writes this for us. He says he's good with writing. We hope it's so.

Your loving sons and brothers, Hugh and Mule

I was thinking on what he meant when he said Pa's regiment got scattered, then Melanie gave Ma a hug around the shoulders and hugged Rayford and me. "You all take care," she said, her words so soft I could barely hear them. It struck me that she didn't say a word about the letter. I reckon as wet as her eyes looked, she couldn't say much or she would've set to bawling, and likely that would make Mr. Foster feel bad. They got on the wagon, Mr. Foster turned the horse around, they waved, and drove off. I suspicion Rayford is bound to have it in his head that a hugging is bad, seeing as how near most every time there is one, someone leaves.

Ma went back to stringing beans with nary a word. I reckoned she was thinking on how I was growed up, some, seeing as how I could shoot the gun, but after a few minutes I glanced her way. She worked those beans like they were set to give her trouble, stabbing them with the needle and pushing them hard onto the string. I didn't know what to make of it, then she made a growly sound.

"Ain't right that Melanie goes off like that. Here I am, her own ma and she is off taking care of some other lady. It ain't right."

"But, Ma, Miss Clara can't even get to the outhouse herself. And if Melanie ain't there, Mr. Foster can't leave, and if he can't leave, we won't get no more mail nor supplies."

Ma stood and brushed the beans off her lap, lickety split, then stomped off into the house. It made me feel like as if she just brushed aside those words I said. I reckon if she could snap her fingers and turn me into Melanie she would. And truth to tell, if Melanie had been here, she likely would've picked up them shucky beans and strung em for Ma, then went in and set with her and been kindly. I wasn't going to do no such thing.

Rayford stared at them beans scattered on the floorboard of the porch like they were evil snakes that would come to life.

"They ain't hurting you a lick," I said and I kept at stringing my own pile. I felt him looking at me scowly and I gave him a mean look right back, of which it ain't like me, but I was getting dadblamed tired of Ma acting like I wasn't worth no more than an old stick. "Pick em up yourself if it don't set right with you," I said.

I strung another handful of beans and Rayford set to rocking and moaned.

"Oh, all right!" I bent over and gathered the beans and pulled them to my lap. Rayford watched me, and when all the beans were picked up, he looked back at the doll in his hand. Then he cut in a little ridge, like as if everything was just fine.

26

Run To The Woods

The last time Mr. Foster came by he said a Yankee general named Sherman took over Atlanta and made folks leave, and he and his soldiers had torn up railroad tracks so supplies couldn't get through. They were stealing and burning what they couldn't take with them, and it was like to keep right on, since the Confederate Army couldn't get him stopped. He said our boys are giving up, and the one good thing about it was that it might could be over soon.

That all came to mind this morning when I was carrying water to Belle and it set me to thinking about how we'd live if what Mr. Foster said was true. I got to hoping we wouldn't have to move north when Pa came back. It's a lot colder there. I recollect wondering how they keep the water for their cows and mules and such from freezing when I heard a noise that wasn't chickens nor Belle. It sounded somewhat like a hoot owl and even though it ain't like them to call in daylight, I looked to the treetops in the woods on McCreedy's Hill. But it was something moving along the road that caught my eye, and of a sudden there were blue coats everywhere, tearing down the hill and shrieking like a flock of crows.

I ran to the house hollering "Yankees!" When I got inside I didn't know whether to bolt the door or grab the gun and head out to the porch. Afore my brain could decide, Ma came out of her bedroom, hollered "Run to the woods!" and pulled me to the back door. I heard Rayford moan, then Ma's face came up to mine, her eyes big and scairt and she yelled, "Git!" I ran out aiming for the path to the creek, then thought better of it and headed into the thick of the woods to the west. As I pushed branches aside, I heard a Yankee yell, "Ain't you got no more food?" then the sound of dishes crashing and tin cups hitting the floor. I took two more steps and heard Ma scream. Then Rayford let out a long scairt howl, like when there's thunder outside. My heart hammered and every thud said, "Run!" but when Rayford cried out again, I turned and through the brush I saw the pitchfork leaning up against the woodshed.

Of a sudden I was back in the kitchen standing over Rayford. He lay curled up on the floor. Blood dripped from his mouth and a smell came from him that told me right quick how scairt he was. One Yankee, skinny and dirty-looking, pointed at him and laughed while two others filled an empty cornmeal sack with the sweet potatoes I had dug yesterday. I gripped the handle of the pitchfork, and when the skinny one took a step towards us, I threw it at him. He jumped back and the pitchfork bounced off the sideboard. When it fell to the floor, the handle hit Rayford in the leg, and he screeched. "Leave him be," I hollered, and I knelt beside him and patted his back to calm him. "He ain't right in the head."

The skinny one grinned and pointed at me, making fun, and I don't know how I done it seeing as how my mouth was dry as a bone with fear, but from somewheres I came up with a gob, stood, took a step closer, and spit at him. He pulled back and laughed. "Looks like we got ourselves a Georgia wildcat."

His hat was pushed back on his head, and greasy hair hung beneath it. He had a small head, too small for his body, and the way his shoulders sloped put me in mind of a weasel. "Hey Joe, I never been with a wildcat," he said. As he turned to look at one of the others, I grabbed the pitchfork again and stabbed at him, but he jumped aside and stood there like a grinning fool.

"You come near me or Rayford, I'll stick you, I will," I said. I looked him in the eye. He wasn't much more than a boy—younger than Hugh, I reckoned—with only a bit of hair on his face like it was just learning how to grow. I didn't see as how he'd had time to get so mean.

"Help me here, fellas," he said, still grinning like all his meanness was just funning. "Gonna bag me a wildcat," he said rubbing his hands together. The other two looked into the sideboard drawers and on the shelves, and one of them said, "L-l-l-l-eave her al-l-l-lone, she's j-j-j-j-just a k- k-k-k-kid." I glanced at him quick, recollecting the night Rayford got away.

"I say she's ripe for picking, and I ain't been fighting this lousy war for nothing," the skinny one growled back. He took little steps, sideways, like he was set to pounce.

"You desperate idiot. Look at her. That snarly head's probably full of lice," a different one said, and after every few words he smashed a dish to the floor. "Sherman said take what we need, not girls." I hated him for breaking them dishes, but I couldn't make him stop seeing as how I wasn't about to take my eye off that Yankee in front of me.

"Who says I don't need this feisty little wildcat," he said, taking a step closer. "Sherman probably ain't had any for so long, he forgot what it's all about. Come here, kitty," he said in a high voice.

I tightened my grip on the pitchfork again and aimed at his heart, when the house filled with the hollering of more men. I reckon if I'd have given it a thought, I might've laid down right there on the floor and gave up, but I wasn't thinking on the whole Yankee army, just that one and I was bound to die before I'd let him touch me or Rayford. He took another step and it came to me I'd best get him in the eyes so he couldn't see. I raised the pitchfork and braced myself to thrust it when there came a voice that sounded different from the others.

"Ramsay, you pig, get out of here. Wyatt, Malone, take the food and get out." The soldiers stepped back and even the skinny one gave him a look that told me he was the head of every one else. "That's an order," he shouted, and when I looked at the head one, the skinny one grabbed my arm and yanked, and I dropped the pitchfork. I tried to shake loose, then the head one shoved him and hollered, "I said get out, Ramsay." The skinny one let go of my arm and stumbled, but caught himself. He snarled at the head one, then made a kissing sound at me and scrabbled out of the kitchen. The head one looked down at Rayford and made a face, and I grabbed the pitchfork again. "Why isn't this coward in the Confederate Army?" he asked. He didn't look to be much older than the mean one.

"Are all you Yankees so dadblamed stupid you can't see he ain't right in the head? Now get." I jabbed the air. "You come near me or Rayford and I'll put this pitchfork right through you. I will. I ain't afeared of you." I had in mind to say it strong, but my heart banged so hard, I squeaked. My stomach rolled and I swallowed hard three, four times, then Rayford set to crying. I wanted to throw that pitchfork down and hug him, but I kept my eyes on the head Yankee.

"I won't hurt you," he said. I didn't know was he trying to trick me, so I kept hold on the pitchfork. He put his hand on the door frame and looked down at Rayford with pity in his eyes, then turned. I heard him walk through the parlor and head outside and holler orders. I put the pitchfork down and knelt by Rayford and rubbed his back. I tried to sing, but my teeth chattered and the words came out skittery. I wondered what they'd done to Ma, but I was scairt to leave Rayford.

"Whoever hit him...they didn't know." I looked up. It was the head one again. He walked around me and out the kitchen door to the back. I heard him call out, "Leave the chickens so these folks have eggs." Some of the men grumbled and argued, but he shouted, "NOW!" I stayed by Rayford, patting him and singing, listening as the voices got farther and farther away, until it was quiet again, except for the chickens, still squawking and flapping around the yard.

I wet a cloth and wiped the blood off Rayford's face and told him he didn't have to be scairt no more. Minutes later I heard footsteps, grabbed the pitchfork, and heaved it when I saw blue come through the door.

"Whoa!" the head one hollered, dodging it. He shook his head and looked at me hard. "I told you, I won't hurt you."

"I was afeared you were that mean one."

"I'll keep an eye on him. He won't be back." He looked around the room, and I saw that pity in his eyes again. "I brought some soap. To clean him up with," he said, nodding at Rayford. "And here's a tin of molasses and a small sack of flour." He set all of it on the sideboard, then took off his cap. "I'm sorry for what we've done here. We took a wrong turn. Wyatt said there was a settlement down this road." He picked up the pitchfork, propped it against the wall, put his cap back on, and left.

27

I Didn't Want To Go To Fosters' No More

Rayford still cowered in a ball, legs pulled up, arms tight to his chest. I dropped to the floor and rubbed his back. He was so scairt and stiff he felt like a big old rock. I sang to him again and he finally loosened up some. He opened his eyes once and the look in them put me in mind of a little baby getting passed round from stranger to stranger, when all he wanted was to see his ma's face. But leastways that baby would grow up and figure things out. Rayford would always need someone to look after him and protect him and keep things the same for him. Of a sudden, the tears came on like a stampede. I cried quiet, but I shook like a wagon on a deep-rutted road. I reckon a year's worth of tears leaked out before I dried up. My nose was so closed up by then I had to take slow, deep breaths through my mouth. I worried on Ma, but I stayed until Rayford's breath came easy, and I knew he'd fallen asleep. Leastways that was a good thing seeing as how I surely didn't want to take him outside to his garden.

I sat up and looked around. Broken dishes covered the floor. If that soldier that gave me the soap hadn't come in when he did, there wouldn't have been a dish left. Pa's voice came into my head about then, saying things could be worse. "Leastways you're alive," he said. I got to my feet and pulled a length of wood from behind the sideboard and set it across the back door, and hurried through the parlor to the front door. Ma says barring the doors means we don't have no faith in the Lord to protect us. But I was afeared that mean, skinny soldier might come back, and I didn't think the Lord would mind if we helped Him out. As I dropped the board in place, I saw that Mr. Foster's gun was gone.

I took a deep breath and shuddered, then looked around the parlor. Ashes from the hearth had been scattered so there was black everywhere, and Ma was laid out on the floor in front of the parlor bench. I knelt beside her. "You all right?" I asked. She didn't move, but she was breathing, and I couldn't find no blood nor bruises, so I reckoned she'd fainted. I had in mind she'd rest easier in her bed, then it came to me the Yankees might have gone through the bedrooms, too. I hadn't been in Ma's room since I went in to tell her Granpappy wouldn't wake up. I pushed the door open and saw clothes and stockings and blankets strewn all over. But the carving of Preacher Abernathy was on her dresser and so was her looking glass. When I saw how the straw in the middle of her bed was matted near most flat, it came to me the mess was likely Ma's doing. I took off the bedding and picked up her mattress to fluff it and straw fell out at one end. I looked to see did it need mending and found a small opening where the thread had been pulled out. When I pushed the straw back in, I felt a folded-up piece of paper. I took it out and opened it. There was a heart shape drawn on it and in the middle it said: Will loves Mae. I got a picture in my head of Ma pulling out that paper every night, and it brung on feelings for her like I ain't had since that time I shaved Rayford and she talked kindly to me. It came to me like a revelation that she surely don't like the way things are no more than I do.

I stuffed the paper back in, went to her, laid on the floor and put my arm around her. I felt more tired than I ever did before...not sleepy tired, but like I'd worked for three days straight. Being scairt takes a lot out of a body. The chickens had quieted and pecked round the yard, like as if it was a regular day. They didn't know nothing but that they weren't in no pot. I listened to them awhile, and I must've fallen asleep.

When I opened my eyes again, Ma hadn't moved and my arm was still around her. I got up and looked in on Rayford. I thought I'd best get Ma settled afore I woke him, so I went back to her bedroom and picked up her straw tick so my hand was over the opening and shook it again to fluff it up good. I made up her bed and hung her clothes on the wall pegs. I went back to the parlor and tried to wake her, again, but she wouldn't move. I dragged her into her room, and wrestled her into her bed, then pulled a sheet over her. I stood back and looked at her, wishing it was me that had fainted.

Rayford's mouth had stopped bleeding. There were brown spots on the floorboards where it had dripped. I looked closer and saw it was his lip that had got cut. He could've been punched, but he could've bit it himself, too. I didn't know which looked worse, Rayford or the kitchen, but he smelled so bad, I reckoned I'd best clean him up first. I stoked the fire and put water on to take the chill off it, then picked up the soap the soldier left. It smelled good, like some kind of flower, not like the strong lye and grease soap we made, and better even than what we got from Miss Clara. It didn't seem right to use it for cleaning up Rayford that way, so I put it with Rayford's carvings on the shelf in my bedroom. It came to me that there might come a time when I could give it to Ma to make her feel better.

When the water got hot, I poured it in the wash basin, then pushed at Rayford til he opened his eyes. "Everything's all right, now," I said, putting a smile on my face. I patted his back and wondered if he'd recollect seeing them soldiers as well as he recollects seeing critters and flowers. He sat up and looked around the kitchen. I watched his eyes go from the broken dishes on the floor by the cupboard, to the pots pulled off the wall hooks and thrown on the ground by the hearth. One of them soldiers must've filled a sack with cornmeal, then threw it back on the sideboard when the head one came in. Meal had poured out in a pile and spilled onto the floor. The little baskets of leaves drying for tea on the sideboard had been tossed around the room. Rayford took one that had upturned on the floor next to him and of a sudden he seemed to recollect what had happened. He grabbed my hand and jabbered and pointed around the room at all the things that weren't where they should be and got himself so riled he took to howling.

I recollected the empty coffee tin I'd hidden under my bed.

I brought it in the kitchen and pulled out the folded-up piece of brown paper inside it. I unwrapped the paper and picked out the five little lemon drops all stuck together and smelling some of coffee. I chipped one off and gave it to Rayford. He sniffed it and fingered it and put it in his mouth. I picked up the baskets and pans and set them on the table, thinking that once things were set right, he'd likely forget. I don't reckon he puts his mind to bad things like Pa leaving and Hugh and Mule leaving and Granpappy passing, and them soldiers busting in. His mind runs more to keeping pictures in his head of things to carve, and I reckon he mostly keeps just the ones he likes.

"All right. I'll clean you up," I said. He took the lemon drop out of his mouth and looked at it, then put it back in. I grabbed his hand and pulled and he got to his feet. As I took off his drawers, of which they smelled worse than the outhouse, I thought as how if I'd had to do such as that last year I would've retched just thinking on it, now here I was, doing it for a second time.

I just about had him cleaned up when he spotted a piece of the bowl we kept on the sideboard to hold the eggs after we cleaned them. He picked it up and held it, like he knew what it was, but couldn't figure what had happened. I tried to take it from him, but he held it tight. When I pulled out the folded-up brown paper again, he set the broken piece on the sideboard and held his hand out for another lemon drop. I finished cleaning him up quick and set him in the parlor and told him he could whittle something for me. He pointed around the room at the scattered logs and jabbered nonsense.

"You help me." I set his knife on the hearth and gave him a log and pointed to the wood box. He put it in, then helped me pick up the rest. When I picked up a small log at the edge of the hearth, I noticed it had a shape to it. I blew off some of the ashes and saw it was one of Rayford's carvings, bigger than regular, a man from what I could see. Likely that one of Mr. Foster he'd been working on. I rubbed away more of the black with my apron and saw he'd done a lot of work on the features. I set Rayford in his chair and he dug in his bucket for something to work on. I took the carving to the kitchen, dipped it in a bucket of water and washed it careful, until I could see the face clear, and I reckon if I hadn't already used up so many tears, looking into those eyes would have started me up again. I brushed my finger over the hair that had a turn to it here and there, and the straight nose, and the smiley creases in the cheeks. I kissed the top of the head, and of a sudden, I recollected how before Pa left he said if I kept growing, I'd be kissing the top of his head time he got back.

I went back to the parlor and sat on the bench across from Rayford. It had been getting harder to bring back the picture of Pa's face in my head, but when I looked at that carving it seemed like he was right there in the room with me. Of a sudden, I felt strong and not a lick afeared of those Yankees, or anyone, and I knew certain I didn't want to go to Fosters' no more, neither. I wanted to stay here, like Ma, and watch for Pa to come down our road. I took the Pa doll to my bedroom and set it on the shelf with the other things Rayford had whittled for me. I thought on how Ma would like to see it, too, and near most took it to her. I studied on it for a minute and decided to let her sleep. I wanted that carving to myself for awhile. I laid back on my bed and looked at it and at the yellow ribbon hanging on the hook below the shelf and asked the Lord to please, please send Pa home soon.

I checked on Ma every half hour or so and mid-afternoon, she woke up. She said she was feeling poorly so I told her to rest. When I swept up the cornmeal in the kitchen, my stomach growled. With all that commotion, we never had no dinner.

I looked over at the basket setting on the sideboard. If we wanted more than cornmeal and flour and molasses I'd have to go out to the garden for vegetables and greens and to the smokhouse for meat, and just like that, the scairt feeling came back. I looked out the parlor window to the east and didn't see nothing except chickens, and then I wondered if them Yankees had taken Belle. I didn't think the head soldier would've let them other ones take her, but I hadn't heard her moo, neither. Part of me wanted to run right out and see was she still over by the barn in the corral, but another part of me didn't want to go nowheres outside. I looked out the parlor window once more, as far to the north and south as I could see. There wasn't a body nowhere. I went to the kitchen window and looked out toward the back by the smokehouse and root cellar. Nothing. From my bedroom I looked out to the west, and saw the hill that led up to the cotton field on the other side, and there wasn't no one there neither. But without I opened the front door and looked out I couldn't see the corral.

Back in the parlor, I lifted the board off the door, and propped it against the wall, wishing Mr. Foster's gun was still there. I pushed the door open a crack, just far enough so I could look out across the road. There was Belle, resting with her back up against the corral fence and chewing her cud. I put my head out and peeked over to the east and saw Rayford's garden. The fence was latched, of which it didn't make no matter seeing as how he was in the house, but it set my mind at ease to see it so.

I went back to the sideboard, grabbed the garden basket and stepped out on the porch. The chickens had scattered and were chirping and pecking for grubs and grass and bits of grain. I went down the steps and looked in every direction, past Rayford's garden to the northeast, up McCreedy's hill, over to the woods east of the barn, across the road to the corral, and west to the cotton and corn field. I walked out into the yard, but when I noticed all the tracks the Yankees had made in the dirt, I got to shivering and near most ran back in the house. Pa came to mind then, like as if to say that since he wasn't here, I'd have to do like he would. I got as far as Rayford's garden and had to lean on the fence to steady my legs. I hadn't counted but eight chickens, so they made off with four, lessen there was some still in the coop of which it ain't like them during the day, unless they are broody. The eggs were likely gone, but there'd be more the next day.

Fresh piles of dirt dotted the garden, and I was afeared they'd dug up the whole thing. I got Rayford's shovel and went to the sweet potato patch. There had been some digging but the head Yankee must've stopped them before they took much. I dug into the ground and after every shovelful of dirt I stopped and listened. I reckon there wasn't no need to be scairt seeing as how I hadn't seen nobody, but scairt don't always make sense. It comes a might easier than it goes. I half filled the basket with sweet potatoes, pulled a mess of greens and threw 'em on top and quick took them back and set them on the steps. I wanted to run right back in the house and throw the board across the door, but I suspicioned if I did, I wouldn't never come out again.

I headed to the smokehouse. It sets back of the root cellar, so you can't see it until you're near most on top of it. I didn't see nary a track there, so I reckon they hadn't found it. I got out some salt pork, ran to the back of the house, grabbed the basket of sweet potatoes and greens and ran up the two steps to the back door. I pushed on it, then recollected I had barred it, so I raced around to the front of the house, tore up the steps and through the parlor to the kitchen. I set the salt pork on a plate, set the basket on the table, hightailed it back to the parlor and banged the board across the door like it was a race. It must have been near 90 degrees but I shivered all over. Shivers are peculiar. I reckon sometimes they come when what scared you is already over and you are safe, but your body has just figured it out, and it can't talk, it just shivers, like as if to say, "that was mighty close."

My stomach set to rumbling, like as if to tell me *it* weren't scairt, just hungry, so I rinsed the salt pork, cut off the rind, chopped it up and put it to cooking with the greens. I made some biscuits, too, and the sweet potatoes, hoping the smell of food would get Ma up and in the kitchen, but she stayed put. After me and Rayford ate, it was time for night chores. I looked out all the windows. I wished I had the gun, but there wasn't nothing for it.

Rayford and me brought up water, threw potato scrapings to the chickens, and brung a pile of corn shucks from the other side of the barn for Belle. I took the cup off the hook on the barn wall and gave it to Rayford while I milked Belle. When I held out my hand, he gave me the cup. I squirted the last of Belle's milk into it, and he hopped back and forth from one foot to the other, like always. Pa trained him to wait and not get ornery. It was so much like every other night, a time or two it almost seemed like them Yankees coming was a dream. But when I gave Rayford the cup, I saw how his lip was cut and I quick looked all around even though I didn't hear a noise nor nothing peculiar. I kept up my listening and watching while we took the pail of milk to the root cellar so the cream could rise overnight.

Some nights I like to sit outside with Rayford and watch the sun go down and the stars come out, but we stayed in. I got Rayford into bed, and looked in on Ma. She said her head pained her and her back hurt more than regular and she didn't want no food, she just wanted to be left alone. I got in bed and as soon as I closed my eyes, Yankees took to running through my head, and I didn't think I'd get a minute of sleep. I made myself think on Ma then, and asked the Lord to make her feel better in the morning so she could help clean up the rest of that Yankee mess. It is a lot for a body that is still mostly just a child.

28

How Do You See It?

Next thing I knew, our rooster was crowing. I opened my eyes thinking we'd be smart to make a stew of him so every morning he wouldn't be hollering to the world that we are here. I listened for voices, but didn't hear nary a one, strange nor regular. I got up and looked out my window. A sparrow flitted into the brush and I heard a woodpecker working off in the trees. I tiptoed to the parlor window and looked out to see a jay on one of the fence posts in Rayford's garden. From the kitchen window I saw a squirrel head toward the creek, but there wasn't a Yankee in sight.

I dressed and went out the back door, stopping for a few seconds at the edge of the woodshed to look around before I headed to the root cellar to get the milk. After I skimmed off the cream and poured it into the bucket I'd been filling all week, there was only enough to make a small crock of butter. Leastways with just the three of us it would last a few days. I took a good whiff of it, and of a sudden I pictured the cream running over a mound of fresh-cut peaches and down into a slab of warm, spicy gingerbread, some of it soaking in, the rest making a puddle around it. I felt my hand pick up my spoon and scoop up a soppy edge of that gingerbread with enough cream to slosh around my mouth. Then my brain brought in a picture of Rayford sitting in his chair, pointing and reaching across the table with his spoon, and I felt mean for ever having such thoughts. I picked up the crock and headed to the kitchen.

I suspicion that seeing as how I didn't drink that cream when the thought came, the devil won't never come round again to tempt me with his ideas. I reckon I have growed up just enough so I don't have the heart to pull pranks no more. 'Course I don't have time for such as that, neither. He likely found some other child to do his evil deeds, like Missy, of which that ain't fair. She's already got a ma who is kindly like Pa, and a brother, Hereford, to bother any time she gets a notion, and a granny and granpappy that live down the road. She goes to their place every other day or so to help them and gets a peppermint or a licorice in the bargain.

I churned the bit of cream into butter, spooned it in the crock, set it on the table, and made hoecake batter with the buttermilk. I got Rayford up and shaved, settled him in his chair in the parlor, and put him to whittling. Then I went to Ma's bedroom and shook her awake.

"Ma, it's morning." She didn't move. "Why don't you get up and have some hoecakes and fresh butter. We even got some molasses."

She opened her eyes and looked at me like she wasn't certain who I was. I expected her to ask on what had happened yesterday and how she got into bed and why it felt so good and fluffy, and not all matted down like it had been. I waited a minute or two for her to say something, then it came to me I'd best get the hoecakes to cooking. When she came to eat we could talk more on it. I got to the door and heard a cheery voice say, "Why, it's Sunday, ain't it?" I turned and she stretched her arms over her head and said, "I best get dressed for church meeting. That Will Wiley aims to sit with me."

"Ma!"

She sat up and and plopped her feet on the floor and looked around like she'd just opened her eyes, and when she saw me she got a peculiar look on her face.

"It's me. Tatum!"

She stared at me some, closed her eyes like when her head pains her, then looked at me again. "Yesterday...are you all right?" I nodded. She looked me up and down, like as if to see was it so. Then she patted her bed. "Come. Tell me what happened."

Her eyes followed me as I came over and sat next to her. I hoped she'd put her arm around me, but she kept her hands in her lap, fists clenched. "I recollect you ran out the back and I went to the parlor to bar the door...then...I don't know..." She clasped her hands, and looked at them, then out the window, but her lips moved, like she was thinking words, just not saying them. After a minute or so she said: "Them men, them soldiers, they rushed in whooping and hollering, and I recollect thinking how could there be such evil men, to break in like that, with our menfolk gone." She looked at me with a question in her eyes.

"I ran, Ma, I did. But I heard Rayford holler...and I promised Pa I'd take care of him." I told her how I'd turned back to the house and saw the pitchfork. I told her everything, how the skinny one grabbed my arm and the soap soldier came–

"The soap soldier?"

"He took pity on us, Ma. He made them others leave and told them not to take all our chickens, then he came back and left us some flour and molasses. And a bar of soap."

"He touch you?"

"No. No, he just brought them things in and said he was sorry about what they'd done to Rayford--" Ma's mouth popped open-- "He's all right. His lip was bleeding some. I don't know as he got punched or bit his lip."

"They came...we're not safe here. Maybe we'd best move to Fosters."

"Ma--" She sighed, like it was too much to think on. "I got something to show you."

I went to my room and took down the carving of Pa and held it to my heart for a few seconds. I wanted it where I could see it every night, but I reckoned Ma needed to see it, too. I took it in and handed it to her. She scowled, like it was just another thing Rayford had wasted his time on, and pushed it away. "I ain't in the mood for none of that."

"Look at it, Ma. You got to look at it."

She studied it, then took it and touched the face and the hair. Of a sudden I felt peculiar, like there were too many folks in that room, so I left.

I put the frypan on the hearth with a spoonful of hog grease, and stirred the batter and made a plate of hoecakes. I set them on the table and called to Ma and brought Rayford in. I piled three big cakes on his plate and buttered them and took out the crock of molasses the soap soldier left and spooned a bit on. I reckoned some family was doing without this morning, but there was naught I could do about it. I gave Rayford a fork and told him to eat, and went to see how Ma was doing.

"Ma?" She still sat on the edge of her bed, holding the Pa carving. "Hoecakes are ready."

"Tatum, I reckon we'd be safer at Foster's, but...I'd like to stay. How do you see it?"

I nearly swooned to hear her talk to me so, like as if I was a growed up person.

"I want to wait for Pa, too...and Hugh and Mule. This is our place. I don't want to be run off it. And I reckon Granpappy would want us to stay." I recollected his stories about clearing the land and building the house. I didn't want no Yankees to take what belonged to us.

"And it's been hard enough for Rayford lately. He ain't never slept anywhere but in his bed. Maybe we best not tell Fosters about them Yankees."

Ma nodded.

"I got them hoecakes on the table. Molasses, too. And Ma?"

She looked at me.

"When Pa comes back, he'll want to know we took good care of Rayford. We got to make sure we keep his gate latched. Pa loves you, but he and Rayford have been together since the day they were born. It would be the death of Pa if we let anything happen to Rayford."

"I'll be out directly," she said.

29

That Carving Ain't Going to Keep You Safe

Fall, 1864

Today is Melanie's birthday, October 20. It's been over a month since the Yankees came and we ain't seen hide nor hair of them. Yesterday I woke early thinking I didn't have a thing to give Melanie excepting a celebration, like Pa would've done. At first I pictured how it would look a might empty around our table. Howsomever Fosters would fill up two more chairs. And we had chicken to roast, and molasses to make gingerbread and sweeten apple cobbler. Then it came to me I could take Rayford's knife and square off the bar of soap the Yankee left, so it looked brand new, and give that to Melanie. I could cradle it in a bed of grasses and set it in the honeysuckle basket seeing as how it was near most finished. Then I rolled over and saw the yellow ribbon on the clothes peg and wondered if Pa had sent Melanie a hair ribbon for her birthday, too.

It wasn't likely Ma'd recollect so I went to tell her. I nudged her: "MA, IT'S MELANIE'S BIRTHDAY TOMORROW." I reckon the chickens heard me, too, but if I don't talk on something loud right off, she gets stuck in her dreams, talking about Pa and calling him Will. She's like to get it in her mind it's Sunday. That was the only day they had for courting, Pa had told me, seeing as how he went off to the foundry during the week and Saturdays he worked at home and helped with Rayford.

She opened her eyes. "WOULDN'T IT BE FUN TO HAVE HER AND THE FOSTER'S FOR A CELEBRATION?" She didn't say nothing. "YOU HEAR ME?"

"Quit hollering. I heard you. My head hurts so I can't hardly talk."

"I thought as how you might like to go over and invite them." Truth to tell, I wanted to go myself, but after what she said about her head, I thought it best not to say as much.

"Might do me some good to get out."

An hour later she headed out the door.

After breakfast and chores, I took Rayford's chair outside. He made cat noises like purring with squeaks in it, and followed me out to the garden like a big old happy bear that got into a beehive full of honey. I put it down to him knowing Ma was gone. He brung out a polecat he'd been whittling on, and set it on his water stand. He stared at it some like he was waiting for it to talk, then he picked it up and set to work. He don't never look out to the road like I do—afeared them Yankees might be coming—so I reckon he forgot how they busted in, if ever he did have a recollection of it.

I got the ax from behind the woodshed, took it to the whet stone and worked it top and bottom til it was so sharp it could've split a hair, like Pa says. I pretended he'd come out and say, "Tatum, that is the best ax-sharpening I ever seen." I set it on the stump on the other side of the wash tub where we always butchered, then I put Rayford to digging sweet potatoes and went in and set some apples to cooking.

I kept on all day, sweeping the floors and the yard, getting vegetables ready, making an apple cobbler, and talking nice to the chickens so they wouldn't suspicion nothing. I even finished the honeysuckle basket and cut up some pieces of yarn instead of grass to make a little nest and put the soap in it. The sun was starting to settle when I got to worrying did Ma get lost or run into a pack of Yankees when I heard wagon wheels. I wished for that gun that we didn't have but before I could think much on it I heard Melanie's voice. When I looked out, Mr. Foster was turning the wagon around. He headed out of the yard and Melanie and Ma were making their way to the house. Even if a body didn't have eyes I reckon they could tell who Ma was talking to by her voice, of which it gets lively and happy sounding when she's talking to Melanie and whiny and cantankerous when she's talking to me. It came to me to pay some attention and make note of the difference and call Ma out on it. Maybe she's been doing it that way so long she don't know any other way, even when I am helping and doing chores and not complaining, of which that is the way it's been lately. Then Melanie walked into the kitchen and all that thinking fell away.

"I swear, Baby, you are gone be tall as Pa. Can't be calling you Baby much longer the way you are shooting up." She sniffed and headed over to the mantel above the hearth.

"Apple cobbler," I said. "For your birthday!"

"I can't hardly wait. Ma Foster ain't been out for awhile, and I said as how we might could have the celebration to home to make it easy on her, but she's got her heart set on coming. She wants to see what all new things Rayford made." I got in my head the picture of that nice Miss Clara sitting with us and all of us talking and such. I reckon I looked like a eejit with a stupid smile on my face. "We'll have such fun." Melanie busted into a smile and hugged me.

Ma was real quiet. I wondered was she thinking on moving back to Foster's so she could be by Melanie. I feared she might go on like as if Pa just walked in the room, but I reckon that talk on having a birthday celebration here tomorrow kept her mind on us.

That night when she got in bed with me, like when she used to live here, it put me at ease like I ain't been in a long time. We generally talk some until we can't keep our eyes open, but she was real quiet, and after waking early I was ready to close my eyes and dream on the next day. My mind drifted to thoughts of Pa sitting with us at the table and laughing and the sleepier I got, the more real it seemed. Then I felt a nudge.

"Baby? You awake?"

"Now I am."

"Ma told me about them Yankees that came." I didn't say nothing. "She said they knocked her down, but she don't think they'll come back."

"That's right."

"Baby?" she whispered with a sadness in her voice that made me sit up.

"What?"

"They hurt you?"

"No."

"They didn't never lay a finger on you?"

"No. One brought molasses and flour and said he was sorry for what them others did. Then he left." Her breath came like a sigh, and I knew what was coming, so before she could start in, I said, "I know what you're thinking. But Rayford made us a carving of Pa. You can see it in the morning. It's in Ma's room. After I showed it to her we talked on it. We aim to stay right here and you ain't like to change our minds. You recollect all them stories Granpappy told how he cleared this land...and all the work Pa has done. They built this very house and I ain't gone let no Yankee come here and burn it down, nor take over our land. I'll shoot em first." And then I recollected I had to ask Mr. Foster could he spare another gun.

Melanie was so quiet, I thought she'd fallen asleep. Then she sat up, too.

"I don't like worrying on you every day."

"We weren't going to tell you about them Yankees."

"Ma made me promise not to tell Pa Foster."

"Well, leastways she did that."

"You know that carving of Pa ain't going to keep you safe."

"But the soap soldier--"

"Soap soldier?"

"He...well, now I reckon it's ruined."

"What's ruined."

"I called him the soap soldier seeing as how he brung us a bar of soap and--"

"He brung a bar of soap, too?" She said it like as if it was a lie. "I don't know as I can believe all that. Are you telling me them evil Yankees busted in, broke dishes, and brung you things?"

"No, just one Yankee, the one that made the others leave."

"So you were alone with him."

"No. Rayford was there, and after I said how he was simple-minded, the soap soldier took pity. The soap was to clean him off. Rayford messed himself bad, but the soap smelled too nice for that. I aimed to give it to you for your birthday, but now the surprise is ruined."

"I don't know as I want soap from some evil Yankee."

"Melanie! That ain't like you."

"Don't forget, them Yankees is why Joram is gone...and Pa and Hugh and Mule."

"But Pa said there's good ones up north and bad ones, just like down here."

"If they're soldiers they're bad ones."

I had to think on that. I could see it her way. But I saw the pity for Rayford in the soap soldier's eyes.

"And they're like to come back. There's Yankees all over these parts now, and rebel deserters, and plain old outlaws running wild with no law to rein 'em in." Melanie hissed in her whisper-ing and for a split second, she put me in mind of Ma.

"But the soap soldier said we were so far from the main road it wasn't likely no one else would bother us. He said they all got lost and took a wrong turn. And you recollect them three soldiers I seen when Rayford got out? How I said one stuttered? Well, a stuttering one came that day. I reckon it was some of them that was up on McCreedy's Hill the night Rayford got out, and they got lost a' purpose to come back during the day to see what was here."

"That means they could come again."

"The soap soldier was the head of them. He told them to leave and not to take all our chickens and they did, so--"

"Baby, you ain't safe here! Fine talk and being stubborn and a carved Pa don't make you safe."

"Melanie, truth to tell, if that pack of Yankees had busted into your house—there were leastways a dozen—you reckon Pa Foster could've stopped them from taking your food and busting your dishes?"

"But, Baby. You're a woman now. They could hurt you, not just bust dishes and take food." I recollected the skinny mean one and how he grabbed at me. It made me uneasy to think of him. "You understand what I mean?"

"Well, I got the jist of it. But like I said, Mr. Foster can't hold off fifteen Yankees. If more Yankees bust in, I'll tell them Rayford's simple-minded and they'll take pity."

"Baby, it is not the way of evil folks to take pity."

"But every Yankee ain't evil."

"Hmmmph."

She didn't say no more, but she tossed around awhile. I laid still. My body was as tired as ever, but my brain wouldn't stop working, thinking about what Melanie said, and how them Yankees knew that we were alone and we still had food and chickens. I wasn't afeared of that soap soldier, and I didn't think he'd let that mean one come back. But I had to keep in mind to ask Mr. Foster for a gun. And keep the door barred at night.

Time passed and I heard Melanie's breath come easy. I got to wondering again if Pa had sent her a birthday letter. She didn't say naught of it, but there wasn't no way he'd forget.

30

I Couldn't Put My Finger On It

I rolled over towards her, and after three pushes Melanie opened her eyes. "It's your birthday and you're here," I said, hugging her. We hung on to each other for a minute, like we did when we were younger. She didn't say naught on what we talked about last night.

"I'm happy to be here, too, Baby. I just wish Joram was back, and Pa and the boys. And we were all together." The morning light shone on the ribbon Pa gave me, and Melanie must have been thinking the same thing I was. "I didn't get a letter from Pa. Pa Foster said it was likely setting in a saddlebag somewhere, trying to get here, but caught up in the war. Regular mail riders can't always get through the lines."

"It'll come. Pa ain't one to forget birthdays. Now, don't be sad.

We'll set ourselves up a celebration to do right by your birthday like Pa would do if he was here. You know how to butcher a chicken?"

"Ewww!" She rolled over. " I ain't never even watched."

"Sorry, I forgot how you are. I hope Ma is up to it."

Mid-morning I got the wash kettle boiling and told Ma to be ready, then took a feed sack out to the yard. We still had eight chickens and the rooster. Pa says you need leastways one rooster to keep the flock going and we only had us the one, so I told him he was lucky he'd get to celebrate Melanie's birthday this year, and I set off after one of the hens. I finally got near one and hid the sack behind my back so it wouldn't spook her, then I dove for her. I caught a leg on the first try and threw the sack on her to quiet her down, but she flapped and squawked and nearly got loose anyway. I grabbed her other leg and she beat her wings and nearly lifted us both off the ground, and by then every hen was flying and squawking and Ma flew out the back door.

"The ax is on the stump," I yelled. We both ran to it and I handed her the chicken and she hollered at me over the squawking, "Get another one. This one's puny." I just stood there, not certain I'd heard right. She'd been fighting the idea of eating them even before the Yankees stole nearly half the flock "Get!" she yelled and I skedaddled out to the yard and tore around after them hens and fell about twenty times. When they get riled they're fast and sneaky, but I finally outsmarted one by chasing her into the henhouse. I cornered her, grabbed her, and ran back to Ma. Ma wrung her neck quick, then laid her on the chopping block and took her head off. The first one was still flopping around, like they do even after their heads are gone. When she finally came to a stop I took her by the feet and picked the loose feathers off and stuffed them in one of the feed sacks. Then I plunged her into the boiling water to loosen the rest, and they came off by the handful. I tossed the wet feathers in a big oak basket so they could dry, then we singed the chickens to get the pinfeathers off. Once Melanie got too close while we were butchering and she said the smell near most made her retch, but it just smells like butchering chickens to me, and brings to mind a picture of a drumstick and mashed potatoes on a plate with gravy poured over all of it.

Just before noon I went out to get wood for the rest of the day, and when I opened the door to come in again, all them good smells of chicken roasting and onions stewing and cobbler warming rushed up my nose.

"Can't Rayford help haul that wood in?" Melanie asked.

"He's settled in whittling. And I like getting outside."

I went out again and even though it was a warm day, the air felt good after the hot kitchen. I couldn't think on which was better, coming out to a breeze, or going back in to the good smells. I set a log in the crook of my arm and heard a noise and as I turned toward the woods, I saw blue.

Before I could move, a hand clapped over my mouth and another grabbed my waist. My brain brought up a picture of Yankees running in the house and grabbing all our food, and I thought my heart would hammer itself right out of my chest. It felt like everything inside me was tearing around like those chickens with their heads cut off, excepting that my feet—of which they could've got me out of there—were like tree trunks stuck in the ground.

"Don't scream," he whispered. "I won't hurt you." I waited for a whistle or a noise that would make a whole woods full of soldiers come running. I tried to jerk loose, but he held tight. I still had the log, but I didn't know if I should drop it so I could run if my feet ever got the notion, or hang on to it so leastways I had something to throw at him.

"I wanted to be sure you were all right," he said, still whispering. "I'll let you go, but don't scream."

He kept his hand over my mouth, not pushing hard, but keeping it ready, then he took his arm from my waist. "I've been worried about you," he whispered. "I was afraid Ramsay would sneak away and come back–"

When I thought about the skinny Yankee, a woozy feeling came over me. I heard: "Tatum?" and there came a thought that said something wasn't right...and the next thing I knew I was in heaven with an angel. At first she was far, far away, then she came closer and closer and her voice got louder and louder and she said, "Baby, what's wrong? Baby, you hear me?"

I opened my eyes and looked around. It wasn't heaven. I was on the ground by the woodshed, and Melanie knelt beside me, shaking me. "Are you all right? You got your monthlies again?" She put her hand on my forehead. "My word, you're white as a haint and your face is hot as a frypan. C'mon." She helped me up, put her arm around me and we hobbled into the kitchen. She set me on a chair and brought a cup of water. "Drink this. Ma, she was laying on the ground out by the woodshed. Must be the monthlies, again," she said, and Ma came up and felt my head.

"She is a might hot."

I drank the water and Ma came back with another cup.

Melanie sat by me and rubbed my back and a few minutes later, she put her hand on my forehead.

"She's cooled down," Melanie said. Once I felt better I rec-ollected what happened, and got a peculiar feeling again, but I couldn't put my finger on it. There was a thing about that soap soldier that wasn't right, but then we heard a wagon coming, and I had to let it go.

"Sounds like Fosters are here. I'm all right." I stood. My legs still felt weak, but I took a few steps to put Ma and Melanie at ease. Then Melanie got up and set the last of the table and Ma took the cover off the kettle to check the roasting chickens. Major Tom whinnied and I wondered if that soap soldier was hiding in the woods watching. I got to wondering if Pa was by a house that had chickens or turkey or venison roasting and an apple cobbler setting on the hearth and smelling up the whole place of cinnamon and spices.

We went out to the porch to welcome the Fosters. Mr. Foster helped Miss Clara off the wagon and commenced to carry her, but I heard her say she could walk. "H'lo there," she said, and she waved and grabbed on to Mr. Foster's arm and leaned on him, but she walked in on her own. We all came through the parlor into the kitchen and Mr. Foster set her on a chair straightaway. She looked to Melanie, first thing, and put her arms out. "Happy birthday, dear," she said and Melanie went to her for a hug. Rayford came by me and stood, like he was a might shy or such as that, but he wasn't scairt and I knew he would be fine, even if Pa wasn't with us.

Next, Miss Clara said Rayford's name and told him she'd like to see his carvings later. I don't reckon he understood what all the words meant with his ears, but I reckon he felt her kindness, and his head bobbed up and down. Miss Clara said that one of her grandchildren had a birthday soon and she'd like to buy one or two for a present.

"We're neighbors, Miss Clara. You're welcome to any of his carvings that you take a fancy to," I said.

"We'll just see. Now we brought a few things, too," and she looked at Mr. Foster. He nodded, then he looked at me. "Tatum, I could use a hand."

I headed out the door after him and once we cleared the porch he asked me why that gun he left for us wasn't setting by the front door. I tried to think of a way to answer that wasn't lying without telling the truth of the Yankees, but before I had anything worked up, he asked again. "You best tell the truth of it," he said, like he could see inside my head.

"Well...Yankees took it."

"What happened?"

"They came in and broke some dishes, but they didn't hurt us. There was one Yankee, must've been the head one, he made the other ones leave. He thought Rayford was a coward, but when I told him he was simple-minded, he took pity and left us. Even said he was sorry."

"I recollect that you and your ma told me you'd come to our place if you saw a Yankee. Now we ain't taking no more chances."

"But Melanie told me how you brush the road and put stones out to make it look like no one lives back here." I thought on how I could say what I wanted to without telling a lie. "And truth to tell, that was weeks ago and they ain't come back." Just the soap soldier, I thought—so it wasn't really a lie. "If you could get me another gun. And a knife. One of them fold-up knives like Rayford's jackknife so I can keep it in my pocket." Mr. Foster gave me a look as if to say he was set to rope us all up and drag us to his place if he had to. Then I got an idea.

"There is a way we could work this out." I said it with an excited voice, like as if this was the most wonderful idea that just came to me out of nowhere, instead of a sneaky move like as if I was playing checkers with Granpappy.

"How's that?"

"Seeing as how Rayford likes things the same, and he has his garden and he knows our place, maybe it'd be best if you and Miss Clara and Melanie moved here. We got room for you all and Major Tom could stay in the barn."

"That don't make sense. I need to be there to take care of things--" He stopped short and looked at me like as if my checker piece just jumped two of his, and he wasn't too happy about it. He didn't say naught for a bit, then he looked around and shook his head. "Tatum, this ain't a game. Them Yankees could just as well have killed you all." He breathed a disgusted snort. "I just hope this stubbornness comes to some good. You bar the door at night, and keep your eyes open."

"I been."

"I have a knife at home I can bring you. And I'll see about getting another gun. They're scarce, but Jeanette's Ryker might know where I can get one. Meanwhile, you be careful. You see someone coming you ring the dinner bell hard, like as if you're calling for help."

"I will. I promise."

He went over to the wagon and picked up a basket and

handed it to me. "You take this in. I'll run that sack of corn over to the barn and put it in one of your feed barrels. I'll set a rock on the cover to keep the critters out. You give a handful or two to your chickens everyday and they'll lay better. Make sure you put the rock back on." He pulled the sack off the wagon and threw it over his shoulder and headed to the barn.

I took the basket in the house and set it on the table in front of Miss Clara. She pulled out a bowl of little onions, not like ours but in a white sauce the likes of which I ain't laid eyes on for a long time, and another with carrots, cooked and spiced, and a full crock of butter as creamy and yellow as I ever saw.

"I'll put them to warming," Ma said, taking the carrots and onions from her. She set them on the stand above the fire, then swung the kettle out and took the lid off and the smell of roast chicken filled the kitchen and I near most drooled. Rayford had his eye on the birds and I grabbed his hand and pulled him to his chair and set him down. Ma took the chickens out of the roasting pan and set them on a platter from Foster's, and set to making gravy. Melanie took the masher off the hook over the sideboard and mashed the potatoes, and Mr. Foster walked in.

"Everything's ready," Ma said as he sat in the chair next to Miss Clara then Ma asked: "Mr. Foster, would you kindly ask the Lord's blessing?"

He bowed his head and we held hands. He said how we were thankful for the good food, the chance to celebrate Melanie's birthday together, and for all the folks that meant so much to us, but weren't with us, and would the Lord please look out for them and bring them home safe. And would He watch over our families and help these kind folks—of which he meant Ma and me and Rayford—to see the wisdom of moving to be with him and Miss Clara and Melanie. I reckon he got leastways one of my checker pieces with that. He went on some and I got to thinking about that soap soldier and wondering if he had a Ma and a Pa up north somewheres saying grace at their own table, and then, like a bolt of lightening it came to me what wasn't right about him: he had called me "Tatum."

Then Mr. Foster said, "Amen," and the rest of us did, too, and we commenced to eating. Miss Clara kept us talking on good things—on Rayford's carvings, and what a good help Melanie is and how the weather ain't been so bad. She told a story on her cousin up north, and how she was hoping to go up for a visit after the war. She asked Ma how she got the chicken so tender and told me that was the best apple cobbler she ever tasted. For a sickly woman, she was lively and smart, and her eyes shone with a brightness that made you think it was foolish to feel sorry for her, seeing as how she was such a happy person.

After dinner Miss Clara pulled out a little package for Melanie, of which it was a new looking glass with wood edges that had flowers carved into it and a matching wood comb and brush. Ma gave her some indigo-dyed yarn and I brought out the honeysuckle basket. When she picked up the soap to smell it, Ma looked at it peculiar, then nodded, like as if she recollected where it came from, but she didn't say naught on it. Then we got to visiting and Miss Clara looked at some of the new things Rayford's been carving, and Ma brought out the carving of Pa. It was the first time I ever saw her look proud on anything he'd done. "Me and Will is gone be together again, soon. I feel it," she said, and I was afeared she'd talk out of her head, but Miss Clara asked to see the carving and went on about how nice it was and she got Ma to talking some on fancy work and such.

Between all that talking and listening, my brain kept going back to that soap soldier. I went over all what happened when them Yankees busted into our house and I know certain there was never a time Ma called me by name—and Rayford can't talk. So how did that soap soldier know my name is Tatum?

31

A Letter

Melanie rode in mid-morning waving a piece of paper like as if she was driving off flies. I set down the ax, of which I had been ready to do since I picked it up an hour or so earlier. I don't miss Hugh a whole lot til it comes to chopping wood. Melanie slid off Major Tom, threw the reins over a fence post and hollered, "It's from Pa." The excitement in her voice put my brain to thinking he must be on his way home. "And I got two skinned rabbits." She pulled off the saddle bag and marched to the house and I took off to meet her. Seeing as how there was a celebrating to go with the letter, I reckoned it surely must have been filled with good news.

Minutes later we were at the table, breathless and eager. Ma's fists were clenched and pulled up to her chest like as if to keep her heart from dashing right out her body. Seemed like it took

Melanie forever to get her throat cleared to her liking and ready, and I near most grabbed the letter from her, but I could see as how she had her heart set on it.

"'To my dearest family,'" she finally read. "'I'm sorry I ain't been writing much of late but paper is hard to come by. I got this in a trade. I hope it gets to you.'" She looked up and said that part made her sad because she reckoned Pa had to trade food or some such for it, but the next part made her feel better.

"Well, get to it then," I said, thinking that letter, all dirty and torn, looked to me like it had fought half the war itself.

"'We are east of home a ways back off a main road where the Yankees ain't like to find us. It puts me in mind of our place with a barely used curved road leading to it, excepting it is up a hill, not down at the bottom. These are kindly folks giving us food from their garden, of which it's the first one we been by in awhile that ain't already been picked clean by the bluecoats. We had carrots and sweet potatoes last night and black-eyed peas with ham. I ain't never tasted nothing so good, excepting for Ma's cooking. They got five sons, three off fighting the war, so they had a big garden and they hoped there was folks somewheres feeding their sons.'" Melanie looked up then and said, "That's good to hear, ain't it? That they come acrost people so kindly?"

I nodded and looked at Ma. I reckon she had taken herself off to be by Pa in that garden. Melanie touched her arm. "Ma, I'm about to read again. You listening?"

Ma sat up and nodded and her eyes looked hard at Melanie, like as if she was bound not to miss a word.

"'Now I can't say as this is my favorite place to be, but it ain't bad neither. I still got my blanket from the parlor, Tatum. I get to laughing every time I recollect when it was setting on the porch and scairt you. I hope old Beauregard ain't giving you no trouble. And boys, you best be getting the cotton in. I reckon it's time.'"

"If he's telling Hugh and Mule to get the cotton in, he must've written that letter a long time ago." I wanted to be as happy about that letter as Melanie, but there was a truth beyond the words of it that kept knocking on my brain.

"Well, there is a date on the letter, 6 September."

"That was over a month and a half ago!" If Pa was so close, I wondered why it took that letter so long to get here.

"He talks on that, just wait." Melanie cleared her throat again and picked up where she left off. 'We had the prettiest sunset last night. We had camped out near the garden and the smell of earth put me in mind of home. I surely do miss everyone there.'" I got a picture in my head with those words, like Pa was sitting right there talking to us. "Now this here is where he tells about when he is writing." Melanie pointed to a place in the letter. "'A week has gone by since I wrote the first part. I aim to write every few days til they say we can get mail through. Now, I got to tell you about a pup that belonged to them folks that fed us. They named it Three-leg and you can likely figure why. It ran a might funny, but it was the friendliest, most playful little pup. Every morning he'd run round and wake us up, licking our faces and begging for food. He could do tricks too, like sitting up and rolling over. He acted like he didn't know he only had three legs. It was a sight.'"

Melanie set the letter down and looked at Ma, then at me. "Don't that sound just like Pa?" It did, and I reckon that is why

I couldn't get as het up over it as Melanie. Pa finds the good no matter what, but I feared that it was all the bad he didn't let on about that kept that letter from us so long.

"Now I'll read the last part. Looks like he wrote it on another day."

"Read it slow," I said, wanting Pa's words to last.

"'There was a call for mail, so I reckon I'll send this out today. We're still by the farm where the folks have been sharing their food. Most of the men is right pleasant. At night we got singing and card playing and all such as that. I think of you all and pray for the day this war is over and I can come home. Your loving husband and father, William Wiley.'"

"When you reckon he got round to sending it?" I asked.

"I suspicion it was the middle of September." I held out my hand for the letter so I could see the words Pa wrote for myself. She handed it over and stood. "Let's get one of these rabbits to roasting and we'll salt down the other so you can have it later."

That poor, tattered piece of paper said as much to me as Pa's words, causing a sadness to worm its way into the happy feeling that came over me when Melanie first waved it around. And I couldn't help but wonder again why Pa hadn't got a letter out for her birthday.

32

An Orange

Each time Ma gets one of them spells where she talks on Pa like they are still courting, or tells me to haul a jug of water to him in the field, or to get his good shirt washed up for prayer meeting, it takes her longer to get out of it and act like Ma again. She never was much for regular talking, but now it seems like the onliest time she opens her mouth is to tell me to do a thing or not to do a thing that has to do with a Pa that ain't here. There ain't no more talk of rain, nor sun, nor naught as that. She ain't said a word on the Lord or the Bible or even complained about Rayford. Her brain ain't working so good neither. Yesterday she built a fire in the hearth in the parlor and put wood on it til she near most set the house to burning. I had to douse it, then build a new one and set the wet wood around the edges to dry. First off I thought she did it out of meanness, but after I put the fire out, she stood back with her hands over her mouth like it was a most awful thing and she wondered however did it come about. I ain't let her do a lick of cooking neither since I saw her spill some cornmeal last week, then sweep up the whole floor and throw it all back in the bowl. I ain't told Melanie about none of this.

I try to get Ma to talk by asking questions that are like funning. This morning I asked: "What if we could ride in to Harpersville and buy any old thing we wanted? What if we could ride in on Foster's wagon and pull up to the general store and Mr. Wright would come out and hold the door wide open and say, 'You come in and load up that wagon seeing as how you are such good folks.' What would you get, Ma?"

It could've been like a game, but she said, "It don't do no good wishing for what won't never be." I told her it was just to get our minds off our troubles, but she said it wasn't no better than lying seeing as how it wasn't the truth about the way things were. Leastways she answered me back. Most days when I talk, she don't say nothing, so I ain't talked a whole lot to her lately, but Rayford's been getting an earful. I tell him everything that comes to mind, and I reckon he likes it when I talk but without he can't say ary a thing back it has come to where some days I'm afeared I'll go crazy with the quiet.

Sometimes I think on what it would be like to live in a city like Harpersville where there's folks around all the time, and if you had a mind to say something, there'd be folks around to listen and say something back. I get a picture in my head of big rooms where folks sit in circles and you pick up your chair and go to any circle you take a liking to, seeing as how they each one talk about a different thing. I'd talk the whole day if they let me. I wouldn't tell about chasing chickens, or that place I set up for

Pa and me in that old hickory tree, but I'd tell about Rayford, and the things he whittles. I'd show his carvings around and trade for a horse and wagon. Then me and Rayford'd go find Pa, and the three of us would traipse all over. But since that ain't like to happen, I'll just stay here til Pa comes down that road. I've thought on it some and I reckon it's like the faith we're supposed to have in the Lord. If I leave, it would be like saying I don't have no faith in Pa coming back, so I aim to stay.

Midmorning I went out for wood and took an armload from the pile on the west edge of the shed. As I turned to go back in, I saw something atop the other pile. It was not much bigger than my hands and was wrapped in brown paper. I picked it up and something heavy inside moved. First off I thought Melanie brung me more paints, but the shape was wrong. I took off the paper, careful, so I could use it to write on, and underneath was a wooden box with carvings on it—fancy curlicues and whatnots, not real things like what Rayford whittles. I took the lid off, and there was an orange inside. Neither Melanie nor Mr. Foster has been here since Tuesday, day before yesterday, so I couldn't figure how it got to be there without I seen it before.

I dug my fingernail into the skin and took a good whiff and it brung to mind the Christmas when I was ten and it was a good year for cotton. Pa had got us a crate of oranges, and we all wanted to set right down and eat them, but Melanie said if we ate three each day and shared, they would last near most a week. Pa didn't want none, but we told him as how it would be more fun if he shared with us. I sniffed that orange and the thought came into my head that Pa brought it and he was hiding to tease me. "Pa?" I called, looking around the woodpile and into the edge of the woods. "You home, Pa?" Then I reckoned Melanie must've gave it to Ma last time she was here and told her to wait a day or two, then set it out for me.

In the kitchen I peeled the orange and the smell burst into the room and my mouth took to watering. I pulled it into three parts and set Ma's aside for later seeing as how she was still in her room, sleeping I reckon, of which that's near most all she does anymore. I cut Rayford's and mine into small pieces to make it last longer. I took the plate into the parlor, and when Rayford saw it he lit up. I reckon it was the smell that told him what it was, seeing as how we ain't had oranges in a long time. I gave him a piece and he put it in his mouth and grabbed for more, but I put my hand up to stop him and parceled them out. With each bite the sweet-tart juice filled my mouth like sunshine. When I got to the last piece, I rolled it around my mouth til it got warm, then chewed it slow to get every last bit of flavor. There were a few drops of juice on the plate, so I let Rayford lick them up, then took the plate back to the kitchen and took Ma's part to her room.

"Ma, we got some of that orange for you. Me and Rayford saved some. Here." I didn't expect she'd answer, but it ain't a smell you can turn your back on. She sat up, took the plate, and sniffed it.

"Where'd you get this?"

"From that box you set on the woodpile."

"I didn't set no box on the woodpile," she said. "Did Melanie come back?"

"I ain't seen her," I said.

"I didn't set nothing on the woodpile."

"Well then it must've been Mr. Foster." I didn't know who else would've left that box there. Lessen it was haints or the devil, but I ain't never heard about such as them doing what is kindly, only about them being up to no good.

33

A Hobbledy Bluecoat Bum

Rayford wet again last night and Ma wouldn't get out of bed, so after breakfast, I washed his sheets. I had just thrown them over the line to dry when Mr. Foster rode up with a gun, a folding knife he got from Ryker, and news on Joram. "We got a letter yesterday. He took bad sick and they're sending him home. Should be here sometime next week."

"Maybe Pa will be back soon, then, too."

"I hope so. And til he does, leastways with Joram home, Melanie can get over here more regular," he said. "Sherman is holed up in Atlanta, dead set on burning it to the ground, it appears. I hear tell he torches every building he comes on, farm, factory, or mill. Leastways he got past us and I reckon we can breathe some easier for that." He looked over to Rayford's garden and back by the wash tub. "Where's your Ma?"

"She's sleeping. Feeling poorly."

"Last time I came by she was feeling poorly. Reckon she needs Doc Waitly?"

I near most told him it was just one of her spells when she talks out of her head and sleeps for a day, but caught myself.

"She had a hard load of work yesterday." I looked around to see what I could come up with for what she'd done. "Washing clothes and such. And we brought a couple wheelbarrow loads of corn down from the field, and shucked them."

"Maybe I best look in on her."

"I don't know as she is up to visitors. I'll go ask does she want you to fetch Doc Waitly."

I reckon I should've invited him in, but I didn't want him to get no ideas about how we were doing, of which he would've if he got a whiff of Ma's room. It was dark and closed up and had a smell of damp and sweat and pee. I shook Ma.

"Mr. Foster's here. He wants to know should he bring Doc Waitly by."

"I don't need Doc Waitly, I need Will and my boys home. You tell Mr. Foster that's who he can bring." I had in mind to tell her if she cleaned her room, and opened her windows, and got to moving around and not acting like a person already passed on she'd be better off. But I went back outside.

"She's said she's feeling better. Just resting now," I told him. If it was Melanie, she would have pushed past me, and I reckon even Miss Clara would've put up a fuss about it, but Mr. Foster, kindly as he is, ain't much for talking. I suspicion he about gave up on getting me to see things his way. He turned his hat a time or two. Pa ain't that way, but it looks to me like most fellers wear hats just so they have something to do with their hands when they talk. "You keep an eye on that gun this time seeing as how I ain't like to get no more of 'em. And don't cut yourself with that there knife. You hit that switch, it pops open quick. You be careful." I nodded and he looked around again. "I won't sleep sound at night til you and your Ma and Rayford are at our place."

I just took a breath and held my tongue. I didn't have nothing to say he hadn't heard before and I was afeared if I told him I was sorry to keep him from his sleep, he'd stick in a few more words like a wedge and work them til I came to see things his way. I can't say as I'm happy to be here with a Ma that's more out of her head than in it, but I can near most hear Pa telling me to hold on. Mr. Foster tapped his hat against his leg a time or two then put it on his head and climbed up on Major Tom.

I watched him ride away. I tucked the knife in one of my skirt pockets and set the gun by the front door. The morning had been cool so I hadn't taken Rayford out yet. When I looked in on him in the parlor, he gathered up his quilt and stood, like he'd been waiting for me.

"All right, Rayford. Let's get you outside, then I'll stoke the fire and come out with you." I put his coat on and took his hand and we walked out to his garden. It is a might peculiar how the Lord made him such a big man but didn't give him hardly no brain, so that he generally won't even go in or out the house lessen I take his hand. I reckon Melanie was right about that time he got out—that it was Ma took him up to the woods. She likely gave him sweets all along the way to keep him moving, sat him down, gave him that peppermint that made him all sticky, then walked away. He'd never think as how she wasn't coming back for him.

I got Rayford settled and leaned back against the hackberry tree aiming my face to the sun. I patted my skirt to feel the knife and it put me at ease. I closed my eyes, then, and had in mind to rest but I recollected I had to stoke the fire. We been out of matches and I keep forgetting to ask Fosters if they could spare some seeing as how there are too many things to think on. It's near most like I'm a growed up person, of which I still ain't ready. Truth to tell, I reckon I'm even less inclined to get growed up now that I have had a taste of it. Maybe if I quit eating, or leastways didn't eat so much, I might stop growing. But I like to eat and there ain't much else to like around here but for eating.

I thought on that some and then recollected I hadn't stoked the fire. If it went out I'd have a need of going to Fosters but I wouldn't have enjoyed it none knowing Ma was alone with Rayford. I couldn't trust her to keep the fire stoked much less leave her while I made the trip to Foster's for matches. I reckon I am near most half way between a child and a growed up person to have thoughts such as that.

I headed to the woodshed and on top of the pile where I found the orange was a sack filled with dried meat, dried peaches, flour, matches, and two candles. I grabbed an armload of wood and took the sack in and put the meat and peaches in crocks and poured the flour into the bin. The candles were long and fat and when I strung them on the candle hooks, they made ours look puny. I reckoned Mr. Foster was sneaking those goods to us so as to let us keep our pride, and I thought how as I'd have to keep in mind to thank him. And matches! He must have read my mind.

But there was a part of my brain tellin' me that as kindly as he was, it wouldn't be like Mr. Foster to think of matches. And to bring candles that looked like store bought. It warn't no comfort to think on it. I had to let it be.

I put a log on the hearth and stayed long enough to see it catch. As I stepped out on the porch I noticed movement on the road, and pulled back inside quick. I peeked out and as it came closer I saw it was a hobbledy bluecoat bum, walking with a crutch, head down. I thought as how Mr. Foster would be a might surprised that he hadn't much more than brought over that gun and left, and here was a Yankee coming already. If there had been a whole passel of them coming at me, I'd have been scairt to death, but I reckoned I could handle one skinny soldier walking with a crutch. I picked up the gun and stepped out on the front porch and swung it halfway up so it was pointing at him.

"Don't you come no closer, mister," I yelled. He stopped, looked up, and took to laughing, and there came a picture in my head of that skinny Yankee who laughed at me and I pulled the gun to my shoulder and sighted him in to get a good aim. "Stop right there," I hollered. The hand that didn't have a crutch came up like as if to wave, and he stood there. "You turn round now and get a move on, or I'll have to shoot."

"Tatum!"

He hobbled closer and I lowered the gun, and gave him a good looking over. Excepting for his voice, I couldn't hardly believe it was Hugh. Until I saw him standing there, I hadn't known how much I missed him. I put the gun down and ran to him, yanked on his long beard and he pulled my hair, and we grabbed each other and held on tight. After a minute we let go and I stepped back and looked at him.

"You're a sight for sore eyes. What happened to your leg?"

"Mule done it."

"Mule hurt you?"

"Not Brother Mule, a pack mule. It took a shot in the shoulder and fell on me."

"Beauregard?"

"Nope. Even the Confederate Army couldn't coax no sense into that stubborn critter. They hitched him with another mule and put him to pulling wagons with a different driver. I reckon I would have felt bad some, but we were working so steady hauling supplies I didn't have hardly no time to think on it." His eyes moved from one thing to another, like as if he had forgotten what our place looked like. "Good to be home," he said with a grin on his face. Then he took a deep breath and looked down at his leg. "This happened near most two weeks ago," he said. "Doc had many worse off to tend so he set it quick and gave me this crutch. I reckoned I'd get killed certain then. There's some what ain't letting none of their men go lessen they're dead."

"Don't look like you would've been much good."

"They would've stuck me someplace with a gun and told me to stay put. But two days later the news came through that Sherman set fire to Atlanta. Captain told me we weren't gone win this war no how and I best go home. When it came to that, I got to be a might thankful that mule fell on it." He put his right arm around my shoulder and leaned on me and we headed over to Rayford's garden.

"I want to hear all about it." We made it near most to the gate before he answered.

"Ain't nothing worth telling. I couldn't wait to get there, but war ain't like how I thought it'd be."

"You sorry you took off and joined up?"

"I did right by going, but that don't mean it was a place I wanted to be. I'd as soon not talk on it. Maybe later...when it don't seem so real no more. Hey, Rayford," he called out when he saw Rayford was watching us. I took the latch off the gate and he asked about Ma.

"She ain't herself. Missing Pa, I reckon. She don't hardly say a word all day, iffen she even gets outa' her bed. You'll see."

"The barn is too quiet," he said looking acrost the road. "Seems like I should hear Granpappy hammering away over there."

I near most told him right then we didn't have no granpappy no more, but I didn't reckon that was a kindly thing to do before he even had a chance to settle. "It's too quiet everywhere." After I said that, I wondered would he ask why, so I quick said what came to mind. "It's good to see you." Made me red-faced to say such as that, but I meant it. "We need you here." I pushed open Rayford's gate.

"I forgot it don't squeal no more." Rayford had been staring, and it came to me he likely didn't recognize Hugh at first neither. As we got closer, Rayford set down his whittling knife and wood and poured a cup of water. Hugh hobbled over and Rayford handed it to him. Then he leaned closer to Hugh and took a couple of whiffs and then he smiled and made a bunch of loud noises, like he figured out who that hobbledy bum was. I don't know as Rayford figured he'd been gone a long time and just now came back, but while Hugh drank, Rayford stood and gimped around. I was afeared Hugh would get riled, but he just laughed. "That's right, Rayford. I got a new way of walking."

Hugh drained the cup, and held it out and Rayford filled it again. He likely figured Hugh had just gone off to Harpersville to get supplies. I reckon Rayford sees time like a dog might. He don't know was it ten minutes or ten weeks that you been gone, but now you're home and he's happy.

Hugh put the cup back down and picked up a coon setting on Rayford's stand. "There's lots of carving going on out at the war at night, but I ain't never seen nothing near as good as what Rayford makes. War surely makes you look at things different." He picked up a half-made flower from Rayford's bucket. "You think that your life is what's regular, that life is the same for everyone. It takes being away to see the good parts of it." He put the carving back and rested his hand on Rayford's arm. Rayford looked at it, and didn't move, but something changed. Or maybe I just imagined it. Hugh tucked his crutch back under his armpit and headed for the house. "Let's go see Ma."

"Joram's home, too," I said as I closed the gate and caught up to him.

"Met Mr. Foster up on McCreedy's Hill and heard all about it. He said as how you were being stubborn and I was to ask you about it."

"Well, now you're here, it don't matter, none. You see Mule afore you left?"

"Yep. Soon's he can, he's heading north. We heard there ain't much work round here. He told me to say hey to y'all. You get the cotton in?"

"In and cleaned, but there weren't much of it. We gave it to Mr. Foster to sell, but there ain't no places taking it as yet. Fosters been inviting us to live with them, but I promised Pa I'd take care of Rayford. Seeing as how he ain't never lived no place else, I'm afeared it might not set right with him if we was to leave. I reckon that's the stubborness Mr. Foster had in mind."

"Ma's hearing gone bad? Seems like she would've been out greeting me by now."

"I'll go tell her we got a visitor. Just so you know, she looks a might different. She's tired and sleeps a lot. Might perk her up to see you again."

"She been like this long?"

"I reckon it started afore Melanie's birthday. After them Yankee soldiers got lost and found our place and--" Hugh came to a dead stop and grabbed my arm.

"What?"

"I didn't mean to let it out so soon. No need to get riled."

"They hurt you?" I shook my head, and he looked me in the eye, like as if to see was I telling the truth.

"They broke dishes and took some of the food that was in the house, and they laughed at Rayford, is all."

"That don't sound like the Yankees I been fighting. Your face says you got more to tell."

"One of them got hold of my arm, a mean, smelly boy, not much older than you." I told about that day, and the soldier who made the others leave. Hugh looked hard at me.

"They didn't lay a hand on you?"

"No. That one...." I near most told him how he came back on Melanie's birthday, but something stopped me. I didn't think through it all at the time, but I reckoned some part of my brain knew a man who just came back from fighting Yankees wasn't like to look kindly on one that broke into his house, even if he was the one that kept the others from hurting me.

"That one what?"

"Well...like I said...he made the others leave." I expected Hugh to ask more about it. He scratched his cheek, then rubbed his hand over his hair. He got a worried look on his face.

"I reckon it wasn't right for me to head out. Truth to tell, I didn't know Mule was coming with me. I made it halfway to Harpersville and I heard a hollering. Mule had been chasing me most of the way. I reckoned I'd get us into town and send him home the next day. We got there and I signed up without no problem, but I told them Mule was too young. He fought me some on it, but then he let it go. One of the recruiting men, he gave us a place to stay for the night seeing as how the next day there was a regiment leaving.

"Come morning I made Mule come with me to Wright's store and asked if Mule could stay 'til there was someone come into town that could give him a ride home. Mule acted like he saw the wisdom in that way of thinking, so I headed to the hotel and was eating the breakfast they set out for us and there was Mule, ready to go. I should've whupped him and sent him back, but I could see he had his heart set on it and I reckoned he would've hid out til I was gone and come along anyways. I didn't think it would get to where the war came down here. Reckon you wrote to Pa that Mule and me joined up."

"Ma said not to. Didn't want him to worry."

"You hear from him lately?"

"We got a letter late October, but it was a might tattered, like as if it been tossed around for a long time."

"He say where he was?"

"East of here. He wrote how kindly folks fed them and they had a three-legged dog that came to be everyone's pet. He didn't have nothing bad to say."

"That sounds like Pa. He's one for looking on the good side of things. I don't reckon he'll look kindly on me and Mule leaving, but seeing as how I am a man now and done my duty, there ain't no call for him to get all het up over it." He looked at his crooked leg and moved his foot back and forth, like he was looking to see did it still work. "You wait on waking Ma. I'd like to clean up some. You reckon Pa's got a shirt here I could wear?"

"I'll look."

"And britches. My other pair got tore up and bloodied bad when that mule fell on my leg. Been wearing these Yankee clothes nigh onto two weeks. I was afeared some rebel soldier might take a shot at me, so I carried a white flag until I got to Harpersville where people know me."

I found one old raggedy set of Pa's clothes and sniffed for sign of him, but all I smelled was lye soap. The britches would be long and the shirt would hang on Hugh, but leastways they were clean. He took a bucket of water and the looking glass back by the woodshed and while he shaved off his beard and cleaned up, I dug carrots and turnips and set them at the edge of the garden. I brought out the last of the ham from Foster's, and thought how Hugh could go hunting and fill it back up with venison and rabbit and squirrel. I put dried plums in water and set peas to boiling while I cooked the vegetables and ham. When everything was ready, I brung Rayford in and set him at the table. Hugh was already setting there with a thinking look on his face. He didn't look like a hobbledy bum no more with his beard gone, but he didn't look like the Hugh that left in the spring, neither. He was lankier, not as tall as Pa, but near most as thin, and there was a more growed up look about his eyes. I went in to get Ma.

"I ain't hungry," she said, her voice not much more than a whisper.

"Well, we got a visitor."

"Melanie? "

"You best get dressed and not keep everybody waiting," I said, like it *could* be Melanie.

When she walked into the kitchen a few minutes later, Hugh stood. "Hey, Ma," he said, and I looked at him as he took a step toward her. "Ma!" I turned to see her crumble like the life had gone right out of her. Hugh lunged and caught her and sat her in a chair, gentle, near most falling himself.

He grabbed the table and pushed himself back into his chair. I reckon she scairt him some. I brought a cup of water over and wet my hands and patted her face til she opened her eyes. I closed her hand around the cup and held it to her mouth. She drank it up, then wiped her face on her sleeve and looked acrost the table at Hugh, setting there nearly as white as she was. Her eyes had a look like Rayford's, like they were seeing something behind them instead of in front of them.

"You hungry, Will?" she asked, her voice soft and sleepy-sounding. It put me in mind of that day she told me how Pa tried to teach Rayford to shave.

"Ma! I'm Hugh!" But Ma wasn't listening. Or leastways she wasn't hearing.

"Ah, Will. Where you been? I missed you. You look good." She smiled at him and her eyes crinkled in the corners, like Melanie's. My stomach rolled and I saw Hugh had the same feeling. "Don't he look good, Sarah?" She turned to me but I reckon it was her long-dead sister, the red-haired one, that she was seeing. Hugh's eyes were big and he pulled back in his chair.

"C'mon, Ma," I said, taking the cup from her hand. I didn't know what else to do so I took her back to her room and set her on the bed. "You rest awhile, Ma."

"Seeing Will makes me wobbly in the knees," she said, and she giggled. Giggled like a girl. "He's sweet on me, Sarah, I know he is. Now you tell him them flowers was real pretty, and I surely will take a walk with him after prayer meeting on Sunday."

"Ma, that is your son in the kitchen, not your husband," I said in a loud voice, but her ears weren't hearing any better than her eyes were seeing. She laid her head back on her pillow with a smile on her face, and closed her eyes, and I went back to the kitchen.

Hugh hissed in loud whispers when I came back in. "She's out of her head! How long she been like this?" He stood and grabbed his crutch and hobbled over to the window and back, three, four times.

"It comes in spells."

"How long they last?"

"It's different every time. Could be a few minutes or a day. She don't hardly eat. Says she ain't hungry, so it don't surprise me none she's so weak. You best get out of them clothes. I'll see if Mule left anything. I reckon they'll be too small, but…it might could help."

Hugh stared at the door. "I ain't had a decent meal in weeks and I ain't gone leave this table til I'm full up. Then I'll bring up water and get a fire going out by the wash pot tonight."

I near most cried to hear him say such as that. Maybe I won't have to grow up after all.

34

The Haircut

It's been a week since Hugh came home. Ma couldn't get it in her head that he ain't Pa, so he moved to Foster's for a few days til his beard grows back. Melanie is working up some of Mr. Foster's old shirts and britches to fit him. Mid-week I told Ma we got word from Hugh and he'd be home soon. She got sprightly and asked about Mule. I said he was heading north to find work. She told of dreams on Pa, and some color came to her face. "It's a sign," she said. "Will is gone be home soon, too." She never said nothing about seeing him in the kitchen, so I reckon she thought it was a dream. She had a good day—got up and ate regular, then made biscuits. Come afternoon she sewed on the shirt she's making for Pa from some madder-dyed homespun she pulled from a chest in her room.

I thought as how the news of Hugh helped her get back to her old self, but this morning she wouldn't get up. It turned out to be for the best. As I was shaving Rayford, Hugh came home. He stopped by the looking glass hanging on the wall and rubbed his beard. "You reckon this is better?" he asked.

"You're still lanky, like Pa."

"These clothes from Foster's help, don't they?"

"But your hair still looks like Pa's. Wavy like his."

"Hmm," he said, nodding, and running his hand over his hair. "I'm better looking, though." He turned to me with a grin on his face. Of a sudden, a laugh spewed out of me and I recollected that day Ma slammed her fork down and it hit her plate. I told about it, and we took to laughing til my belly hurt. We ain't had near enough laughing around here.

"Soon as you finish with him, you best cut my hair. Hurry. Afore Ma gets up." He stood there watching me like as if his eyes could make me go faster, but I ain't accustomed to no one watching me and I reckon it made me go slower, and Hugh took to pacing back and forth like a caged animal.

"Might help some if you was to shave Rayford now that you're back."

"You think I don't recolllect what Pa said in that letter? Be-sides, I see you're doing a fine job, and I don't aim to–"

He stopped short and I turned and looked at him. He had a sneaky look on his face that I didn't like.

"I don't aim to go against what Pa said."

But the way he said that made me uneasy, like he had more to say but wasn't about to say it. My brain was ready to think on it, but Hugh was right. I needed to get his hair cut afore Ma got up, so I had to let it go, but I tried to put it in the back of my head to work on later.

When I got done with Rayford I set him in the parlor. Time I came back to the kitchen, Hugh was in the tall chair with Rayford's shaving towel round his neck. I picked up the scissors and gave his hair a look. At first I didn't see as how it would be any harder than cutting Rayford's, so I took off a couple inches then gave him the looking-glass.

"No, you got to cut it close to my head. I still look like Pa. Get it so it looks more like how the Driscoll boys have theirs—so my ears show and my neck, too."

"But I ain't never cut hair short, just kept up with the trimming."

"Can't be that hard."

I picked up a hunk and put the scissors close to his head, but I got weak-kneed and pulled the scissors back. I cut it so a bit of his neck showed in spots, and you could see the bottoms of his ears, then I handed him the looking-glass again.

He made a face at what he saw, then looked at me and looked back at himself again. "If I warn't a growed-up man, I reckon I'd set to crying. Can't you do better than that?"

"Well it's a different matter entire to start with long hair instead of taking off what just grew back."

"Here," he said, grabbing the shears and handing me the looking-glass, "hold this." I put it up in front of him and he cut some hair from above his forehead. "See? What I done up front, do on my whole head, but make it the same all over."

I took a deep breath and looked at how he cut it above his forehead, then set out to do the rest of it. It wasn't near as easy to do a whole head that way. I'd start good on one side and work my way around but time I got to the other side of his head, it didn't match, so I went back and tried to get it the same. Three, four times I did that til finally I had it near most the same on both sides, of which it was because there wasn't no more left to cut. Leastways he didn't look like Pa no more. Truth to tell, he didn't look like Hugh neither. He looked like a sorry boy that had too much hair on his chin and not enough on his head.

Hugh held up the looking-glass again and rubbed his head and made an awful face. "That is the worst haircut I ever seen," he said shaking his head.

"Hugh?!"

Ma stood in the doorway looking more like a scarecrow than a woman. I got used to seeing her boney-looking, but she looked like she'd gotten even thinner since Hugh came back.

"Yeah, Ma," he said, jumping up with a smile. "I'm home. Got a bum leg to show for it, but leastways I'm home." He hobbled over and hugged her. With his arms around her she looked even smaller, like she was wasting away, but leastways she knew her son.

35

A Fine Gift

Hugh took Foster's gun and went hunting this afternoon. Ma slept and I sat in the parlor with Rayford, thinking on what gift I could make for Fosters seeing as how they had invited us to their place for Christmas dinner. Every idea that came to mind had to do with knitting or crocheting or such, of which I don't like to do none of that. I suspicion the Lord had in mind to make me a boy, but Ma wanted another girl like Melanie, so He made me look like a girl, but be like a boy. I reckon that's what comes of all this time to think. Truth to tell, I am more like Pa than Ma: I got a good aim on a gun, I am shaving off whiskers every morning, and I am not one for fancy work like most womenfolk. Granny tried to teach me, but my hands didn't want to learn. When Granny took out her knitting, them needles hopped back and forth like long skinny crickets that had got stuck to that yarn. She'd tell me to keep an eye on this and put my hand so and move the yarn like that so as to make a stitch. Then she'd say, "Now you try it," and she'd hand everything over to me and first off I'd get my fingers tangled. Before I could get my hands around them needles proper, one was like to escape, like as if it knew I didn't have no business messing with such as that. But only one idea came to me for a gift for Fosters and it had to do with knitting. I suspicioned if I set my mind to it, I could recollect one or two of the easy stitches.

I found Granny's needles and some yarn in the chest in the loft and after some tinkering one stitch came back to me. An hour later I had a blanket a foot square, more or less, of which that was plenty big enough. I couldn't recollect how to finish it off, but after some studying, I came up with a way to tie knots to keep all the stitches from letting loose when I pulled out the needles. That edge was some uneven, and there was a place or two where the stitches were too big or too small, but by stretching and smoothing it, I got that blanket near most square. Lessen you looked close, of which I didn't reckon them kindly Fosters and Melanie was like to do, it came out to be a right fine piece of work.

Next I got the carved wagon that I'd tied the chickens to, took off the wheels, broke up a handful of straw, laid it in the wagon and set the blanket on top. Then I picked through a barrel of Rayford's old carvings out in the barn. Every so often he gets stuck on carving one thing and we keep out the best two or three and put the others in that barrel. Near the bottom I found a half dozen baby carvings that Rayford made one time after prayer meeting when Miss Carrie Pritchart had brung her new baby and sat in front of us. It was the onliest time I know of that Pa had to haul Rayford outside before the meeting was over. Rayford takes to babies something awful, so as he can't just look at them peaceably, but he wants to get his hands on them. I reckon he thinks a baby is like a kitten that you can hold and pet and all such as that and its ma don't mind a lick, like when Rayford holds Cleopatra's kittens. He'd sooner jump off a cliff than hurt them babies but there ain't nary a ma around that ever lets him hold one.

I couldn't figure why Miss Carrie sat right in front of us, excepting she was kindly and took to Rayford some and maybe she thought he'd be happy just to look at that little baby. Halfway through the preaching, she brought the baby up to her shoulder. Rayford squealed and reached over, just to pat it on the head I reckon. Pa suspicioned Miss Carrie wouldn't take kindly to such as that and pulled Rayford's arm back, and then there was a tussle and the end of it was Pa took Rayford outside and waited til we came out and we headed home directly. Of a sudden we had little carved babies everywhere, til Pa picked up a piece of wood and mooed, of which it wasn't like Pa to do since he always let Rayford do what he liked, but I reckon Pa saw a need of it. Time Rayford had made two or three cows, he had forgot about them babies and got on to other things like he always does.

When I set the carved baby on the blanket in the wagon it had some resemblance to pictures of the manger they laid the baby Jesus in when he was being born in that stable. Then I took one of Rayford's carvings of which I reckon was meant to be Preacher Abernathy because the mouth was kind of big and wide open, and one that was a gal, of which I am a might sure was meant to be Missy's Ma because of the way he had done the hair up all braided and stuck to her head. I set the two carvings on the side board next to the baby to be the pa—Joseph—and the ma—Mary. Rayford never carved camels nor sheep, but I found a mule and a cow and two polecats and a wild turkey and a possum and three coons. All set up it looked near as nice as the Bible pictures.

After dinner a wagon came down the road and only because Melanie was with him did I get the idea that man whose face was covered with hair was Joram Foster, come back from the war. Joram helped Melanie off the wagon and she ran over and gave me a hug like always, excepting she just used one arm and kept the other behind her back. Then Joram came at me and I near most ducked, but he caught me and hugged me good, of which that is not his way. Before they got hitched Missy's Ma said they'd likely court til they both fell into their graves lessen Melanie took the first move and she ain't much more bold than he is. I suspicion Melanie asked did he want to ask her to get hitched, and he nodded, and Melanie said she was willing. Joram ain't that way with Melanie no more but he's always been that way with me, so that hug came as a surprise. I ain't been too happy there is a war, but seeing as how both Hugh and Joram came back more kindly, leastways some good has come of it.

Melanie's hand came out from behind her back with a little box wrapped in pretty paper with trees drawn on it and tied with a red ribbon. "But it ain't Christ--" I started to say, and Melanie grabbed my hand and pulled me around to the back of the house while Joram headed to the barn where Hugh was working. On the way she asked where Ma was.

"She's in the parlor embroidering away on a cloth that I

reckon she will turn into a handkerchief. She has stitched 'William' on it." I was headed to the back door, but Melanie grabbed my arm.

"Open it here."

Now there ain't no part of Melanie that is mean, but when she told me to open that package there was a look on her face that took the fun out of it, more like she was telling me to gather eggs quick before the hens ran off with them. "Hurry!" she said and she sidled up to the back door and leaned against it, like as if to keep anyone from coming out.

As I untied the twine on the package I glanced at her seeing as how she was wringing her hands like as if a snake would jump out at me. I near most handed it back and told her to open it herself, excepting that Melanie is not the kind to play pranks. I unwrapped the paper careful and kept my face way back, and of a sudden, I was holding what I didn't think I'd see til the war was long over.

"Now you and Rayford can paint pictures to surprise Ma and Miss Clara for Christmas," Melanie said. Of a sudden, I thought as how we could put color on them carved pieces I was giving to Fosters. Seemed like the whole world got brighter as I looked at that little box of paints with two nice new brushes, right up until I recollected what Rayford did to the sideboard.

"What if Ma don't let us do no painting?"

"I got that all figured," Melanie said, her eyes all a sparkle. "I'll take Ma to Fosters today, and Joram will come and get you and Hugh and Rayford on Christmas morning."

There wasn't no more talk on it, and an hour later they headed out of the yard. As they rounded the curve of McCreedy's

Hill, Hugh went back to the barn and told me not to come out there so I reckon he was working on a contraption that had to do with Christmas. I ran to the woodshed, took the paints from their hiding place behind the west woodpile, set up the table, and brought Rayford in. When he saw the paints and paper he snorted and squealed and skittered around the table like a happy hog. I generally hush him up when he takes to acting like that so Ma don't lay into him, but with her gone, I let him go til it looked like he'd knock something over. Then I set him down and straightaway he recollected how to use them paints and how to clean the brush.

I set to painting the pa carving for the manger and didn't see nor hear nothing til I painted the last of the shoes and looked up and at the same time Rayford set down a polecat. It was a wonder. He had painted the stripe down the back and the nose and eyes and such like as if he had been learned by them folks that paint pictures in books. It looked so real I could near most smell that polecat, excepting that Rayford had painted it green with a white stripe. I had in mind to tell him polecats are black with a white stripe, but Rayford knows that. Truth to tell, he had mixed in some black so it looked more like the way it is on animals, like how sometimes their fur is white but the tips are grey or tan.

I picked up the ma carving and time I finished painting her, Rayford had done up a coon that was mostly yellow but had some blue and white, and a purple mule that had some grey mixed in. I reckon he thought as how we had all these nice colors, he might as well use them. Now if I had me a camel and a sheep like what I saw in that picture in the Bible, maybe I wouldn't feel so kindly about Rayford picking his own colors for animals, but seeing as how we didn't have all the regular animals, I reckon it didn't make no matter that we didn't have the regular colors neither. I could see as how some folks might think it was Rayford that got it right and the Lord that got it wrong. And I ain't seen Rayford look so happy in a long time.

36

Christmas Dinner

We hadn't much more than got in Foster's kitchen and said our hellos when Melanie pulled me aside. "I got something to show you," she whispered, grabbing my hand. It seemed a might peculiar, but everyone was talking and carrying on about the food and the weather and all such as that, so I traipsed out of the room after Melanie and when we got to the door of her bedroom she closed it and set me on the bed.

"Me and Pa Foster wrote a letter to the Confederate Army," she said pulling open a dresser drawer. "We asked could they look for Pa since we ain't heard from him. This came last week," she said, handing a letter to me. I held it for a minute without moving. I didn't know as I wanted to read it.

"Go ahead. It ain't bad news."

"But if it was good news you would've told me already."

"It ain't neither." I looked to her face—for comfort, I reckon—and she nodded at the paper in my hands.

The letter said Pa was likely in a Yankee prison up north and that the Confederate Army is looking for him and lots of others still missing. It didn't make me feel a lick better.

"We have to keep on praying," Melanie said. "And not give up hope."

I tried to think on something kindly and hopeful to say back, but what came to mind was Pa telling me the north was a mighty big place and how it got cold in the winter, with water freezing and everything getting covered up with snow. Mr. Foster had got hold of a newspaper a few weeks back that had a piece on the prison southeast of here called Andersonville. It said how Yankees are dying left and right from starvation and sickness. I shivered to think on Pa in a place such as that and my stomach balled up hard. If it weren't Christmas with a parlor full of folks that had their minds on celebrating, I reckon I would've gone off in a corner and cried. I handed her the letter, and as she put it back in her drawer, I got up to leave, but she grabbed my arm.

"Has Ma been acting peculiar at home?"

I shrugged, still fighting tears from thinking about Pa.

"I mean does she act like Pa is still here, or like they are courting?"

That took me out of the sadness, some, and I made a face like as if to say I never heard of such a thing, seeing as how if I did, Melanie'd like to tie me up at their place and not let us go home.

"Maybe she just had a bad day." Melanie put her hand on my arm. "We'll find Pa."

My mouth smiled and I nodded, like as if I believed her, but the rest of my body headed down a path of worry.

When we went back in the kitchen Ma was setting plates at the table and the grin on her face got me to wondering was she just happy to be with us all at Fosters or was she seeing Pa in her head. Melanie had done up her hair so she looked better than she had in a long time. "Ma," I said, loud enough to bring her back, "Your hair looks nice braided and put up like that." Her grin got bigger and she set another plate on the table, but she didn't speak a word.

Soon the table was laid with fresh venison and carrots and rutabagas and stewed onions and sweet potatoes and biscuits flecked with green, likely some new thing from Miss Clara's daughters, of which it gave a new smell to them, peculiar, but to my liking. There was a fresh pitcher of thick cream from their milk cow, Brownie, to go with the apple cobbler I brought and the plum pudding made by Melanie, of which it steamed up the kitchen with a spicy sweetness. There might have been some thought of sadness for all the folks that weren't round that table, but Miss Clara kept up a chatter on the food and the mild winter and tender venison, and how it warmed her heart every time she looked over on the sideboard at those two kittens a playing that Rayford carved and kindly gave to her. Seemed like we went on eating and talking until my belly was set to explode like a stick of dynamite. When Miss Clara said we might wait on our sweets, I wasn't a lick sorry.

We headed into the parlor for the Christmas celebration and Mr. Foster brought out his fiddle, of which I haven't heard him play it since before Pa left. We helped Miss Clara sit at the piano and she played songs and we sang Christmas carols and Rayford got to caterwauling with us like he does sometimes at prayer meeting. It came to me as how we ain't been to prayer meeting since Pa left. I don't reckon they even been holding them. I'll have to ask Mr. Foster on it. I can't say as I miss it none, but I reckon it wouldn't be so all fired bad to lay eyes on Missy again.

After the singing, out came the gifts. Seeing as how there ain't been no extries these days, I didn't know as we would have much, but I reckon it will take more than a war to stop Christmas. When Fosters unwrapped the nativity scene, I told how it was Rayford's idea to paint the polecat green and the coon yellow and blue and the mule purple and I was sorry he hadn't made no camels nor sheep but they all said it was the best nativity scene they ever saw.

I gave Melanie a mix of dried leaves to make a tea to rinse her hair, and I put in the ribbon Pa gave me, seeing as how her hair is more the kind that goes with a ribbon. I didn't have a whole lot of sweets left, but most of what I had, I split up and gave to Joram, Hugh, and Rayford.

Fosters gave Ma a shiny new green bowl. There was a present for Rayford—his own set of paints—and even though he ain't one for talking or handshaking, the look on his face was the most thanks I ever saw on anyone. Course we had to set him up for painting lickety split, but I reckon Fosters had that in mind all along.

I got a box of writing papers from Fosters that Miss Clara said could be for painting or drawing or writing or whatever. Melanie gave me a book called *The Rose of Georgia*, about a kindly woman who went around to teach children that couldn't get to regular school. And the Fosters and Melanie gave Hugh a walking stick that I reckon is store bought and has carvings on it, not likenesses, but curlicues and such. I aim to ask Miss Clara can we get hooked sticks like that for Rayford to carve and maybe we could trade them for things we need, seeing as how we still ain't sold the cotton.

Hugh gave Ma a butter churn with a spring in the dasher that made it bounce up and down so churning would be easier. Ma always thought his tinkering was a waste of time, so it done Hugh good to see her crow on a thing he made. He gave Mr. Foster and Joram pipe holders with a place in the bottom to catch the ashes that opens up when you press it. For Miss Clara and Melanie and me, he made pretty little wooden boxes with hinges.

Melanie got a store-bought calico dress from Joram, and new hankies, and a book from the Fosters. Mr. Foster gave Miss Clara a bottle of perfume, of which it was a might spindly to my eyes, but he said it came from France. I reckon what happened next was the best part of the whole day. Miss Clara give Mr. Foster a shirt with ivory buttons. He asked how she sewed that shirt, and she said she came up with the idea mid-summer and kept at it, slow but sure. I reckon tears came to his eyes, but he was blinking so hard, we didn't know certain. He went over to Miss Clara and gave her the biggest hug—not a hug that's done with quick, but one that lasted for a minute or two—and, excepting for Ma who still held on to that bowl like it saved her life, and Rayford who was smelling his paints, you might've thought we were chopping onions, there was so much eye blinking going on.

A knock at the door put an end to it, and in walked the Driscolls, Mr. Driscoll, Miss Arnetta, and their sons, all six of them, including Silas and Jeremy back from the war, both a might thinner, but each whole, excepting for a scar along Jeremy's forehead. The Driscoll's are a quiet lot, and even though their land is only across the creek from us, their homestead is on the northwest corner. You can't get to it from McCreedy's Road, only from the Harpersville Road. You have to head west, then it's a ways back in, and once you're there all you have is a pack of mumbly boys, near most afeared of their own shadows, so we ain't mixed with them much, although they are kindly folk. The younger boys sat quiet, all in a row on the floor in front of the fireplace like stood-up logs, and they done it in such a way that I reckon their ma put the idea in their head.

We went back to singing Christmas carols again, and I recollected the Driscolls had got a name for singing. I heard tell it's a thing they do regular, all of them together singing parts, and truth to tell, with them extry voices, we sounded like a prayer meeting full of folks. I reckon we did right by them carols and time my throat got parched, Miss Clara called us for sweets.

Arnetta Driscoll had brought a cider cake, and laid that out along with the cobbler and pudding. She and Melanie dished up a bit of each one, topped them all with plum pudding sauce, then poured on the cream. I reckon even fancy kings and queens and the richest Yankee that ever lived don't have nothing better.

While we all filled ourselves to the point of misery, there were stories about the war by Joram and Hugh, and once they got to talking, Silas and Jeremy joined right in. I reckon being at the war gave them a chance to use their tongues, and they got accustomed to it, seeing as how Jeremy turned out to be the biggest storyteller of all. He told of a time they were in camp with

some boys from North Carolina. One of them was always brag-
ging on how he was so strong, so they told him to pick up a load
of wood that was on a wagon. Course they didn't tell him they
had nailed it down, and he pulled and pulled but he couldn't lift
it. Jeremy said that fellow never bragged on how strong he was
again, and he looked at me and smiled, of which I don't reckon
he ever looked straight at me in my life. It was peculiar.

The stories and laughing and talking went on until the sun
set, then Driscolls took their leave with thanks all around, and it
was time for Joram and Melanie to bring us back. It was a hard
thing to quit that house where I ain't ever heard nothing but
kindly words, and ain't never seen nothing but smiles and goodness. Miss Clara has her trials and I reckon they all get feisty at
that place too, but there is a feeling that comes on a body when
you walk through that door and I aim to carry it with me. Some
day I'll have me a house like that, where people want to come
and want to stay. I ain't figured how to go about it, seeing as
how I ain't never getting hitched or raising a mess of children,
but it will be a thing to think on in front of the fire on a winter
afternoon.

Hugh climbed up on the buckboard with Joram, and Melanie
and I sat on the back of the wagon with Rayford and Ma. Melanie and me talked most of the way home, but I heard Hugh and
Joram say something about prisoners and I had one ear on their
talk. I couldn't make it all out, but the jist of it was there are
fellows called bribes who can get folks out of prison, and they
are real big, from what I heard, or leastways the big ones are the
best. When we got to our place, Hugh and Joram went off to the
barn. I milked Belle and fed her and the chickens, while Melanie

put Rayford to bed and undid Ma's braid and brushed her hair. When I came in, Ma said she was tired and she headed to bed. Melanie started a fire in the parlor, so we sat and had us a nice visit, and we talked on how Hugh had growed up some since he left and all such as that. I said as how she must be right happy Joram came home, and she smiled and got red-faced. I ain't never getting hitched, but it surely does set well with Melanie. I reckon an hour passed til Hugh and Joram came in. They set and visited a spell, too, then Melanie and Joram headed back.

After they left, Hugh went in to sleep in Granpappy's bed, like he's been doing seeing as how it's hard for him to climb the ladder to the loft with his bum leg. I put out the candles and went to bed. Half an hour later I took my quilt, wrapped up in it, and went out in Rayford's garden. I looked up at the sky and watched thin clouds drift past the stars like flying curtains. In my head, I wrote out a message for Pa and floated it up and dropped it in the stars. I saw Pa fly up there, pick it out, and read it. Then he smiled and swooped down beside me. Of a sudden, I swear I felt his arms around my shoulders and heard him wish me Merry Christmas.

37

We Got To Have Us A Talk

New Year's Day, 1865

It is a new year. If Pa was here, he would've set me down this morning and told me we had to start it right. "What is the best thing that happened to you last year?" he'd ask and I'd tell him it was likely the first time I laid eyes on them paints Melanie gave me for my birthday. Then Pa would say, "Did you do right by that best thing?" And I would say, "Yes, I done right. I shared them with Rayford and we had us a time and made presents. And there might even be more good to come of them if we can paint Rayford's carvings and sell them up north." I got to wondering if folks will take to green polecats and purple mules. I'll have to ask Miss Clara.

Then Pa would ask, "What was the worst thing that happened last year?" I would say when he up and joined the Confederate Army. And he'd ask, "Did you do right by that bad thing?" I would think on how it went after he left, how it took awhile for me to put my mind to it, but when Rayford got lost, I went after him, and I'm shaving him and caring for him. And I'm caring for Ma, too, most days. I reckon there are times when Ma is sleeping that I just sit when I could be mending stockings and working in the garden and making biscuits and being more careful with stews and washing clothes better and such. And Pa would say, "Well it's a fresh new year. We'll try to do more of the good and we'll forget the times we didn't do right by a thing, excepting that if the chance comes again, we won't do it the same way." I pretended he was looking at me with his face full of love and I told him I would try my best to do right by the good and the bad of things. I wish I knew where he was so I could tell him in a letter.

I got Rayford ready for the day and set some shucky beans to boiling so they'd be tender time dinner came. That talk with Pa was still in my head and got me to thinking he'd likely ask me to be extry kindly to Ma and do for her some. I picked up the brush with a mind to braid her hair and if that set right with her, I'd help her get dressed, and if she took to that, I'd take them smelly sheets off her bed and wash em, and get the broom in there and pull down the cobwebs and sweep the floor and such. I reckon I should've done it before but excepting for that time after them Yankees came, she chases me out the minute I set foot in there. Since Christmas, she ain't been near so ornery. Truth to tell, she ain't been much of anything except quiet.

Time I got to her door, I heard Hugh holler. I set the brush down and went out the back door. "Shot a deer back in the woods," he said, and I heard the pride in his voice. "You come help me pull it home." I quick looked in on Rayford then headed out and followed Hugh along the path toward the creek. He was moving a might fast, even with a bum leg, but when he hit a stone or a stump sticking out of the ground, it stopped him short and he cussed some. I near most told him to slow down but he don't take to nothing that sounds like pity.

The doe must have been drinking at the creek seeing as how she was laid down alongside it. We gutted her, dragged her back, and Hugh strung her up by the woodshed near the wash pot. He built a fire to keep the wild critters away at night while she hung. The way Hugh tended to it all, even with his leg paining him, it came to me he was a man now. If he got hitched and lived here with his family, we'd have a full house again, like I wished on at Fosters. It put a smile on my face to think of it.

I reckon it was the smell of cooking that got Ma up. She came out like a haint, hair flying wild and her nightgown worn so thin you could near most see through it. It bothered me some that she don't even know it ain't proper to walk around in such as that with menfolk in the house. I took her back in her room and got her dressed, and she let me, like as if she wasn't no more than a child. I brushed her hair and put combs in it, but she was still a sight, all white from staying inside all the time and more spindly-looking than ever.

I'd cooked up the liver with a bit of salt pork and onions, and thought of Pa again, seeing as how it was one of his favorites. He would've been proud of Hugh and me for providing for his family. Ma didn't take naught but liver, and took it twice and ate on it til I reckoned she'd get sick from it. Then she looked at everybody like she didn't never see us before. I took her in the parlor and gave her that pile of stockings to darn. Leastways she is still good at that. I brung Rayford in, too, and there was a time she might've made faces at him or grumbled, but she kept to her darning stockings and Rayford set to his whittling and there weren't nary a sound from neither one of them.

I went back to the kitchen. Hugh was still setting, like he was thinking on things. I reckon seeing as how it was a new year and I was thinking on all what would come, I told Hugh Mr. Foster would help us plant the corn and cotton and maybe we could get us a better crop this year. He laughed—not funning, but mean—like as if I didn't have a lick of sense. Then he aimed his eyes at me like they were torches and he had in mind to burn me down.

"What you want with cotton?" His whispered words came out like a holler. "There ain't no market! Ain't no way to haul it! No place to haul it to. Fosters still got last year's cotton!" He rubbed his chin and quieted some. "You best plant something you can eat and trade for other things. Plant corn to feed a hog or two for butchering in the fall."

"I had in mind we'd grow enough cotton to trade for a mule...to help with planting and get us to town and such. We can't ask Mr. Foster to do our trading forever." He looked away, then turned back with a sad kindness in his eyes that didn't set right with me. He reached across the table and put his hand on mine.

"I didn't mean to get riled and carry on like that. Truth is, it ain't good for you and Rayford and Ma to stay here. Ma ain't right in the head no more, and the rest of her don't look so good neither, like as if she's ailing. You best move on over to Fosters."

"We can handle Ma and Rayford just fine. " I pulled my hand away. "Pa asked me to take care of Rayford and I promised and he didn't say naught about taking him to Fosters." Hugh dropped his head. I went to him and put my hand on his shoulder, but he still didn't look at me. "I'll help. We'll plant the cotton and corn and find us a place to take it in trade for a mule. War or no war, I reckon the mills need cotton."

"Mills are all burned down."

"But up north? And in England? Pa said they buy a lot of our cotton, too. Pa don't want us to give up," Of a sudden, it was all I could do to keep the tears from falling. Hugh looked down, shook his head, then finally looked up at me.

"Tatum, we got to have us a talk," he said. He pushed himself up off the chair and limped over and looked out the window. "I hate to leave you here with Ma and Ra--"

"No! You ain't leaving. There ain't no one to talk to and I can't hunt and fish and take care of Rayford and Ma and put in a garden and do everything else." I didn't care if Ma heard me or not. "If you leave, I might just as well go lay in the creek face down til I'm dead." Tears pushed up in me, and I pushed them back, riled that Hugh would even think of leaving.

"Or you could move to Fosters!" he hissed, looking at me. "I got a plan," he said in a softer voice, then he turned his head back to looking out the window of which that told me it was a plan I wasn't going to like none.

"You ain't leaving," I said again, sniffing back tears.

"Tatum, you got to listen." I folded my arms and made noises and he talked louder so I set to singing "Jesus Sweet and Jesus Mild" like when Rayford's ornery. I sung it through and when he set to talking again, I set to singing. When he stopped I said Pa wouldn't want him to leave and neither would Granpappy and I stomped off and he yelled, "Tatum, look at me." I glanced back, saw his britches were down and shut my eyes quick, but I'd seen where his leg had got tore up, and the bones were crooked, and how the skin pulled over them where it had healed.

"Til Pa gets back, I reckon I'm the man of the family, and I'm willin' to do my part, but I got me a bum leg. I can't hardly sleep at night for the pain and I can't walk everyday like I been doing to find game. Even if there was a place to sell our cotton, I couldn't do the work it takes to raise a crop. You don't like to hear it and I don't like to say it neither, but I'm the one wakes up every day with this leg. It ain't a leg that can do farming no more." He let out a sigh that gave me to think he was near to crying himself. Then he started in again, his voice soft but strong, his words putting me in mind of Pa. "In the war, there was a time or two I got ideas for contraptions that came of some use. I reckon there is a place somewheres that's already got men with two good legs to do the heavy work that would take me on to do ciphering and such as that. Maybe down the line I could come up with a thing or two to make the work faster and easier. I can stand and work some, but there ain't no way I can get around on this leg all day long. There's men that go back to hard work after their leg's been broke, but my leg didn't get set right and that's the difference. Look at my right foot. It ain't going straight like the other one. Look!"

I turned and saw clear how his foot splayed out to the side, and it made me wince to look at it. He pulled up his britches and came to me and put his hands on my shoulders. "Soon as I get the deer butchered and hung for smoking, I'm heading north to get a paying job."

What was worse than hearing those words was knowing he was right. "Where you aim to go?" I asked.

"Got a place in mind." He put his hand in his shirt pocket, pulled out a piece of paper, and handed it to me. "It's a letter from Mule. Mr. Foster picked it up the same day he got the letter from the Confederate Army about Pa. I didn't want to show it til I had things figured out. I hoped my leg'd get better, or leastways I'd get used to the pain, but..."

I took the letter and read:

"To my family,

I reckon Pa and Hugh and Joram is back by now. Write if they ain't. Found a job at this horse ranch in Kentucky. It's hard work, but the food is good and plenty of it. Didn't go further north seeing as how I hear they don't look kindly on rebels and they got no use for us, just like I ain't got no use for Yankees. I reckon it is a hard life there from what I hear. I would send money, but I ain't got much yet and I hear there ain't nothing to buy. I'll save up and you write and tell me what you need. I will try to send it. The man I work for trades at the general store. He gets his goods cheap. If Hugh is home, he might could

try to come here. I reckon, big as this ranch is,
    they'd have a place for him.
Your son and brother,
Mule Wiley

If all this had happened when I was twelve, I would've laid down on the floor and thrown a fit and kicked and hollered til I got my way. But no good would come of it now, and it would only make Hugh feel worse. He took the letter back and held it up.

"I aim to get work at that horse farm, too. After working with mules in the war I got some ideas for contraptions they might could use. If they let me stay on, leastways I could take care of myself. A man's got his pride."

I had my eyes on my hands, but when he said that I looked up. There was a time I never looked ahead, thinking we'd all stay like we were, the Ma and Pa and Granpappy being the growed-up ones and Hugh and Mule being the sons, and me being the child. I reckon Rayford's the only one that ain't changed.

38

I Didn't Hold Naught Against Her

It was likely Bright's Disease that took Ma. Doc Waitly said it had to do with kidneys that didn't work right. Her headaches and being high strung and those pains down low in her back were all part of it. Mr. Foster shook his head, recollecting that day he came by and asked on Ma. "There wasn't nary a thing I could've done to help her," Doc Waitly said, putting his hand on Mr. Foster's shoulder. Then he turned to me. "Your Ma has been headed to this day for years, Tatum. Truth to tell, I didn't reckon she'd make it this long. You best move in with Fosters, now. I hear you been fighting it, but Rayford is too much to take on alone."

Finally, with Hugh gone again, I was the head of us, but of a sudden it was a thing I didn't much care for.

Mr. Foster fetched Melanie and she laid Ma out in the parlor. I asked should I help and she said no. I was glad of it then, but I got to thinking I should've done it anyways so as to let Ma know I didn't hold naught against her. But there was Rayford to care for and the fires to stoke and cooking to be done. Leastways with all her praying and steering clear of funning, Ma is likely in heaven with Granpappy, and it eases me some to think on that.

This morning Fosters came, even Miss Clara, of which she's been getting stronger ever since Jeanette came across an herb woman visiting Harpersville early in the year, who got a name on her healing up in the mountains. She had come down to nurse her son that near most got killed by Yankees. She told Jeanette that Miss Clara should eat a handful of walnuts every day, and take a spoonful of tonic she'd made. I can see it's helped just by looking at her.

There wasn't no funeral, same like with Granpappy. Ma wasn't one for being neighborly, leastways not as far back as I can recollect, so it was only Mr. and Mrs. Driscoll that came by. They paid their respects and stood at the grave with us while Melanie said a piece, then Mr. Foster and Joram lowered the box. Seeing Ma go into the ground set the tears to rolling and brought on a sadness that shook me and took my breath. I recollected the time she talked soft to me when I first shaved Rayford, and the time after them Yankees came and Ma and me sat on her bed and talked some. That was the kind of ma I had always wanted, and just when it looked like she might turn softer and I might get a ma like that, she took to talking out of her head. I reckon my tears had as much to do with losing the chance to have a good ma as losing the one I had.

As we walked back to the house, Melanie's arm came round me, and I felt her readying her thoughts. Right off I told her I'd been taking care of things and we had the venison from the deer Hugh got. "Mr. Foster said Sherman's already through Georgia and into South Carolina. There ain't no need to fear for us."

"Baby, there is gone be a change," she said, her arm tighter, like as if she had a grip on my brain instead of my shoulders. I shrugged loose of her, and she hissed at me. "If I got to drag you to Foster's, so be it." We had got to the porch and I opened the door, but Melanie pulled me back. "It ain't the days that worry me, it's the nights. And it ain't only Yankees. There's men coming back that lost a lot—their homes, their way to make a living, their pride, their good sense. Some come home mean. I've heard tell of it. Now you listen to me, Baby."

"I ain't got my ears stopped up, have I?" I slammed the door.

"I mean you drop that stubbornness and think on my words. I got an idea that might suit us all. Specially since I might be needing your help with the baby."

"What baby?"

"My baby. The one that's gone come to me and Joram."

I should've said something, but my brain must've tipped over in a faint.

"Your mouth is open," she said, and I wrapped her in a hug. Of a sudden, I felt better, like the good part of things had made some headway toward overcoming the bad part again, and it was about time. "Here's my idea," she said, squirming under my hug, but I hung on for dear life. "Baby, you're holding a might tight to me, and I need to breathe."

I let her go, stepped back and gave her a good looking at

to see was she different. I couldn't see no sign to tell a baby was coming, but if Melanie said it was so, it was so. She was still speaking on it, or something, but my brain had got itself uprighted and headed off on thoughts of how Rayford would take to a new baby, and how happy Pa would be, and how I might teach it a thing or two.

"Baby! Did you hear me? I got an idea to let you stay here with Rayford, after a fashion, and still be safe at night."

"I'm listening," I said, but my brain went straight back to thinking on all the things I tried to learn Rayford that never came to naught—like how to shoot a slingshot. He didn't take to it, and when Pa caught me trying to get him to settle a stone and aim and pull back on the leather, he said if Rayford ever did get the hang of it, he might hurt someone and I best let it go. But I reckon I got a teaching streak in me that ain't never had a chance to show itself and was way past ready for it.

"Tatum Louise Wylie. Are you that excited over a baby coming that you can't pay me no mind for one minute?"

"I surely am. I aim to learn it to climb hickory trees and weave honeysuckle baskets . . . and look for sassafras root--"

"Now Baby, you recollect how they start out small and can't do none of that. For a year or two, all they need is caring for. But I'll need help with that, and that's why I got this idea. I see the wisdom in keeping Rayford here for his garden and all what he is accustomed to, but leastways you can spend the nights with us. Since Granpappy passed on and Hugh left, I can't barely sleep for worrying on you. And I don't reckon it's good for me to be worrying so with a baby coming."

I put my loneliness up against the promise I made to Pa

and thought on it. "Me and Rayford'll come back here every morning?"

"Ain't but three miles between us," she said waving her hand off to the south, her eyes smiling. "There'll likely come a time when Major Tom is limp or we get a downpouring, or such as that, when you won't get back for a day or so, but Fosters got a parlor same as here and if Rayford has his quilt to set on and his bucket of carvings, I reckon it will suit him."

"I told Pa I'd care for Rayford. You think I'll still be doing right by that promise?"

"You think Pa'd want to worry on you every night, with him not here to keep watch?"

"Then I'm willing to try it. If Rayford takes to it, we'll keep it up regular." The smile on Melanie's face took hold on my insides and I felt a relief.

"We'll take things so Rayford feels to home—like the shaving stool--" Melanie said.

"And the stand at the head of his bed where he always puts his knife afore he sleeps. You got a place set up for him to sleep?"

"We'll put him in that corner room they been using for storage. It's got two windows so the air can pass through, of which that will be better than the middle room he sleeps in now. And if you ain't against it, you can sleep in the loft."

"I recollect when I first came to visit after you and Joram got hitched, how we slept up there—you and me—when Ma let me come and stay the night." With a baby coming, she'd likely miss Ma more than I would. "Ma ain't been right in the head for a long time. But I was afeared if I owned up to the truth of it, you'd make us leave here."

"I suspicioned as much ever since fall. I put it up to her missing Pa, but even Miss Clara made note of how she didn't look nor act regular."

"I got a thing to say that I need to get out, but I ain't proud to say it."

"What's that?"

"I ain't real sorry Ma's gone. I reckon that makes me evil, but I don't see as how I can change how I feel. There's been a time or two when she's been kindly, and I was glad of it then, but truth to tell, it only made it more clear how she ain't been the kind of ma I wanted. Like Miss Clara. She is always so kindly. Even flat in bed. Ma's always been harsh with me, but of late—with her talking on courting Pa and calling me Sarah—she's been more like a stranger than a ma."

Melanie aimed her eyes on her hands and put them together like she was thinking on what I said.

"You and Ma were cut from the same cloth—leastways when it came to knitting and cooking and such as that. I took after Pa—even Granpappy said so. But I'm sorry on your account that she ain't here, and that she can't see her first grandbaby."

"I been trying to look on it somewhat like how I looked on Granpappy's passing," Melanie said, her eyes as soft and sad as her voice. "It eased their pain and they're in a place of comfort now. Ma was down to skin and bones and she was gray as old wood. I hope she's found peace." She took a deep breath and put her hand on her stomach. "Makes this baby more of a blessing, giving us new life to think on and keep us looking ahead."

For all that she took to the same things as Ma, she sounded like Pa, certain. I reckon she got the best of both of them.

39

A Different Plan

I ain't never moving Rayford to another place again. If ever I take off to look for Pa or visit Hugh and Mule, Rayford is staying right here at Foster's with Melanie.

The first night I didn't get a lick of sleep. After supper at our place Joram came to get us with the wagon so we could take Rayford's night stand and his quilts and pillow. He likely thought it was a celebrating and we were headed to Fosters for eating and would come back home for sleeping. He ate like usual, then we took him into Foster's parlor, of which it is a lot like ours but bigger and is a sight better looking with a picture on the wall and a rug on the floor and such. It didn't have his twig chair, of which we bring that in for the winter, but we had his bucket of wood and set the quilt over one of Foster's parlor chairs so he'd have a soft place to sit that was like at home, and we moved him close to one side of the fireplace. Miss Clara sat on the other side seeing as how she always likes to be by the fire for the warmth of it, howsomever she no longer sits with a quilt over her lap. She took to fussing with her fancy work and Rayford sat and looked at the fire, of which their hearth has a ledge on it and I reckon that didn't set right with him. After some time of him sitting there I picked out a half-finished critter that could have been a bird or a chicken, and pulled his knife out of the pouch and handed it all to him and told him to get whittling. He took the knife, but then rested his hand on his thigh and stared at that fire, like as if to say we weren't going to fool him—we had the hearth set up wrong.

Melanie had some stitching in her hands, Pa Foster was cleaning his gun, and Joram worked a tool that made marks on a leather belt—to gussy it up some, I reckon. I picked up a basket I'd just started, of which that is the only kind of fancy work I can keep my mind and fingers on, both. I worked at it, but mostly my eyes were on Rayford who kept looking at that fire. It worried me some, but I reckoned he'd come round and get to where Foster's fire was the regular one at night and ours was the one that wasn't the same. Leastways he wasn't ornery, of which I was grateful, seeing as how Foster's have been so kindly and have tried hard to make us feel to home at their place.

There was some talking, mostly from Melanie and Miss Clara and me, about books and such as that. Thoughts came on Pa or Granpappy or even Ma, but I kept them to myself. Time passed, an hour or so I reckon, and Miss Clara said she was ready to turn in. Mr. Foster said he was some tired, too, then everyone stirred and set things aside, but Rayford still stared at the fire. I put his knife back in the pouch and took the half-finished bird from his hand and put it back in the bucket. I took him to the outhouse, and in the dark with just a lantern to light the way along with a smell that don't change much one outhouse to another, he didn't put up a fuss. When we came back in I took him into his new two-windowed bedroom. He tried to look at everything but directly I unbuttoned his shirt and unhitched his pants and got him undressed and pulled his nightshirt on over his head—of which all those things were the same as usual—so as to keep his attention away from what was not.

Then I took his hand and pushed it over to the night stand we'd brought from home and I tried to open his fingers so he'd set the knife down. He pulled his hand away and held tight to it in its pouch, then stood and walked from the bed to the wall over and over. Then he sat on his bed and looked to where Granpappy's bed would have been if we were at home.

"This is for the best, Rayford, and you're just gone have to get accustomed to it." He generally looks up when I talk, but not this time. I sat next to him and sang and held the lantern up to his face to see did his eyes look tired. They did not.

I sang three more songs, then stood him up and pulled back the coverlet and the sheet and picked up his pillow and pushed it to his nose so he could smell it. Sometimes smells help to right him, but he pushed the pillow away. I turned him around so he could see me set that pillow on that bed, then I pressed on his shoulders to get him to sit, of which he let me do. Then I tried to push him back so as he'd lay on the bed, of which he did not let me do, and truth to tell, he got some ornery and shoved my hand away. I thought on it and recollected the twine in my pocket. It is a thing about Rayford that he can't turn away from a knot, so I tied up the twine in four places, gave it to him and set the lantern on the night stand so he could see easy. Time he finished it seemed like some of the spunk had gone out of him. I tried to push him back on the bed again, and he shoved my hand away again. It looked like a durned predicament to me.

I let him be, figuring he'd likely wear himself out with all that staring, then flop over and fall asleep when he got tired enough. I sat on the bed til my back got to aching, then I scooched up against the wall so I'd have something to lean on. Each time I was near most asleep, Rayford groaned. There wasn't naught I could do but sing another song.

He finally tipped over with his knife still tight in his hand. I set it on his night stand so he'd see it when he woke up, of which that would make it a thing he was accustomed to. I put a cover over him and headed for the loft. Then it came to me I best stay by him for the first night. I piled quilts on the floor and brought my pillow and coverlet from my bed in the loft and laid there beside him, eyes closed but sleep nowhere near for worrying how this arrangement would ever work.

The next day when we went back to our place, Rayford fell asleep in his chair and slept most of the morning, of which that was fine with me, seeing as how I dragged my mattress in the parlor and slept, too.

That night we were both wide awake and Rayford fought sleep again. I sang til I was hoarse and knotted the twine three or four times, all to keep him quiet so he wouldn't bother them kindly Fosters. It came to me I needed a different plan, so when Joram brought us home to our place the next morning I kept Rayford moving. I hauled him up to the cornfield and down by the creek and back to the barn, then up McCreedy's Hill. It took all the lemon drops and licorice sticks and horehound I had hidden from the last time Mr. Foster brung them, but I kept him moving and every time he near most fell asleep, I sang loud. I was afeared he'd get ornery, but I reckon he was too tired. Time we got to Foster's that night, he didn't have much fight left and when I took him into his new bedroom, he let me take off his clothes and get his nightshirt on and push him back against the pillow. I pulled the knife out of his hand and set it on the night stand. Then I went up to the loft, directly. I reckon Pa is right. I got me a good thinking brain.

40

Ain't Gone Be No Good Fellers Left For Us

If Missy had come down the road a year ago, I would've run and hid in the woods before Pa could collar me and make me sit and be neighborly. The last time we were both at prayer meeting she asked who I thought was more handsome, Miles Auckleigh or Farley McMasters. I said both of them were about as ugly and pitiful as a duck's hinder. Truth to tell, when I saw Missy in that wagon this afternoon with her brother Arlo I got to wondering what kind of story she'd tell that didn't make no sense, but seeing as how we've been a might short of visitors, it came down to where even Missy and Arlo were welcome.

When Missy hugged me and said she was sorry to hear Ma had passed, out of the blue I recollected a time Ma made me a family of corn husk dolls and played with me and turned her voice tiny for the baby and old for the granny and such as that. Of late, my brain's been coming up with good pictures of her, of which they make me more sorry she is gone, howsomever if she was still with us, I reckon I wouldn't have them kindly feelings. It is peculiar.

I steered Missy to Rayford's garden so he could give us water. She said she'd been wanting to come by, but her ma wouldn't let her travel til Arlo came home. She told about her brother Benton who lost a leg, and how they traded firewood to buy one. I thought: there it is, there's the story that don't make no sense. I reckon she saw it in my face. "You ride into Harpersville, you'll see. The Yankees emptied Wright's store and burnt it clear to the ground so he's set up in a barn now. He ain't got much for goods yet seeing as how the Yankees tore up the railroads, but there's a man over by Marietta been carving legs to sell. Makes you sick to look at a pile of them that ain't attached to bodies."

Arlo had tied their horse to a fence post and stood outside the garden. He had a hang dog look on his face like there wasn't no sense in pulling pranks on folks no more. Hugh talked on such as that, how being in the war made boys grow up right quick. But it still didn't set right on Arlo, like as if he had got new skin, and he wasn't accustomed to it. He turned his hat round and round in his hands. Finally he came out with: "I'm sorry about your ma, and you being left alone to fend for Rayford." I reckon it was the first thing he ever said to me his whole life, and he still didn't look me in the eye. Before he went to the war, he'd run up behind me and pull my hair or throw dirt at me or some such. I put it up to him being like Rayford, but mean, til Missy said he talked at home. "You got anything round here needs fixing?" he asked.

From what I recollected hearing, Arlo Tarkan wasn't no better with a hammer and nails than he was with words. Missy told me once that he could handle a mule or a horse better than anyone, but if he got aholt of any kind of tool, like as not he'd break something or get hurt. I saw he had it in his heart to help me out so I told him about the rail on the east fence of Rayford's garden that had got knocked loose when a branch fell on it. I didn't see as he could cause no harm with that.

"There's tools and such in the barn," I said, and he headed over without so much as a gander at that rail to see what he needed.

"He's been near most as het up about coming here as I was. I don't know as he's sweet on you, or just ain't settled in to home life yet." Missy whispered, then she gave a little jump. "Oh, I near most forgot," she said, pulling a letter from a skirt pocket. "We were in town yesterday and I asked Mr. Wright if he had anything for you. It came tattered."

I took the letter, praying it was from Pa, and she put her hand in her other pocket and came out with a small brown-wrapped package and handed it to me. "Peppermint sticks for Rayford and you from Mr. Wright. He recollected you like them lemon drops and licorice, but he can't get none of that, just the peppermint."

I reckon it was all of it together—Missy's visit and the letter and Mr. Wright's kindness—that near most brung on the tears. I dropped my eyes to the letter, tore it open, and read how Hugh had found Mule working for that fellow that owned the horse ranch in Kentucky and got a job there, too. It was part writing and ciphering so as he could sit some, and the stable master said he'd pay for contraptions that made it easier to take care of the horses, but til he proved himself, he'd have to do the work on his own time.

"It's from Hugh," I said, sniffing back tears, wondering where Pa was. "He's found work and aims to send things we need since there ain't much for goods round here."

"Ma says there's fellers that'll get you ary a thing you want, long as you got money. Blockade runners they call 'em—but what money we got is no good. Course Ma says you can't trust the mail neither. There's some along the way what open packages and take what they want."

Her words set me to thinking on all the things that weren't right in the world, until Arlo's hammering pulled me out of it. Here there was a body to talk to and I was letting my brain take over. "Let's go set a spell. I got some fresh-baked gingerbread. I had to mix cornmeal with the flour, but it ain't bad if that's all you got." I looked over at Arlo, and when he set the hammer down, I called to him. "We'll be in the kitchen, Arlo. You come in when you're finished."

I cut three slices, thick like they do at Fosters,' and Missy and me set to talking on this and that. I showed how Rayford had gussied up the sideboard with flowers and told how Ma had got all riled and such as that. I asked her what was her ma reading in the newspapers. She said they weren't coming no more regular than the mail, and it didn't matter none to her nohow. "Don't see as how what them folks up north, or in England, or nowheres else is up to has naught to do with us."

"If we got newspapers here, I'd read em. Someday I aim to go north and travel to England. Ain't you curious about the world?"

She gave me a look like Ma did when she saw a thing as foolishness. Then she sat up in her chair, her face bright like as if the sun came out from behind a cloud. "Did you hear Miles Auckleigh got himself turned into a corporal." The way her words bounced, it put me in mind of womenfolk talking after prayer meeting. "He's sweet on Jenny Wright, and ain't it peculiar that she is near most three years older than him. Heard tell he was sweet on her afore he left for the war, and they got en-gaged and didn't tell no one. Not even her ma. Her Granpappy, you know, that's Mr. Wright who runs the general store, such as it is, he was so proud, he gave a dance for Miles when he came home and they told everyone they aim to get hitched. I reckon there ain't gone be no good fellers left for us." Her tongue near most ran her out of breath.

"I don't care much for fellers," I said.

"Why Tatum Wiley! You mean to tell me there still ain't no fellers you're sweet on? You just ain't had a chance to get out none. Next time Mr. Foster comes to town, you come, too. What with the war and all, it ain't like it used to be, but leastways folks still gather in the barn Mr. Wright took over for his store. You recollect how the MacDaniels had that big house? Well after Mr. MacDaniel got killed up at Chickamauga, his missus had in mind to sell out and move to Alabama by her daughter. But when the Yankees burned down the hotel, she took to inviting traveling folks to stay at her place. Every once in awhile, some nice-looking fellers come through on the way to Atlanta." She stopped for a breath. "Why's that grin on your face?"

"You sound all growed-up. Reckon you'll be getting hitched any day now."

"Well you're like to turn into an old maid if you don't never get to meet no fellers," she said, red-faced. "You come stay with us a day or two real soon. Ain't but two miles to Harpersville from our place. It's an easy walk."

"Once Pa gets home, I'll come."

"I'd like that," she said, thumping the table.

Arlo came in and I told him to pull out a chair. I set a slice of gingerbread and a cup of tea in front of him. I thanked him for fixing the fence rail and he nodded, then dropped half the gingerbread on the floor, finally got some in his mouth and choked on it. He rustled about like as if he was sitting on a porcupine instead of a chair, but he never did say another word.

We talked, Missy and me, a little longer. After they left, I took a gander at that fence rail, of which it looked like it had been attacked by a hammer. He must've used a bucket of nails and didn't get a one of them in straight. I surely hope he ain't sweet on me, seeing as how there ain't no way I aim to get sweet on a feller who can't talk and don't even know how to pound a nail.

41

A Thirsty Soldier

Rayford's been wandering in the garden. I suspicion it's the smell of early spring that sets him to working it again. I sat on Jenny's Stump this morning, pondering how he fusses over that garden like a family, like them plants that come up are his children and he makes sure they grow up right. I caught myself wishing he could do all kind of things he can't do now—like talk. But if he was like everyone else, he'd be off at the war, like Pa, or come back already and be home with his wife and children. Then I wouldn't be here taking care of him...and Ma would've been different, then maybe Hugh—or leastways Mule—might never have joined the war. I was daydreaming, one thought coming after the other, when I heard a noise back in the woods. I turned and watched a dirty, ragged Confederate soldier come round the corner of the house and stop about twenty yards away.

"Spare some water for a thirsty soldier?"

I stood and took a step backwards, thinking about that gun inside the door.

"You alone?" I asked.

"Yes, Ma'am," He sounded peculiar and then it came to me it wasn't no Confederate soldier, it was that soap soldier wearing a grey jacket. I took another step backwards and would have backed all the way to the house, but I tripped over a bucket and hit the ground hard. He came at me, and I shut my eyes and kicked, but I never hit nothing. Once I caught my breath, I opened my eyes just enough to see him staring at me like I was touched in the head.

I scrambled to get up and my foot caught in my skirt. He grabbed for me and I batted at him and stumbled and hit the ground again and he backed off with his hands up. "I won't hurt you," he said.

"Get! You get! Rayford! Rayford!" I had in mind to scream the words, but truth to tell, they came out like squeaks.

"Here." He held out his hand. I shook my head and got up, more careful, and brushed myself off. "I'm alone. I won't hurt you. I just want to talk to you," he said.

"Why you got that there Confederate coat on?"

"So I don't get strung up by one of these rebel bands out running around. That's why I came through the woods. I try to stay off the roads. I'm parched. Could I get a drink?"

"In the garden. But go through that gate over there, or Rayford'll get riled. He'll give you water." He nodded and walked to the garden, and I went up to the porch, so I could get the gun, need be. I kept an eye on him as he went through the gate.

Rayford looked up, lumbered over to his table, dipped the

ladle in the bucket, poured a cup of water, and handed it to him, like as if that soap soldier stopped by every day. I never saw Rayford afeared of nobody, excepting Ma. The soap soldier drank it down, held out the cup and asked for more. While Rayford poured it, the soap soldier picked up one of his critters. "Did you make this?" he asked. 'Course Rayford didn't answer but you would've had to be the biggest plumb fool eejit in the world not to know what that smile meant. The soap soldier drank that water down and put his hand on Rayford's shoulder, then nodded and thanked him. There ain't many folks who'll touch Rayford and there ain't many strangers that can put a hand on him without he swats at them or bellars.

"I've got something for you," he called out. "I'll be back in a few minutes. I promise I won't hurt you."

He left the garden, shut the gate behind him and disappeared into the woods behind the house. It was maybe five minutes later he came back leading a small, near-black horse that he tied to Rayford's fence. I would've liked to get a closer look at the horse, of which it looked strong, even if it was a might puny, but I didn't want to get so far from the gun. The soap soldier pulled a sack out of his saddlebag.

"My name's Frank Werner," he said walking back to the yard. "I come from southern Illinois—north of here a ways. My sister, Hattie, she's your age, maybe a year or so younger."

"I'm thirteen."

"She'll be thirteen in April." He stood about ten feet away and fidgeted with the sack like it was a bother, but he couldn't let go of it. He took a hard breath that made his shoulders go up and down. Of a sudden there was a pitiful look about him.

"You all right, mister?" He glanced at me and smiled, but it wasn't a happy smile. "You best sit," I said, pointing to the steps. "You're white as a haint. If Ma was here, she'd likely make you drink some of her tonic."

"Let's both sit. Up there, if it's alright with you," he said, looking up at the rockers on the porch. He was so kindly, I would've felt foolish getting the gun, but I put my hand in my pocket and felt for the knife. I nodded to the rockers, but I stepped back, and let him pass, so I could take the one closest to the steps—and the gun.

"Your mother gone for the day?"

I shook my head. "She passed on. 'Bout a month ago. Bright's Disease, Doc Waitly said. It has to do with kidneys that don't work no more. But for the last few days she wasn't right in the head neither."

"I'm sorry," he said, and I could see the pity clear in his eyes. He lowered himself careful, like an old man, then leaned forward in the rocker, and held the sack, his hands around the top where a piece of twine held it closed. I moved the chair closer to the door and sat, too.

"It was for the best. She'd get to talking crazy—how her feller brung her flowers and such as that, like as if she was just a girl and my pa was courting her. He's still at the war, likely in a prison up north somewheres." The soap soldier looked past me over at Rayford for the longest time, his shoulders moving up and down like his nose was stopped up and he couldn't get air. He finally looked back at me.

"You're taking care of him by yourself?"

"He ain't no trouble."

"He's a big man." The chickens took to squawking and I looked out to see Cleopatra run across the yard. She ain't never hurt no chickens, but they get riled and take off flapping when she tears by them.

"He ain't hard to care for lessen there's a storm," I said, turning back to the soap soldier. "Thunder scares him a might, but I sing Jesus Sweet and Jesus Mild, or the song about the faithful horse, or the fox and the chicken, all such as that, and he calms down. Winter he whittles and such. When it's time, he works his garden. He can't talk."

"Don't you have any relation you could move in with?"

"Every night we head to Fosters. My sister, Melanie, lives there. She married Joram, their youngest. They live the other side of McCreedy's Hill, off to the south. Right close. I like to keep Rayford here in the day. The way he is, he likes everything the same. He likes his bucket of carvings sitting right there by his twig chair," I said, pointing, "and he likes to pull up water from the well and pour it into cups when we come in the garden. When he's in his garden, you best come and go by the gate if he's watching. It's a rule Pa set up so he wouldn't get out."

"Looks like he could crawl through the fence if he wanted to."

"To Rayford, there's just one way of things and if you try to change it some, it don't set right by him, and he gets ornery."

"Your fath…your pa teach him to carve?"

"Granpappy taught him some. How to do it, leastways, but Rayford works at it most all the time." It came to me I was chattering like a squirrel, talking as easy as if he was someone I'd known all my life. "He can draw, too. Pictures of ary a thing he sees. And paint. He painted Ma's sideboard, and I reckon if she wasn't so weak, she would've killed him. She cried and carried on like he burned the house down. Granpappy said she was strung tight and couldn't help it, then the war came. Pa left to join the Confederate Army and then my brothers took off and joined up, too, and a time later Granpappy passed on. Then you all busted in."

"So much trouble in such pretty country."

It was quiet but for the sound of Rayford kicking his foot against the shovel, doing his first digging of the year. The soap soldier held up the sack and opened his mouth like as if to say something but the words got stuck. He had the durnedest look on his face, like that sack weighed a ton, but he couldn't set it down. Even though he was a Yankee, I got a sorry feeling for him.

He cleared his throat a couple minutes later and finally set the sack at his feet. I looked to his eyes for sign of relief, but his head was down. He untied the twine and took another deep breath that shook his shoulders again. Then he put his hand in the sack and when he brought it out, it was holding a carving of a girl with a wild mess of tangled hair. I don't know that a thought went through my head, but of a sudden I couldn't scarce get a breath.

"I have something to tell you...I don't know that there is a way to do it right . . ."

It came to me one of them other Yankees must've stole it when they busted in. I recollected a time Rayford was carving on such a thing, but I figured he picked it up one day and turned it into something else, the way he does. I got a picture in my head of that skinny soldier running out to Rayford's garden and going through his bucket of carvings. It made my stomach roll to think on it, then the soap soldier puffed air out loud enough to hear it.

"Your father...your pa...I got this from him."

"Pa? Pa gave it to you?" I jumped up to look for him, but the soap soldier grabbed my hand. I reckon that's when I should've been most afeared, but I wasn't. I closed my eyes and everything fell away but the warmth and roughness of his skin, and I felt his thoughts pass through me like wind through the trees. I reckon if he had told me with words right then, the truth of it would've killed me, but his hand kept me there.

He stood and steadied me and helped me sit again, his hand tight on mine. I looked over at Rayford, toward the road, across the way, up the hill. Everywhere I looked I saw Pa—Pa carrying water out to the barn for Belle, Pa leading Beauregard up to the field, Pa leaning back against the tree in Rayford's garden, Pa coming up the path to us. I pulled loose of the soap soldier's hand, and he gave me a worried look, like as if to see if I'd be all right. Then he sat again, his eyes on the carving he held, his elbows resting on his knees. He took in another breath, blew it out.

"Our regiment was guarding the supply line at Allatoona Pass, southeast of here. It was the fifth day of October. Hood and his men attacked, but we pushed them back. We chased them til we were running through the end of their line, stepping over..."

He let the words go, and rocked the carving back and forth, then went on.

"Off to my right, someone cried out. I followed the sound and spotted a young boy. Couldn't have been more than ten or eleven, I'd guess. Too young to be on a battlefield, but there he was, sitting up against a tree crying for water. He looked too scared to move. There was a man lying on the ground next to him, reaching for a canteen—but his legs had been—they'd been hurt somehow. Hard to see, you know, out there in the evening...late evening coming on to dark.

"Orders were to stay away from the Reb wounded. It was dangerous for us, and the sooner we got out of the way, the sooner their own would be up to help them. I took a last look around to make sure none of our men were out there and turned back to our line. Must have gone twenty or thirty yards, then I ran back and picked up the canteen and handed it to the boy. He'd been hit above the knee, on the side of his thigh. I tore back the leg of his pants. It wasn't bad. Just grazed his knee. He said he'd just come out to watch and got caught up in the fighting.

"I stood, and the man that had been trying to give the canteen to the boy pushed himself up on one elbow and reached across and grabbed my pants leg. 'You make sure my family is all right,' he said. I was afraid he might have a gun or a knife, and I pulled back, but he kept talking. 'Got a brother who's a might slow," he said. 'My wife, Mae, is waiting for me. You tell her I'm sorry, and I love her, and tell my daughter, too. She's real special to me." He fell back on the ground, and I turned to leave. 'Mister,' he said, 'take care of her.' I thought he was crazy to ask such a thing. 'Please...please promise you'll take care of my daughter,' he asked again. I said I would—to give him peace. I didn't think anything would come of it. Then I heard horses and looked back to see the Rebs coming through for their wounded."

He stopped and took a breath, held it, then blew it out again, like leastways he'd said the worst.

"I took off, and the boy hollered, 'Wait!' He pointed to the man's haversack. "Something in there you should have," he said. I tossed it to him and he dug around in it and pulled out this carving and held it up to me and said, "It's his daughter." I grabbed it and ran, and the boy called out, 'Tatum! He called her Tatum.'"

I wanted to be dead then. Not taking a rope and playing with it. I didn't want to live as long as it took to die. I didn't want to feel anymore. Then I heard Rayford's ladle hit the side of the bucket and looked over as he took a drink. I thought as how that is what the rest of my life would be. It would pass one minute, one movement, one noise at a time, and of a sudden, I recollected how that soap soldier had jumped out of the woods and put his hand over my mouth on Melanie's birthday. "That's how you knew my name...." He nodded, but he didn't look up. It came as a surprise to hear the words come out of my mouth, to know my voice still worked. Truth to tell, it helped, like as if some of the hurt came out of me with them words.

"I stuffed the carving in my knapsack then ran back to our lines to help shore up our defenses in case they came at us again." He stopped for a minute, like as if to recollect the rest, then he went on. "Later that night we were sitting around the campfire and I went to my knapsack and pulled it out. Didn't look at the face at first, just...just thought what a shame it was that a man who had this gift, who could carve so well...I thought he was the one that had carved it...then I remembered that day we came here." He looked out at Rayford. "And him lying on the floor...you standing over him with that pitchfork. At first I thought it was an unlikely coincidence and you couldn't be the one, but then I recalled what the man had said about his brother...that he was slow. I held the carving closer to the fire for a better look, then I knew. I knew you were the girl that Reb was talking about."

A chicken squawked and we looked out to see it had wandered into the garden and Rayford had took off after it. It seemed like everything should have changed. The sky should have growed dark, and the air should have turned ice cold, and the earth should have swallowed us up. But Rayford looked the same— the chicken squawked and fluttered around and finally ran out of the garden. At first it hurt some to see such a regular thing as that—like it didn't even matter that Pa was gone. But then it seemed like a good thing, because Pa wouldn't have wanted the sky to turn dark, and all of us to disappear. But he'd never brush his hand over my hair again, or race me to the oak at the curve of McCreedy's Hill, or sit in our tree. He'd never see that door I put up there, or play the mouth organ--

"He looked happy...after I promised. You were the last one he thought of."

I closed my eyes and pictured Pa and a breeze ruffled my hair. The way my tears rolled out easy, it was like as if they knew all along and had been resting back of my eyes, waiting for my ears to hear. I pictured Pa to ease my mind, and saw him in heaven, he and Ma together, sitting on steps somewhere, Ma shelling peas and Pa finally sitting beside her. She had a happy look on her face. Pa, too. In that picture, he looked at me and said me and Rayford were going to be all right, and of a sudden, my whole body shook. I wanted to run away, but I didn't know where to go. Away from me, I reckon. Away from the rest of my life. Of a sudden my back was getting patted, and the soap soldier was saying kindly words. He went on, but my head was filled with thoughts of Pa, and I didn't pay him no mind. Then I heard Rayford. He stood at the fence rail looking at us, and I wiped my face on my apron and waved. It came to me to wonder how I'd ever make him understand.

"I'm sorry," the soap soldier whispered.

Of a sudden a noise came up out of me like the wailing of a wild critter. It was near most like retching, excepting it was sounds that kept rising to my throat, over and over and I let them out, til there was nothing left. Then the soap soldier stood and walked past me, then down the steps and the tears came. I cried until the lap of my dress was wet with tears, and I knew that even if I cried forever, it still wouldn't be enough.

Time passed and I had no heart to move. My pa. My pa, gone. I closed my eyes, willing lightning to strike me or a tree to fall on me, or the sun to burn me to ashes. I felt a hand on my arm. I kept my eyes shut.

"I'll take care of you," the soap soldier said. I opened my eyes then because he sounded so far away, but he'd just touched my arm. There ain't never been nothing peculiar like that again, but I'd swear on a ten foot stack of bibles that he'd touched my arm. But he couldn't of seeing as how he was standing by his horse. He had one hand on the saddle but he'd turned back to look at me. I know as how it don't make no sense, but I think I know whose hand was on my arm. I ain't never told no one out loud, seeing as how it puts me in mind of the way I thought about Ma at the end. But my brain works fine. And I know whose hand that was.

"I promised," the soap soldier said then. "I'm taking you home with me. To Illinois. Soon as I find a way." I heard him, but my brain didn't want to think on what he was saying. "I wrote to my father about you, and about my promise, and he agrees."

I put my hands to my ears.

"I can't take care of you here. I'll get killed. My father runs a general store, and I work with him. We'll take good care of you...and Rayford."

My mind was moving now, thinking, fearing his words. "No," I whispered. "No."

"Things won't ever be the way they were--"

"I made a promise, too." My words felt small and quiet, but hard as rock, and of a sudden, I had a need to be by Rayford. I stood, not sure my legs would carry me, but I made it to the edge of the porch, down the steps, acrost the yard, and into his garden. He had come back to his chair by then. He poured water, and I drank it and gave the cup back to him, shaking my head to let him know I didn't want no more. He set the cup down and I put my arms around his shoulders and hugged him. He sat there stiff, til I let go, then he went back to his carving, something so small his fingers hid it. "Pa's gone," I whispered. "He ain't never coming back."

I looked for something to think on that didn't hurt so much, but every thought ended in wanting. I felt it in the tips of my fingers and my forehead and my stomach, so much in my stomach, but in my elbows and knees, too. Everywhere. It was like as if I didn't have a body no more, like as if I was turned into a feeling, a feeling of wanting and I got a picture in my head of everything in the world pouring into me, people, houses, critters, mountains, rivers, but nothing filled me, nothing eased that wanting.

I sat on the ground, then laid down on my side on the dirt starting to warm in the early March sun. I rolled onto my stomach, feeling the smallest bit of comfort in laying on the earth, and turned my face to look out to where Rayford would soon be planting greens and carrots and peas. The ground felt warm and bumpy on my cheek, and when my tears hit the dirt, it brought up the smell of spring and a recollection of that day almost a year earlier when Ma told me to get the sassafras and I took Rayford up on the hill where Pa was plowing.

I got up on my knees and crawled, staying low to the ground, that feeling of wanting pulling me along. As I moved acrost the garden, I saw where Rayford had dug up the dirt, then patted it back down. That wasn't like Rayford. He always planted in rows. I pushed my fingers into one of the newly planted places and felt around to see what kind of seed he had gotten hold of. He doesn't plant until we give him the seeds. Pa taught him and we always help him plant.

I pulled out a carving, maybe four inches long, of a man with creases in the face around the mouth, and hair that had a turn to it here and there. I reached around to another patch of fresh-packed dirt and pulled up another one. I crawled forward and found another, and another.

"Tatum," the soap soldier said, in a kindly voice, and I looked up to see him standing outside the fence, his hands on the top rail. "I think he knows."

I shook my head.

"He must know. He must feel it. Otherwise, why would he bury them?"

A shadow came over me and Rayford knelt beside me, took the carvings, and pushed them back into the ground. Then I understood.

I put my hand on his back and of a sudden, I felt something like a spark inside me. I closed my eyes and let it build like a fire warming my insides, and I recollected that time I sat in Rayford's garden after Pa joined the Confederate Army. It seemed like there had been a pot inside me set to boil that day, too, when my feet took me to the barn, and I found the rope, and I recollected how it went from a noose to a thing I could use to build something for Pa and me in the hickory tree. That feeling came back and I could near most hear Pa put words to it: "That's hope, Tatum, rising like ashes from the fire of despair."

"We ain't leaving," I said, my voice stronger now, with that fire in my words, and I recollected those times there were two voices in my head. One would've sat there and cried all day, but the other was the voice of the girl that pulled that door out to our tree, and went after Rayford in the middle of the night, and stood over him with the pitchfork when the Yankees busted in. "I ain't setting foot off this here place with a mind to leaving." I pushed myself up and looked around at our land, and of a sudden, I had the strength to stand. "This is my home. And Rayford's. You go on now and get back to your own kind. Me and Rayford will do fine," I said, recollecting Pa's words when I got that picture in my head of him sitting with Ma on the steps of heaven and looking down at me.

"It will take years to rebuild. The railroads are torn up. No supplies are getting through. There's hard times ahead. I can't change that, but you come north and there'll be food, and you can get to school. There's nothing left down here. I've seen it."

I shook my head. To leave this land? Pa's land? Never.

"I'll get another horse and a wagon. We'll take everything north—your furniture, his table over there and carvings, that bucket, your clothes. I can't leave you here."

"We'll make do. I see now it was you brung that orange and them supplies. I ain't been proper grateful, seeing as how you risked your life to provide for us. But you done your part, now I got to do mine."

"My word means something to me, Tatum. I understand you feel you've got to keep your word to your father—your pa—but you're just a child. Thirteen. Thirteen is still young."

"Don't have to be old to keep your word." He didn't have ary a thing to say against that.

"I can't stay here any longer. I've tried to take back roads, but there's a group of local boys that spotted me again this morning. This coat won't fool them for long."

"Well, you best get, then."

"Tatum, you could starve down here."

"I won't starve."

Minutes passed. I thought about the big carving Rayford made of Pa. It would help me recollect his face.

"You know how to write?" The soap soldier looked over at his horse. "Will you promise to write letters, so I know how you're doing. And tell me what you need. Will you do that?"

"Your kind killed my pa. Don't see as how I got to promise

you nothing." I stood tall when I said it, and looked straight ahead, acrost to the barn.

"You've got a right to be angry...and sad. I can't change what's happened, all I can do is try to help you. Tatum, look at me, please."

He had come to Rayford's gate. I looked him in the eye, and I saw his goodness, but I knew Pa didn't mean for him to take us north.

"I'd like to keep this," he said, holding up the carving of me. I nodded. He stuffed it into the sack and went to his horse and put it back in his saddlebag.

"When I get back, I'll write and tell you where to send letters. But I'm going to stay for one more day in case you change your mind."

I gave him a look to let him know that'd never happen.

"Just think about it." He untied the reins, grabbed the saddle horn, and pulled himself up. From inside the garden I watched him walk his horse to the path at the edge of the woods that led to the creek. When he got to it, he stopped and turned in his saddle.

"Tatum, if you tell anyone about me I'll be dead by morning."

42

The Doe

I wanted to tell Melanie about Pa that night, but I didn't want nothing to happen to that soap soldier, and that's what it came down to. And if I told her, all that would change is there'd be two of us fighting the need to talk on it.

In bed the sadness came over me again like a heavy blanket. My brain looked everywhere for something good to think on, but in the dark quiet, all my thoughts ran to Pa. I'd slip into sleep and see him falling out of our tree or being kicked in the head by Beauregard, or getting hurt in the woods and calling for me. I'd go after him, but of a sudden there was a mountain, or a deep river, or a gorge that I couldn't get acrost, and I'd wake up again and again all night long. I don't reckon I had a moment of peaceful sleep, and then I heard movement beneath the loft.

I crawled down the ladder and got Rayford up like always. I shaved him, we ate breakfast, and Joram brought us back home, like as if it were any other day, excepting Pa had passed on and I couldn't tell no one about it.

The soap soldier didn't come round. I figured he took me at my word and went home after all.

Noontime there was a doe laying at the edge of the woods, mostly hidden by brush, with just her head sticking out. I likely wouldn't have noticed but for Rayford standing at the north fence staring out into the thicket, his hands splayed out and gripping the top rail. I had come to bring him in for dinner, and looked out to where his eyes were aimed. I still might have missed her but for a movement, likely the flick of her ears. She had a grey cast, not a winter coat, but a sickly hue that made me recollect Ma. When I looked closer I saw thick red patches around her eye and at her snout—fresh blood, still bright—and the palsied quiver of her head brought on by breath coming quick and shallow. Likely a coyote attack laid her low, and I felt her fear and a longing to comfort her that I couldn't rightly figure.

Rayford's eyes were so hard on her he didn't know I was there. I looked over at him and saw he was lost in some kind of thought that had nothing to do with talking or listening or the knowing that comes from them. He was bound to that doe in a way I can't put words to, but I could feel, like heat rising from a fire. I can't account for it, nor for the pain that shot through me of a sudden from the side of my head that was near Rayford, like as if he got it from the doe and passed it to me, and it bound me to her, too, so that we were all three strung together in a sadness that gave me to understand there is more to this world than what we see, or hear, or smell, or taste, or touch.

I shook my head, wondering how that carving could've worked loose of that sack and crawled out of that saddlebag and jumped to the ground.

"Days go by and there ain't nothing different, everything the same," he said, startling me. "Truth to tell, since I got a taste of excitement at the war and seeing new places, well..." He looked down at his hat and waved it a bit, like as if he had no claim to excitement or new places and he was a fool to even think such as that. "What goes on around here day to day is a might tame. I ain't saying I got a taste for war, but I'd like to head out and see things I ain't yet seen. I don't let myself think on it much, but when I saw that carving, seeing as how it was something different, it got me to thinking along those lines again. Reckon I sound like a fool. "

I shook my head. "I've thought on such as that, too," I said, recollecting how Pa had wrote some on Tennessee and the mountains up there and how pretty they are. "I got Rayford to care for now, but some day I aim to travel and see this country and Europe, too." I don't know where the words came from. It was like as if my mouth recollected what it might've said months ago and went off in that direction while my brain worried over that soap soldier, and my heart broke all over again to think on Pa, and I couldn't let on about none of it.

"You got to sail there," he said, like as if that would make me think twice.

"I know. I ain't afeared of them big ships." I was near most surprised at my mouth carrying on like that, all on its own.

He looked off to the east, and sighed, like as if he was thinking on one of them big ships himself.

"Pa'll think I got lost. It sure has been nice talking to you, Miss Tatum. I never suspicioned a girl would think on such as travel and adventure."

"You think girls ain't curious?" I near most called him a fool.

"Oh, no. No I surely don't think that." He got red-faced quick, and dropped his eyes. "Guess I ain't never talked to girls much. Excepting for Ma."

"Didn't you see no girls off at the war?"

"Saw some. Never talked to any." He looked up then. "I'd like to," he said, his words quick and certain. "I reckon I just never learned how."

"Ain't no learning to it. What kind of a critter you think you're talking to now?"

He grinned and shook his head, like someone pulled a prank on him. "Reckon you're right," he said, smiling.

"Ain't *that* hard, is it?"

He shifted his weight and took a breath, then looked me square in the eye. "It's downright enjoyable," he said with a laugh, of which it got *me* red-faced. "Well. I'll be heading back. You need anything?"

I need my pa back, is what I wanted to say, but I shook my head.

He had his hat halfway to his head but pulled it back down and gave it a little push toward me. "Near most forgot. Ma said to say she hopes you and Rayford are well and it eases her mind to know you head to Fosters' come nighttime, lest more Yankees come round."

"More Yankees?"

"Didn't you hear? There's been a Yankee sneaking round these parts." I dropped the carving, and quick picked it up. "Passed himself off as a rebel with a broke jaw that couldn't get a word out clear, til Whit Whitlow heard him talk to his horse. Then they knew he was a Yankee, certain, and chased him down and bloodied him some to teach him a lesson. They trussed him up and took him over to Whitlow's. Reckon they would've killed him, but Whit's pa studied on preaching back a few years ago, and said even if he is a dadblamed Yankee, he's a child of God all the same."

"What're they gone do with him?"

"They're looking to send him down to that Yankee prison they got set up past Macon."

"Andersonville?"

"That's it." He pointed at the carving. "Sure is strange how that carving got all the way out on the road like that. You want I should ask round Harpersville on it next time we head over that way?"

I nodded. "It's a mystery, certain."

"Leastways it's a good mystery," he said, and he put his hat on his head and turned and headed back to the woods.

I stared at the likeness. There was a look of feistiness about it on the face, like as if it was thinking on Ma. Or on something that didn't set right with it. I took it to Rayford. He set down the piece he was working on and turned the carving of me over in his hand a time or two and saw fit to alter it in some way. I let him be and headed in to make some tea to settle my stomach.

44

An Idea

I couldn't scarce look Melanie in the eye last night, afeared it would all come out. But, I owed that soap soldier something. I didn't have it all thought out in my mind what it was I owed, or what I intended to do about it, or what it all had to do with telling Melanie about Pa, but I wasn't ready to tell nothing, yet. Thinking on it, and trying to look at it like Pa would've, gave me some comfort.

It takes a lot of work to act regular when your heart is set to grieve, but you can't get to it because there's a thing you have to tend to first and your brain is tearing around your head and bringing in guns and nooses and fighting and throwing in a picture of a doe with a bloody face. The end of it was I kept quiet most of the night, of which that didn't set right with Melanie. Afore I headed up to the loft, she asked was I ailing. That got my brain to thinking all over again. I told her my stomach had a peculiar feeling.

"You got your monthlies again?"

"No, it ain't that. It's more...higher, I reckon," and I made a face of discomfort to go with it. It brought out the goodness in Melanie's eyes of which I reckon I would've felt some shame over, if my brain hadn't been so busy working out a plan. I was glad of that seeing as how when I was scheming, I wasn't as sad.

Once I got in bed and had an idea of what I aimed to do, my thoughts went back to Pa. I reckon if a brain was left to itself, it wouldn't do naught but scheme and think on things, but seeing as how a body has a heart, it has its own idea of what a brain should be thinking on. I reckon the brain is more like Hugh—it don't want to mess with feelings, it just wants to make new ideas and such as that. The brain likes a thing it can sink its teeth into and work on some, like a dog with a bone. But if a feeling of sadness comes along, seems like your heart gets in it and the tears come, and your hands don't know what to do, and your legs don't want to work. If a happy feeling comes, your heart gets your mouth to smiling and wanting to tell on it, and your hands move, and your feet want to run in an excited way. And if you're het up and ornery, your heart puts out an anger, then you have a need to whale on someone or hit something. I reckon thinking comes from the brain but when you get to mostly feeling something, that comes from the heart, then *it's* the boss of the brain. The end of it was I didn't know which was running me, my scheming brain or my feeling heart. But leastways all that thinking tired me out, and I slept for an hour or two. When I heard stirring below, I sat up and near most put my feet on the floor. Then I recollected my plan, and didn't move. A while later Melanie called up to me.

"Tatum. It's morning."

I didn't answer.

"Baby, time to get up."

"I'm ailing," I whispered loud enough so she likely heard something. A minute later the ladder creaked, then her head came up through the floor, and she looked over at me.

"You don't look good."

"I don't feel good, neither," I said. It likely helped that I hadn't slept but an hour or so the last two nights and had rubbed spit on the hair around my forehead so as to make it look like I had a fever.

She came on up the rest of the way and bent over me and put her hand to my head. "Your head's sweaty, but you don't feel hot."

"I feel cold." I shivered as best I could.

"Your stomach still hurting?"

"Something awful." Then I recollected how pains hit Ma. "My back hurts, too. Down low. And my head. About here," I said, rubbing my temples like I'd seen Ma do.

"Oh, Baby. We best fetch Doc Waitly."

"Melanie?" She looked into my eyes and I near most went red-faced with shame. "You reckon Mr. Foster could take me to town to see him?"

"I don't know as that is a good idea.."

It wasn't. I had to come up with something better or Mr. Foster would be off fetching Doc Waitly for naught. Melanie walked to the ladder, and I set my brain to working on it. She was backing down when it came to me.

"Melanie, I can't take Doc Waitly away from them soldiers he's tending at that hospital he's got set up at Tuckers."

"It won't take him but an afternoon."

"No, Melanie. All them brave fighting soldiers what got hurt protecting our way of life need Doc Waitly there. I reckon I can make it. Mr. Foster can wrap me up in a blanket and lay me on the back of the wagon." I scrunched up my face in such a way as to make it look like a pain had taken hold. I reckon it could be called lying, but I had in mind to tell the truth of it as soon as I had it all figured out.

She gave me another look of pity that near most wrung the truth from me right there, but then my thoughts went to my promise to Pa. "You take good care of Rayford for me whilst I'm in town. Don't let him get out on his own, and help him right his buttons after he gets dressed, and see that he gets shaved--"

"You just get yourself better. You know I'd never let no let no harm come to him. Ain't no need to worry on that account."

An hour later I was laying next to a couple sacks of corn in a straw bed Mr. Foster had made in the back of the wagon with blankets spread over it. I laid atop them and he threw a quilt over me. I whispered my thanks, like as if it was all I could do. But once we topped McCreedy's Hill I called up to him that the pain had let loose some, and could I sit up with him. I hadn't been to town since before Pa left, and I wasn't about to miss it lying on my back. He whoa-ed Major Tom and came back and helped me and I hung onto him hard, like it still hurt some to move. "It comes and goes. There's times I don't think I can stand it, then it eases up some," I told him. He is so kindly, like Pa. I leaned on him and he walked slow to the buckboard, then near most lifted me up. Once I got on the bench, I gritted my teeth and pulled air through them. He went white and froze. I held that face a minute, then let it go. "I'm alright. It was that last step pulled up a pain in my back."

I reckon the Lord is considering eternal damnation for me, seeing as how I have turned into a lying fool and am pulling the wool over everyone's eyes, but I reckon if the devil can give you ideas, the Lord can too, and lessen he comes up with a better one, this is the only one I got.

The Harpersville Road headed straight west for four miles til it met the railroad line, and I always thought of that part of the road as belonging to us and the Fosters and the Driscolls, seeing as how there wasn't generally no one else likely to use it. It looked the same as ever, but then the road turned north and ran alongside the tracks into town. Just beyond was a small settlement, five houses clustered together. I don't recollect a time we passed without we saw chickens scratching in the yard, and a dog or two, and mules and cows grazing in corrals outside the barns, and heard the sounds of wood being chopped, or pounding in a work shop, or voices outside at battling boards or in the gardens. The quiet struck first. I looked for movement—a hen, britches waving in the wind, or some such, but nothing stirred. It filled me with an uneasy fear before I even saw the charred walls of the houses, near most burnt to the ground. I grabbed Mr. Foster's arm, and that soap soldier's words telling of hard times ahead came back to me.

"There was one Yankee had a real mean streak. After he stole what he wanted and put an ax to furniture, he'd throw all the clothes he could find on the beds and set fire to the lot." He had slowed Major Tom and we drove past the houses at a walk. "The more the womenfolk begged him to leave them be, the more he'd pile on, and when they got to crying and wailing, he'd poke fun. But the story was that not even his own men liked that one. After he left one place, some of the Yankees sneaked back and helped the women and children pull up water and try to put the fires out. They said time that Yankee got to this place, he was riled at his men and ornery over a jug of corn squeezings he got his hands on that was too strong to drink. He opened it, poured it over the clothes, set fire to it all and stayed right there til he was sure it caught good. Then he made his men march together in front of him back north to Harpersville. By then he'd got into more liquor and was too drunk to go on. His men put him on a wagon and headed to the main road and on down to Atlanta."

We could've had our place burned down, too. Or been hurt by that awful skinny Yankee. The closer we got to town, the more I thought on the soap soldier...and that doe...and the carving Jeremy and his pa found along the road.

As we rode into the south end of Harpersville I saw that most of Mr. Wright's general store was gone. The hotel next to it was gone, too, and so was the bank, with nothing but charred wood and chimneys left to mark the spot.

"They were built too close," Mr. Foster told me. "Once the fire took hold, it ate its way from building to building." Across the street, the livery stable was still standing, but there was a scattering of boards out front, white and fresh-smelling, and sawhorses set up. A handful of men and boys scurried here and there sawing and carrying lumber, and such as that. As we got to the north end, we saw how that wall had burnt, and they were rebuilding it.

"The hay was stored along the north wall on this end. It caught fire quick and took the wall with it. They had the water troughs to draw from so they were able to wet down the other walls and save them. Can't get many supplies, but leastways there are still trees standing, and a sawmill on the way to Rome that can turn them into lumber." Of a sudden, it hit me how I'd been thinking it was only me that was hurt so bad by this war that took Pa, but seeing what other people lost took me out of myself and filled me with pity.

"You know Arlo Tarkan took a job here?"

"They best keep him tending horses and not let him near them boards and nails," I said. Despite I still felt the sadness, I snickered to think on how that rail on Rayford's fence looked after he'd had at it. Mr. Foster turned to me in such a way as to make me recollect I was meant to be half dead. I coughed a time or two, and said the pain had let go for awhile, and it was helping some to think on the troubles of others. He clucked to Major Tom, and headed past the mill, where new wood met old here and there. "They took axes to the building but didn't hurt the working parts," he said, looking over at it as we passed.. "They likely had in mind not to burn it down til they took out what grain was already ground to feed their own horses. Reckon if that one Yankee hadn't got drunk, he would've made them burn down the rest of the town."

Across the street and down a ways hung a new hand-painted sign that said "Hotel." I told Mr. Foster what Missy had said, and he nodded. "The Yankees holed up there and put Mrs. MacDaniel to cooking and washing their clothes. She got a big new wash pot out of it of which them Yankees stole it from somewhere. We heard tell how some of them young bluecoats came to her like as if she was their mother, with britches needing patching, and stories of home and family to tell. I reckon her kindness helped saved the town. After they left she opened up the house to travelers, and has been taking in the few that pass through."

He shook the reins and walked Major Tom on up to Tucker's, of which it sat just south of MacDaniels. It was the first house ever in Harpersville and had been built big to hold two brothers and their families. Some Tuckers still lived on one side and the other was turned into the hospital. Mr. Foster jumped down off the buckboard and tied Major Tom. He put his hand up and helped me to the first step, then lifted me down. As I hit the ground, I bent over some, like Ma used to, and baby-stepped to the house. Mr. Foster ran ahead and knocked. A minute later Jenny Wright came to the door.

"Tatum Wiley here is ailing, and I'm afeared it could be what took her ma." He looked at me sheepish then, like he shouldn't have said it for me to hear. After he left I thought on it, and reckoned the Lord marked another strike against me, causing that poor man such worry, of which I ain't proud, but I was only doing what I didn't see no other way of getting done.

Miss Jenny looked at me and I hunched more and squinted and she stepped up and took my arm. "Doc Waitly is looking in on Ches MacDaniel. He come back just yesterday with a foot near most blown off. He'll be back directly. Tatum, you come with me."

"You want I should stay here, Tatum?" Mr. Foster asked.

"No, you get your corn ground and such. I'll be fine, now I'm here."

"You need help?" he asked Miss Jenny.

"Not as long as she can walk."

"You take it slow, I can walk," I said, hobbling along beside her. She took me into a room with another bed and a girl lying in it, unfamiliar to me. She didn't look bad hurt, and the thought passed through my mind that she might have what I had—a good case of lying—but then Miss Jenny whispered.

"That's Miss Laura Hattersly. She got burned something fierce on her legs. Doc doped her up so she don't feel the pain. Poor girl ran in a burning house to fetch a dolly her Granny gave her, and got caught in the fire. Her ma had gone to the well for water and didn't see her go in. The poor woman near most lost her mind. For a time I thought we'd have them both in here, til Doc Waitly promised Laura would live. She'll have bad scars to show for it, but she'll walk."

I felt some shame then, me with not a thing wrong next to a poor girl that near most died.

"You reckon you'll feel better sitting or laying?"

"I'd best lay. Curled up on my side eases the pain some," I said.

"Where is the pain?"

"Around my head—here above my ears. And in my stomach and back, too, down low."

She put her hand to my head.

"No fever."

"I reckon I had one during the night. This morning my hair was wet, and I was cold . . . chilled through."

"I'll send Doc Waitly in soon's he gets back. You want a cup of tea?"

"Reckon I'd just as soon rest." Leastways that was God's truth certain. Laying down in that bed felt right good. "Didn't get ary a minute of sleep last night."

I must've fell asleep straightaway, and when I opened my eyes, Doc Waitly was standing over me, Mr. Foster at his side.

"Child, I hear you're ailing."

I nodded and took on the most pitiful look I could muster.

"Well, I'd like to check you over, see what we got."

He turned and talked low to Mr. Foster, who left then. Laura Hattersly was still quiet in the bed next to me.

"Miss Jenny told me some of what you told her, but I'd like to hear it from you."

I went through it all again, and he pressed on my head and my stomach and back and every time I felt his fingers pushing on a part of me, I moaned. Then he put his hand across my forehead and held it there. He peered into my eyes and had me open my mouth wide and looked me over good, like I recollected Pa did with Beauregard the day he bought him.

"I can't figure it." He rubbed his hand over his face, then pressed his mustache back in place. "Harley," he called out to Mr. Foster, "you can come back in now." Then he peered at me again. "Is the pain easing up some or getting worse?"

"Comes and goes. Times I don't think I can stand it, then it eases some."

"Is it achy and long, or quick and sharp?"

I thought back to when I had the monthlies. "Feels like a

hot knife slicing through my innards front and back, then every once in awhile, it goes through my head."

"Quick, like a lightning strike?"

"No. It goes on some."

"A few minutes?"

"Longer. Then it eases and builds up again."

"Hmmm. You say you didn't sleep good last night?"

I shook my head.

"I'll fix up something to ease the pain and help you sleep. Can you make it back to Fosters?"

"I don't want to be there if it comes on again like it did last night. With all them pains and the sweats too, I thought I was dying."

Mr. Foster's eyebrows rose like as if a thought came to him and I recollected that time I showed up at their place afore sunrise to talk to Melanie, and told him I was dying. He whispered to Doc Waitly.

"Well. You best stay til tomorrow, then. Miss Jenny's sister comes at night to keep an eye on things here. I moved my family over to MacDaniel's whilst I got patients to care for, so I'll be nearby if I'm needed." He heaved a sigh, looking more tired than me. He straightened up, and they walked out, talking low. Likely on the monthlies, of which I got red-faced when I thought on it. Leastways it gave me a night to do what I had to do. Of which I still wasn't certain what that was.

45

The Back Door

Miss Jenny's sister, Miss Leona, came in round supper time and brought me a wooden tray with a bowl of rabbit stew, a fat, buttered-up biscuit, and a cup of tea on it. I sat up and took the tray, picked up the spoon and swirled it in the stew, mixing greens and sending up a smell of onion. I dug in until I saw how Miss Leona looked at me, of which it made me recollect I was near to dying with pain. I made a face, handed her the tray, laid back careful, and asked her to leave it, in case I felt some better, later. She set it on the table between the beds, and said seeing as how I was staying the night, I'd best put on my nightgown if I brung one. I pointed to the haversack Foster's lent me, and she went to it and pulled out my gown. I put it on, then she hung my clothes on hooks and helped me get back in bed. She smoothed back my hair and patted the bed sheets and pulled them around some, so as to try to make me feel better I reckon. Then she gave me a bell and told me to ring it if I needed her seeing as how she'd be sleeping on the cot in the office. I asked where the outhouse was and she pulled a chamber pot from under the bed and set it on the low shelf of the table. I wondered if Miss Laura Hattersly ever used one. She hadn't stirred since I got there.

Miss Leona said she had to tend to her and I might not want to look, so I rolled over and faced the wall. I heard her pull back the bedding. Fresh smells filled the room, sharp and strong— some kind of dressing I reckon—but also the smell of pee, of which it made me think they had put a big cloth on Miss Laura Hattersly's bottom. I hoped none of that smell was getting into that stew. I ain't never had in mind to do work of a nursing nature, but after seeing Hugh's leg and knowing what Miss Leona was up to, I didn't reckon I had the stomach for it. Cleaning up Rayford was bad enough but leastways he was a relation. Whilst she worked, I gave more thought to things and said I was afeared Yankees might bust in.

"They're long gone, but for that one they got tied up over at Whitlows'."

"You got a back way they might sneak in during the night?"

"There's a door down the hall, on past those other two rooms . . ." She groaned a bit, like as if she was lifting something heavy, then went on, ". . . but it's got a lock on it and a bar besides. Ain't no one getting in, so you get some sleep and don't worry."

"That puts me at ease, " I said..

"All finished. You can turn your head, now." I rolled over. Miss Laura Hattersly was all tucked back in, and Miss Leona was holding a bundle of cloth of which I didn't want to think on what was in it. "I'll be back directly with the medicine Doc Waitly set out for you."

"Well, I don't know as I need it now. I'm so sleepy, I don't reckon there's ary a pain that could keep me awake." She made a face.

"Doc Waitly had orders on it." She said it like as if it was as good as done, but I didn't want to take nothing that would put me to sleep.

"I'd best try to sleep first," I said. "You can save that medicine in case them soldiers need it."

"Well...we are short of everything. "I'll keep it ready, then. If you need me, or if Miss Laura here stirs, you ring the bell."

"Thank you, kindly.".

"You rest now," she said, patting my feet. "You'll likely feel better come morning."

"Reckon I will," I said, as she headed out. There was a door on the room but she left it open. First off I wished it would've been closed but then it came to me open was better—one less noise to make.

I closed my eyes, and stirred some. I should've been too tired to keep my eyes open, but I felt as awake as if I'd slept a week straight. I heard quiet talking from the other rooms. I guessed there were leastways four or five men in them, howsomever it's hard to tell voices when they're low. It put me in mind of nights when Hugh and Mule talked long after dark, of which that wasn't often, although that was surely the way of it the night before they left for the war.

I must've fell asleep awhile, and woke later to darkness and quiet. I sat up, felt for the tray, and brought it onto my lap. The biscuit had dried out but I ripped it in two, dunked it, and ate the rest of the stew, sopping up the last of it with the biscuit. I set the tray back, and laid down again. When I judged it to be near midnight, I pushed back the covers, and as I sat up, I threw my legs over what I thought was the open side of the bed, and hit the wall with a thud. I near most howled from the pain, but caught myself and stifled a groan, of which I wasn't even to the end of it when Miss Leona's footsteps skittered across the floor.

"That you, Tatum?"

"Yes, ma'am," I winced, still thinking that nothing but a full-out holler would ease the pain.

"You fall out of bed?"

"No. Forgot which side the wall was on."

"Are you alright?" I near most hollered to her that this time I was really in pain, but I took a deep breath and whispered yes. "You need to use the chamber pot?" she asked.

"Yes, ma'am." I reckoned I needed some reason for why I was trying to get out of bed.

"I'll help you," she said, and I quick told her I could do it my-self, now that I knew where I was. "Well, I'll let you be." She left and by then I could hear the men in the other room were awake. I heard her footsteps and then whispering. She was likely telling how I just needed to use the chamber pot, of which it made me hope I didn't have to look any of them in the eye.

She came back a few minutes later with a lit candle, picked up the chamber pot and headed out. I heard her walk along the hall, heard her take the bar off the door, put the key in the lock, open the door, and head out. A minute later I heard her again, then the sound of water pouring, and her going out and coming back again, of which it was likely her rinsing and emptying the chamber pot. Then the flickering light from the candle grew brighter, I heard her steps move closer, and in she came. She set the candle on the table, and the chamber pot on the shelf beneath. She glanced at the tray and saw I had eaten the stew.

"You must be feeling better."

"Some, " I said, thinking how with my throbbing foot, it was the worst I felt since I got there. It came to me that might've been the Lord's way of helping me, and I told Him right off I didn't need no help with recollecting how pain feels, I needed help with ideas for setting that Yankee free. Miss Leona took the tray, and left. I laid back down and wished Pa was with me. I recollected that day he left and how sad I was that he'd be gone for weeks, maybe even a month. I would've cut off my own legs to keep him there if I'd known he wasn't never coming back.

Right off it came to me that soap soldier likely had a family up north who loved him near as much as I loved Pa, so I pushed the covers back slow and this time, set my feet down quiet on the right side of the bed. I stood careful, then took a step, and then another. With each footfall I listened for the creak of boards before I put down my full weight. Took forever just to get to the hook where my clothes were. I dressed quiet, and stuffed my nightgown under the sheets and arranged the bedding so it would look like a body laying under there if Miss Leona got a notion to look in on me. There was just enough light from the candle to lead me to the doorway. I walked down the hall, past a door on the right, and past a door on the left. I took two more steps and one of the men let out a snort and scairt me good.

I stayed put, thinking on what story I'd come up with if

Miss Leona came. A minute passed and I took another step, then another, looking ahead at the door and recollecting how I'd heard the sounds of Miss Leona taking down the bar, then turning the key in the lock. It was the noise that worried me—I hadn't thought about where the key might be. It was likely hung in the hall, maybe atop the door, or to the side. I took another step, still moving slow so that if I hit a creaky board, I could pick up my foot. Then one of the men snorted again, and set to snoring loud and steady. As long as he kept it up, it would cover any sound I made. If the Lord was next to me, I would've patted Him on the back for that.

Of a sudden there was an opening off to my right, wider than the other two, of which that didn't make sense seeing as how Miss Leona said there were two rooms, but I wasn't about to go back and take it up with her. I got to the door, pushed the bar up slow, took it off, and propped it in the corner. I felt around for the key, but couldn't find it. It came to me Miss Leona might've kept it in her skirt, but with Miss Jenny and Doc Waitly work-ing, there, too, they'd likely keep it where everyone could get to it. I thought back to what I'd heard when Miss Leona emptied the chamber pot, and recollected the sound of pouring water. I went back to the opening and felt my way along the inside of it. It was a shallow room, maybe six feet deep, with shelves at the back, of which that was likely where she got the water. I ran my hands along the top shelf and right off I knocked over a bottle, a small one that made only the tiniest tick of a sound. I uprighted it and it came to me it didn't make no sense to set a key on a shelf lined with bottles that could be tipped by hands reaching in the dark. I brushed my hand along the wall inside the opening closest to the back door and found the key on a hook at head height.

The snoring kept up, but I recollected the loud click of the key turning in the lock and pulled my skirt around it to muffle the sound, then waited for a snort. A few seconds later one of the soldiers obliged me with a long one, and I turned the key and opened the door, both. I pulled it shut behind me and left the key on the ground, where it could be seen easy, need be.

Clouds covering the sky shed some light but it was still dark enough that I couldn't do no more than stand there and wait for my eyes to accustom themselves to the night. A breeze blew cool acrost my face, soothing the heat that came with the fear of waking Miss Leona. Near as I could figure, I faced east. Whitlows' would be off to the north an eighth mile or so. I still didn't know what I'd do when I got there, but leastways I wanted to know if that Yankee they had trussed up was the soap soldier.

I reckoned I'd best stay behind the buildings, so I took off to the left, still setting my feet down soft so as not to cause a crackle in the brush. I passed MacDaniels' place and just beyond was the road heading north out of town. Crossing it to Whitlows' would bring me into the open where there was more light and I'd be easier to spot so I said a prayer and just as I was about to step out into the road, someone touched my hand. I reckon my heart would've shot out the top of my head if bone hadn't stopped it. I turned and when I didn't see no one, thoughts of haints and bears and such as that near most laid me to the ground with fear. A rough wetness covered my fingers then, and there came a whine. Looking down, I could just make out MacDaniels' old collie, Scottie. I would've thought he was dead by now, seeing as how he looked ready to pass on the last time I came to town with Pa. My breath came out in a shudder and I petted him, grateful that the fear had stopped up my throat or everyone in town would've been out hunting me. "Go on, " I said, shooing him away, but he held tight to me like as if he was deaf, or didn't have nothing better to do. Leastways he wasn't a barky dog. Truth to tell, once I saw he meant to stay close, it put me at ease some.

I crossed the road to Whitlows' heading to the darkness at the back end of the house, a big old two-story like MacDaniels'. It had likely been built on the same order and I thought as how there might be a room out back off the kitchen where they could keep a trussed up prisoner. I let my eyes adjust again until I saw the back entrance with two steps that led to a door. I went up and peeked in. A soft glow gave just enough light that I could make out a chair and shelves and cupboards. It appeared to be storage, maybe a fancy-house pantry I was looking into. I looked up at the sky and put a message in the stars asking Pa what to do. Scottie knocked his snout against my hand, likely thinking if I was just going to stand there, leastways I could pet him.

Of a sudden there came a noise. I heard it again—a cough. I followed the sound around the corner to the north end of the house and saw a window too high for me to reach. I thought back to how the Whitlows' place was set up and recollected their woodshed was a west-facing lean-to off the carriage house. I made my way back to it, thinking I'd bring over a load of flat pieces of firewood and pile them up to stand on. With a roof and three sides walled in, it was real dark and I had to feel my way around. Right off I came across a couple of logs, each near most a foot and a half long, of which, set end to end, they'd likely get me high enough to reach the window. I put one under each arm and as I headed out of the woodshed, it came to me I'd need a step to get up on them. I went back in and felt around until I found another log. I laid them all in my skirt, and pulled it up around them like a sling. Scottie followed me, of which I came to see as a help. If someone came, he'd likely take off or whine or some such to warn me. And folks accustomed to him roaming would likely think it was him, if they heard prowling.

Back at the window I set up the logs. I got up on the low one, lost my balance, and my bottom hit the ground with a thud sending a grunt out of my throat that sounded loud as a crack of thunder. I laid still, listening, while Scottie licked my face. After a minute I got up and felt the ground for a flatter spot closer to the house so I could lean against it. I put the fattest log down and turned it some to push it in the dirt. Then I got the next fattest log and set it atop centering it over the bottom one. I rocked them and they felt sturdier than before. I did the same with the other log, turning it until it set more solid in the ground. I stood on it, put my hands against the house for balance, then hoisted myself up on the tall log and grabbed for the sill. As my head came up to the window there came a tap from the other side, and I yelped and jerked away and thudded to the ground again, landing on my back. I don't know if it was fear or the wind knocked out of me, but I couldn't breathe. I pushed myself up on my elbows and Scottie whined and I gasped for air. I reckon my eyes were as big as moons and I thought how as, any minute, I'd see the barrel of a gun come round the corner and there'd be a loud shot and I'd be dead, lessen my breath never came and I died first on my own.

Of a sudden my lungs filled up, and I took a deep breath, then another, and another, until the air came easier, and I heard a loud whisper: "Tatum, is that you?"

"Yes," I whispered back and Scottie whined again, like as if he wanted to have his say, too. I set up the logs quick and climbed back up, then put my forehead against the glass and peered in. I couldn't see nothing but blackness. "How'd you know it was me?"

"When your head came up over the window sill and I saw the hair, I was pretty sure it was you."

Right then I reckoned if I could gather everyone I knew and put them in a big hall and tell them that my tangly mess of hair they'd all been telling me to put a comb to had likely just saved a life...well not yet...and truth to tell it was a Yankee...and I reckon I would've wasted another ten minutes thinking on it when the Yankee talked again.

"I'm roped to a cot but I can move some, but my wrists are tied together. Do you have a knife?"

I pulled the knife out of my skirt pocket and tapped it on the glass.

"Work it along the edges and pry the window up."

I opened the knife and pressed it between the sill and the window near the bottom. I worked it around the edge in both directions as far as I could reach, but it wouldn't move.

"Wait," he said, and seconds later I made out the faintest light at the window. "I got a pillow. I'll press it against the bottom pane and you hit it with the knife handle."

I was afeared the sound of the glass would wake someone.

"Did you hear me?"

"It'll make a noise," I whispered, loud as I dared.

"No. The pillow will soften the sound. Hurry."

I closed the knife and gripped it tight. I grabbed the sill with one hand to steady myself and smashed the knife handle into the pane with the other. The glass shattered with a small crinkling sound, then dropped to the ground, falling on itself with a plink, plink.

"I'll put my hands through and you cut the rope." With the glass gone, I heard him easy, and saw his hands come close, but the opening was too small for his tied-together fists.

"I'll put *my* hand through," I said.

"Pick away the glass first." I pulled shards out of the wood and tossed them off to the side in the brush, where they fell quietly. "How'd you get all the way into town?"

"I made like I was ailing and Mr. Foster brought me in and left me at Tucker's—that's where Doc Waitly set up a hospital. They found that carving of me out on the road. That's how I figured it was you they had locked up."

"Fold this up and lay it across the opening, so you don't cut yourself," he said, pushing a shirt he had clasped between the heels of his hand at me. I did, then opened the knife and pushed my hand through.

"They were sending me to Andersonville. You saved my life."

"You ain't free yet," I said, slicing at the binding between his wrists. The rope was thick and I had to saw on it, but finally I cut through the last of the strands. He unraveled the ropes and freed his fists, stretching his hands open and rubbing them together. "You're more like to need this than me," I said, handing him the knife.

"Get back to Tucker's. I won't forget this, nor my promise to your pa."

"How you aim to get north?"

"My horse is at the livery."

My brain got excited, passing along one idea after another of how I could help. "I'll get your horse," I said.

"No. It's too dangerous. If anyone sees you, they might think it's me and shoot."

"They see you with your horse, they'll capture you again, lessen they kill you right off. I got a plan," I said, warming to this adventure.

"No. This isn't a game for a child."

"A child! I been caring for Rayford, and Ma, and I just set you free. I'm thirteen. I ain't a child no more." I could scarce believe it was me claiming I wasn't no longer a child. "Leastways let me tell you my idea."

"Alright, I'll hear you out."

"You stay here, and I'll bring your horse."

"That's your idea?"

"The dangerous part will be crossing the main road, getting the horse out, and getting it back here. Once you got the horse, you can head on out."

"What if they catch you?"

"Well...I'll think on it. I got a good thinking brain. Leastways if I get caught, they won't take it out on you, and you'd still have a chance to get away. You just stay put and be quiet, so as no one knows you're set free."

"My horse's name is Homer. If he gets jumpy, call him Homer

Boy and scratch him below the right eye, not the left. He's touchy on the left. And be careful!"

I jumped down off the logs and hightailed it to back to Tucker's. I passed the door I'd escaped from and rounded the corner at the south end of the house so if anyone saw me, they'd think I'd just come out the back way of the hospital, and I'd make like as if I was just walking in my sleep. I crossed the road and made it to the livery stable without no one seeing me, and went around to the side where the wall was only part way built, and found a place to sneak in. I kept quiet so Arlo wouldn't hear me. He had a room at the front of the livery where he slept and handled what business there was—like Mr. Holsum used to do. Scottie had given up on me, of which I was glad since he might've riled the horses. Thinking on that and wondering if Arlo would grab a gun and start shooting if he heard a noise, my heart got to beating hard and my face grew hot again, and my mouth went dry. I reckon it was part from fear and part from knowing I was about to steal something. Or leastways that's how it would look.

There were eight stalls, but only two horses. I peeked up over the edge of the doors and right off I saw which one was smaller. Just enough light came through to see he was the same dark color all over, like the horse the soap soldier had in our yard. so I figured he must be the soap soldier's horse and I headed back to the saddles. I recollect times when I came to town with Pa and we'd stop by to pay Mr. Holsum a visit. Of a sudden another recollection came, of how Mr. Holsum would pull open a drawer in his desk in the office up front and ask, "You want a swig there, Will?" Pa told me that since his wife died, old Mr. Holsum had taken to drink. Ma likely would've walked out or busted him in the jaw, but Pa turned him down as polite as if he'd just offered Pa a piece of cobbler. It brung tears to my eyes to think on Pa and I near most sat and cried but for that soap soldier waiting back at Whitlows'. Leastways I reckoned now I had a better idea of how Mr. Holsum felt, and I could see as how he'd take to drink if it eased his pain some.

Back then—before the war came—he had saddles all along the wall for sale. Now I only saw two. I picked up the smaller one. It wasn't as heavy as Major Tom's so I figured it was the right one for that little horse. I took it into the stall and whispered my plan to Homer, who was a might jumpy, but I scratched him under his right eye and called him Homer Boy and told him we'd met before. He tossed his head a time or two then settled down. I grabbed the saddle and as I was about to lift it, I heard steps in the straw.

"Arlo?" I whispered, letting go of the saddle. I stood up, and a hand went over my mouth and another came round my chest, pinning my arms to my side.

46

Scheming

"Keep quiet." It was a voice I didn't know. I felt his breath on my ear and he squeezed my face til it hurt. "What need you got of this horse?" he asked. Even if I did have an answer, his hand was so tight on my jaw I couldn't move it. "You deaf? I'm talking to you." He yanked my head, and my knees buckled. He hung on and dragged me out of the stall, let go, and I hit the ground hard, like as if I fainted.

I still didn't recollect the voice, but, mean as he was, I suspicioned it was Whit Whitlow. I was afeared he'd come to the livery knowing I'd tried to set the soap soldier free. He stood over me and I made myself stay limp. He called me a name and kicked me in the shoulder. I let it jerk from the blow, but I didn't make a sound.

I heard him move back across the straw, then Homer snorted and his hooves pawed at the ground. Whit told him to be still, cursing a time or two, of which it only made Homer snort louder and toss his head more and stomp harder.

"Who's there?" It was Arlo's voice with a strength to it I'd never heard before.

"You keep your nose out a' this," Whit hollered. There was a thud and a grunt, then Homer let out a cry and hooves crashed against the walls of the stall. I rolled into the shadow beyond the light coming in from the opening in the end wall, and with all the commotion and noise of Homer kicking, Whit swearing, and Arlo coming our way, I crawled into one of the open stalls without no one noticed me.

"Whit, what're you doing here?" I heard.

"Claiming my horse."

"That ain't your horse and you know it. You been whaling on him with that board? Put it down and get on out of here afore I shoot you," Arlo said, not sounding a lick like the clumsy boy that came to visit with Missy. I reckoned this job had done him good and given him some pride.

"I told you to keep your nose out a' this. Leave me alone or I'll shut you up for good," Whit snarled and I peeked out just for a bit to see him fling a board at Arlo.

"I'm here to keep these horses safe and I aim to do my job. You wouldn't be the first man I shot."

Whit took a few steps towards Arlo and he backed up to where I couldn't see. Then Whit said, "I brung that Yankee in and I'm claiming--"

There was a loud smack, then a groan, and next came a thud. Of a sudden it was quiet but for the skittering of Homer's hooves in the straw. I held my breath and ducked back into the stall.

"Easy, boy," Arlo said. He must've knocked Whit out. "Easy, now." I reckoned Arlo had gone into the stall to calm Homer. "Ain't no one gone hurt you." Homer made some soft snorting noises and then it was quiet but for Arlo walking across the straw.

I near most popped up and hollered for joy, but seeing as how I didn't know what to do next, I figured I'd best stay quiet til it came to me.

"Whit, you ain't never been nothing but trouble," Arlo said. I listened again for Whit to answer, but what I heard was a sliding sound. I peeked out of the stall and saw Arlo dragging Whit up to the front of the livery. "I'll tie you up and we'll talk about this in the morning," he said to Whit's body.

With Whit tied up, I figured I could take Homer and get him to the soap soldier. Unless Arlo heard me. And if he did, I wondered would he let me head out with that horse. I thought it through this way and that, and it came down to where I had one chance and I had to be certain Arlo wouldn't mess it up.

Once he'd dragged Whit into his office and shut the door I crawled out, staying low to the ground and in the shadow so if Arlo came back out he wouldn't see me. I felt along the wall where I recollected Mr. Holsum kept lengths of rope on hooks. I found one, tied a slip knot in it, then headed to where lantern light glowed around the door of Arlo's sleeping room and office and I knocked quiet. "Arlo, it's Tatum Wiley. I got to talk to you."

"Tatum?"

"Yes, sir. You let me in?"

The door opened. "Ain't you sick at Tucker's?" he asked.

"I feel some better. Wha–?" I stopped and stared down at

Whit like I had no idea there was a trussed up body in there on the floor. "Who's that?"

"That durned Whit Whitlow. He brung in a Yankee soldier and now he's got some fool idea he gets to claim his horse. Mr. Holsum says it belongs to the Confederate Army, such as it is, and I told Whit as much, but he can't get it through his stubborn skull."

"What're you gone do with him?" I acted just as sweet and kindly and curious as I could.

"Reckon I'll hand him over to Mr. Holsum and let him decide. It's still his stable."

"Looks like that rope ain't tied so good."

"Where?"

"That one round his chest."

Arlo leaned over and looked close—just like I hoped he would—then he put both hands out to fiddle with it. He didn't suspicion nothing of me, so when I slipped the rope over his head and down to his elbows and pulled tight, he just looked at it. I don't know what he thought, but likely it wasn't that I had in mind to truss him up like he done to Whit.

"Tatum, what're you doing? You take this here rope off of me," he said, finally jerking his arms.

"Wait, don't move yet, please." He relaxed, trusting me like I figured he would. "Let me tie you up so I know how in case some Yankee comes sneaking round and I grab a skillet and hit him over the head, and I need to tie him up afore he comes to."

"Have you gone plumb crazy? It's the middle of the night, you're supposed to be grave sick at Tucker's, and I got Whit here to keep an eye on."

"I couldn't sleep. I feel some better, and Mr. Foster won't come for me til morning."

"This is the craziest idea I come across in all my borned days."

"I ain't gone *leave* you tied up," I said, like as if he was crazy to think I would.

"Well, I ain't never heared of such a thing. Hurry it up, in case Whit comes to."

He held still for me and I got his hands tied up together with the rope wound round his fists like they did to the soap soldier so he couldn't get himself untied. Then I steered him over to the chair and set him down and tied each of his legs to a chair leg and wrapped the rest of the rope around his chest and tied him to the chair back. It got to where I couldn't believe he was letting me do such as that, but he is a trusting soul until you let him know otherwise. Of which I was about to do.

"I'm about as trussed up as a body can get. Now take these here ropes off."

"See can you get free first, so I know I got you tied right." He tried to move and the best he could do was to slide the chair an inch or two.

"You did a fine job, Tatum, now set me free."

"Oh, I near most forgot. What if that Yankee took a notion to call out to the other Yankees? I best tie a kerchief round your mouth, then we'll be done."

"Tatum, this is pure foolishness. No Yankee is gone set still while--" and that's when I put the kerchief in his mouth and he kept mumbling, and I got around in front of him.

"Arlo, I got to help that Yankee soldier get free. I ain't got time to tell the whole of it, but soon's I get his horse to him and he heads out of town, I'll be back directly to take them ropes off. And if you want I'll even marry you just to show I ain't got no hard feelings toward you."

His eyes got big and scairt-looking, and he shook his head so hard I was afeared he'd tip himself right over.

"You ain't sweet on me?"

He shook his head hard again, his eyes as big as if he saw a whole roomful of haints.

"Hmmm," I said, and I blew out the lantern and went back to saddle up Homer.

47

Another Promise

Homer was still a might skittery from what Whit done. I rubbed under his right eye and called him Homer Boy and told him how his Yankee was in trouble and we needed to get back to Whitlow's and get them both headed north, and that horse leastways let me get the saddle on him. I would've liked to ride him over there—I missed riding—but I didn't know how he'd take to that, so I just took the reins and walked him out through the back door of the stable, and stayed in the shadows as much as I could. Homer came along quietly, like as if he knew what I was up to. I figured it was some past midnight, so I didn't worry on no one being awake to hear us, but I was afeared of what Whit had done to the soap soldier. We headed beyond the mill to where we were across from Whitlows, then dashed into the open, acrost the street, and to the north end of their house. Scottie was waiting and whined some, but he shushed after I petted him. I walked Homer to the window I had broken, then whispered Frank Werner's name loud as I dared. I waited for an answer, then called again. Pictures of him lying dead in that room filled my head, and then I heard footsteps behind me, and I knew Whit Whitlow had sprung free, and Arlo couldn't stop him and I ducked and threw my hands up over my head to protect it.

"Homer Boy! Shhhhh! Easy, boy," I heard. It was Frank Werner, and I near most cried with relief.

"Where've you been?" I asked.

"I hid out in the woodshed."

"Whit came for your horse..." I said, and then I told him all what happened and of a sudden his arms were around me and he kissed my forehead.

"You saved my life, Tatum."

"Not yet. You best get and make it so."

"I'll never forget this."

"I won't neither, specially if you get killed."

"I'll write you letters. I'll help you and Rayford whatever way I can. I intend to keep that promise I made to your father." His arms came round me again. "Thank you," he whispered in my ear, and he took the reins and grabbed the saddle horn and pulled himself up on Homer, then leaned over. "Good-bye, Tatum," he whispered.

"Just GET!" I hissed.

He pulled on the reins, Homer turned, and they headed east to the road that would take him home.

48

Not A Lie Outright

Of a sudden I felt my tiredness and recollected it had been three nights since I had a good sleep and near most three days since the soap soldier told me about Pa. I would've dropped right there and cried myself to sleep, but Arlo was still tied up. I headed back to the livery stable, felt my way to Arlo's office, and opened the door. I was sorry I'd doused the lantern—I couldn't see a thing—but I recollected how the room was laid out.

"Arlo! It's me, Tatum."

He mumbled back in such a way as to let me know he wasn't too happy about being trussed up. I followed the sound, felt of his head, then leaned over and whispered.

"I aim to let you loose, but you got to know why I did what I did. I'll take the gag off, but if you make a noise, I'll have to put it back on. You understand?"

He nodded, so I untied the kerchief.

"Tatum Wiley, you are in a heap of trouble," he hissed. "You took that Yankee's horse. I heard you!"

"Now you just simmer down, or I'll put this right back on you."

"Well, I'm like to lose my job with that horse gone."

"No you won't. That soap soldier saved my life and he brought news of my--"

"Tatum! That horse is gone. My job is to not let such as that happen. If you had a good reason to take that horse, why didn't you tell me first, and we could've gone to Mr. Holsum--"

"I didn't have time to take no more chances."

"Well now it'll look to Mr. Holsum like I can't do this job. It would've been different if I'd have let him go, but no, I got trussed up by a girl and she stole that horse."

"No one knows that. We'll just say I came to you and told you all about what happened, of which I am right now, and you let me take the horse, of which you did in a manner of speaking, seeing as how you knew it was the right thing to do. So it won't be a lie outright, just a rearrangement of the truth."

"What about Whit. He knows that ain't the way it was."

"Who's gone believe Whit?"

"His pa, for one. And them friends of his that caught the Yankee in the first place."

"Well, I'll tell them how you saved me."

"Saved you?"

"I was already back there when Whit came in."

"You were?"

"He grabbed me and threw me aside and kicked me just to get that horse."

"He did?"

"And you came and saw me on the ground and Whit standing by me and you knocked him out and tied him up and brought me back here to tend to me.

"I did?"

"You got Whit trussed up, didn't you?" He didn't say nothing. "So now I'll untie you and we'll just keep quiet about all this til morning, in case there's a body or two out there who don't see it our way."

I took the rope off him and he didn't move, he just sat there like as if he was thinking the whole thing over. "I still think Whit is like to cause trouble. He don't like losing."

Of a sudden, I recollected that bottle Mr. Holsum kept in his desk. I felt my way to the bottom drawer and when I pulled it open, Arlo went wild.

"What're you doing. You stay out of there. Mr. Holsum gave orders that I ain't to go snooping in--"

"Shhh. I'll just spill some of this on Whit so as to make it look like he was stinking drunk and no one will believe a word he says."

"You won't never tell how you left me here all tied up?"

"Never. Setting that Yankee free is all I wanted to do."

"Why'd you want to do that?"

Melanie should've been the first to hear it, but I reckoned she'd understand how I had to tell it to keep folks from chasing that soap soldier down. Then I told Arlo the story—how the soap soldier saved me from that mean, skinny one, and how he found Pa and promised to take care of me, and how he came back and left supplies, then tried to take us north, but I wouldn't go, and that's when Whit and them other boys captured him.

"I'm real sorry about your Pa. I didn't know."

"Nobody knows. I was afeared if I told, they'd go after that Yankee and string him up."

"But if you told what he done for your Pa--"

"That wouldn't have mattered to the likes of Whit."

"I heard a ruckus when they brought the Yankee into town," Arlo said. "I went out to see what it was about and they made Whit bring me his horse. That Yankee begged me to take good care of him, and not hurt him. A man that loves his horse and treats it right is a good man in my book, even without all what you told me."

"Pa said there's good ones and bad ones, North and South."

"That's the way of it. I saw it out at the war."

"Well, I best get back to Tucker's. I ain't slept but a few hours in three nights."

"Tatum?"

"What?"

"Now that I see all of it, you done right."

"Reckon I did. Leastways I got a good feeling about it."

I headed to Tucker's, went in the back way, locked the door, set the bar back in place, put the key on the hook, made my way back to the bed, and flopped down in it. I was too tired even to cry.

49

A Wide-Eyed Look

The next thing I recollect was waking to a knock on the open door and there stood Jeremy Driscoll, his face lit up like he'd just stumbled on a fortune. I looked out the window to see the sun high in the sky and figured it was past noon. There was a peculiar feeling in the air I couldn't put a name to, but I didn't get a chance to think on it.

"Arlo told me what you done," Jeremy whispered, coming to the foot of the bed. "It gave me gooseflesh to hear of such an adventure." The way he stared put me in mind of the way Joram looks at Melanie. It also told me he didn't know the whole story yet—leastways not the part about Pa. Of a sudden he snatched off his hat, like he just recollected it had come in on his head, and he worked his fingers around the edge of it. Then he stammered some, like his tongue had got tangled and when he finally got it untied, he wrinkled up his face and said, "Folks say you're sweet on that Yankee."

"I ain't sweet on nobody."

His shoulders relaxed and he let out a sigh. "Well, you're still a might young," he said, like as if he was an old man instead of a boy barely four years older than me.

"Be fourteen come summer. I just don't see no sense in getting sweet on no one. I got Rayford to care for, and I don't aim to have no feller standing around telling me how to do things." I put some spit on my words and Jeremy stepped back with a hurt look on his face. But I figure if he aims to get sweet on me, he'd best know what he's in for.

"Now I'd take a feller for a friend," I said, thinking on that day he came though the woods with that carving of me. "Leastways if he let me go hunting and on adventures. But I don't aim to be stuck in a parlor doing fancy work the rest of my life. I ain't much of a hand with a needle. Poke myself leastways as much as I poke the thing I am working on. If you was to pour water in me, I'd likely empty right out from all them holes." He laughed, and I did too, of which that surprised me some, like that laugh had pushed through all them sad and cantankerous feelings and took its place right next to them. "No sir, I ain't got no plans to get hitched, nor nothing like that, but I wouldn't mind me a friend who could talk some on interesting things and who knows how to work a hammer."

"Me and Pa and Silas are building a new barn," he said, and his eyebrows arched high.

"And he should know how to read and be some curious about the rest of the world." I talked on the curious part and he stood there serious, nodding ever so often, like as if he was putting himself up against my words and figuring he held up to the measure.

"I aim to have a place of my own soon, and work it," he said, when I let off talking. "And set something aside so as to travel north or west, or . . . well, I got a book that tells about them big steam ships and how long it takes to cross the ocean. It's real interesting, and has drawings of countries over there."

"Has it got a piece on England or Scotland?" I asked.

"Them and more. I'll let you look at it, if you want."

Then it came to me what I liked about Jeremy Driscoll. Some folks look at the world with their eyes near most closed. They don't hold no stock in curious and ain't about to let in nothing extry. Ma and Missy Tarkan are that way. But other folks—like Pa—have a wide-eyed look and want to take in everything they can. Jeremy Driscoll has eyes like that.

"Doc said to let you rest." He backed up and put his hat on. "Once you get to feeling better, I'll bring that book by."

"I'd like that," I said. He left and as I listened to his boot heels hitting the floorboards as he walked out, in came Miss Jenny with a tray smelling of roast meat and onions. It set my mouth to watering and then it came to me as how I'm still here. I'm still alive. When I heard Pa was gone, the hurt was like a thing outside me pushing on my skin and I thought I had to get shed of it or I couldn't go on. It felt like I was in a prison of hurt. Then the soap soldier needed help, and three whole days went by. I reckon whilst I had my mind on setting him free, that hurt made its way inside. It was still a sad, sorry thing, but it had a strong part to it, too, and the end of it was I didn't feel like I had to always let things happen. I could make things happen. Likely that was the feeling I couldn't put my finger on when I first woke up this morning. It wasn't in the air. It's in me.

Of a sudden, I recollected that day down by the creek when Pa told me he was joining the Confederate Army and I tried to make him stay. I can still hear his words in my head clear as when he said them: "There's times you got to do a thing you don't want to do. But it's the right thing and you do it so at the end of the day you can sleep in peace. It ain't always easy. I reckon that's why I been trying to protect you from it. But there's a good feeling that comes of doing what's right, and maybe I kept that from you, too."

I surely do feel good about freeing that Yankee. I know I did right by him.

I picked up the fork and whilst I ate, it seemed like a new thought came with every bite. I got to pondering whether it's always hard to do what's right. But truth to tell, it ain't hard to care for Rayford. Leastways not all the time, and I'm surely willing. It might be that when you do a thing you want to do, the good feeling comes aforehand, but when you do a thing of which it ain't easy, the good feeling finds you after the deed is done. That's the part of growing up I could never make peace with. It seems like Pa was forever doing what he didn't want to do, but now I see it different. I see why he had to join the Confederate Army.

I reckon he's up in heaven laughing on how he asked that Yankee to take care of me, but the end of it was I had to help him. And I can near most feel Pa's hand ruffling my hair and hear him saying he's proud of what I done. 'Course it ain't over yet. I still have to tell Melanie how the soap soldier found Pa and made a promise and how he was true to it. And I'll have to write all that to Hugh and Mule. I wish I could write it to Melanie instead of telling her outright, but that ain't the way Pa would want it.

I recollect how he promised something special was waiting for me. I ain't thought about that promise since he left, seeing as how I took him to mean a five-pound sack of sweets that I could keep all for myself, or a horse of my own, or a pile of gold pieces. And I had in mind he'd be the one to bring it, whatever it was. But now I see he likely wasn't talking about a thing that came to me on the outside—a thing that could get lost or stolen—but something I'd have on the inside forever, that no one could take from me. I reckon that's why he made me be the one to shave Rayford. Each time I had to face trouble, I got a little closer to it. When that Yankee got caught I was near most there, I just needed one more nudge.

Now I got my own ideas of right and wrong. I got my own ideas about a lot of things these days, things a body who is only a child ain't like to ponder. I reckon when I set that Yankee free, it set something free in me, too, a part I didn't even know wanted to get out. Likely that's the special thing Pa promised was waiting for me. It wasn't a thing at all, it was a way of looking at things.

When I was just a child it seemed like steering clear of Ma and her chores and doing whatever I wanted all day was the best thing in the world. I reckon it was back then. But seems to me that line of thinking would have kept me stuck in that small world of our farm. As much as I like being in Rayford's Garden, now I see there's a whole other world out there, a world too big for a child to handle.

Tonight I'll look up at the stars. I reckon it won't be just Pa looking down, but Granpappy and Ma too. I'll tell them I miss them, but I'm grown up now. I'll take care of Rayford. We'll be okay.

ABOUT THE AUTHOR

I've always loved and been fascinated by words. I began my writing career in business communications, but as an avid fiction reader, I was compelled to try my hand at short stories. They met with moderate success---publication and some small awards---but when one turned into a novel, I realized that while writing is my strength, fiction is my passion.

ACKNOWLEDGEMENTS

My gratitude flows in so many directions. First, for the gift of imagination that compels me to write for the same reason I read...to find out what happens next. That surely happened in *Rayford's Garden* when Tatum's adventures spilled onto the page as fast as I could type.

Second, to my husband who's helped me with this story beginning with our research trip to Georgia and continuing through countless hours of reading and listening to countless versions. Whew! It's done!

Third, to the many generous folks staffing Georgia's museums and historical sites who shared time, ideas, and information and made Tatum Wiley and her world come alive. Early in my career I was careless about noting sources, so I can't give them the credit they deserve, but I'll be forever grateful, and will do better next time.

Fourth, to family, friends, and book club members for their feedback, support, and encouragement.

Fifth, to Sharon Vincent, graphic artist, mind reader, hand holder, and path clearer. The cover is amazing!

Last...although writing stories has been my passion for nearly 40 years, it's been difficult to value it as little more than something I love to do. But recently my husband stepped into my office and insisted: "You have to do this. This is your legacy!"

This story came from my heart. I hope it touches yours.